PRAISE

Nora Roberts Land
"Ava's story is witty and charming."
—Barbara Freethy #1 *NYT* bestselling author

Selected by *USA Today* as one of the Best Books of the year alongside Nora Roberts' *Dark Witch* and Julia Quinn's *Sum of all Kisses*.

"If you like Nora Roberts type books, this is a must-read."
—Readers' Favorite

Country Heaven
"If ever there was a contemporary romance that rated a 10 on a scale of 1 to 5 for me, this one is it!"
—The Romance Reviews

"*Country Heaven* made me laugh and cry...I could not stop flipping the pages. I can't wait to read the next book in this series." —Fresh Fiction

Country Heaven Cookbook
"Delicious, simple recipes... Comfort food, at its best."
—Fire Up The Oven Blog

The Bridge to a Better Life
Selected by *USA Today* as one of the Best Books of the Summer.

"Miles offers a story of grief, healing and rediscovered love."
—*USA Today*

"I've read Susan Mallery and Debbie Macomber...but never have I been so moved by the books Ava Miles writes."
—Booktalk with Eileen Reviews

The Gate to Everything
"The constant love...bring a sensual, dynamic tension to this appealing story." —Publisher's Weekly

MORE PRAISE FOR AVA

The Chocolate Garden
"On par with Nicholas Sparks' love stories."
—Jennifer's Corner Blog

"A must-read...a bit of fairy magic...a shelf full of happiness."
—Fab Fantasy Fiction

The Promise of Rainbows
"This is a story about grace, faith and the power of both..."
—The Book Nympho

French Roast
"Ms. Miles draws from her experience as an apprentice chef...and it shows...I loved {the} authenticity of the food references, and the recipes...looked divine." —BlogCritics

The Holiday Serenade
"This story is all romance, steam, and humor with a touch of the holiday spirit..." —The Book Nympho

The Town Square
"Ms. Miles' words melted into each page until the world receded around me..." —Tome Tender

The Park of Sunset Dreams
"Ava has done it again. I love the whole community of Dare Valley..." —Travel Through The Pages Blog

The Calendar of New Beginnings
"A funny, inspirational friends to lovers story to pull on your heartstrings." —Cullen House Reviews

The Fountain of Infinite Wishes
"A beautiful story... I love going back to Dare River."
—Goodreads Addict

The Grand Opening
"Ava Miles is fast becoming one of my favorite light contemporary romance writers." —Tome Tender

Also by Ava Miles

The Dare Valley Series
Nora Roberts Land
French Roast
The Grand Opening
The Holiday Serenade
The Town Square
The Park of Sunset Dreams
The Perfect Ingredient
The Bridge to a Better Life
Daring Brides
Dare Valley Meets Paris Billionaire
The Calendar of New Beginnings

Daring Declarations: An Anthology Including
The Holiday Serenade & The Town Square

The Dare River Series
Country Heaven
Country Heaven Song Book
Country Heaven Cookbook
The Chocolate Garden
The Chocolate Garden: A Magical Tale
(Children's Book)
Fireflies and Magnolias
The Promise of Rainbows
The Fountain of Infinite Wishes

Once Upon A Dare Series
The Gate to Everything

Non-Fiction
The Happiness Corner: Reflections So Far

Home

Sweet Love

THE DARE VALLEY SERIES

AVA MILES

ISBN-13: 978-1-940565-55-2

www.avamiles.com
Ava Miles

DEDICATION

To all the healers in the world—Eastern, Western, natural,
conscious, and unknowing. Thanks for doing your part and sharing
your gifts with all of us.

And to my divine entourage, who continues to show me how best
to share my gifts with the world and
all that is possible.

Acknowledgements

Team Ava and all the beautiful people who continue to sign up to support implementing my highest vision in the world.

My amazing editor, Angela, who is my divine partner in more ways than we both realized when we first began.

T.F. For being a man to love.

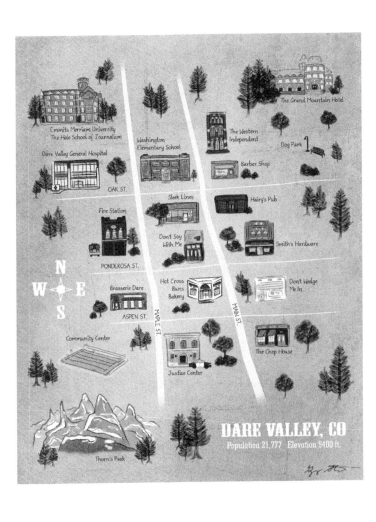

CHAPTER 1

CHASE PARKER DIDN'T LIKE THE THOUGHT OF RUBBING elbows with his mortal enemy.

Certainly not at the invitation-only fundraiser he and his work colleagues were planning. Moira Hale, the intriguing new director of The Artemis Institute of Innovation, was the one who'd made the ludicrous suggestion. Of course, he couldn't exactly blame her. She had no way of knowing Maurie Wallins, the CEO of K-Barker, was his mortal enemy or why.

The asshole had slept with his wife. His now ex-wife.

Which was not the kind of thing a professional could mention in a business meeting.

Chase and Moira were sitting in a conference room at The Grand Mountain Hotel with the man who had brought them together—Evan Michaels, their boss. He and Moira represented the two branches of Evan's work. While Chase was the chief financial officer of Quid-Atch, the global defense contractor company that had made billions with Evan's inventions, Moira would be running Artemis, Evan's pet philanthropy project—a private institute designed to foster young inventors with seed money and training. So far, Artemis was in the start-up phase.

This team-building weekend in Dare Valley, Colorado, where Evan and Moira both lived, had been Evan's idea. He'd wanted them to plan Artemis' first fundraiser together to ensure they were all on the same page.

Right now they were not.

"I can't believe you want to invite Quid-Atch's competitors to Artemis' first fundraiser, Moira."

Chase shifted his gaze to Evan, who was wriggling like he was sitting on the hot seat. If he was considering Moira's lamebrain idea, he *was*. He knew better than anyone that Maurie Wallins was toxic.

"When Evan endowed Emmits Merriam University with the largest gift anyone has ever given a U.S. university to support young inventors," Moira said, tucking a lock of her brown hair behind her ear, "he put Artemis on the map. We have to invite Fortune 500 company executives who support innovation, and that means going to companies like K-Barker and Longburrow. We'll lose credibility if we don't."

"But they're Quid-Atch's *competitors*," Chase repeated, pushing back from the table and crossing his arms. "You don't know the kind of dirty tricks we have to guard against when we're competing for defense contracts, and we have a huge U.S. Defense Department bid going on right now, Moira. To the tune of seven hundred million dollars. Tell her, Evan."

Even though Evan was technically the chief executive officer of Quid-Atch, he left much of the day-to-day work to Chase. But he knew about the big bids, the kind that could cause layoffs if they didn't win. This was that kind of bid.

After over a year of preparation, they had eighty-seven days to put all the remaining pieces together. The project management leader they were putting forward for the bid was the best candidate out there, and they'd paired him with a first-rate team of subcontractors. Chase never settled for less than a winning strategy.

"Chase is right in saying a seven-hundred-million-dollar bid is a *really* big government bid for us," Evan said in a neutral tone. "I could barely talk him into taking time off for this team-building workshop, but Artemis' first fundraiser is critical."

Moira's eyes widened like silver dollars, likely because of the amount of money they were discussing, but she immediately narrowed them again. She really was one determined woman. Chase usually admired that about her—it was why he'd approved hiring her for the director job even though her experience, while impressive, was limited to human resources.

He'd be better off if it were the *only* thing he admired about her. Truth was, he was having a tough time fighting his attraction to Moira Hale. She was funny and no-nonsense, smart as a whip, and sexy to boot with her clear green eyes, curly brown hair, and petite figure.

It was a unique experience for a man who'd sworn off romantic feelings after his divorce.

It was also a problem.

While Chase could have delegated his work with Moira to someone else, the grant Evan had given Emmits Merriam for the Artemis Institute was high-profile news. Everyone knew the institute was tied to Evan, which meant it reflected on Quid-Atch. Besides, if he hadn't agreed to come to Dare Valley this weekend, Evan might have given Moira her way. It reaffirmed Chase's need to oversee the center's ongoing business.

"I see Moira's point about credibility, Chase," Evan said, making him want to growl. "But, Moira, I also hear Chase's concern about inviting our competitors to the fundraiser, especially when we have such a huge bid in the works."

"One we're not assured to win outright, Evan," Chase

reminded him. Since Moira looked puzzled, he glanced her way, trying not to register how pretty she looked in the green ski sweater that matched her eyes. "On some bids, we're in a strong position to win, either because we had the preceding contract or because we've done a lot of work in the area in which we're competing. Not this time. It's a wide open field."

And his mortal enemy was gunning for them like always. Chase hated competing with Maurie Wallins. He played dirty, but he knew how to skirt the line between unethical and outright illegal, which was how he'd made K-Barker so successful. Chase simply didn't do business that way, and luckily Evan agreed.

Moira folded her hands and looked intently at them. "I appreciate your point, but if Artemis is going to be seen as an independent center, we need to be neutral about who we invite to our fundraisers."

Chase was ready to snap back at her, like a taut rubber band, but Evan slapped a hand on the table and stood up. "I think we need to table this discussion for a few days while I consider the pros and cons. Is everyone ready to hit the slopes?"

Chase didn't like that suggestion. "I think—"

"I'd love to," Moira said, standing up and smiling as though she'd won a minor victory.

Maybe she had. Evan usually fell in line with Chase's wishes. Whenever he delayed giving an answer, Chase knew they were destined to go back and forth on the topic for days.

"Fine, let's go," Chase said, keyed up with nervous energy from the discussion. He would talk to Evan later.

They left the conference room and headed to the small private room holding their ski gear. The hotel was a destination for skiers, so there were several rooms like this right on the slopes. Chase did his best not to watch Moira get dressed. Oddly, it was arousing to see her putting *on* clothes. He forced himself to keep his gaze away from her as he clamped on his ski boots, picked up his skis, and walked out into the snow. He put on his skis and waited for Evan and Moira to join him. When they did, they moved in tandem to the ski lift.

Growing up in Wyoming, Chase had cruised down his fair share of slopes, whenever he could scrape enough money together. Money wasn't a worry now, but time was. It had been a long time since he'd gone skiing.

Chase continued to fight the urge to look at Moira as they all hopped off the ski lift at the top of the hotel's luxurious ski slopes. Finally, as they stood at the top of the hill, he let himself look his fill. She met his gaze and held it. There was a sea of white behind Moira, and in her red suit, she looked like a lone flame that could melt everything in her wake. Including his resistance.

Her mouth tipped up at the corners as she continued to stare right back at him. Sometimes he thought she engaged in staring matches with him because she was competitive, and she wanted him to know she wouldn't back down. Chase had a good poker face, and he could out-stare even the most trained politician or defense minister in the military business dealings he conducted for Quid-Atch. However, a few times he caught a softer glint in her eyes, the kind a woman had for a man she found pleasing.

That softer glint kept him awake at nights and made him analyze all the reasons why he'd be an idiot to ask her out.

Chase Parker didn't date. He made deals. Ran a corporate empire. Had sex occasionally with an interesting companion he'd selected to look good on his arm. He certainly didn't date colleagues, even peripheral ones like Moira.

"I'll see you at the bottom," Chase said and turned to fly down the slopes.

The blue sky was brilliant—even through his ski goggles—and he loved the punch of cold air on his face as he wove his way down the slopes, making sure to keep clear of beginner skiers.

He pulled up at the bottom of the slope and took a deep, cleansing breath. Skiing was invigorating. He wished he had more time for it, he realized. There were a lot of things he didn't have time for, but that's what happened when you spent every waking moment working.

Someone punched him in the shoulder.

"Why didn't I realize you were a pro at skiing like you are at everything else?" Evan asked after skidding way too close to him. He was wearing a lime green ski suit with black racing stripes.

Only Evan could pull off a ski suit with racing stripes.

"Because we've never gone skiing together," Chase answered, causing Evan to roll his eyes behind his dark ski goggles.

Moira, who'd just pulled up beside them, shook her head. "How is that even possible? I thought you two were known for hanging out at Europe's finest ski resorts."

Chase snorted. "That was all Evan—in his playboy days—before Margie."

"My one and only," Evan said, a charming but dopey smile on his face.

"I only visited Evan in Europe when he needed to get his head out of his ass," Chase continued. "I sleep better at night these days knowing he's all grown up. It was a burden to remind him to eat before he met her."

It was meant to be a joke, but it was mostly true. Chase had helped Evan grow up, and yes, while it galled him to admit it, there were times when he'd needed to remind the sometimes-forgetful inventor to eat. And shower.

Evan made a dramatic show of looking over his

shoulder. "My head doesn't seem to be up my ass anymore, Chase."

Moira laughed again, and they slowly made their way back to the lift. Evan and Moira were chatting about the view and how wonderful it was to be living in Dare Valley. Evan was new to the small town, but Moira had been born here. While she'd lived in Denver for a while, this was home to her. She had plenty of family here—a family Evan was now connected to through his wife.

Yet another reason Moira was off limits.

"Don't have anything like this view in the D.C. metro area, do you?" Evan said, clapping him on the back as they sat in the lift.

It was obviously rhetorical, but Chase answered him anyway. "No, but we have the Smithsonian museums and a heck of a lot more restaurants."

Evan cracked his neck. "They had all that and more in Paris, but I still prefer it here."

"Because the woman you love is here," Chase said with a grin.

When they crested off the lift, Chase skied to the right and stopped, waiting for the others to catch up with him.

Evan flashed a smile to a few skiers as he passed them, and one of them whisper-shouted, "Isn't that Evan Michaels?" As a billionaire inventor and the only man in town in possession of both a red Ferrari and a black Lamborghini Reventon, Evan had achieved a weird celebrity status among some Dare Valley folk. Being Evan, he enjoyed every minute of it.

"Good thing they can't ask for your autograph," Moira joked as they joined Chase.

"Oh, they could ask for it," Evan said. "You wouldn't believe the kinds of places I've had...ahem...models ask me to autograph."

"If anyone suggests something super inappropriate," Moira said, "leave them to me. I'm good at kindly brushing those sorts of overtures off."

Chase wondered about that. She was beautiful, but she wouldn't be an easy mark for the kind of guy who picked up women at bars. She was too confident, too no-nonsense. It was part of her appeal.

"I'm thirsty," Evan announced, planting his poles in the snow. "See you guys at the bottom. Chase, you won't catch me this time."

There was a sluice of snow against skis as Evan pushed off and sailed down the hill. Honestly, there was no way Chase was going to race Evan. There were some lines work colleagues and friends didn't cross.

"Afraid to race him?" Moira asked.

"No," he replied, feeling a sheen of snow cover his face and melt as the wind rose up.

"I didn't think so," she said matter-of-factly. "I'm not sure anything scares you."

You do sometimes, he wanted to say, but refrained. Getting older meant knowing when to keep his mouth shut. "Fear pisses me off," he said instead.

"Oh, I like that. Do you mind if I use that?"

"Not at all."

Then she tugged her yellow ski goggles up, giving him a clear view of her green eyes. Clearly she was in no rush to ski, and neither was he, it seemed. The edges of her brown hair curled around her white stocking cap, and his eyes narrowed on her lush, red lips, slightly cracked from the cold. He didn't want to stop looking at her.

"Why aren't you afraid of me?" he asked. "Most new hires are. God's honest truth." He worked hard to overcome that with each new executive hire. If they didn't stop walking on eggshells around him, they were reassigned. Fear had a way of creating obstacles in the best of working relationships.

She took her time, keeping her gaze on him. "I've

never been afraid of anyone, really. What's the point? It's like my Uncle Arthur says. Everyone puts their pants on the same way when they get up in the morning."

Chase knew about her uncle, Arthur Hale, one of the legends of modern journalism. He supposed with an uncle like that, she was used to powerful men. "Except nudists," he said as a joke.

Joking was one of his tools to make other people more comfortable around him.

Her mouth curled. "*Ah...*I see what you did there. No pants."

He shook his head, knowing he was bordering on flirting with her. "None whatsoever."

"Do you think nudists ever ski?" she asked, grinning now.

He rolled his tongue around his teeth. This conversation proved the old adage he'd heard from his father. The topic didn't matter—a man and woman could flirt about anything.

"Be a cold proposition," he said, unable to stop himself from smiling back.

"I suppose we should probably follow Evan," Moira said, not making any move to pick up her ski poles.

Her green eyes continued to gaze at him, as if waiting. That was when he was sure of it. She *was* waiting for him to make the first move. If anyone was going to make it, it had to be him.

Moira had been a human resources manager before. She would understand his dilemma.

He'd never dated an employee.

Moira isn't my employee, he told himself.

But they would still have to see each other professionally if things didn't work out. He'd seen other people date at work, and when things went south, it usually ended up in reality-TV drama territory.

He hated drama.

But he knew Moira did too.

What are you thinking? He gave himself a mental slap. After his marriage to Trisha, he'd learned every painful thing one person could do to another. There was no going back.

Still, rather than suggest they follow Evan, he found himself asking, "Are you having fun?"

"Skiing as part of a work day at The Grand Mountain Hotel? Knowing the famous Chef T is going to make us lunch? Are you kidding? I have the best job in the world."

That snagged another smile out of him. "I feel the same way. You're still happy you've moved back to your hometown? I heard what you said to Evan, but is that the truth? Leaving the big city can be a big transition for anyone."

She rubbed her gloves together like she was cold. "I miss things about Denver, but there's plenty to do here. I have my family, which keeps my social calendar full. And I have a home, a real home. Apartment living sucks. I'm happy to be here, Chase. Truly."

"I'm glad. I want you to be happy." He cleared his throat, realizing it wasn't a common sentiment for one co-worker to share with another. "I would have hated for you to return to your hometown and regret it, no matter how much you love your job."

Unhappy employees tended to leave their jobs, he told himself, but he knew that wasn't why he'd said it. He just wanted her to be happy—Moira, with the encompassing laugh, the green eyes, and the challenging stare. The woman who'd suggest they invite their competitors to the fundraiser and stood her ground in the face of his disagreement.

He realized he was seeing her less and less like an employee and more and more like a partner in Evan's vision. Except for the whole inviting their competitors to the fundraiser notion, which he planned to nip in the bud with Evan later. Moira's mind was set for reasons he understood. Artemis was establishing itself as the premier invention center in the world, so they needed to include *all* of the companies that applauded and recruited innovation to make themselves legitimate.

But it was a goddamn corporate nightmare for Quid-Atch. Chase was always worrying about safeguarding the secrets in their government bids and contracts and keeping their highly skilled employees from jumping to a competitor like K-Barker. That was why they offered them the sun, moon, and stars.

"You can't imagine ever moving back to Laramie?" Moira asked, refocusing his attention on the present.

"No," he said flatly.

Because he and Moira were so linked by their gaze, he saw the ripple of shock crest across her beautiful face. Had he sounded too harsh? When she finally broke their stare-off, he felt bereft, and found himself struggling with the sensation. He was acting like a moonstruck boy, and he didn't like it one bit.

"What is it?" he asked.

"There's smoke over on the bench," she said, raising her hand against the sun. "A lot of it."

He'd seen the bench on his previous visits. It was one of the flatter areas cut into the mountain to make room for new housing developments.

Chase followed her gaze, squinting against the bright light reflecting off the snow. What he saw was enough to make his insides roll over in his gut. "Fire."

He knew that thick, black smoke. Had seen it before in the hometown she'd just mentioned. It had destroyed his family's ranch when he was twelve—and everything they'd worked so hard to build. Worse, it had destroyed their pride. The loss of it all had driven his father to take his own life six months later when the insurance check arrived, not enough to help them start over.

His mother had never been the same. *He* had never been the same.

A sharp pang ricocheted through his chest and down his left arm, and he stumbled enough that he had to plant his ski poles to regain his balance.

"Are you all right?" Moira asked, walking sideways in the snow to reach him.

His gaze was focused on the smoke. "Someone's house is on fire."

Her hand touched his arm. "Let's pray the fire department comes quickly."

Another sharp pain rocked through his chest, but he bit his lip hard enough to keep from making a sound.

"Chase?" Moira asked, her eyes scanning his face. "Are you okay?"

He was sweating inside his blue ski suit, and his heart was pounding in hard, painful beats. "I'm fine. We should ski down and meet Evan. He doesn't like to be kept waiting."

Then he pushed off with his poles.

"Hey!" someone called in panic, and when he swung his head to the right, he saw a woman with a pink fleece cap gliding into his path. He turned his skis inward hard to avoid hitting her and felt the snow give underneath him. Losing control of his skis, he sailed off the path down a hill. The sharp descent increased his speed, but he was too off-balance to turn or stop. He was hurtling toward the wooden fence with the yellow caution tape on the side of the mountain, a marker designed to keep skiers from journeying into an unskiable area. He made one last effort to use his poles to avert disaster, but his skis slid out from underneath him. All he saw was the fence.

He struck it hard.

CHAPTER 2

"CHASE!" MOIRA SHOUTED AS HE CAREENED INTO THE fence.

The sound of him thudding into—and then through—the wood slats made every hair on her body rise up. His skis flew off in opposite directions and then one of his poles vaulted through the air like a spear before sinking into the snow yards away like a punctuation mark.

"Oh my God!" she heard people saying around her.

Shaking off the shock, Moira dug her poles into the ground and skied toward him, crouching lower as she passed the broken part of the fence. It was a dangerous fifty-foot drop, and possibly a stupid move on her part, but she had to do something. Chase was down there, and she was a good skier. She took it slow, using steady mogul-like maneuvers down the hill. When she reached him, he was lying at an odd angle on his stomach.

"Chase!"

His head was turned to the side, and with his goggles on, she couldn't see if his eyes were open. Scared to touch him should it hurt him, she gently placed her hand on his back.

"Chase! Are you okay?"

She scanned his body, and that was when she noticed his leg twisted under him, something that made the gorge rise in her throat.

"Get a medic!" she shouted to the skiers up the hill.

"Is Chase okay?" Evan shouted down to her.

"He's hurt," she yelled back. *Badly.*

"I'll get help," he called back.

She watched him ski off and then turned back to Chase. He hadn't moved. Hadn't so much as groaned. Fear drove an ice pick into her belly. Was he unconscious? A fall like this could certainly have caused it. Goodness, how she wished her brother were here. Andy was a doctor—he would know what to do.

"Help will be here soon, Chase," she told him, deciding her best course was to take off her skis and sit beside him.

His right arm was turned underneath him in a way that made her queasy, but his other hand was palm down in the snow.

"Wake up, Chase," she told him, laying her hand gently over his. She took off one of her gloves and touched his jaw. He didn't stir. She checked her watch, thinking it best to keep record of how long he was out. Minutes passed, and with every single one of them, she grew more afraid for him. What if he didn't wake up?

He groaned then, and she jerked her hand back before resuming their connection.

"Chase, it's Moira," she told him. "You've had a bad fall. Try not to move. The medics will be here shortly."

She looked up the hill. There was still no sign of Evan or a red-suited medic, but more people were gathering. Time continued to pass, heedless of her worries, as Chase lay there unmoving. She found herself rocking in place, offering up snippets of prayers.

"Oh, Christ," he finally said, sucking in a breath. "What...happened? Where?"

He sounded completely disoriented. "You had a skiing accident. Help is coming. Lie still."

"What? Fuck, shit, damn. This...hurts."

When he tried to roll to his side, he cried out in agony. She fought off a shudder at the raw pain in his tone.

"Don't move," she made sure to say in a gentle voice, noting his right leg was lying listless and...bent like a broken stick. *Oh, God.* "I think you broke your leg."

"Ah, fuck," he groaned. "My arm too, feels like. Jesus Christ."

She was unfazed by his language. "Just lie still," she repeated. "Evan went for help." She stood up and cupped her hands against her mouth so the sound could carry. "Where's the medic? Any sign?"

"Your friend said he'd get them," a tall snowboarder shouted back. "Do you want me to come down and help you?"

"No," she shouted back. "There's nothing you can do. He's broken his leg, we think. And his arm maybe. We'll need a stretcher."

"Fuck that," Chase called out. "I'm not a goddamn baby."

With two brothers, Moira was used to tough guys. She crouched back down beside him. "You think you can ski out of here with a broken leg and maybe a broken arm?"

He pounded his good hand in the snow. "I can fucking do anything I set my mind to. Help me up."

From their very first meeting—her job interview at this very hotel—she hadn't minced words with Chase. "Don't be some stupid He-Man. Have you looked at that hill? I barely got down here." Okay, that wasn't completely accurate, but she didn't want to encourage him.

He tried to lift his head and groaned. "What the hell were you thinking? Skiing down that drop after me? You should have left me alone."

"Couldn't do it." Gently, she took off his ski goggles.

"Does your head hurt?"

"Are you kidding?"

"I mean, do you think you can turn it?" She kept her gaze on him as he moved his head slowly to the right and then the left.

"It's fun making snow angels with my face," he quipped in a hoarse voice. "God, I feel like I took a few punches to the jaw. But yes, I can move my head. Satisfied?"

"Yes." She dug out the snow near his head and then gently settled his head on her thigh. "You'll be warmer without your face planted in the snow."

"This doesn't qualify as appropriate behavior," Chase muttered. "Oh, Christ, I can't believe I took a fall like this. I never fall."

Something told her that he wasn't only talking about a physical, time and space, disaster. Chase Parker didn't fall down in life like most people, she imagined. He wouldn't allow it.

"Maybe the fire across the valley distracted you," she said, looking over in that direction. Black smoke was still rising in the sky unchecked. She hoped the family was safe, if they'd been home.

"It wasn't the house. I just didn't fucking see that woman... Oh, fuck this hurts. Shit, damn...ignore my cussing. Not appropriate."

"Oh, shut up about that already. I fucking wrote the human resources manual for Artemis. These are not normal conditions. You're lying here with broken bones and likely a concussion."

"I was out?" he asked, his head heavy on her thigh.

She was tempted to put her hand on his head in comfort, but felt it would be weird. Plus he probably had a huge robin's egg under his black fleece ski cap. "Yes, and we both know how dangerous that can be."

"Good thing I have excellent health insurance," he

quipped and then sucked in his breath again. "It's like a hot poker is burning my right side and the left is freezing from the ice."

"Let's pray the medics bring blankets. And yes, you have great health insurance."

"Negotiated the plan myself," he muttered.

"Of course, you did," she said agreeably, finally resting her hand gently on the back of his damp neck. "This doesn't hurt, does it?"

He was silent for a moment. "No."

His words were gruff, and she found herself blinking back tears—unusual for her. Must be the shock of the situation. Good thing she and Caroline were getting together tonight. She'd been looking forward to it, mostly because her sister had a mysterious lunch date with their great uncle and they were both dying to know what it was about, but now she had another reason. After the morning she'd had, she would need to vent.

"You're going to be okay," Moira told Chase.

There was a swoosh of activity above them, and then she heard, "We're coming down for you guys."

Two red-suited medics skied around the wrecked fence. She spotted Evan at the top, his head bare now, peering anxiously down at them.

"Help is here," she said.

Chase nestled his face more comfortably into her thigh and let out a pained sigh.

"About goddamn time. I'm turning into a popsicle."

"Maybe we could market that," Moira said, knowing she was rambling but unable to stop. "An executive popsicle—"

"Shut up," Chase muttered. "I have something to say before those yahoos get here."

She shut up.

"Thanks for coming after me, Moira."

That shut her up even more.

CHAPTER 3

EVEN THOUGH IT HAD REQUIRED HER TO TAKE A VACATION day, Caroline Hale hadn't even considered ignoring her uncle's invitation for lunch at Brasserie Dare. First, Uncle Arthur rarely took a lunch. Everyone in Dare Valley knew he'd eaten a sandwich, pretzels, and a green apple at his desk for some sixty years, with red hots for dessert, as he liked to joke. Second, the only time Uncle Arthur ate lunch out with someone was either for a story or to drill some sense into a person.

Since she'd spent practically every moment of the last couple of weeks working on a new show for the art gallery she curated for in Denver, Caroline couldn't think of any stories Uncle Arthur could wrest from her for his famous newspaper, *The Western Independent*. Moira had told her to keep on her toes around their uncle. They'd concluded he was planning to drill some sense into her.

For the life of her, she couldn't imagine why. Caroline was doing great right now career-wise. Of course, there were currently no prospects in the dating department, but that could change any day. She was an eternal optimist.

Uncle Arthur was already seated at his special table

when she arrived—he was the restaurant's primary investor, after all. There was an untouched basket of steaming hot baguette in front of him, accompanied by a wad of butter in a small clay dish, reminiscent of Provence. The chef and her cousin by marriage, Brian McConnell, paid attention to details like that.

"My dear," Uncle Arthur said, rising half out of his chair. "You honor me with your presence."

When Uncle Arthur kicked off with bullshit like that, Caroline knew she was in trouble. Just like she and Moira had thought. Best be plain speaking about it. He'd run over her otherwise. "Honor you? Did you forget to take your medication this morning?"

He harrumphed, which made her smile as she pulled out her chair and sat down across from him.

"Why can't I say something like that?" he asked, his white, bushy eyebrows pinched closer together with his glare. "Didn't you drive all the way from Denver on a work day to have lunch with me?"

"You know I did," she said. "You're usually not so mysterious. Besides, you wouldn't budge on shifting this to a weekend."

He made a rude gesture with his hand. "Too much family around. Everywhere I turn on weekends, there are happy couples making goo-goo eyes at each other and babies everywhere. Even Rhett and Abbie's new girl is being shoved in my face every time I turn around. Do I have to adopt all the children in this town as my grandchildren?"

He loved every minute of the attention, and he damn well knew it. "You're just being ornery. And Rhett and Abbie's little girl is the sweetest baby ever."

"Bah! You young people say that about every baby. In my day, we just stuck them in a drawer with a blanket and told them to go to bed."

She bit her lip. He was in a mood. "The good ol' days

before modern cribs. Have you ordered a drink yet?"

He gestured to his coffee cup. "They're always pushing that sparkling water when I come here. Like I want fizz all over my face."

"Well, I'm going to have a glass of wine since I'm staying over with Moira." She and her sister had plans to watch *Magic Mike* for the hundredth time and drink at least one bottle of wine while consuming an entire pepperoni pizza. Bliss, to her mind. After they conferred about her mysterious meeting with Uncle Arthur, of course. Damn, but she missed having her sister in the same city.

"Be irresponsible of you to drink and drive back to Denver," Uncle Arthur said, shoving the breadbasket her way. "Might as well have some of this fancy bread too."

She signaled the server, who seemed to be waiting, and ordered her wine and the sparkling water just to get Uncle Arthur's goat. He narrowed his blue eyes at her, and she tried and failed to hold back her smile.

The waiter was just walking away when Brian came striding across the restaurant toward them, the kitchen doors swinging shut behind him. "Hey, you two. Caroline, I heard you were meeting Uncle Arthur about something secret."

"Secret?" Uncle Arthur scoffed. "Stick to cooking, kid. Journalism is safe without you pursuing stories."

But Brian wouldn't have used that word—*secret*— unless he had a reason. Did Jill, his wife, know something Caroline didn't? Or had Moira said something? In a big family, sometimes it was hard to know.

"What do you recommend for lunch, Brian?" Caroline asked.

He hung his thumbs in his pants. "For you, I would suggest the grilled octopus with lemon tarragon sauce for an appetizer."

"Octopus! Good Lord. What is the world coming to?"

Brian didn't even look in Uncle Arthur's direction, but she saw his mouth twitch. "For an entrée, I would go with the lamb chops. Grilled to perfection with a black pepper cream sauce and a side of frisée."

"Sounds delicious." She wanted to purr, it sounded so good.

"If you're over your gastronomic ecstasy, Caroline, I'll order." Uncle Arthur rested his elbows on the table. "French onion soup and a croque-monsieur sandwich."

Brian sighed. "Arthur, you always get that. Why not try—"

"Do I look like I'm interested in trying anything new? I'm in my final years here. The routine of life comforts me."

Usually Caroline would have called bullshit, but there was something in his voice. Brian glanced over at her, and it was obvious he'd sensed it too.

She reached for her uncle's hand. "You look better than ever to me."

"Yeah," Brian said, rocking on his heels. "I want to be as alive and hopping as you are when I'm your age."

The side of Uncle Arthur's mouth tipped up before flattening out. "That's my order. Go make it happen, Brian. You've been shooting the breeze with me long enough."

Brian rolled his eyes. "All right, I'll head back to the kitchen, but your soup is coming out with Caroline's appetizer, Arthur. Don't fight me on this."

Uncle Arthur muttered to himself as Brian headed away from the table. "I hate all this pomp and circumstance."

"Yeah, two courses is so stuffy," Caroline teased. "You've been to dinners at the White House, for Pete's sake."

He looked down his nose at her over his glasses. "My

dear, this isn't the nation's capital, and you aren't the First Lady."

"Something I'm grateful for every day," she quipped as the server brought her wine and sparkling water. "Now are you finally going to tell me why I took a vacation day to meet you for lunch?"

"A friend of mine could use your art expertise," he said without blinking. "I hoped you would be amenable to helping him."

For a man who wrote succinct ledes for a major newspaper, it was a vague request. She imagined deliberately so. "Tell me more."

"It's for J.T. Merriam," her uncle said, picking up his coffee cup and taking a sip. "Emmits Merriam's great-great grandson."

"Wasn't he the kid who threw mud at me when I was five?" she asked, recalling the scrawny older boy who'd ruined her dress when he'd missed hitting his twin brother.

"Sadly, yes," Uncle Arthur said, scratching his jaw. "I was hoping you wouldn't remember that. Emmits would be appalled that's all you remember of his kin."

She didn't doubt that he was right.

"Why does his great-great grandson need my help?" Caroline asked, picking up her wine.

"Because he wants to bring the Merriam family art collection to Dare Valley," her uncle told her. "Emmits would be over the moon, and so am I."

"Didn't Emmits come to Dare Valley the same year you started *The Western Independent*?"

Arthur shook his head. "Good heavens no. You young people and your memories. I've got more brain cells firing. Emmits and his wife built a summer house here long before that. He was my mentor and my friend. Encouraged me to go to Columbia University's journalism school and helped my career and this newspaper when I was first starting out. I owe that man a whole heck of a lot—even though Emmits always said a man makes his own fate. He'd want his art to rest here. I know it."

His impassioned tone made her smile. "Where is he planning to display the collection?"

"He's working with the university, of course," her uncle said. "And that's strictly between us, even if you choose not to help."

"Of course. Do the Merriams have good taste in art?"

Her uncle snorted. "Impeccable. If you meet with J.T., you'll see for yourself. Excited yet?"

She lifted her shoulder. "Sure, but I'm still not clear on why he'd want my help." The Merriams had oil money and were richer than Croesus. She imagined J.T. could have the best of the best in the art world.

"J.T. can tell you more himself," her uncle said as the server brought their appetizers. "As for why he wants you, I told him he does. He needs someone with your skills. Plus, you're from Dare Valley."

"But I live in Denver, Uncle Arthur," she said, popping a bite of octopus into her mouth. "Delicious. Sure you don't want a taste?"

"I stopped eating things with more than four appendages in 1962," he replied, totally deadpan. "Can I tell J.T. that you'll meet with him? He's happy to set something up in Denver if that's easier for you. He has to fly in anyway."

"Where does he live right now?" she asked.

"Rome," her uncle replied. "The art capital of the world to many intellectuals."

"I couldn't agree more," Caroline said. "What does J.T. do?"

"He's been managing the Merriam oil and gas division in Africa and the Middle East. Lately, he's been thinking about doing something different."

"Hence this art collection," she said, sipping her wine. It was quite a shift, and that intrigued her. "All right, I'll meet him, but I make no promises. You're being oddly vague here, and my alarm bells are ringing."

"I don't know what you're talking about." He tapped the melted Swiss cheese covering his soup, and the steam escaped.

"You aren't thinking you'll be able to lure me back to Dare Valley like the rest of my siblings?" To her mind, there'd be no purpose. Denver wasn't far away, and she worked at the city's finest gallery.

"I'll leave major life decisions to you," Uncle Arthur said. "But it makes me happy to think about more of Emmits' legacy returning to Dare Valley. The university is one thing, but it doesn't reflect his heart anymore. No one had a bigger heart than that man."

His gruff tone told Caroline he was getting choked up. She rose from her chair and went over to kiss his weathered cheek. "Except you, perhaps."

"Bah," he said again as she returned to her chair. "I'm just an old man who's done the best he could with what he had. That's all any of us can do."

When he was like this, there was no arguing with him. "Give J.T. my number and tell him to call me."

Her uncle gave her a radiant smile and slid two red hots across the table to her. "One for the kiss and the other for making an old man happy."

"You're a sweetheart," she told him with a wink.

She'd meet with J.T. Merriam a dozen times if it would make Uncle Arthur smile like that again.

CHAPTER 4

CHASE'S ARM AND LEG WERE THROBBING WITH PAIN when he was wheeled into a hospital room after going through the agonizing ordeal of having both his tibia and humerus put in separate casts. Like the overachiever he was, he'd broken both major bones on his right side clean through.

And he had a major concussion to top it all off. Capital news.

Which meant he had to stay in this godforsaken hospital in a stupid white-patterned gown with his backside exposed.

"This is ridiculous," he protested again to Moira's brother, Dr. Andy Hale, who had taken charge of him at Dare Valley General Hospital. "I'll follow whatever directions you want, but I'm not staying here. Evan, tell the man we can hire a nurse."

Evan stood at the edge of his hospital bed, pasty white from anxiety. Moira was as composed as a swan.

"I know you want out of here," Evan said, worrying his lip, "but we need to listen to Andy. He's the doctor. A serious concussion like yours requires overnight observation."

Andy was a nice guy. He was Moira's brother, after

all. But he was standing between Chase and freedom. "I can be observed in the privacy of my hotel room with adequate medical supervision."

Moira narrowed her eyes. "If that was advisable, Andy would advise it, Chase. Stop being so bullheaded and let the professionals take care of you."

"Look, man," Andy said, "I don't blame you for wanting to be sprung. If I didn't work here, I'd feel the same way. But let's review the situation. Your scan showed a serious concussion, which will be plaguing you for the next four to six weeks at least in the form of headaches and possible mental confusion. You're going to have to take some time off. No working on a computer—something you do a lot of, I'm sure—and no travel."

If Chase's head hadn't been pounding, he could have convinced Andy to see reason. "I'm sure that's for extreme cases. I have a multi-country European trip planned, and we're working on a crucial government bid. I can't shut down for four to six weeks."

"The world will end as we know it," Evan interjected, making Chase frown, which only added to the pain in his head.

"I'm going to check on my other patients," Andy said, staring him down like his sister was so adept at doing. "Push the call button if you need anything. You should be pretty good with pain meds right now."

Except it hadn't helped his head much. Wasn't that something to be worried about? He could work through it. He knew he could. His blurred vision would go away if he concentrated hard enough.

Moira put her hand on her brother's arm. "Thanks, Andy."

He kissed her cheek. "Sure thing, Mo. Can't have one of your bosses keeling over."

The moment the door closed, Chase said, "Dammit,

Evan! I want out of here."

His friend's face bunched up. "I know you're upset, but I'm holding the line here. You scared me, Chase. I mean...look at you."

Chase didn't have to look. He had a pretty good view of his massive body draped in an ugly hospital gown with his casted upper arm and lower leg hoisted up in slings. If any of his hardcore Defense Department folks saw him now, they'd reconsider working with Quid-Atch. This was not the respected corporate executive who'd graced the cover of *Fortune* magazine.

"I still don't understand how this happened, Chase," Evan said. "You're an incredible skier."

"I wasn't looking, and then things got out of hand," he replied, hoping Evan wouldn't press him.

"It wasn't a question of skill, Chase," Moira said, giving him a pointed stare, just like her brother had moments ago. "You were as distracted as I was about the house that was on fire across the valley."

A ripple of shock crossed Evan's face. Damn. Chase had hoped Moira wouldn't say anything about that. Evan would connect the dots.

"Moira?" Evan asked with a gentle smile. "Let me talk to Chase alone for a bit."

They shared a look of understanding, and Chase saw how things were going to go form here. Evan and Moira were a united front, and they were going to tag team him until they got their way. He wanted to hurl his plastic cup of water across the room.

"I'll see about getting us some real food," Moira said, looking back his way.

Her concern was obvious, but right now, Chase had bigger fish to fry.

After she left, Evan pulled the utilitarian visitor's chair up to his bedside. Like they were about to have a man-to-man chat straight out of *Good Will Hunting*.

Chase looked away. "Whatever you're about to say, don't."

"I have to," Evan said quietly. "You're my best friend."

Chase curled his good hand into a fist. "I don't want to talk about this, Evan."

"Which is why we never have," Evan answered, scraping the chair closer. "I've known about what happened to your ranch since the beginning. When I wanted to hire you, you told me to do a background check on you. I learned about everything, from the fire to your father's suicide. I guess you wanted me to know upfront so I'd never ask. And I haven't. But Chase...if it's still bothering you enough to get you this distracted and hurt, maybe it's finally time."

Chase turned to look at Evan. "There's nothing to discuss here. I've dealt with it, Evan. Anyone who'd lost their home that way would be a little thrown to see another family going through the same thing. You're like a brother to me. Don't act like my shrink."

"I wouldn't imagine myself qualified for that," Evan said. "But I'm worried about you. This accident was serious, Chase."

"Tell me about it."

"You're going to have headaches for weeks," Evan continued. "You won't be able to travel by airplane, and you're going to need to be in a wheelchair until the casts come off."

Andy had told him the same thing earlier, but hearing it from Evan took the wind out of him. Not be mobile? Not travel? Basically, it meant he couldn't be himself.

"I'll find a way to work, Evan," he ground out. "We have big things going up. My trip to Europe, the bid—even this fundraiser now since you're considering inviting our competitors like Maurie—"

"Didn't you hear anything Andy said?" his friend

asked. "Your brain—*your one-of-a-kind human brain*—has to recover. It's a heck of a lot more complicated than your broken limbs, although you did a number on them too. You *have* to cut back on work. I'm going to *insist*. Heck, this accident might be your wakeup call to deal with the past. Like coming to Dare Valley was for me."

A wakeup call? Who was Evan kidding? He was a grown man. "Don't compare me to you, Evan. You still had some growing up to do. I'm closing in on forty."

Evan was silent for a while, and Chase forced himself to look out the hospital window. That was when he saw the smoke, and his chest contracted painfully again.

The column of black smoke was smaller now, but it was unmistakable. That poor family.

"I'm putting you on medical leave starting today until Andy determines you're ready to ease back into work."

Chase swung his head to gape at Evan, which made pain shoot across his skull. "No way! You can't force me to take leave."

Evan leaned back in his chair and gripped the arms. "When Moira comes back, she'll tell you that I can. When a doctor advises it."

"You actually read the Quid-Atch human resources manual?" Chase scoffed.

"I called Janice at headquarters while you were being swathed in plaster," Evan said. "You aren't going to want to fight me on this, Chase. Focus on getting better."

Being out of commission was a death sentence. Why couldn't Evan see that? Quid-Atch needed him—and it went both ways.

"You're serious, aren't you?" Chase levered himself up and fought a curse when pain shot through his head again. "Evan, I run your goddamn company. I can't do that on leave or part-time. No one can do my job but me. Not even Darren."

"I agree no one does it better than you," Evan said,

"but the rest of us at Quid-Atch will have to do our best. Darren is your VP of Operations, for Pete's sake. He'll do great. He can take over your role on the bid."

That didn't assure him one bit. "We're undermanned right now—"

"I'm going to draft a workflow plan, which you can give input on orally. You're not supposed to read anything in the early stages of a concussion. Your travel can be assigned to other members of the executive team, including myself. We'll keep you involved with critical issues—"

"Everything I do is critical, Evan. I won't let you sideline me. I can work through the pain. We need to win that bid." He wouldn't talk about how the thought of being caged in a wheelchair made him feel. He hadn't processed that yet. But nothing had ever stopped him before, and he wouldn't allow anything to stop him now.

"The bid will continue without you. We have almost ninety days to turn it in, Chase. I'll be waiting for your input when you're better."

"Are you kidding me? Every day counts. You have no idea how much work goes into this kind of thing. The proposal team sometimes clocks in twenty hours a day on a bid like this." That was a regular day for Chase, but Evan knew that.

"I'll rent you a house here," Evan responded instead, standing up and going over to the window, shaking his limbs like he was feeling the anxiousness of his decisions.

As well he should. Evan had never tried to limit him. Chase was the one who took care of Evan, or at least that's the way it used to be. He wasn't going to let his friend reverse their roles.

"I can take a car back to HQ," Chase said.

"No way," Evan said. "Andy said it would be a horrible trip across country. Plus I won't be able to monitor your well-being as easily if you go back to D.C.

And your well-being is my number one priority right now, alongside my wife's."

Chase couldn't let those words affect him, but he felt it happening all the same. "Fine. But you can just extend my reservation at The Grand Mountain Hotel." He would find a way to work in secret.

"You'll like the privacy of a house better," Evan said, pulling out his phone to type in what Chase expected were notes. "Judging from the mausoleum you live in by yourself, you like space."

It wasn't the space so much as it was having the kind of house people thought you should have. He lived in Great Falls because it's where all the richest global executives lived in the D.C. area. Not that he spent much time there, or even considered it home. If he could have gotten away with living in a hotel his whole life after the fire, he would have. Only people who'd been through an experience like that could understand what it felt like to have everything destroyed, from family photos to cherished heirlooms like the lace tablecloth his great-great grandmother brought from Boston when she came West on the wagon train as a mail-order bride. His entire childhood had gone up in flames with the ranch. His family's history too.

He didn't consider his current residence a home. Trisha, his ex-wife, had understood that.

"Fine," he grumbled, "find me a house if you're going to be so bull-headed about it," he said, knowing Evan was barely listening to him now.

Chase would do what he could to make the situation suit his needs. Evan was busy working on his current invention and the launch of the Artemis Institute, not to mention his domesticity with Margie. He'd have little time to keep an eye on Chase, and no one who worked with them at Quid-Atch or elsewhere would rat him out.

"I'll personally go to D.C. to oversee the packing

of some of your things. I think you're going to be here awhile."

Then his friend looked up at him and gestured to his current state. They should take a picture and title it, Powerful Man Cast In Plaster. They could show it in the MoMA.

"Since I know you and the way you think," Evan said, "I'm also talking to the staff about your condition and making it clear they will get into trouble if they help you work on the sly, especially on this bid. I mean it, Chase."

Shit, Evan had out-foxed him there. "This isn't a good executive decision, Evan. Our staff will likely freak out if I'm not around to lead them on this seven-hundred-million-dollar bid." They both knew the money involved, of course, but it couldn't hurt to remind him.

Evan's eyes darkened. "I'll blame your irritability on your current condition and hope it improves as your body heals."

He and Evan had always been plainspoken, but he'd taken it too far by besmirching his friend's ability to lead. "I'm sorry, but you're taking away everything I love, everything I live for." He hated the plaintive tone in his voice.

"No, I'm ensuring you don't make your condition worse." Evan shook his head. "I hate being the bad guy, but I will. I'm also going to shut down your ability to send emails from your work account for the moment. And your phone. I'm going to tinker with it so you can't use it to call, text, or email."

Being the genius inventor he was, Evan could alter anything technological to suit his needs. "What the hell am I supposed to do? Sit around and stare at the wall? I can't live like this, Evan."

"You're going to have to find a way," Evan said, sighing deeply. "Otherwise, you'll delay the body's natural healing process or make things worse."

Chase didn't buy that. He'd always beaten the odds, and nothing and no one was going to keep him from doing what he did best.

Not even a stupid concussion.

CHAPTER 5

"GADS, I'VE HAD A HORRIBLE DAY," MOIRA SAID THE moment she opened the door to Caroline.

Her sister stepped inside and wrapped her in a strong hug. "I heard all about it from Andy when I popped in to see our nephew. And here we thought I'd be the one with all the news. I'm so sorry about Chase. Sounds like he did a number on himself."

That was one way of putting it. He'd shown her so many facets of himself today. Before they'd hit the slopes, they'd had their first showdown over inviting Quid-Atch's competitors to the fundraiser. Then, after the accident, he'd gritted his teeth through the pain instead of crying out. The strength of will that must have required... At the hospital, he'd immediately turned surly and stubborn, insisting that he could recover faster than anyone in the history of head injuries. Goodness, that man had a stubborn streak a mile wide. Could he not see that he needed to heal?

But he'd also been vulnerable, and that had shaken her most of all. Her heart still pinched at the memory of how he'd thanked her for not leaving him alone. That couldn't have been easy for him.

"Evan made me go home," she told her sister as they

separated. Icy air was wafting in from outside, so she shut the door with a shiver.

"You can still go back to the hospital if you want," Caroline said, shaking the snow off her coat and hanging it up in the closet. "I'll come with you if you'd like—once I warm up."

"Evan said he'd stay with Chase until it was lights out." Besides, her relationship with Chase was different. They were work associates who were becoming friends. And then there was the whole strange smoldering thing between them. She still didn't know what the hell to do about that.

"Okay, then we really need to get you some wine and Channing Tatum. Maybe we'll just fast-forward to the sexy parts tonight."

"I've already started on the wine," she said. "Which is dangerous since we both know I can't hold my liquor."

"I can't either, so you're in good company. Are we changing into PJs?"

Moira looked down at her clothes. She still had on the ones she'd worn under her ski outfit. "Yes. I probably have hospital cooties on these clothes."

Her sister narrowed her eyes. "Eww. Not the cooties!" She said it the way their nephew did. "All right, let's change, and then you can tell me more about Chase."

"No, I need a break from my day. I want to hear all about your lunch with Uncle Arthur."

"Righto," Caroline said. "You aren't going to believe it."

They headed down Moira's hallway to the back of the A-frame house where her three bedrooms lay. *Her* hallway. Gosh, she loved saying that. Before, she'd only rented, but owning a home had allowed her to fully express herself. She'd painted the hallway a vibrant orange because...why the heck not? It had brightened up the dark space and brought out the orangey tones in her hardwood floors.

Moira slipped into the first bedroom.

"Hey!" her sister called out from farther down the hall. "You hung the painting I bought you in my room away from home. You're the best."

Caroline sometimes stayed with their mom, but now that Moira lived in town, she usually slept here on her overnight visits, enough to warrant her own dedicated guest room. She'd earned it after helping Moira decorate the newly purchased house. Caroline had a great eye for decorating and had helped her pick paint colors that would liven up her space with her existing furniture while adding cost-effective touches from some of the more popular discount stores like new curtains, knee-high vases, and fluffy pillows. Lots of pillows.

When she finished changing, Moira padded out to the open living room/kitchen area and found Caroline pouring herself a glass of wine.

"Did you order pizza yet?" her sister asked.

"Nope. What are you in the mood for?"

"Honestly, Brian stuffed me to the gills at Brasserie Dare, so I'm not super hungry. You pick the toppings."

It only required her a minute to consider her choices. "I want meat lovers."

"You always do," Caroline said, laughing. "I'll order a salad so I feel good about myself in the morning."

That was so Caroline. Her sister could be such a moron when it came to body image.

"I don't know why you say things like that," Moira said. "You look fabulous. If I were a man and not your sister, I'd be *so* into you."

"That's just gross."

"Okay, I'm ordering," Moira said, grabbing her cell phone. "Then you can tell me about our dear uncle."

Once she'd put in the order—thankfully, there wasn't a long wait for the pizza—she grabbed her glass of wine and hooked her arm through her sister's. "Grab your wine. I'll make a fire in my new fireplace while you fill me in on your lunch."

Moments later, she was hunkered down in front of the hearth, lining balled-up newspapers under the grate. Man, it was nice to have a freaking fireplace. She hadn't been lying to Chase earlier—when it came to moving back to Dare Valley, she had zero regrets.

"So?" she said.

"So, Uncle Arthur wants me to help one of Emmits Merriam's great-great grandkids with some art," Caroline told her from the couch. "You aren't going to believe who."

"Tell me."

She snorted. "J.T., the infamous mud slinger."

Laughing, Moira said, "You're kidding! Whatever happened to him? Is he living a life of crime?" She arranged some sticks on the grate.

"No, he's fairly respectable, it sounds like, and this art thing...I'm not supposed to technically tell anyone, but please...Uncle Arthur knows how family goes. Even Brian alluded to some 'secret' when he came out to take our order."

Moira grabbed a couple of logs from the wood pile, plopped them down with a thud, and then reached for the matches. "We Hales wrote the book on family intrigue. I didn't think the Merriams had ties here beyond the university. I remember playing with them in the summers when we were kids, but they suddenly stopped coming. Never knew why."

"Me either, but I was little," Caroline said, lifting up the navy cashmere blanket she'd wrapped herself in so that Moira could join her under it. "From what I could learn online, J.T. and his siblings lived in California until they graduated from college. Most of them run some part of the Merriam conglomerate."

"Oil, right?" Moira said.

"Yeah, and they still have those operations, but Emmits' descendants branched out. Big time. We're talking technology, skincare, pharmaceuticals, and—oddly—organic products and super foods. They even patented a special organic strawberry that's widely sold in grocery stores. And that's the short list."

"I guess they're still rich then." Moira laughed. She wondered if Chase or Evan knew the Merriam family. Sounded like they might run in the same high-powered executive circle.

"How did Uncle Arthur get reconnected to them?" she asked, reaching onto the coffee table for her glass of wine. The red wine she'd selected tasted of nice, dark fruit and a healthy balance of spice and leather. On a cold night, it was heaven.

"It sounded like he's been in touch all along," Caroline said, fitting her legs under her. "You know Uncle Arthur. The way he talked about Emmits being his mentor...he practically had tears in his eyes."

Uncle Arthur could be pretty gruff, but he had a soft heart. "So this art...tell me more."

"J.T. wants to bring the family art collection to Dare Valley. Uncle Arthur thought I was a good resource since I know the community."

"Hmm," Moira said, wondering what their uncle was plotting. "Where does J.T. live now?"

"Rome." Caroline leveled a glance at her. "And I found out something else from my Internet sleuthing. He's no longer a scrawny boy. Never have I seen a finer dressed man. He's swoon worthy now." She heaved an audible sigh.

"Is he *really*? The mud slinger? Where's your phone? I want to see."

Caroline leaped off the couch and brought it back to Moira. After tapping on it for a few seconds, she handed it over. "Here he is. All in all, pretty impressive. He has an MBA from Stanford, but he's currently running the Merriam oil and gas operations in Africa and the Middle East."

Moira grabbed her phone and gasped. "That's him? You weren't kidding. My God, he's like a walking Gucci commercial with those green eyes and pouty lips."

"I thought more Fendi," Caroline said, fanning herself dramatically. "From my little looksee earlier, he seems to be well regarded. There was even a picture of him with the president."

"Okay, I'm a little impressed," she said, "but aren't they letting anyone into the White House these days? I think I heard Uncle Arthur say that when the president was photographed with that hideous pop star with the pink hair."

Caroline laughed. "I told Uncle Arthur to have J.T. call me. I figured why not talk to him? Maybe I'll get a long overdue apology."

"Why not, indeed!" Moira said. "Cripes, Caroline, if the art stuff isn't interesting at least he'll be pretty to look at. Did it say what J.T. stands for? I can't remember."

"Julian Thomas."

"No wonder they called him J.T. You'll have to tell me what he says when he calls you."

"Of course!" Caroline said with a smirk. "You know I'm going to dial you the minute I get off. Now, are you going to stop deflecting and talk about your day?"

She mulled it over while staring into the fire. "It was awful. Chase scared the shit out of me. I didn't tell him or Evan, but when I saw him crash through that fence and go down the drop—it was fifty feet at least—I...couldn't move at first. I froze up. He looked *lifeless*. But then I pushed through it and went to him."

Caroline took a sip of her wine. "Andy said the hotel medics were shocked you'd skied after him. Sounds like it was pretty dangerous."

She shrugged. "It wasn't easy, but I'm a good skier. I had to make sure he was all right, Caroline." Suddenly her throat was thick, and she found herself getting emotional. The image of him lying there in the snow had resurfaced in her mind, and she couldn't shake it.

"Hey!" her sister said, rubbing her arm. "He's going to be all right, Moira. You did a good job."

"Shit, I don't even know why I'm blubbering." She wiped her eyes on her sleeve and tried to pull it together.

"You know why," Caroline said softly. "I've seen the look on your face when you talk about him."

"So, I'm attracted to him. It's complicated with work."

"I agree," her sister said, setting her wine aside. "But it's not just attraction. You like Chase. And you admire him. That's a powerful combination."

She blew out a long breath. "I know it. I think he feels something too, but he's as aware of the work thing as I am. I...can't do anything about it."

"Right," Caroline said. "You're a new employee, so you don't want to mess that up. While he isn't technically your boss, it sounds like he and Evan are a package deal."

"Indeed," Moira said. "When he was lying in the snow, I put his head on my thigh so his face wouldn't get cold. After I checked to make sure he could move it, of course. And I felt..."

Her sister waited as she formed the words.

"I felt like he was...I don't know...special to me. I liked being there for him when he was hurt. It was so weird."

"And you like being with him when he's well," Caroline finished. "Sounds like you've fallen for him. Traumatic moments like the one you had today can sometimes crystalize our feelings."

Moira grabbed her wine. "I don't want my feelings

crystalized like this. Caroline, when he didn't answer me when I called his name, I was afraid he'd..."

She couldn't finish her sentence. She hadn't even let herself consciously think about it while she was out there with him in the snow, but the fear had been there, looming in the back of her mind. The possibility that the fall had broken his neck. That the behemoth that was Chase Parker was just...gone.

"But he didn't die, and he's going to get better." Caroline shifted to face her. "Repeat after me, Moira Hale. Chase Parker is going to be fine, and I'll be open to my feelings for him."

She shot her sister a look. "I notice how you snuck that last part in there. That can't happen, Caroline."

"Yes, it can. Chase can't work for the next few weeks, and he's here full-time with practically no friends. This is the perfect time for you to get to know him on a personal level and see if it's worth the risk of the potential business complications."

Maybe Caroline was right. The attraction she had for him hadn't gone away, it had only gotten stronger. Maybe she owed it to herself to see if there was anything to it.

"We'll see. He was a bear today, arguing with Evan and Andy about taking a car all the way back to D.C. Plus, he's laid up with a broken leg and arm. How does a man make a move on a woman under those conditions?"

Caroline bit her lip. "From what you've told me about Chase, he doesn't let anything stand in the way of getting what he wants."

But he didn't steamroll over anyone normally. He listened. He negotiated. He compromised. It was part of what she liked about him. "We'll see. I have to help Evan find him a place to live. I promised I'd look out for him when Evan goes to his house in Virginia to pack up some of his stuff."

"That sounds like a good opportunity," Caroline said. "Now, how about we stop discussing complications with men and watch *Magic Mike*. You can't get any less complicated than a movie about male strippers. Plus, it will get your mind off Chase for the moment."

Moira wasn't so sure about that.

CHAPTER 6

HOSPITALS SUCKED.

There were no two ways about it, to Chase's mind.

Sure, he had never stayed in one before. Honestly, he'd never even visited anyone in a hospital. But one day of incarceration in Dare Valley General was enough for him to blaspheme hospitals everywhere with confidence.

How did anyone get well in a place like this? Maybe it would be different if he had a VIP suite or something. As it was, he was grateful for his private room. He'd been shocked to hear some patients had to room with strangers. Strangers! What kind of a wellness plan was that? Every hospital administrator in the United States should be embarrassed.

Then there was the crying and the moaning he could hear from a patient down the hall. When he'd asked a nurse about it, she'd told him the man was badly injured. No kidding. It was horrible to listen to someone's suffering and not be able to do anything about it. Shutting the door hadn't helped.

The view out of his window was the icing on the cake. He was sure he could still see a faint trail of black smoke from the house that had caught fire the day before.

God, he wanted out of this place.

According to Dr. Andy, he needed another night of observation—just to be sure his head wasn't going to fall off or something.

His nurse, a middle-aged woman named Nancy, entered after a brief knock. She had on blue scrubs and her dishwater blond hair was pulled back in a rubber band. "Hello, Chase. Time to take your pill."

The pain meds made him groggy, and they didn't take away the pain completely. He could still feel it, as if pressing from another place inside him.

He downed the pill with the water in the plastic cup she handed him. But his gaze was drawn to the window again. "Nancy," he said. "There was a house that caught fire yesterday on the bench. Just over there."

When he pointed in that direction, she nodded her head. "Yes, it was terrible."

"Do you know who the family is? I'd like to help them."

She took his plastic cup back and looked at him. Really looked at him. "I know who you are," she said, surprising him. "I'm sure Roger and Cora—their last name is Drepe—would be grateful to you. Their little boy is with us, and I heard they're really worried about the medical bills."

His chest tightened. "He was hurt?" God. His mother had told them over and over again after the fire that they were so lucky none of them had been injured.

"Yes," she said sadly. "He was taking a nap upstairs. I can't imagine what Cora is going through. He's their only child so far, just four years old. What would make you want to help them? If you don't mind me asking."

"I have a sense of what they're going through," Chase said. "But it's important to me that you keep this quiet."

A smile flickered over her lips, and suddenly she looked less rushed. "Of course. Would you like to meet them? They're on this floor."

Part of him cringed. Could he really face these people when their pain was so raw? Did he even want to?

"I'm sure it would mean the world to them," Nancy added. "I can wheel you down there."

She was practically beaming. He almost said no, but then he thought of the boy. He'd remembered how desperately he'd needed reassurance after the fire had destroyed his world. "Only briefly."

After helping him into a wheelchair—a horrible experience—Nancy took him down the hallway. He passed other rooms, hearing the cries of pain from the one man, patients' conversations with visitors, and the chattering of the medical personnel. When they arrived at Room 222, his insides seemed to roll up in his gut at the faint smell of smoke hovering in the air. A woman was sitting beside the hospital bed, gripping the hand of the little brown-headed boy lying there with an oxygen mask covering his nose and mouth. Pain flashed through Chase's chest.

"Cora," Nancy said softly. "I'd like you to meet Chase. He works for Evan Michaels and heard about your troubles. He wants to help you guys."

The woman finally turned her head, and Chase noted she hadn't had a shower yet. There was a streak of ash in her brown hair and another across her neck. He gulped. His mother had looked like that after wading into the wreckage to see if anything was recoverable.

"Hello, Cora," Chase said. "I'm sorry I'm not more presentable, but I had a small accident myself. Nothing like what you and your family have been through. What is your son's name, and how is he?"

Chase didn't see any burns, but clearly things were serious if he was in the hospital.

"I'll just leave you," Nancy said quietly and stepped out before Chase could ask her to stay.

"His name is Alfie," Cora said, tears filling her

red-rimmed eyes. "He got smoke inhalation. I couldn't get to him fast enough. The fire..."

"Spreads so fast," he said, remembering how it had seemed to flash through their house and then the outbuildings with the speed of wild mustangs. "I'm sorry for your loss. I saw the fire yesterday, and I wanted to help you and your family recover. I know it's an incredibly difficult time."

The boy made a sound when his mother put her face in her hands and started to sob. Chase sat there in his wheelchair, feeling helpless.

"Hi, Alfie," he decided to say to the boy. "Your mom is okay. She's just sad about your house. I'll bet you are too, huh?"

There was the slightest of a nod from Alfie, and Chase heard Cora sniff repeatedly, trying to pull herself together.

"I was a little older than you when my house burned down," he found himself saying. "We're going to make sure you're okay. You're going to have another beautiful house, and all your toys and then some will be returned to you. Okay?"

Tears were pouring down Cora's face, and Chase found his throat growing thick.

"Thank you," she whispered and reached for his hand, squeezing it like he was a lifeline.

He understood. How different might his life had been if someone had been his family's lifeline? Would his dad have had the will to rebuild if he'd had the necessary funds? Well, they'd never know.

"Can you tell me how to get something to you? I'm going to call my financial manager now and have him send you a check to get you up and going."

He didn't know about their personal circumstances or whether her husband would accept it, but he was going to give them a million dollars, he decided. That should be enough. He would ask Nancy to give him their temporary address if they had one. Either that or he'd have the check sent to the hospital.

"You're...you're..."

He waited while she let out another sob. "It will be fine," he said. "I'm happy to help, Cora. Truly."

"I'll...tell...tell...Roger," she said, fiddling with her pocket and pulling out a tissue to wipe her runny nose. "He's off doing... God, there are so many people to meet with. Things to see to. It's..."

"I know," he said when she couldn't finish the sentence. "The next few months are going to be hard, but you're going to get through this. You have support, Cora, you and Roger. You just focus on your little boy."

Her face crumbled again. "We're lucky, really. Alfie is going to be okay. It could have been so much worse."

He gripped her hand, not wanting to utter any pathetic clichés. He'd said what he wanted to say. That was all he could offer beyond helping financially. The rest would be up to them.

When Nancy came back for him, Cora let go of Alfie's hand—a monumental move, Chase knew—and turned to face him. She leaned in and gently kissed him on the cheek. He found his throat growing tight again.

"Mister, I don't know how we got so lucky to have you as our guardian angel, but I'm really grateful. You can't know how much. I'll have Roger come to your room when he gets back to say thank you."

Chase didn't want to see the man, didn't want him to have to suffer any of the indignities that had broken his own father. "No need. Roger has plenty to do right now, and so do you. Plus, I'll be out of the hospital soon and focused on my own recovery. You don't have to say thank you beyond what we've said today, Cora. And I'm not your guardian angel. I'm just someone who understands what you're going through and is in a position to help.

My privacy is important to me, though, so please don't tell anyone. Make up a story that works for you."

She wiped her nose again and nodded. "Of course. Thank you, Chase."

He took one last look at the boy. "Hang in there, Alfie. You're lucky to have a mom who loves you so much. All right, Nancy. Let's go."

Turning him around, his nurse wheeled him back to his room and helped him into his infernal hospital bed, smiling the whole time. Once she'd fluffed the pillows behind his back and under his casts, he settled back with a sigh.

"Would you be able to dial this number for me?" he asked, frustrated that the phone was out of reach. "I want to arrange things for Cora and her family."

"This is so kind of you," Nancy said, her hand on her heart. "It's a miracle."

He'd had enough of all this miracle and guardian angel nonsense. "No, it's just one person helping a family who needs it right now."

Taking the receiver she gave him, he suffered through his wealth manager's initial concerns about his condition—apparently Evan had already spread the news—and then he shared his plan to help Roger and Cora and their son. Victor assured him he would handle everything.

When Chase hung up, he looked over at Nancy. "All right, since I'm on a roll, I'd like to donate some money to a few organizations that support people with disabilities. Being impaired like this has given me a new outlook on what they go through daily." Plus, he needed to do something rather than lie here all day. God!

"You're invoking a lot of good karma today," Nancy said.

That was the last thing on his mind. "Can you help me with that? Do you have a laptop handy?"

Her grin was conspiratorial. "Be right back."

Chase looked out the window. The trail of black smoke that had haunted him all day could no longer be seen. Granted, his vision was a little blurry, so he couldn't trust that his reprieve would be permanent.

He settled back deeper against the pillows, suddenly exhausted. Must have been the exertion of getting in and out of the wheelchair. Then he thought about Cora and her sorrow and that little boy lying in the hospital bed, lucky to be alive.

Chase realized that maybe he was a little lucky too. If he hadn't seen the fire yesterday or been in this hospital, he might never have found out about the Drepes' troubles. He wouldn't have known to help them.

CHAPTER 7

WORKING IN A TEMPORARY OFFICE SITUATED IN THE heart of a university campus sometimes made Moira feel old.

She passed baby-faced students on the quad on her way to Emmits Merriam's Department of Physics. Since they'd only broken ground on Artemis' future building three months ago, Evan had worked with the university to find them a place to hang their hat until the facility was complete, hopefully by summer. The various science departments had offered up temporary space, and after looking over both their lab space and security, Evan had selected the third floor, west corner in the physics building. For now, it served their purposes.

They had six offices, a conference room, a break room, and a high-tech lab, one Evan could use for his projects while his own private offsite lab was being finished. Moira knew they had a long way to go until they reached Artemis' full potential, but she was fully committed. Sure, it was a little frustrating sometimes to be in the start-up phase, but she reminded herself daily they were building Artemis from the ground up.

She only had one part-time employee helping her right now, but she was finalizing additional positions to hire along with the organizational chart.

Said part-timer was waiting for her when she opened the door, an ever-eager smile on his face. Honestly, it was hard to miss Gary Frehlich. He was six foot seven— one of his favorite jokes was about being too clumsy and gangly to play basketball—with blond hair that practically glowed. Being a PhD student in electrical engineering, he totally geeked out on all things technology.

"Hey, Moira," he said. "How's it hanging today? I heard about Evan's friend, Chase. Man, that's rough."

While Gary was prone to say awkward or inappropriate things like "how's it hanging?," he was one of the most easygoing people to work with, had an incredible attention to detail, and would do anything to help Artemis. One, because Evan Michaels was his hero. Two, because he'd rented a room from Evan's wife before she and Evan had gotten married. And three, because Gary was graduating in the spring and hoping to apply and gain acceptance into Artemis' first inventors' class— or get a real job, as he liked to joke, if that didn't work out.

"In time, he's going to be all right," she told him.

"Are we working on invites today? I have a couple of hours before I meet with my advisor."

Gary never seemed to let her take coat off before he asked for his marching orders. "I'm going to finalize the design for the invitation, but we're waiting on Evan's approval for the guest list." She made sure not to frown. Gary would only get anxious and ask about it.

"Okay, I'll work on drawing that org chart you gave me for the institute," Gary said. "I know you and Evan don't have all of the positions finalized yet, but we can always add them in later."

She wanted to sigh. Evan had a vision, all right, but he was short on details most of the time. Like how many people they would need to run the center full-time besides her and what their annual budget would be. He always told her they'd have enough. Not exactly helpful.

They were still learning their rhythm with each other—and while she'd realized there were many things she could handle on her own, without running them by the perpetually busy Evan, some of her ideas and plans required his feedback. Like the organizational chart. They'd already met to discuss it, but he'd grown fidgety after about thirty minutes and told her she needed to talk to Chase. She'd decided to put her ideas on paper first—with Gary's tech help, of course. Chase struck her as the kind of man who responded better to ideas on paper. But Chase wouldn't be in a position to comment on her org chart for some time.

"Maybe you should finish up the budget for the fundraiser instead," she said.

"Do we have a final count yet?" Gary asked, his right leg bouncing, an ongoing sign of his hyperactive personality.

She mentally tallied up the competitors Chase was opposed to inviting with their plus ones. There were fourteen invites in question, more or less. She did the math. "Let's run one budget for one fifty and one for one sixty-four."

"Sweet!" Gary exclaimed. "Can I get you a coffee?"

He asked her every day, and while she knew he was happy to do it, she didn't feel comfortable with it. "I told you you're not an assistant like that, Gary."

His shoulder lifted in a shrug. "I know, but you look like you had a tough night."

She and Caroline had consumed a bottle and half of wine, snickered like school girls over Channing Tatum and his stripper moves, and then fallen asleep on the couch. If it hadn't been so fun, so *needed*, she might have been embarrassed.

"I'm fine," she said, making a shooing motion. "Go

work on the budget."

He saluted her and darted off. She chuckled all the way down the hall to her office. As she was taking off her coat, she heard, "Hey," and jumped a foot.

Turning around, she gaped at Evan. "You scared me. I didn't hear you come in."

He made a face. "Sorry. It's these Italian shoes— I could be a cat burglar. Thought I'd pop by before I headed to the hospital. I was up there late with Chase, and then I spent the rest of the night breaking the news to everybody at Quid-Atch and redistributing his work for the next couple of months. It's...a lot."

She finished taking off her coat and hung it over her chair. "What can I do to help?" she asked.

"Whew! I was hoping you'd ask. Can you look into finding him a furnished rental house? I've got back-to-back calls and emails up the wazoo. I knew Chase did a lot, but Jesus... Sorry. It's a little overwhelming, trying to figure out how everything is going to work without him. But we're going to do it. Somehow."

She knew he was saying it more for himself than for her benefit. "Do you have any suggestions for a style of home he might like?"

He scratched his jaw. "Yeah, I've been thinking about that. I'd like to find him something that looks like a mountain cabin minus the Lincoln-Logs look. You know. Rustic. One story with wide windows and a large front porch. Open floor plan. Big hearth. Homey."

Her brow rose. "That doesn't sound like something Chase would want. He strikes me as more of a modern—"

"That's what we're going with," Evan said quickly. "Assuming you can find one on short notice. Margie assured me it's a common style of home in the West."

"It is," she said, guarded. "Are you sure, though? Chase—"

"May complain about it," Evan said, "but he doesn't

like anything right now. Ignore his negativity. When you find the house, give me a holler. This is my main priority. I convinced your brother to keep him in the hospital for another night, perhaps two, to give us time to secure a house. If we put him up at The Grand, he'll refuse to leave. I know him."

She bit the inside of her cheek. He'd convinced her brother to keep Chase longer? Wow. That must have been an interesting conversation. She wasn't going to ask.

"I'll call the real estate broker my siblings and I used to find our houses," Moira said. "She knows all the properties up here like no other."

"If Margie and I weren't so keen on building a new house, I'd ask for her name and number," Evan said. "Okay, enough of that. I'm off. Make your call and let me know what you find. You have full power to rent the place in my name. If we find something today, I can tinker with the house to make it more Chase-able. He won't be able to do things normally for a while in that wheelchair."

Which was going to annoy the crap out of him. "I'm on it."

The smile he gave her was probably intended to be encouraging, but his own worry showed through. "Trust me, Chase is going to be a hard case for a while, but he'll grit his teeth and rise to the occasion. He always does."

CHAPTER 8

MOIRA WAS THE ONE GRITTING HER TEETH AS SHE wheeled Chase into the rental she had found for him. As Evan had predicted, he was being difficult about it.

If you asked her, he was lucky. The one-story cedar plank house was situated at the end of the valley, and it boasted a marvelous view of mountains and water from its wide front porch. There was a snow-covered dock where the mostly frozen-over Black Lake touched the edge of the property line. The property management crew had gone to considerable effort to clear all the snow and salt the sidewalk and porch.

Chase was in such a mood, he was even bitching about the sleek, automated wheelchair Evan had bought him. Moira didn't consider it a normal wheelchair—it was equipped with all-terrain tires for the winter season, for goodness' sake—but he had just about bitten her head off for saying so. Only the constant visual reminder of his injuries gave her the patience to put up with his attitude. His arm cast lay on the metal rest while his leg was extended out in front of him on the corresponding leg rest. Evan had offered to write on Chase's cast, something Chase hadn't found funny. His former good humor was a thing of the past.

"I don't like this house," Chase growled again, awkwardly tinkering with the automatic controls on his wheelchair to turn and face her. "Take me to The Grand. Dammit, I need to get back to work."

She was supposed to ignore him when he talked about work, Evan had told her. Since he kept beating the same drum, she'd gotten pretty good at tuning him out. It only seemed to piss him off more. She felt a little guilty about it, but as Evan said, it was for his own good.

"This is a lovely house," she repeated for the umpteenth time.

"This one is too homey, and I hate homey. I want something modern, with lots of glass and metal. Or marble. Anything but this."

Hadn't she thought that? But Evan had been emphatic about which kind of house she should rent. She'd followed orders. This wasn't the time to show weakness.

"It's going to be a long few weeks if you keep fighting Evan and me, Chase."

He harrumphed as good as Uncle Arthur as she unlocked the door and gestured for him to go inside. When he didn't budge, she crossed her arms.

"We can wait out here all day. I don't mind the cold." Had a man ever had his head so far up his ass?

"No, you're a regular firecracker, breathing up my ass."

He didn't say it in a way that was nasty, so she didn't take offense. "I was just thinking about your ass," she said with a tight smile, making him bark out a laugh.

"Best news I've had in days."

"Not like *that*," she quipped, but since she *had* thought about his ass like that in the past, she couldn't protest too much. Sue her. He had a nice one.

"And here I was thinking that if I finally asked you

out, you'd say yes."

Every hair on her body rose straight up. *He was going to ask her out. Now?* The air in her lungs froze, and she found herself waiting for him to continue.

"What the hell else am I going to do in this godforsaken town?" His good hand was gripping the side of the wheelchair so hard his knuckles were white.

The dart struck her heart, and she flinched. "Well, that's the least complimentary pickup line I've ever received, you'll be interested to know," she said in a hard tone, one he deserved. "I honestly didn't think anyone could top the jerk who grabbed my arm at a bar a couple of years ago and said, 'Hey, you're not bad. Wanna fuck?'"

His gray eyes locked on hers, and he frowned. "I'm sorry, Moira. That came out wrong."

"No shit," she said, shaking it off. "Let's forget you said it."

"No...I need to explain myself."

She glanced at the lake, not wanting to look at him. "I don't know that I want to hear this. It might be better—"

"I was thinking about asking you out before this... travesty happened," he interrupted. "I've been weighing the pros and cons because we work together. You amuse me—except when you're siding with Evan—and you're smart and beautiful. If my head didn't hurt so much, I could probably say this better." He paused and then added, "You're right. Never mind."

She took her time to consider his words, still staring at the lake. Chase's words had hurt. A whole heck of a lot, and that scared her. She was feeling way too vulnerable with him.

"I don't date crabs," Moira said, as a way of retreating from the seriousness of the conversation. She finally returned her gaze to him. "Or stubborn-minded bulls."

His mouth twitched. "So I'm screwed either way, huh?"

On some level she knew the question wasn't rhetorical. He was *asking* her. She thought about it some more. Like she had a hundred times since meeting him. Beyond their work responsibilities, he didn't live in Dare Valley permanently. Judging from all of his grumblings about small towns, they never would. They wouldn't have to see each other often if things went bad, and besides, they were both professionals. Neither would let a...what would she call a thing with Chase? A liaison? Certainly not a fling.

"If you resort to your happier self, there's hope for you yet," she said, meeting his steady gaze.

His eyes narrowed. "Then I guess it's a good thing for both of us that I'm laid up. I couldn't even put my arms around you."

Her brow rose at his comment. "Guess so, but you strike me as a creative type. All right, wheel yourself in, boy wonder. Or do I need to go and find Nurse Ratched?"

"One named Candy would be preferable," Chase shot back. "And thank you for allowing that I might be creative."

It seemed best to ignore that statement. For the moment, anyway, they were at an impasse. She wouldn't go out with him unless he properly asked her, and he was obviously not in a place to be courteous about anything.

"Are you going to go inside finally, or are we going to have a tussle on the porch?" She laid her hands on her hips. "If you want a fight, I'll give it to you. I'm out of patience, Chase."

He looked down in his lap, rocking his chair forward with one clockwise motion of the controls. "I'll go in, but I'm going to talk to Evan about finding a new place when he gets back from Great Falls."

"Fine," she said as he wheeled past her and into the house. "You do that."

"This is eerie," Chase said, directing his wheelchair

into the cozy den. "It reminds me of..." He cut himself off abruptly and said, "You don't have to stay with me."

She wondered what it reminded him of, but since he was being so disagreeable, she wasn't about to ask. Personally Moira loved the floor plan. The den and dining room were connected in an open layout, just like Evan had requested, while the kitchen and three bedrooms were situated in the back of the house. It wasn't the biggest house in Dare Valley, but it had been both available and furnished.

"You're lucky Evan is an inventor," Moira said, walking over to the coffee table and picking up the specially wired remote control. "He only had a day to tinker with the place, but he programmed the refrigerator to open for you, and the lower shelves extend and retract now. I know he's a genius, but watching him modify basic appliances like that... It was amazing."

"Yeah, Evan is pretty amazing."

Since his tone was less than enthusiastic, Moira crossed her arms. "You're also lucky he's your friend. You've been hurting his feelings, Chase."

"And he's hurting my feelings by limiting my ability to my work," Chase shot back. "If he can modify a refrigerator, he can modify the tools I use to work. Isn't the backlighting of electronic devices the only problem with me answering emails?"

She saw where he was headed with this. "No, I believe it's the mental concentration writing and reading require. Your brain is hurt. It needs rest to heal. No invention will fix that—only your body."

He hung his head. "I know the nurse Evan hired is scheduled to swing by soon. You have a real job. I suggest you get back to it."

His comment raised her hackles, and she had to bite back an angry retort. "If you hadn't been so adamant about not letting the nurse stay here with you full-time, you'd have no need to keep up with her schedule. How are you planning to bathe and dress?"

"I don't know yet," he said, putting a hand to his head. "Maybe I'll just sit in these clothes for the next couple of weeks."

"Rot, huh?" She fisted her hands at her sides. "You're being impossible!"

His eyes shot fire at her. "I told you. Get back to your real job, Moira. I don't need a babysitter."

She laid the remote back on the coffee table, close enough for him to reach it. "All right, that's it. No, I'm not a babysitter, although from the way you're acting, you need one to tell you to take a time out. I *am* a professional, but I'm also your friend. Evan is too. Are you really going to keep yelling at us because you're mad this happened to you? Because if so, I'm going to come to check on you with ear plugs next time. As it is, I'm starting to consider myself a modern saint for putting up with your shit."

His hands fell to his lap. "I'm sorry. You're right, Moira. I have no right to speak to you that way." His voice was softer now. "It's just...I feel like you and Evan are taking my whole life away. Work is my life."

She unclenched her fists. "We're only trying to help, Chase. Truly. Maybe this time off will help you figure out there's more to life than work." She was sad he didn't know that already.

He winced when he tried to narrow his eyes, telling her a lot about the pain he was experiencing. "Do *you* believe there's more to life than work? From where I'm sitting—or from where I'm stuck—you work a lot too."

"But I balance that with family time and fun," she told him. "Sure, I work hard and I love what I do, but it's not everything."

"Well, not all of us are lucky to have a family like yours, but we make do. I'm not ashamed of the way I live my life. Most people are jealous of what I have. I've worked damn hard for it."

She wondered about his family, but this wasn't the time to ask. Something told her the topic was off-limits. "Maybe this is a good time for you to figure out what else you like to do besides work."

"Besides having sex occasionally and eating good meals?" His growl was impressive. "I'm turning forty in a few months. I think I would have found it by now."

Apparently this was another conversation it would be best to postpone. "Let's table this. How about I help you out of your wheelchair? Evan and I practiced with my brother until we got it right." She wasn't as strong as Evan, but it mostly came down to leverage anyway.

"I practiced it too, and while it's not pretty, it won't embarrass me as much." He sighed deeply. "I'd get all surly again, and you don't deserve that."

"Surlier than you already are?" Moira asked, saying it dramatically in the hopes of scaring a smile out of him.

One side of his mouth twitched, and that was all she got. "I'm...not good at being...impaired like this."

She crossed the room to stand near his wheelchair. "Imagine what someone who's permanently in this chair must feel."

"I have. I've already given a hefty donation to a few organizations for people with disabilities."

"That's lovely of you," she said. With that one comment, he'd reminded her of all the reasons she liked him. Only...

"Wait. How did you do that? I thought Evan rigged your phone." Temporarily disabling his phone's major functions hadn't been enough. This proved it.

"I talked one of the nurses into helping me make donations on her laptop."

"What else did you do?" she asked, gazing at him suspiciously. "If you worked on Quid-Atch—"

"I can't work on a non-secure computer, Moira. You know that."

Chase was the last person she'd suspect of breaking that rule, so she let the subject drop. "How about a tour of the house?"

"I'm sure you and Evan made sure everything is in order." He ran his hands through his dark hair. "Go. I don't need you."

The edge in his voice was what made her decide to stay. Dammit, she hated being the bigger person. "I'll get you a drink. What do you want?"

"Bourbon. Neat."

"Not on your approved list of beverages."

"Moira, I meant it when I said you could leave. The nurse will be here in another hour. I'll be fine. I won't drive around with scissors or anything."

The joke made her lips twitch. She sat on the couch and picked up the TV remote on the coffee table. "Good plan. Andy said you could listen to TV if you wanted. How about ESPN?"

"How stereotypical of you to suggest a sports channel," he said, wheeling close to her. "I can *listen* to TV? Am I supposed to turn my chair around while it's on?"

"Evan disabled the TV screen so all you have is audio."

"He thought of everything." Another heartfelt sigh. "CNBC would be nice."

Of course he wanted the news. "You should listen to the Hallmark Channel. Some warm fuzzies might improve your mood."

"If you turn the TV to the Hallmark Channel, I'll find a way to run you down in this contraption." He glared at her, and even in a wheelchair with a broken arm and leg, Chase could be pretty intimidating. But she had a brother whose nickname was Matty Ice. He wasn't going to break her.

"Good thing I can outrun you."

He harrumphed again.

"Besides, if you kill me, you won't be able to ask me out once you remember how to be nice." She gave him a smirk just to get his goat.

He rolled his eyes and winced, likely from the pain it caused. "I think I changed my mind. I'm starting to think you *are* Nurse Ratched."

He was full of shit. He'd be lucky to get her to go out with him. Especially after seeing this side of him. If they ended up being an ongoing thing, how would be react to a common cold or the flu? God help her.

She clicked through the channels, lingering on the Hallmark Channel for just long enough to tease him before continuing to CNBC. "Your loss. I do rock a nurse's uniform." Okay, maybe it was a little mean of her to throw that out there, but he'd exhausted her higher nature.

As the commentator began to discuss the Asian markets, she saw him smile and heard him all but purr, "I bet you do."

CHAPTER 9

"HELGA!" CHASE SAID THE MOMENT EVAN WALKED into the sickeningly charming cabin that had become his prison. "You hired a nurse named *Helga*?"

"No one else could stand up to you," Evan said, shutting the door after he set two large suitcases on the den floor. "Besides, Andy says she's the best nurse in the state. He was a gem to help me find her on such short notice."

The cold air that had been wafting through the door was the first fresh air Chase had experienced in over a day. There was snow on the ground, and—laid up like he was—he couldn't exactly go for a hike. He'd been nauseous from the concussion, which only aggravated everything. Thankfully, the throbbing in his head was dull at the moment. In the middle of night, he'd tried to roll over and almost cried from the pain. It was nearly impossible to sleep with his head injury and all this plaster.

"I'm going to go crazy being cooped up like this. With Helga! She could win a Sumo wrestling competition."

"That's the point," Evan said. "She won't take any of your shit, and trust me, she won't be inclined to accept any inducements either."

Like money, Chase realized he meant. Yeah, he'd thought about bribing his nurse. "I would never insult her that way."

His friend had the nerve to chuckle.

"I also can't stay here," he told Evan. "I hate this house. You need to find me another one."

Of course, he couldn't tell Evan the real reason, which he'd almost spilled to Moira. The damn house was an almost exact replica of his family's ranch house in Wyoming. Of course, it was a common floor plan and style in the mountains, but still. Every time he looked at the massive flagstone hearth, his chest felt tight. While the furnishings were nicer, there were still too many homey touches. Every time he swung his chair around, he expected to catch a glimpse of his mother and father. His little brother. There was no question—being cooped up was messing with his head.

"Trust me, this is the best place we could find," Evan said. "I brought what I thought you might want, but with those casts, we're going to have to make some slits in your shirts and pants. And I felt weird packing your underwear. I deserve a Best Friend Medal for that alone."

"Funny," Chase said, doing his best to ignore the urge to itch at the edge of the cast on his leg. "Yesterday, Moira suggested tear-away stripper apparel. She wasn't even joking. How many more indignities must I suffer?"

"Yeah, she told me," Evan admitted. "Margie thought it was a great idea. Then they bonded over cinnamon rolls and Channing Tatum's abs...and dance moves. I kinda hate that guy. He's made it hard for every man in the free world. What other guy can get on the floor and hump it like that without making his woman laugh hysterically?"

Chase had enough use of his brain to realize Evan must have seen the movie in question at some point. He allowed himself a groan. "Are we really discussing *Magic Mike*? Evan, I'm cooped up here, and I'm serious about hating this house."

"I know!" There was that look in his friend's eyes—the one Evan always had when he'd brainstormed a potential invention. Only this time, Chase had a feeling *he* was the invention. "Close your eyes."

"Give me a break." He stared back at him in a silent refusal.

"Do it! Work with me."

He gave in.

"First thing that comes to mind. Favorite thing to do as a kid."

A vision of riding fences with his dad on horseback flashed through his mind. After they lost the ranch, he'd never ridden horses again, only bulls. "Nothing."

"Try again. Did you make anything fun?"

"This isn't a therapy session, Evan. Come on."

The hardwood floor squeaked, ostensibly because his friend had walked toward him. "C'mon. When I was a kid, I was always tinkering around. There must have been something you liked to do back then."

An image came to mind—another memory with his dad. "I used to smoke meat," he found himself saying.

"Really?"

Chase opened his eyes to see Evan crouched down in front of him. "You know I lived on a ranch. We butchered our own meat. My dad smoked some of the parts while my mom cooked the others. You can make anything taste better with a good smoke. Even tongue."

Evan made a gagging sound. "Tongue! That's disgusting."

"You lived in France, Evan," Chase said. "They use offal in everything."

"Doesn't mean I tried it," Evan said. "So you smoked meat. What was your favorite?"

Chase decided to play along. After all, he had nothing better to do. "Bacon." Largely because it involved time with both his father and mother. "And ribs. Nothing better than smoked ribs."

"Did you ever draw?"

Chase shook his head on reflex, and pain shot across his skull.

"Paint?"

"No," he said in exasperation. "We ranched, and trust me, that means you're up before dawn milking cows and feeding animals. Then I'd go to school and come home to more chores, after which I would do homework and go to bed."

"What about music?" Evan asked.

There had been singing during chores. He lifted his shoulder. "My parents liked music. My mom had a fine singing voice." The last time he'd heard it had been at his dad's funeral. They'd sung "Amazing Grace," and Chase had fought tears at how raspy and halting his mom's normally angelic voice had sounded.

"Do you play an instrument?" Evan asked.

"You're not going to give up, are you?" His friend didn't blink once. "I played a little guitar, and I sang. Happy?"

"As a clam," Evan said, standing and rubbing his hands together. "Beyond your clothes, I also brought something I found in your closet. At first I thought it might have been an old girlfriend's. Wasn't Trisha's style."

Chase watched as Evan unzipped one of the suitcases and drew out a pillow. His heart stopped.

"The more I looked at it, the more I realized the stitching wasn't from a factory or anything. In fact, the pillow smelled a little off to me. Then I realized why."

His friend held up the pillow his mother had sewed by hand. The backing was a simple cream fabric, but it was the front that garnered the attention. On a bold blue fabric, his mom had cross-stitched *Home Sweet Love* in the center in white thread. Pain shot through his heart, and Chase had to bite down to keep from crying out.

"You shouldn't have brought that, Evan," he ground out, suddenly sweating.

"Who made it? Your mom?" He brought the pillow over and set it in Chase's lap.

"Take it away, Evan. I don't want it here."

"Why not? It was in your closet." Evan sunk to his haunches in front of him. "Tell me about the pillow, Chase."

Instead, Chase used his good arm to hurl it across the room. It hit the wall. But the words his mom had cross-stitched still taunted him.

"I'm going to put this pillow on the couch for the moment," Evan said, walking over and picking it up. "I'm hoping someday soon you'll tell me about it. I'm quite fascinated with its origin, you see. It's the first homey thing I've ever seen in your house."

Which was why he'd stuffed it in the back of his closet. "You're crossing some pretty big lines here, Evan."

"Perhaps," he said. "But I have this feeling in my gut that I'm on to something. And now, since you're all worked up, I'm going to give you my surprise."

"I don't want anything," he said, hating how petulant he sounded.

Evan opened the front door and disappeared. The cold wind stole over him, and while it felt good to be exposed to fresh air again, it hurt to shiver when you had two broken bones and a concussion. When Evan reemerged, he was driving a sleek, four-wheel, all-terrain mobility scooter. The door was just wide enough to accommodate it.

Chase made sure to lock his jaw so his mouth didn't gape open like some idiot.

Evan's smile was practically beaming sunshine. "I thought this baby would soothe you some. I made some modifications to the design. The scooter can travel up to eleven miles an hour, and it'll even tilt you up to help you get out of it easier."

He demonstrated these functions by pushing on what looked like a simple keyboard.

"Evan—"

"Oh, and check this out," he said, grinning. "You can call or text me, Moira, Helga, or Andy about anything related to your recovery by using this keyboard. And the screen isn't backlit, so it won't hurt your head."

"How quaint," Chase drawled. "You're not completely taking my phone away, but I can only call or text my jailers."

"I guess I should be wearing a guard uniform then," Evan said, swinging off the scooter. "You can also adjust the arm and leg rests with the punch of a button."

"Can I order room service too?" he quipped.

"I've already talked to both Chef T at The Grand Mountain Hotel and Brian at Brasserie Dare. They're setting up meals on wheels for you."

Chase clapped his good hand against the side of the wheelchair. "Goodie!"

Evan sucked in a steady stream of air, signaling he was losing his patience.

"If I can listen to CNBC, why don't you fly out Gerdie?" Chase pressed. "She can read me emails, and I can dictate responses. I can work on the bid." His executive assistant would be more than happy to help him, he was sure.

"Because listening to CNBC is different than the mental concentration your work requires," Evan answered. "Especially on a complex bid like this. It's a hotbed of stress."

He wasn't wrong there.

"I've done the medical research myself, Chase," Evan said with a sigh. "Do you think I like having you laid up like this? That I'd insist on you taking a break if it wasn't what's best for you?"

Chase shook his head and then winced. Dammit, he needed to remember that hurt. "I know you don't. It just seems like we could come up with a better plan."

"Right. Plan. I've drafted how we're going to reallocate your work for the next four weeks—" Sensing Chase's objection before it was voiced, he raised a hand to keep him quiet. "Just to be safe. Even if you can work sooner, you'll have to ease back in. Would you like to hear what I came up with and comment?"

Work, real work. "Please."

"First, tell me about that pillow."

It seemed Evan wasn't the only one in the room who could drive a hard bargain. "No. I don't negotiate with terrorists."

"Funny," Evan said, heading into the kitchen. "I'll pour us some water and then we can make sure all my reallocations are suitable."

A half hour later, Chase had to concur they were. Evan had done an excellent job of dividing up his workload, even though it put extra pressure on his already hardworking staff, especially Rajan and Darren. It should have made him proud that Evan knew his own company so well—he'd come such a long way from the untried genius kid Chase had met a decade ago—but instead it sort of galled him. Made him feel expendable.

"You'll be back in no time," Evan assured him. "Without the headaches, surliness, and nausea."

Chase wasn't so sure about that, but he let Evan help him into his new all-terrain scooter. With those wheels, maybe he could run away from home at eleven miles per hour.

Except he'd have nowhere to run to. For the first time that felt like something of a problem.

CHAPTER 10

EVAN HAD A WAY OF WRANGLING PEOPLE TO HIS CAUSES, and since Moira was concerned about Chase going batshit crazy, she was helping her boss with a project she would never have conceived of on her own.

They were buying BBQ equipment so that Chase could smoke meat—apparently a pastime of his. Who would have thought Mr. Corporate liked making his own bacon? Chef T, The Grand Mountain Hotel's nationally famous head chef, was acting as their cooking consultant on the project.

He'd even popped over to Artemis' temporary offices on campus to meet with them. Gary didn't seem like the type of guy who sat around watching cooking shows—he could hardly sit still for a minute *ever*—but he was a constant surprise. He'd completely wigged out upon meeting Chef, and Evan had asked him to run out and grab them sandwiches to distract him from his suggestion that Chef T do a cooking show for college students about the best way to create a gourmet meal on a hot plate. Fortunately, Chef T had been amused—he'd even promised to consider the idea.

"Don't worry about choosing and ordering the cuts of meat," Chef T assured her after Gary left. "Natalie is going to handle that. She'll add it to Chase's catering account."

Right, Evan had set up a regular account with the two best restaurants in Dare Valley for Chase.

"You're going to need wood chips," Chef T said. "You should ask Chase what he wants, but honestly, it's pretty standard—hickory, mesquite, apple, cherry, and oak. Then there are the rubs. He'll need spices. Are you taking notes, Moira?"

Was she taking notes? Evan smirked at her from his position at the computer in their conference room. He was selecting the best smoker on the market.

"Do I look like a BBQ secretary to you?" she asked Chef T. The question was rhetorical, so she didn't wait for an answer before turning toward Evan and asking, "Are we really doing this? Did you ask Chase if he *wanted* a smoker?"

Evan had returned his attention to the screen, and he didn't look up.

"Hey over there! Genius inventor! Did you ask Chase if he wanted to spend his convalescence smoking meat?"

This time her boss gave her his attention. "Chase talked about it in the way I talk about racing hot cars. He might not have smoked meat in a long time, but he'll be happy to resume the hobby."

Smoking as a hobby? Suddenly she felt like she was living an episode of *Pioneer Woman*. "I think all of you are crazy. He's the CFO of a global conglomerate. Not Billy Bob BBQ."

Chef T snorted. "That's a good name. Maybe I'll call myself that in my next cooking show if I don't go with Gary's idea, which isn't bad, by the way. Evan's right, Moira—Chase needs a distraction. Andy said smoking meat isn't on the concussion no-no list, so we should help Chase get his smoke on."

"Of course it isn't on any list," she said, rolling her

eyes. "What self-respecting doctor would think to add it? Honestly, you two. Shouldn't we just ask him?"

Evan gave her a playful wink. "Trust me, this is a good thing. Chef T, I want you and Natalie to have a gift box ready tomorrow. Everything a man would need to smoke meat. Chips. Spices. Equipment. And, well, meat. I'm having a couple smokers shipped overnight."

The next morning dawned cold and snowy, typical for January, but Moira found herself standing next to Evan in the freezing wind as they knocked on Chase's front door.

When he shouted, "Enter," Evan blessedly turned the knob. Inside, a fire was blazing in the hearth. Chase wheeled himself over from his position by the fireplace. He'd been listening to the radio, more investment news from what she could hear. His gray eyes zeroed in on what they were holding, and he frowned.

"We brought gifts," Evan said, hefting the boxes he'd personally wrapped in giant red bows. Of course, Evan's bows had been terrible, so Moira had retied them after he'd picked her up at the institute.

"I have a gift bag since Evan is apparently sexist when it comes to letting women lift heavy boxes."

"Suddenly, I'm terrified," Chase said dryly.

Moira took a moment to study his face. There were dark circles under his eyes and grooves around his mouth. She'd bet anything he was still having trouble sleeping. The casts were obviously uncomfortable, and he'd admitted his pain meds had been wearing off in the middle of the night. Poor guy.

He was growing a beard, and while he looked pretty rough compared to his normal clean-cut style, somehow it only made him hotter in her estimation. If he'd been wearing a plaid shirt...she'd be in trouble.

"You should be terrified," Moira said, deciding to navigate a middle road between Chase and Evan. If he hated Evan's idea, he'd have a friend in her.

"We brought you everything a man could want to smoke meat," Evan said, setting the boxes on the floor and opening the lids. "An assortment of the finest wood chips, an array of amazing spices, a chimney starter, a fire stick...and meat, of course. Chef T and Natalie have procured and will continue to procure for you the best pork belly and pork shoulder and whatever cuts you want. Come see."

Chase's frown grew darker. "You think I'm going to cook with a broken arm and leg? From a scooter no less? Evan, you're out of your goddamn mind. Sorry about the cussing, Moira."

She gave him a smile. "Cuss away. I told Evan he should ask you about all this first."

Evan shot her a scorching look. "I also bought you two kinds of smokers: an electric one so you don't have to work as hard and an old-fashioned one that needs a real old-fashioned fire. They're set up on the back deck as we speak."

Chase wheeled off in that direction, and Moira and Evan followed.

"You're supposed to be on my side," Evan said softly.

"I'm on Chase's side," she said. "Someone needs to be."

Evan's mouth pinched. "I am too. He *wants* to do this. We just need to give him permission."

It seemed like a laughable idea—Chase wasn't the kind of man who would ask for permission. "Chase does what he wants. Besides, he isn't going to become some weekend grill master."

"Perhaps not, but he's going to do it because he's bored stiff, and it's going to reconnect him with something from his past. For reasons I can't talk about, he needs that right now, Moira."

She was intrigued. How would messing around with

a couple of smokers connect Chase to his past? And why wasn't Evan willing to talk about it?

"This isn't a bad smoker," Chase said when they emerged onto the deck.

Fortunately, the delivery crew was nowhere in sight. Evan had possessed the foresight to ask them to assemble it at the store, something she'd laughed at. Since it was winter, she expected everything got assembled inside. He was such a newbie sometimes.

Chase ran his hands over the cast-iron frame like it was the finest treasure. "The electric one is pathetic, Evan. I would never use it."

"You might when the weather is cold enough to freeze your balls off, Chase. It takes some doing to keep a fire hot enough to smoke meat in the winter. From what I read, it's a hell of a lot harder to smoke meat in cold temperatures."

"You forget I'm originally from Wyoming," Chase said, wheeling his scooter over to the end of the smoker, where a chimney-like opening was located.

Yeah, Chase wasn't a hard winter newbie like Evan. He seemed built for the cold.

"We did just fine. Sure, the cast iron absorbs a lot of heat in warmer months, but things like bacon do better with a cold smoke."

A cold smoke? Was that even possible?

"What kind of chips did you get me?" Chase asked, raising and lowering the smoker's lid and giving it a thorough inspection.

"All kinds," Evan said.

He gave Moira a knowing smile. She thought about sticking out her tongue at him, but figured it would be crossing a line. Instead, she rolled her eyes dramatically.

"I'll need corn cobs too," Chase said, turning to face them. "They give a fabulous flavor to bacon and ham. It's from the Native Americans."

"I'll find some," Evan said, grinning. "So I did good?"

"I haven't decided." Chase looked over in her direction, his gray eyes intent. "Show me the meat."

"Be right back," Evan said, taking off for the house.

"No, we'll go inside," Chase said. "Moira is cold."

She was surprised he'd noticed. Chase was a details man, but with all the pain he was experiencing, he hadn't been in his usual fine form lately. "I'm fine. I still have my coat on."

"We're going inside," Chase ordered, and his tone sounded like the old Chase.

He pressed a button on his scooter, and the door slid open. Another button press closed it behind them once they were all back inside.

"Aren't the automated doors awesome, Chase?" Evan said as they headed back to the boxes he'd brought. "I knew it would be easy to rig them to open and close with a remote. My buddy, Wayne, at Smith's Hardware store is my go-to in Dare Valley."

Despite Wayne's constant hale-and-hearty jokes, which drove all the Hales nuts, Moira was glad Evan had bonded with the nerdy store owner. Even if it was weird.

"You've outdone yourself, Evan," Chase said. "This house is a laboratory experiment of invention for invalids."

Evan's smile faded, and Moira shot Chase a look.

"He's worked hard to make it more comfortable for you." *Be nice.*

"I know," he said, looking down in his lap. "I'm sorry if I sound surly again. I'm still adjusting to having all this time on my hands. Helga isn't the most charming of companions."

"Well, now you can smoke meat to your heart's content," Evan said, forcing cheer into his voice. He reached into one of the boxes and emerged with a package wrapped in brown paper and a plastic bag full of what looked like salt. "Here's the pork belly Chef T picked. He included curing salt. Said you'd know what to do with it."

"Can't make bacon without it," Chase said, holding out his hand. "I'm going to need some cookie sheets... hell, I'm going to need help...with all of this." Frustration twisted his features, and he let his hand fall. "Oh, who are we kidding? I can barely dress myself. How in the hell am I supposed to prepare and smoke meat? Forget it. Forget all of it."

"I'll help you, Chase," Moira said, stepping into his path when he began to scoot away. "If you want to smoke meat, we'll smoke meat. You don't have to do everything alone."

"As I've said before, you have a full-time job." Chase jerked his good thumb in Evan's direction. "So do you."

"I *like* bacon," Moira said. "Thick, smoky bacon. If you can make it, I'll help you. I'll consider it payment enough."

"A woman who likes bacon," Chase mused, stroking his beard with his good hand. "Imagine that."

"I also like pork shoulder and pretty much any other meat out there," Moira said, putting her hands on her hips. "Here be a carnivore."

"Me too!" Evan said, patting his chest. "We'll help if we can eat what we make."

It touched Moira to watch them together. Evan obviously understood how important Chase's pride was to him.

The gruff man in the scooter gave them the makings of a smile. "Fine," he said. "We can't all starve in the wilderness. I'll tell you what I need, and we'll make this happen. The bacon is going to take about a week to cure, but we can smoke the pork shoulder tomorrow if you'd like to swing by."

"I'd love to," Moira said, happy to see the change in

him. "If that's all right with Evan."

"We'll make sure everything at the center is running smoothly before we leave. If it's okay, maybe Margie can join us for dinner? She'll bring a baguette."

Chase pointed to the kitchen. "She already dropped off her own gift basket stocked with more bread than any one man can eat. I know you sent her to check on me, Evan."

"Then we're covered on the bread front," Evan said, clapping his hands. "I plead the fifth on the rest."

Moira let out a laugh, which made Chase glance her way. His intense gaze sent electricity skating down her spine. Even sitting there in his scooter with casts on his arm and leg, he managed to be compelling. His mouth quirked up on the right as if he were reading her mind.

"Bring a few bottles of wine too, Evan," Chase said. "I can't drink yet, but the rest of you can. And I imagine we'll need some side dishes. We can't just eat meat and bread for dinner."

"We can in my world," Moira said, making Chase smile wider. "Don't worry. I'll cover the sides."

"So, it's a date then," Chase said, his husky voice offering all sorts of promises a man in his condition had no business throwing out there.

She caught Evan smirking in her peripheral vision and decided it best not to engage.

"A date it is," she found herself responding.

CHAPTER 11

THE NEXT DAY CHASE WAS FEELING EVERY STINKING limitation of his current condition. His head was hurting non-stop, and damn it all if there wasn't a constant throb in his leg. He could feel it swelling, pushing against the plaster cast. He'd kept it propped up on a pillow all day.

He wasn't a man prone to self-pity, but today he had to admit that he was sorely tempted to wallow in it.

His nurse, of course, didn't let him. Helga had told him in no uncertain terms that he was taking a shower today. Since it was an excruciating, degrading process, he'd decided to do it only every couple of days. It wasn't like he was getting sweaty or dirty since he was basically just sitting around hurting all day. They'd wrapped his casts in plastic tied off at the end to prevent moisture from wetting them. He could wash himself with one hand, but it was a bitch. Still better than Helga getting into the shower with him and washing his balls, which he'd assured her was never going to happen. Her smirk had only made him more determined, and he was glad she hadn't pressed him.

Somehow Helga was managing to preserve his dignity the best she could.

She'd even surprised him by agreeing to open the spice bottles for him, something he'd discovered he couldn't easily do with one hand. Then she'd turned into his sous chef extraordinaire by curing the bacon for him and hefting the pork shoulder out and arranging it on a cookie sheet so he could rub the meat. That he could manage with one hand, but the process of making a rub was haphazard at best. He'd thrown spices into a bowl by eye—using black pepper, dried lemon, chili powder, and sage—and stirred them awkwardly.

His dad had always said the best rub was one you wanted to lick off your fingers, the meat notwithstanding. Sadness had overwhelmed him at the memory, and so he stirred harder. When he was satisfied with the flavor, he rubbed the meat, oddly enjoying the process of transforming the plain pork into something more.

A rub and a good smoke would do that.

"Cooking will be healing for you," Helga said when he removed his hand from the meat.

"What did you say?" he asked, still coming out of his childhood reverie. He wiped his hands off with the wet cloth she'd brought him.

"Food makes people happy," she said, her full face transformed by a rare smile. "Happy people heal faster."

Chase knew medical professionals talked about such things, but it was hard to imagine it in regards to *him*.

"Are you trying not to laugh?" she asked, ever perceptive. "Maybe you should. It might make you happy."

His mouth was tugged into a smile. "I don't think I expected anyone to ever include my name and healing in the same sentence."

She started laughing, enough that her shoulder-length, straw-colored hair bobbed with the movement. "Even tough cookies like you need to heal. You're resisting it. The body is a healing instrument. It's made to heal."

Cocking his head to the right to study her sent a spear of pain through his head. "I thought the body started to break down after a certain age."

"You look pretty decent for your age," she said, chuckling. "So do I."

He studied her, for the first time. She was five-ten and large-boned, but despite his Sumo joke to Evan—which he now regretted—she wasn't fat. He'd guess she was probably in her early sixties, but her muscles were more than impressive. She'd helped him out of his scooter a few times when he was in too much pain to do it himself. While she was tough, she was also kind. Evan would have looked for that.

"Do you cook?" he asked her.

"Every day," she said. "It's one of the ways I relax after a tough time at the office."

He thought about what a tough day might look like for a nurse. Dealing with people's physical issues and emotions couldn't be all that easy.

"Thanks for helping me, Helga," he said.

"Any time, Chase," she said, washing her hands. "Your friends can take over when they arrive."

Yeah, Evan would help him, and so would Margie. And then there was Moira...

He found himself excited by the prospect of seeing her.

"Enjoy the rest of your day," Chase said, which made her smile again, softly this time. Like she'd won a victory.

Maybe she had.

They were finding their way together in this horrible life event called convalescence. He decided to be grateful for that. Since he'd been in the accident, he hadn't been grateful for anything. Hadn't felt like he'd had a win.

Well, he planned to have another one. No, two more. He was going to smoke the shit out of this pork shoulder, and he was going to enjoy seeing Moira.

Maybe he could get her to talk about the institute. He was dying for any talk related to work. After he'd approved Evan's reallocation of his work and travel—with a locked jaw, mind you—Evan had deflected any and all of his questions about company business, saying they'd talk about it when he felt a little better. Chase hadn't liked that answer one bit.

He wheeled himself over to the stack of wood chips Helga had opened for him. All the different varieties were set out on the counter. He was going to use mesquite, he decided. The flavor would be edgier for the pork shoulder. Chef T had been inspired in his spice selections, even going so far as to include lavender, which really intrigued Chase. What meat and smoke might work with lavender? Surely the French had tried something. They incorporated lavender into food as though it were an art form.

If only Evan would let him go online and do some research. Maybe he could talk his friend into it when he arrived.

A few hours later, Evan held the line again on Chase using a computer. "I'll find you some BBQ rub books."

"I'll help," Margie said, her smile eager and genuine.

She really was a sweetheart, and the perfect match for Evan in so many ways. But he needed an ally in this. He looked over at Moira, who was pouring a bold Chianti into three wine glasses.

"Don't look at me," she said. "Evan agreed to be the technology bad guy."

"But I want to look up how the French might use lavender in a rub or marinade," Chase said, refusing to be embarrassed. Some men would feel compelled to give up their Man Card for even talking about lavender.

"I'll bring you some printouts," Evan said.

It felt like someone had turned his burner on to

simmer, but Chase decided not to let this minor setback diminish his mood. He was about to smoke meat for the first time since before his family's ranch had burned down. Pain shot through his heart, and he must have winced because Margie darted over and put her hand on his good shoulder.

"Are you okay, Chase?"

"Just a pain," he said, trying not to worry. He'd thought the pain he'd felt in his heart before the accident had been a psychosomatic reaction to his memories of the fire, but he was smart enough to know he should get it checked out.

Andy had agreed to check in on him at Evan's request—likely accompanied by a fat donation to Dare Valley General—and Chase planned to confidentially ask him to take a look at his heart. His first home visit was tomorrow. As his doctor, he couldn't tell Evan or Moira anything.

"I know you can't have any wine, Chase," Moira said, "but I wondered if you'd like some sparkling water with lime?"

"That would be great," he said, looking forward to the day he could have his first bourbon. He wasn't a big drinker, but he felt like a kid at an adult party, not being able to enjoy a drink with their meal.

When she handed him the glass, she lifted hers in a toast. "To a speedy recovery."

"That I can drink to," he said, and everyone crossed to touch glasses with his.

It was hard not to feel awkward in the scooter. He was used to being a commanding presence in the room, not a pitiful one. He shook it off. He'd entertained self-pity enough in the last few days to last a lifetime.

"Let's get the chimney starter going. Moira, will you help me?"

Her eyebrow rose a fraction before she smiled.

"Of course. Let me get my coat."

"Grab some newspaper by the fireplace too," Chase told her.

Evan put his arms around Margie. "We'll observe from the door. Warmer here."

If Evan knew why he'd asked Moira and not him, he wasn't giving anything away. Margie, however, was studying him carefully.

"Thanks for bringing the bread," he said, hoping to distract her.

She smiled immediately. "Of course. I'll make sure you have some delivered every day."

"You'd better get a move on, Chase," Evan said, kissing the top of Margie's head. "This one goes to bed early since she starts her bread making before dawn."

Bakery hours weren't the only reason they went to bed early. They were newlyweds, and Chase couldn't be happier to see his friend so happily married. *Good for them*, he thought.

"Moira, you ready?"

"As a clam," she said, sauntering over, ruffling the newspaper.

"I think it's 'happy as a clam,'" Chase said, his lips twitching.

She shrugged. "Lead on."

He fought embarrassment as he wheeled to the back patio doors in his scooter and then pressed the button to open the door. But when he reached the smoker, a new peace settled over him, drowning out his nerves. It had been so long since he'd smoked anything. But somewhere inside, on some deep intuitive level, he remembered what to do. Some of his favorite, and earliest, childhood memories were of smoking meat outside with his dad, and they'd done it together until...they hadn't.

Helga had set everything up for him before she'd left. Bless her. The bag of coals lay open by the patio table.

He gestured to the chimney starter, eyeing the funnel designed to hold the coals.

"Can you ball up some newspaper and put it under here? Then we'll add the coals on top."

"I've helped light coals before, with my brothers," she told him, to which he nodded.

She was efficient—just like she'd proven herself to be with everything related to Artemis. Her newspaper balls were precise and laid out in a perfect circle under the chimney starter. Then she added the coals up to the top. He handed her the torch lighter, but she shook her head.

"I think you should do the honors," she said.

He clicked the black button and the flame appeared. Touching it to the paper, he watched, entranced, as everything caught. The coals started to simmer and pop, and he realized how much he used to love that sound. It was primal of him perhaps, but there was something about fire.

He wasn't afraid of it, oddly—even after what it had done to his home.

In an odd way, he respected its power. It could warm a home as well as destroy it.

"Once you pour the coals into the smoker, we need to use the tongs to arrange them in a circle," he said. "Then we put a few of the wood chunks on the outside of the coals. It's called the snake method."

"So long as you don't plan on smoking snake for dinner," she quipped, reaching into the bag of wood chips.

"I've smoked a lot of meat—rabbit, elk, venison—but never snake."

"You're a wise man," she said dryly. "Okay, let's do this."

He wheeled closer to the side of the smoker, careful of the popping and sizzling chimney starter on the side grate.

"Wait. Use the heat protection gloves," he said, pointing to the gloves slung over the railing.

Her brow wrinkled as she put them on. "I've always wanted to wear giant rubber gloves in prison orange."

He found himself smiling. "I wish I could take a picture of you like that."

She did jazz hands with the gloves and made a face. "I'm sure I look adorable."

As she picked up the chimney starter, he found himself saying, "You do. Maybe you should wear prison orange more often."

"Your mood is much improved," she said, carefully emptying the coals into the smoker and arranging the coals and wood chunks to his specifications, again with precision. "Is this right?"

"Yes."

"You should smoke more often."

"Funny," he said, but she was right. He did feel better. The anger that had become his constant companion these last several days had finally loosened its grip.

He was actually enjoying himself. "Time for this baby to get up to temperature."

Leaning over, he checked on the coals one last time. Small ribbons of smoke were already trailing up from where those white-hot briquettes were touching the wood chunks. Mesquite smoke tickled his nose, and he inhaled deeply.

"I'm getting hungry already," Moira said. "When is the pork shoulder going to be ready?"

He'd had Helga cut the one Chef T had delivered in half to ensure a faster cook time. "About two hours."

"Two hours," she exclaimed. "Seriously?"

He let his mouth tip up. "Yep. I thought you and Evan could fill me in on the Artemis Institute in the meantime. It's only talking. My brain can handle that, according to your brother."

She put her hands on her hips. "You are a devious man."

Sue him, he'd planned to maroon them for a few hours. "You guys can drink wine. I want to circle back to the guest list for the fundraiser."

"You're still chomping on that bone?" she said, meeting his gaze and holding it. "Cripes. I'm going inside to tell Evan we've been set up."

He eyed the smoker and closed the lid. "You do that. I'll stay out here until we have the right temperature." The shoulder needed to be cooked at around two hundred and twenty degrees, plus or minus ten degrees.

She walked inside, and pretty soon Evan came out to the patio with the seasoned pork shoulder on a cookie sheet. "I hear you had a bigger plan than dinner."

"We have to talk about things, Evan," Chase told him as Evan placed the meat on the cooking ledge to the right of the smoker. "Like the guest list for the fundraiser. We didn't get the chance to discuss my concerns after the accident. Did you really think I wouldn't circle back?"

"I was hoping you'd rest your brain so it wouldn't explode," his friend commented, rubbing his bare hands together to generate warmth.

"I haven't exploded yet, and if it hasn't happened by now..."

"The brain is a complicated organ," Evan said. "You can't push it."

He hated hearing that. "You cut me off from my team. Rajan and Darren even. It's hard for me not to be able to even talk to them."

"Since Rajan is our head of R&D and Darren is our VP, I thought it best," Evan told him. "They know you'll pump them for information."

"Rajan has a lot going on, finalizing your new invention," Chase said, referring to the revolutionary invisible paint Evan had created. "And prepping the bid."

"I've got MAL-77 in hand," Evan told him. "You need to trust me."

"I do, but I've never been cut out of things like this."

Evan put his hand on Chase's good shoulder. "Our counterparts are going to survive without you being in the picture. I know you were worried about delegating the contract renegotiation with the Germans to Darren, so I've pushed it back. It can wait until you're better."

Darren wasn't as chummy as Chase was with their tight-assed counterpart, and given how sticky the situation was, chummy gave him the edge. Postponing still chapped his hide, though. "We'll lose money because of it."

"So what?" Evan said like only he could. "You and your well-being are much more valuable."

He looked away, beset with messy emotions, and checked the temperature to give himself a moment. "The smoker is ready."

"What do I do?" Evan asked as Chase lifted the lid again.

"You put on the prison-orange gloves, as Moira called them, pick up the shoulder, and place it on the grate in the center. You never smoke meat directly over the coals."

"Good to know," Evan said, following his instructions. "These gloves really are an abomination, aren't they? I'll bet the French have much sexier looking gloves to use for grilling."

Chase snorted at that. "You're probably right. Maybe you can look into that the next time you head that way."

"All right, let's get you inside," Evan said. "Your cheeks are red from cold."

"I like this kind of cold," Chase said. "It doesn't get this way in northern Virginia. The cold is different in the mountains. It's drier somehow." And it felt good on his skin, like a kind of fabric he hadn't worn in a long time. It was another thing he hadn't realized he'd missed.

"See, you already dig living here," Evan said. "Maybe you'll want to move to Dare Valley. Like I said, I'm much happier in my new town."

"And like *I* said, that's because Margie is here," Chase said, following Evan to the patio door in his scooter and wheeling inside.

"But I'm here," Evan said, "and you love me."

"I should never have told you that," Chase said. "My compassion got the better of me because you were so miserable from being apart from Margie. Besides, you know I don't love you like *that*."

Evan started laughing as he closed the door. "What a bromance we'd have, though."

"You two would be a good bromance," Margie said, joining him in laughter.

"Shut up, Margie," Chase said, eyeing the row of sliced baguette she'd arranged on a long wooden plate.

Evan pulled his wife in for a kiss, and Chase looked away, only to lock gazes with Moira, who had removed her coat. Her brown hair curved around her neck in a way that made him long to brush it aside and kiss it. Suddenly Chase's heart was beating faster. He shook himself, wary of the way she made him feel.

It wouldn't be smart to let Moira into his heart.

Even so, he had to admit to himself that some of his old bitterness about marriage had leached away after Evan and Margie had found each other and begun a wonderful life together. Somewhere in the back of Chase's mind, he'd wondered if it might still be possible for him.

Until Margie, Evan had hung out with models and a nouveau-riche crowd. Chase hadn't imagined Evan ever wanting a wife, a family, a home. And yet here his friend was, the winning lottery ticket in hand. Margie wasn't the kind of woman who'd do to Evan the things Trisha had done to Chase. They were true partners, and he had no doubt they'd be there for each other no matter what life threw at them.

For the first time in his relationship with Evan, Chase envied him.

Trying to shake off this line of thought, he said the one thing guaranteed to push Moira away rather than pull her closer. "Let's resume our discussion about the guest list for the fundraiser."

Moira's shoulders visibly tensed up. "All right, but I'm pouring more wine."

"Good idea," Evan said. Turning toward Chase, he added, "I have a rare bourbon for you when Andy gives you the go-ahead."

"That's something to look forward to," Chase said. "Let me check on the meat and then we can talk."

If he hadn't been so attuned to Moira, he wouldn't have seen her release a slow breath of relief. He told himself to go easy on her. She was only doing what she thought best. Problem was, she didn't have any experience with corporate espionage.

Chase added more coals to the fire to keep the temperature up while they were chatting. If it ran a little hotter in the beginning, it wouldn't hurt anything. The wood was smoking nicely. He felt a rare pride in the task. It was helping to calm him, anchor him. Sure, he might be laid up in a scooter, living in a home in Dare Valley that reminded him too much of the house he'd had as a boy, but standing out here in the night air, over the heat of the smoker, everything felt okay.

That sense of calm disappeared like the newspaper in the chimney starter as soon as he went back inside. They had all gathered around the hearth, and it took all of a minute for Moira to start outlining the reasons she felt it necessary to include Quid-Atch's competitors.

"Moira, I know you think this is only a fundraiser," Chase said, wheeling closer to the fire and facing her. "Let me tell you why I disagree. If we invite our competitors, they are going to find out everything they can about our plans for the center, including which benefactors we're courting. Then they'll go home and plot ways to capitalize on what they've learned."

"That sounds pretty paranoid to me," Moira said. "It's only one night, Chase."

"All it takes is one inadvertent thread of information," Chase said. "Spoken casually over cocktails. They'll send people who are trained to ferret this stuff out, Moira. Government contracting is a nasty business. Everyone is looking for an edge."

"But this isn't Quid-Atch, Chase," Moira said. "It's Artemis, and we're not competing for any funds."

"But we might be competing for grants in the future," Chase said, glancing over at Evan, who was observing them from the couch. "Right?"

"No," Evan said emphatically, squeezing Margie's hand. "The whole point of the center is to allow inventors to develop their inventions and talents without being subjected to outside influences."

Chase wasn't so sure about that. "Let's see how things progress."

Evan gazed at him uneasily. "Between my money and the private benefactors we're inviting to the fundraiser, I don't believe we'll need to compete for grants."

"But you don't know yet," Chase said, pressing. "You'll thank me if it's a path you end up wanting or needing to take later. Haven't you thought that some of Artemis' inventors might want to apply for grants in addition to what the center can give them?" he asked. "It might be good training for them."

Evan rubbed his chin. "You're right about that. A lot of inventors survive on grants to keep their research going. We'll only be helping them for a short time."

"Right, it's only a two-year program," Chase said. "You're training them to apply for patents. Why not grants?"

"I still don't see why it matters whether the center or one of our inventors might want to pursue grants," Moira said. "What does that have to do with inviting Quid-Atch's competitors to the fundraiser?"

"Because we'd potentially be competing against those companies," Evan said. "They have research centers too. Not like Artemis exactly. K-Barker has a research institute, for example, which isn't technically under its corporate umbrella—"

"But is still linked to them," Chase said, grateful Evan was finally hearing him.

"Okay," Moira said, standing up as if too anxious to keep sitting on the ottoman next to Chase. "So what you're saying is that we'll have to train our inventors in what they can say and what they can't say, like to our competitors at a fundraiser." She turned to her official boss. "Evan, I thought the whole purpose of Artemis was to encourage innovation through invention. What you're describing seems to stifle some of that. Why enter grants into the equation at all?"

"Welcome to the fine line of making money out of innovation," Chase said gruffly. "No one really invents for the sake of it, Moira. Certainly not the initial applicants we'll select for the program. We're only going to fund invention ideas with social value. If they can turn that idea into a reality, they should make money from it. The public will benefit. Why not them?"

"And us, obviously," she said with a tinge of sarcasm in her voice. "So is your vision for Artemis to be a farm team for Quid-Atch? Because no one mentioned that to me before I took this job."

Even Margie squirmed in her seat at that comment.

She'd appeared to be ignoring their argument up until then.

"Is there anything wrong with us finding young talent and nurturing it in the hopes it might fit within the Quid-Atch family?" Chase asked.

Her green eyes locked on his. "No, but—"

"Before you take this any further," Evan said, interrupting them, "let me point out that we are not prescribing the kinds of things our inventors invent. People can come to us with all sorts of ideas that might have social value. Not all of their ideas will have an application to our work at Quid-Atch."

"What if one of Artemis' inventors creates an invention that could help the defense industry?" Chase pressed. "And Quid-Atch?"

Evan shrugged. "I see your point, Chase, but I don't think we can circle the wagons around the center or our inventors like this. Moira is right. As much as I hate to admit it, we need to invite companies like K-Barker and Longburrow."

Chase wheeled his scooter forward until he was brushing knees with Evan, who was sitting on the couch. "You know how I feel about K-Barker, Evan. I wouldn't allow the person who cleans their fancy toilets to show up at our fundraiser."

"I heard what you said the day of your accident, Chase," Moira said. "And I'm hearing you now. Sounds to me like you have a personal issue with K-Barker."

She couldn't be more right, and it wasn't just because Trisha had slept with the smarmy CEO. No, she'd done much worse than that. The reason Chase was so nervous about security breaches was because one of the biggest ones in Quid-Atch history had happened because of *him*.

No one but Evan and Quid-Atch's legal team knew, but Trisha had stolen papers related to a government bid and sold them to Maurie Wallins. Her lover.

It still pissed him off that he hadn't seen it coming. He'd brought the papers home and put them in his safe, thinking they would be secure until he returned from a work trip. Trisha had taken them out from under him while he was gone, along with most of the possessions in their home, leaving him with a note that simply said:

I found a better offer. You'll hear from my lawyers shortly.

K-Barker had won the billion-dollar bid out from under Quid-Atch by a hair. Either way, he had to give Maurie credit. He'd used Trisha and dropped her after she'd completed her purpose for him. Still, she hadn't gotten off too badly. Despite the corporate espionage suit his lawyers had slapped at her, she hadn't gone to jail. To add insult to injury, she'd be receiving a hefty alimony check from him for the next thirty years. The bitch.

"K-Barker isn't as ethical as we are, Moira, and Chase is being cautious," Evan said. "Chase, let's go check on the meat." He kissed Margie and flashed a smile to Moira, who didn't return it.

Evan didn't bother with a coat. Neither did Chase. Once they were outside, he turned to face his friend. "If you invite one of our competitors, you have to invite them all. I don't want K-Barker there."

"We'll just have to keep an extra set of eyes on whomever they send," Evan said.

Chase's jaw popped. "You *know* who they'll send."

"I do," Evan said, crossing his arms. "I hate Maurie almost as much as you do, but this is still the right move."

"On that we disagree," Chase said, his full attention on Evan. "This is a bad idea. You give Maurie an inch and he'll—"

"Fuck your wife," Evan said crudely.

Chase couldn't have said it better himself. "I'm lucky to be rid of her," he added, meaning every word.

"Moira can't know what happened with K-Barker, according to the terms of your settlement with Trisha." Evan ran his hands through his hair. "I still hate being out here talking about this without her. Margie too. She knows Trisha was a piece of work, but—"

"As you said, the case is sealed," Chase said.

"I still hate leaving Moira out in the cold," Evan said, rubbing his hands together to generate warmth. "Haha. I need to get back inside before I get frostbite. Look, Chase, I say we invite Maurie and those other assholes to the fundraiser and stick it in their faces that we came up with the idea for this center and they didn't. K-Barker's research center is nothing compared to what we're going to accomplish with Artemis."

"Let's stick it to our competitors by beating them on this bid," Chase growled. He wheeled over to the smoker to check the temperature and took a deep inhale of the hickory. Man, it smelled good. "Grab some more charcoal, will you?"

"You want me to put my hands in there?" Evan asked, rustling with the bag. "It's filthy. I'm wearing Gucci."

"Oh, for Christ's sake," Chase said, wheeling over toward his friend. "A little dirt never hurt anyone. In fact, it usually improves a person's character."

As Chase shoved his good hand into the bag, he realized his dad used to say that. The charcoal dropped from his hand, but he firmed his muscles to scoop up some more.

No amount of dirt in the world had helped his dad stay strong after the fire.

Chase still couldn't reconcile himself to what his father had done. His dad had been such a strong man, but losing everything had broken him. Alcohol and depression had taken what was left. Even so, Chase had never forgiven him—didn't think he *could* forgive him. How could a man leave his wife and two sons to deal with a fall-out like that?

He shook off the thought and wheeled over with a handful of charcoal.

"You can have the dirt," Evan said, smiling. "Margie says I have plenty of character, and she's a good judge."

"She is indeed," Chase agreed. "Can you open the firebox chamber?"

When Evan lifted the metal bar, Chase carefully placed the new coals on top of the existing ones he could reach. "Let's go back in. I know when your mind is made up."

"I hate being at odds here, Chase," Evan said, clapping a hand on the shoulder of his good arm. "You know that. Moira makes the right points because she's unbiased. As far as I'm concerned, that's an asset."

"Maurie will find a way to use this against us," Chase said. "You know I'm right."

"It's only a fundraiser," Evan said. "There will be hundreds of guests, and I meant what I said. We're going to keep a close eye on Maurie. Happy?"

Chase wheeled himself toward the patio door. "No."

Evan opened it for him. "I'm going to have Moira send out the invites tomorrow, Chase. We can't wait any longer."

"Wonderful," he said, crossing the floor and heading back into the den. Personally, all he wanted to do was speed off into the night and forget about the damned fundraiser.

Margie and Moira had their heads together, but they jumped apart as soon as they saw him.

"I don't like being shut out of a conversation about a fundraiser I'm in charge of," Moira said.

"You knew when we hired you that there were things we couldn't share for security reasons," Chase said. "What you need to understand is that none of our competitors should be trusted. Ever. Especially

K-Barker, and especially when we're putting together a seven-hundred-million-dollar bid."

Moira's cheeks had flushed an angry red, and dammit, it only made her more attractive. "Maybe you should send me over a dossier on all the people I need to be wary of."

"Maybe I will when Evan lets me back on my computer," he shot back.

"Are you always this much of a conspiracy theorist?" she asked.

Evan put a hand on his shoulder before he could bark off another response. "Chase has a good understanding of what Quid-Atch faces when it comes to competing for government contracts. He's also an excellent judge of character, with some of the strongest ethics I've ever come across in a corporate executive."

Chase appreciated the support, but he could speak for himself. "I don't believe in conspiracies, but we've seen a consistent lack of ethics from some of our competitors. Especially K-Barker. Do you want to know how far they're willing to go? We're talking hiring strippers or call girls to persuade consultants to go with them on a bid. And then there was the time—"

"The strippers and call girls are probably good enough examples, Chase," Evan said wryly.

He sure as hell hoped so. "Moira, their practices have made me...cautious." And sick to his stomach, but he wouldn't add that.

"I appreciate you giving me a fuller picture of the odds you face in the defense industry," Moira said. "If it makes you feel any better, I'll make sure they have a shitty table, far from anyone important."

As a slight, it was a good one. "No, stick them up front," he said. "That way I can keep an eye on them myself."

Because when Maurie came to the fundraiser—and

he would—Chase wouldn't rely on anyone else to keep an eye on him. He would be watching him the whole time.

Chapter 12

MOIRA COULDN'T RISE ABOVE THE FEELING THAT CHASE was studying her as they finished dinner.

Everything had been delicious—especially his hickory-smoked pork shoulder—but she hadn't been able to relax enough to enjoy it. He was angry with her, and it couldn't continue. She wasn't going to let their disagreement over the guest list for the fundraiser hurt their relationship, working or otherwise.

When Evan yawned in an exaggerated fashion after dessert, Moira made her decision. She wouldn't take her leave with the newlyweds. No, she and Chase were going to have a friendly chat.

"You two go on home," Moira said, giving them a smile. "Margie, I know you have an early morning. I'll clean up."

"No, we can help," Margie protested.

"I insist," she said, giving Evan a good look in the hopes he'd get the message.

He stood up quickly. "She means it, Margie. Let's get you home so you don't fall asleep facedown in your bread dough."

Moira's mouth twitched. "Not sure if that would be a good facial or not, Margie."

The woman winced. "I don't plan on finding out. All right, I'll let you clean up this one time. Chase, thank you so much for smoking the meat for us. It was a treat."

"Yeah," Evan said, "I can't wait to tell Rajan, Darren, and the others you have a domestic side."

"Tell them and you die," Chase said.

"If I didn't know you, I'd believe you," Evan said, walking over and putting a hand on his shoulder. "Good job on the new hobby."

Chase rolled his eyes. "It won't last when I get back to work."

"You never know," Evan said. "Come on, babe."

Margie went over to Chase and leaned down and kissed him on the cheek. "Take care of yourself and listen to Helga."

Her lips were still twitching with a held-back smile when she pulled Moira into a hug. "See you later."

Evan hugged her too. Even though he was her boss, they'd met through her cousin, Jill, and saw each other socially at the extended Hale family parties. She wondered what Chase thought about that.

"Bye, kids," Evan said as he closed the door.

Moira shook her head and started to clean up. Chase's scooter wheeled after her.

"You don't have to do this," he commented as she picked up the plates and stacked them. "Evan has cleaning people come in daily to take care of things like this."

"It's no bother," she said, walking into the kitchen. "Besides, this gives us some time to sort through your unhappiness with me."

His scooter stopped immediately. "My unhappiness?"

She finished loading the plates into the dishwasher. "I know you're angry with me about the guest list. I don't want that hurting our relationship."

His gray eyes darkened to storm clouds. "Are you

questioning my professionalism?"

"I don't know why, but this issue is obviously personal to you." She headed back to the table and collected the glasses. "You also don't like Evan agreeing with me."

"We've been known to disagree before," he said, not bothering to deny it.

After she placed the glasses in the dishwasher, she leaned back against the counter. "I don't want us to be at odds over this. I also don't want you to stop trusting my judgment."

"Is that what I'm doing?"

The derision in his voice was unmistakable. "Your opinion of me and my judgment matters."

"Not enough to back down when I disagree, it seems." He gave her a pointed look.

"I told you I wasn't going to hold back with you. You said you wanted that. Have you changed your mind?"

"No," he said, putting his hands to his head like it was paining him. "Christ, do we have to talk this out? You're making this more personal than it needs to be. I don't question your judgment. I just think you're wrong on this one point, okay? It doesn't change my faith in you or your abilities as the center's director."

"Bull," she said. "You looked at me as though I was public enemy number one earlier. I thought we were work colleagues...and friends."

"*Friends?*" he asked. "Is that what we're calling it?"

Her throat dried up. "Do you really want to talk about this?" Shit.

"Isn't that why we're both so keyed up?" he asked, frowning. "Let's grab a drink and sit down like adults. I don't care what your brother said. I'm having a half glass of wine. It won't kill me."

Her legs seemed rooted to the floor.

"Moira, if you'd pour a glass for each of us, I'd be much obliged." He wheeled over to the couch. "I refuse to talk about this in a goddamn scooter."

She watched as he maneuvered his body out of the chair and onto the cushions. Then, spurred into action, she jogged off for her glass, found him one, and poured more than a half glass of wine for both of them.

Setting the glasses on the coffee table, she sat down next to him, leaving a cushion between them. Her nerves stretched in the silence as he picked up his wine and drank deeply. Then he turned his body toward her.

"The fire...needs more wood," she said, jumping up.

God, she was acting like an idiot. She took her time adding a log to the fire. Hoping her pulse would normalize, she grabbed the poker to rearrange the wood.

"Moira, the fire is fine. Sit down."

His tone was commanding, sexy. Still, she took her time returning to the couch and situating herself. He studied her as she reached for her wine glass and took a sip.

"You're nervous suddenly," he mused, leaning back against the cushions. "You surprise me. Usually you're all up in my face about things. Why not this attraction between us?"

Oh, dear Lord, he was really going to do this. Was she ready? Were they ready?

"I don't want this to hurt my position at Artemis," she said honestly. "We both know the dangers of...an office attraction."

His chuckle sounded dark and humorless. "I'd rephrase that. We have an attraction that happens to coincide with working with each other. It makes all the difference in the world."

"What exactly does that mean?"

"I've seen an attraction crop up between people over work items. A shared passion for something. Like wanting to win a government contract. The attraction you and I feel for each other would have happened outside of work. It just...is."

She nodded slowly before taking another sip of wine. "Right."

"I didn't want to be attracted to you," he said in a deep voice.

His stormy gaze made her stop breathing.

"I didn't want to like you either," he added softly.

She lowered her wine glass until it came to rest in her lap. "I didn't want this either. It...doesn't...we..."

"Yes?" he asked, moving closer to her with a great deal of effort.

Should she scoot away? Suddenly she was unsure of everything. In her professional life, she always knew what to do, always knew what she wanted, but now she felt adrift. All she knew was that the attraction neither of them had asked for was very real.

"My career is one of the most important things in my life. I don't want anything to mess that up."

He shifted to make his casted arm and leg more comfortable. "I feel the same way. It's not like it can go anywhere, if that makes you feel any better. Once your brother says I'm 'healed,' I'm going back to Virginia and my crazy schedule. This would only be an interlude."

She found herself wetting her lips in the face of his intense gaze. "If it's going to be so short, then why pursue it? From where I'm sitting, there aren't as many pros as there are cons."

"There's an expiration date, sure, but that doesn't mean it wouldn't be enjoyable," he said. "Even though I'm technically laid up, it could still be fun."

He was talking about sex. Her lungs seized up. Of course, she'd thought about it. Wanted it. Wanted him. But was she really willing to go through with it? She'd never had a relationship that was mostly sexual.

"We'd have an agreement about remaining friends and professionals, something I think both of us can handle." He reached for his wine and took a drink. "Once I leave Dare Valley, it's not like we'll see each other that often. Maybe once a month at best, and even then, I'll be interacting more with Evan than with the center."

But he was on the board of directors for Artemis, she thought. And there would be meetings. More parties like the fundraiser. They would continue to see each other.

"I don't know," she said honestly.

"In your shoes, I wouldn't be sure either," he said, clenching his good hand in his lap. "Plus, I'm not my usual self. That's something a smart woman would take into consideration."

He might have a concussion, but she didn't think he'd let a couple of casts get in the way. She gripped her glass. "If we did anything, no one could know. Not Evan, for sure."

"Evan already sees the attraction between us," Chase said. "He knows me. I...it's been a long time since I've been interested in a woman like this. Like you."

Chill bumps broke out over her arms. "How long and what do you mean 'like me?'"

He reached for his glass and took another drink. "Since... It doesn't matter. All you need to know is that my attraction to you is unique. If yours is that way for me, then maybe we do something about it."

"Or maybe we run in the opposite direction," she said.

"You don't strike me as that kind of woman," he said, meeting her eyes. "The Moira I'm attracted to, the Moira I like, is the one who skis down a dangerous hill to help an injured man because she didn't want him to be alone. She's the woman who always speaks her mind and doesn't take shit from anyone, especially me when I'm being a bad patient."

She could feel herself softening from his words as much as his steady gaze.

"And she's the woman who looks so beautiful and uncertain in the light of the fire right now," he said softly.

Oh, she was a goner when he talked like that.

"You swear we'll be okay?" she asked, wetting her lips. "Work and friends?"

The corners of his mouth tipped up. "Yes. I swear. No one will hear about it from me. I'll assume the same for you since you're the one with all the siblings and cousins in town. I've already been warned about Jill's... what did Evan call it? Rambunctiousness?"

"Jill is definitely...high-spirited." Crap, he had a point. No one kept a secret in her family. How was she supposed to do that here?

"Why don't you take some time to think about it?" he said, reaching for her hand with his good one.

Sparks shot up her arm, leaving a trail of heat. "Maybe I need an example of how this is going to work with you...all laid up." Gosh, had she just said that?

His mouth curved. "I like a woman who asks for proof. I'm a cynical man myself. How about a kiss? One all-in kiss? That should be self-explanatory. Afterward, we'll be completely honest with each other."

The idea had merit. "I haven't played truth or dare since I was in junior high."

"Are you in or out?" he asked.

She took a deep breath. Was she crazy? "In. Evan would approve. He's always talking about testing things."

Chase laughed. "Let's forget about Evan right now. Come closer to me. I hate being plastered up, but one thing is certain. My lips aren't impaired."

No, indeed. She turned her body to face him, and he brought his good arm up to fit around her waist and tug her closer.

"Come here, Moira."

Seductive words. His kiss had better live up to it. With his two casts, the whole thing was a little awkward.

She scooted until she was flush against him. Normally on a first kiss, she wouldn't be this close.

As his lips lowered and touched hers, she knew it was going to be good, *really* good.

Heat gripped her belly, and she couldn't breathe. While his good hand was firm around her waist, his lips were soft and teasing. Playful, if she were asked to analyze it. Then he kissed the right side of her lips and teased the corner with his tongue.

Suddenly, his lips were as firm against hers as his hand was around her waist.

She relished it.

Leaning in, she placed her hands on his chest, enjoying the play of muscles there, as their mouths opened and connected. That was the best word for it. She grew lightheaded as their tongues met and twined.

When he cupped her face to change the angle of the kiss, a soft moan escaped. He seemed to like that, taking the kiss deeper, wetter. Her heart rate increased, and from the pounding she felt in his chest, so did his.

He sucked on her bottom lip, causing everything south of the Equator to go haywire, and she fought the impulse to crawl into his lap. Things were getting out of control.

She made herself edge back and stared at him, panting.

His eyes had darkened to a smoky gray, but it was the intensity in them that caused her to shiver. He wanted her.

She understood. She wanted him too.

"From that demonstration," she said, trying to keep things light, "it seems like exploring this briefly might be worth it." *Jesus, Mary, and Joseph.*

His brow rose. "That wasn't very honest of you."

"It wasn't?" she asked.

"That was a hot kiss," he said with a knowing smile.

"Especially for the first time."

He was preening. "Since you've been laid up like a mummy, I'll ignore your arrogant assessment and simply agree. It was a great kiss."

"It was better than great," he said, giving her a pointed look. "Admit it."

"Jeez, is it always going to be like this? With you pushing for more?"

"I only push when I'm right," Chase said, settling back on the couch. "That kiss was even better than I expected it would be."

It was pointless to argue when she agreed. "Fine. Now what?"

"You should go home," he said, taking her hand. More sparks showered through her. "Take more time to think things through. I want you to be sure you're okay with this. Moira, I don't want you to get hurt."

"Why would you think that?" she asked. Unable to think clearly with him touching her, she pulled her hand free. "I own my own feelings."

"For some people, it's easy to fall in love when they—"

"Make love?" she asked, trying to remain neutral. "Not you, though?"

He shook his head. "Sex has always been sex for me. I don't do love."

"But you were married once," she said, surprised. "Surely—"

"I had a genuine affection for my ex-wife, but I didn't love her," he said, looking off into the fire. "She didn't love me either. We both knew what we were getting into. I was wrong to think that kind of an arrangement was going to work."

Arrangement? "I don't understand."

"Trisha knew I was on the fast track to become one of the most powerful executives in the U.S., even the world.

I needed a wife who could fulfill the roles required for that position, everything from being a good hostess to looking good on my arm. She was smart and powerful and knew how to be an asset."

Moira had heard of such matches, but had never met anyone who'd experienced one personally. "You don't believe two people can marry for love?"

He turned his head slightly, but not far enough that she couldn't see his locked jaw. "I believe it's right for many people. Just not me. The price of having that kind of relationship is too high for some."

Something had happened to him to make him believe that. Maybe whatever past Evan kept cryptically referencing. "My parents weren't always happy, and I'm glad my mom finally left my dad. She's happier than she's been in years. But I've seen people truly love and support each other. It's a beautiful thing."

She thought of how much her brother Andy had loved his first wife. Her death had devastated him, but he'd eventually moved on with his childhood best friend, Lucy. She had so many of examples of supporting, loving relationships in her life, and she was grateful for it.

"Some people are luckier than others," Chase said, turning to her. "And now I think you should go home. If you want to pursue this, come over after work tomorrow. We can have dinner. I'd ask you out to a restaurant, but clearly I'm not in a position for that right now."

His hair had fallen across his forehead, making him look boyish in a way she imagined he wouldn't like. She had the odd urge to brush it aside. "All right, I'll go home and see how things settle."

"After that kiss, I have high hopes for how things might settle. Good night, Moira."

She realized he couldn't walk her to the door, so she stood, gazing down at him. The firelight highlighted the strong frame of his body, the breadth of his shoulders.

"Good night, Chase."

When she let herself out the front door, she realized how much she was looking forward to kissing him tomorrow night.

It looked like she'd already decided.

CHAPTER 13

CAROLINE EYED THE NEWEST PAINTING IN THE LEGGETT Gallery's collection. The famed Southwestern artist, Milo Francovich, had sent them a brilliant landscape of the Sonoran Desert. Unlike his other rugged landscapes, this one showcased a starry night during a full moon. The outlines of cacti against the dark flats looked more like dish antennas, Milo's play on the encroachment of technology in nature. An environmental activist, Milo was concerned about the spread of satellite stations like the Goldstone Deep Space Communications Center in the Mojave and beyond.

"It's pretty good," she heard a male voice say behind her.

She jumped. The painting had so drawn her in she hadn't heard anyone enter the gallery. Turning around, she gaped. "J.T. Merriam."

He smiled immediately, the rugged planes of his face softening. "You recognized me. Hello, Caroline. I decided to swing by in person to introduce myself after your uncle told me you were open to speaking with me. I thought it might also help you forgive me for the horrible mud incident. Uncle Arthur told me you remembered. I'm really sorry about that."

The shock of his presence jarred her as much as his good looks did, but there was no denying he was a feast for the eyes—even more so in person. With wheat-colored hair, mischievous green eyes, and a camel-colored wool coat trailing down to his knees, he did indeed look like a European model.

"You flew all the way from Rome?" she asked. "That's quite—"

"Impetuous?" he asked, flashing her another smile.

Oh good heavens, he has a dimple. She was a sucker for men with dimples. "Well, yes."

He took his gloves off and slid them into his pockets. "I had another meeting, one I didn't feel I could do over the phone. It's with Evan Michaels. I believe you two are acquainted. He tells me your sister, Moira, is working for him at Artemis."

Now she was really off balance. "Yes, she is. I—"

"I've thrown you a little by showing up like this, haven't I?" he asked. "Can we chat? I don't see too many people milling around the gallery right now."

"Wednesday is usually a slow day, so it's just me here. Would you like to sit down? I can make you some coffee."

"Coffee would be great. If someone comes in, we'll just take a break and start up again once they leave. How much for Milo's newest, by the way?"

He was already taking his coat and scarf off and hanging them over his arm. She noted the fine navy wool suit underneath, paired with the bright white shirt and gray tie. The man had an ideal body for fine clothes. Not super built, but lean and muscular.

"Let me stow your coat, J.T.," she said, holding out her hand. "I'll be right back with your coffee."

"I can hang up my coat and help make the coffee," he replied. "I'd offer to take you to a cafe, but you're the only one here."

She wished it were otherwise. "I wouldn't feel right closing the gallery."

"Of course not," he said, flashing her that winning smile. "You didn't tell me how much the Milo was."

"Oh, right," she said, feeling the need to hold onto one of the gallery beams while talking to this man. "It's twenty-three thousand."

"Sold," he said with a playful wink.

She was sure her mouth had opened a fraction. Sure, some people paid outright—a rare few—but usually they tried to negotiate with her on the price, which she had leeway on. "Are you serious?"

"Completely," he said. "If you ask my siblings, they'd say I horse around, but never about art. I like the painting. The theme of it appeals to me. As someone who runs part of an oil company, I deal with my own struggles about how technology interrupts the flow of nature. Oil rigs don't look too different than parabolic dish antennas at night, do they?"

Parabolic what? Who was this man?

He took her elbow. "Is your break room in the back?"

Was he leading her? She needed to get control of herself. "Yes. The coat room is there as well."

She showed him where to hang his coat, but he didn't follow her. Instead she looked over to see him touching the fabric of hers. "Ah...what are you doing?"

His smile lit his eyes. "You like cashmere. I like a woman who likes cashmere. I'm an unapologetic clothes whore after living in Rome for the last ten years."

She felt a ping of attraction race down her spine. "Where did you live before Rome?"

"Stanford University," he said, shutting the coat closet.

She wanted to kick herself. Hadn't she read that in her research? "Of course."

"I was finishing my MBA," he continued. "Never

room with your twin brother. Total mistake. Trev and I decided to stay close to home so we could see the rest of the family on the weekends."

The affection in his voice was evident. She expected he was teasing about his twin. "There's seven of you, if I remember," she said.

"Yep, we're a handful," he said. "And you've got four siblings. Andy, Natalie, Matt, and Moira. You're after Natalie."

"Yes, but it's been ages since we've seen each other. How did you—"

"I have a good memory, especially since one of my singular worst punishments as a kid involved you." His smile was almost lop-sided. "Technically I was trying to hit Trev with the mud, but no one seemed to care about that. I really want to apologize."

It had happened at a big party at Uncle Arthur's house. A couple of older boys had chased her and gotten her pretty dress all dirty. "There's really no need to apologize."

He held up his hands. "The fact that I've been called The Mud Slinger most of my life suggests otherwise."

"Your family—"

"*Everyone* called me that," he said, rolling his eyes. "Uncle Arthur said my fame continued in your family too. What can I say? We were ten and mud was our superhero protoplasm. You were five, as I recall. You're twenty-nine now, right?"

Nodding, she watched as he leaned against the counter in the break room and unbuttoned his jacket.

"You had a yellow dress on with a white cowl and looked adorable. The adults—Uncle Arthur especially—busted our butts for getting you dirty. I made you cry."

"You did," she said, rolling her eyes in embarrassment. "I was a peaceful kid."

"Andy and Natalie weren't peaceful, as I recall. After

your mom took you inside to clean you up, they jumped out of a tree and attacked Trev and me in retaliation. Your sister knocked my loose tooth out. I got gypped by the tooth fairy that night after being given my first spanking. Now I know it was my parents' way of driving home a lesson about not throwing mud at people."

She could feel her lips twitch. "It's a good life lesson."

Some of his sparkle died, and she wondered why. "Indeed. Where's the coffee? I'll make it while you keep watch to make sure no one sneaks into the gallery and steals a masterpiece."

"That's nice of you," she said. "It's in the cabinet. I hate those pod things."

"Me too. Living in Rome has made me a coffee snob. Go on. I've got this."

She left him in the break room, deciding a moment away from his engaging personality would be good for her. The man had charisma in spades. Taking some calming breaths, she walked over to the orange couch in the corner of the gallery and sat down. J.T. was acting like he knew her, which was weird. Other than the mud incident, she couldn't remember him.

When he appeared with two coffee mugs and that engaging smile, she looked up. "Why don't I remember seeing you in Dare Valley after the famed mud incident?"

He sat down beside her, close enough for his thigh to brush hers. "We stopped going there after that summer. I really missed it. Some of my happiest memories were our summers there. You know, your cousin Meredith and I used to pretend she was a reporter and I was someone famous. She'd interview me, scribbling down notes in her spiral notebook. Then there was Jill. She was a pistol."

"Still is," she said. "She just posed like a Picasso model in the town's calendar to raise money for cancer."

"Uncle Arthur told me. I need to get a copy."

"You call him Uncle Arthur," she observed.

He picked up his coffee. "Everyone in the Merriam family calls him that. Even my parents and grandparents. He's been an honorary member of the family ever since he and my great-great grandfather, Emmits, became friends. I wish I could have been a fly on the wall when they talked about their visions."

There was something wistful in his voice. "You're running your family company's oil and gas operations in Africa and the Middle East," Caroline said. "That sounds pretty visionary to me, especially in these times."

His shoulder lifted. "It's not as exciting as it sounds. For a while now, it's been pretty dangerous and really depressing. There are a lot of good people getting hurt by politics, and it's a struggle not to feel like shit about it."

She paused in sipping her coffee and glanced sharply at him.

"Don't mind me," he said, waving his hand in the air. "Trev says I'm certifiable right now. Which is a great segue to why I'm here. I'd like to fly you to Rome to look at part of the family's art collection."

Taking a fortifying sip of her coffee, she leaned back against the couch. "Fly me to Rome? Just like that?"

"Well, it's a great city, and the best place to start. We have more art in Napa, but my parents live there. I'd rather not bring you around the family just yet."

She wondered why, but refrained from asking. "Uncle Arthur said you wanted to bring the collection back to Dare Valley. What made you... Well, why did you suddenly decide to do this?"

"When Evan announced Artemis, it kinda got me thinking," he said, taking another sip of his coffee. "Our family has been receiving pressure for years—and I mean decades—to give the bulk of our art collection to a museum. You wouldn't believe the lengths to which some of the museum curators have gone. One of them even propositioned my mom. My dad was outraged."

"As he should have been," she said. "I've been surprised by some of the things I've seen in the art world."

"Yeah, it's a small community. Plenty of petty jealousies, artistic rivalries, feuds." His mouth pursed. "Then there are the sexual interludes. So many people have slept with the same people. Good thing I realized that after my one moronic dive into that pond."

She had to bite her lip to keep her mouth from dropping open. "Ah...well, not everyone acts like that."

His mouth tipped up to the side. "Uncle Arthur said you were smarter than that. Although, trust me, I learned my lesson. Trev is on call to warn me away from any art or painter temptresses."

His jaw was tight, and she suspected there was some personal edge to all this, something she wasn't privy to. "Anything I need to know?"

He shook his head. "Nope. I just need an unbiased expert to peruse our collection and work with me on arranging it by theme. Uncle Arthur thought you'd be the right person for the job."

"But I have a job," she said, gesturing to the gallery.

"I know that. I was going to suggest a long weekend in Rome to kick things off. You can decide if you want to continue. But I'll warn you. Once you see what I have in Rome, you're not going to be able to stop there. You'll want to come with me to my parents' house in Napa."

A long weekend? Why did she think he was underestimating things? "How many paintings do you have in Rome?"

"With the acquisition of the Milo today, the count is three hundred and thirty-three."

She gasped. "You're kidding! You have to be kidding."

"We have one hundred and eighty-two painting in

Napa," he said. "I got the lion's share as I'm the only one of my siblings who cares about art."

"How is that possible?"

"They're cretins," he joked, his dimple winking. "All six of them."

She doubted that, but she was still in shock. "Let me get this straight. You have over five hundred paintings in your collection."

"Well, we have close to seven hundred, but my dad's sister is a bitch. She stole some art from the house in the Hamptons the day my grandma died. We're leaving that alone for now, although I have some ideas on how to force her hand."

Creating a Merriam Art Museum might change her mind, especially if the press heard there was more to the collection. "Long weekends? Are you crazy?"

"I told you Trev thinks I'm certifiable," he said, holding his hands out in a charming way. "Don't worry. Everything has already been catalogued. The provenance is in place. I discovered one painting had been stolen by the Nazis and later sold to Emmits with fake provenance. My lawyer found the family and returned the painting."

She sat back, stunned. "You tracked down a family the Nazis had stolen art from and gave it back? Who *are* you?"

"I take stolen art very seriously," he said with a glower. "Despite my laid-back attitude about a lot of things, I have a code, and I don't break it."

Laid back? He was putting her on, right? "A long weekend isn't going to cut it."

"Of course it will," he said. "We'll work long hours, but you'll see everything. Trust me, it will help you form your initial impressions. I can give you my thoughts, and we can go from there."

"How long have you been working on this idea?" she asked, noting that his wheat-colored hair curled at the ends.

"Since last May," he responded with a wink. "I had some time on my hands. Trust me, it's going to be great. I'll have my private jet bring you over. You can stay at a hotel or with me. I have a four-bedroom flat near the Piazza di Spagna. You'll love it. We'll look at art. Drink wine. Eat awesome food. And I can tell you more about the museum."

Private plane? Piazza di Spagna? She shook her head. "I'll need to think about it."

He checked his watch. "Of course. Look, I hate to dash off, but I need to meet with Evan. I'm leaving for Rome shortly afterward, but here's my number. You can call me when you've thought it through."

She took the card he handed her. His name and mobile number were engraved in gold. "This is pretty grand."

"I'm old-fashioned," he said, standing up. "I like personal calling cards. I told you. Rome changed me."

Coming to her feet, she found she was suddenly a little unsteady on her three-inch black boots.

His hand cupped her arm. "Easy."

She firmed her shoulders. "I'm fine. J.T., when did you fly into Denver?"

"This morning," he said with a smile before walking toward the break room, likely for his coat, she realized.

He was shrugging into it when he returned.

"You flew in from Rome for a few hours?" she asked.

"Welcome to my world, Caroline."

CHAPTER 14

HELGA ARRIVED IN HER USUAL GOOD MOOD, WHICH didn't irritate Chase for once.

"I see you're already dressed," she commented as she took off her coat and hung it in the closet.

"It only took thirty minutes. I'm improving my time. Five minutes less than yesterday."

"The pants I altered helped, didn't they?" She looked smug.

"I still have to contort my body like I'm playing Twister to get into them," he said, "but it's good to do it myself." It humiliated him to even think about how much he'd needed to rely on her in his first few days home from the hospital.

"I can't imagine you playing Twister," she said with a twinkle in her eye.

He couldn't either. The game was frivolous.

"How was the pork?" she asked.

"Excellent," he told her. "You should have some. Maybe make a sandwich later with the leftover bread Margie brought?"

"Sounds wonderful." She approached him. "Are you looking forward to Andy's visit today?"

"If he can spring me from this prison faster so I can

return to work, yes," he said. "You don't call him Dr. Hale, I noticed."

Her round face was transformed by a soft smile. "Andy asks everyone at the hospital to call him by his first name, from the lab techs to the nursing staff. He doesn't have an ego like some doctors do."

Chase liked hearing that somehow. It was nice to know Moira's brother was a good guy. The mere thought of her was enough to remind him of that kiss. Would she show up later?

"How do you know Andy?" Chase asked.

The smile faded from her face. "I was his first wife's home health nurse before she died."

"I remember Evan mentioning something about that in passing," he said, wishing he'd paid more attention. "But I don't remember what he said."

"That's okay," she said. "It's in the past now. Kim died of cancer and left him with a beautiful little boy. She was a lovely woman, and it broke his heart to lose her. But he's a strong one. I couldn't be happier that he's found love again."

"Lucy, right?" His brain was still a little fuzzy when it came to obscure details like this. He followed her as she moved into the kitchen.

"Yes," Helga said, beginning to make them coffee, as she regularly did when she arrived. "She's also lovely."

"Two chances at love." Chase whistled. "That defies the odds."

"You strike me as a man who defies the odds as a point of pride," she said, giving him that penetrating look of hers.

Helga and Moira could bond over their fondness of staring him down. He stared right back.

"In the business world," he said, reaching for the cup of coffee she extended to him. "You make damn good coffee. Didn't Andy live in Denver before?"

"Yes," she said, sipping her coffee after adding a splash of milk. "What would you like to do until he gets here?"

"Wait," he said, his brain finally putting the pieces together. "Helga, where do you live?"

"In a suburb outside Denver," she said. "How about we do some leg and arm exercises?"

He wheeled forward in his scooter. "Are you driving here *every day* from Denver?" The trip was anywhere from an hour to an hour and a half, depending on what part of town she lived in.

"Yes," she said. "Evan offered to put me up in a hotel here, but I like my things. And my kitties. Don't you dare pretend to be surprised that I have cats. You could benefit from one, let me tell you. They're natural healers. Did you know their bodies' rhythms are opposite of humans'? They can help a person's energy flow better. Everyone focuses on recovery dogs, but they're missing out when it comes to cats."

"Helga, my brain is too concussed to deal with everything you just said." He set his coffee cup on his good knee. "Why take a job this far away? That's a horrible commute." And he was used to D.C. traffic, second only to Los Angeles.

"Andy called and asked me," she said simply.

"Just like that?" he asked. "Didn't you have other patients?"

"I retired last year," she said. "Working with you has only confirmed how wise I was to do so."

He couldn't tell if she was kidding or not, and he was getting to know her enough to guess she'd probably intended it that way. "But it's so far away." No way did he want Helga sleeping down the hall, but surely he could convince her to stay at The Grand Mountain Hotel? "You should work from here. We can put you up—"

"Evan already did everything he could to convince

me, Chase," she said, patting his good shoulder. "The drive is lovely."

She arrived at eight a.m. every day. "But you must get up at the crack of dawn."

"Always have," she said matter-of-factly.

So had he. He wasn't going to ask if Evan was covering her transportation expenses. He knew he was. "All right, if that's the way you want it. Now, I want to pick up what you said about cats."

"I can bring you one, if you'd like," she said with a sly smile.

"I'm not that desperate for a cure," he said, but then he wondered. Wasn't he? Every morning he woke up with a thousand worries. How was Rajan handling the final testing of MAL-77? How was the bid going? How had his European trip been split up between the team members? Were the meetings going well? And on it went.

"Of course," she said in a neutral tone.

"The other day you mentioned the link between happiness and healing faster," he said, wanting to kick himself. "I couldn't stop thinking about it. Now you're talking about cats. What else... I can't believe I'm about to ask this."

There was a smile lurking in the corners of her mouth. "Yes?"

"What other kinds of healing modalities can I try to heal faster?" he asked, letting go of the preconception that such things were woo-woo and unscientific. "I've heard a lot about acupuncture, of course. I've even read about some of the energy stuff. Plenty of medical professionals have come out and said alternative healing modalities are effective. Dr. Oz, for example. Then there's Deepak Chopra, also a physician. What do you think?"

She took another sip of coffee. "I've seen them be very effective. I'm glad you're open to them. Certainly it will work wonders on the nausea you have from the concussion."

"It's getting better," he said, trying to focus on the positive.

Of course, he had rolled over wrong in the middle of the night and almost gotten sick from the pain.

There was no way Moira was going to be able to stay the night if they went that far. Some moments he wondered what the hell he was thinking. How in the world was he supposed to pleasure her like he wanted to? A kiss was one thing—and it had been awkward as hell before he'd put his mouth on her. But sex? He kept trying to focus on being creative—where there was a will there was a way, right?—but self-doubt crept in. What if he couldn't pleasure her in his condition? What if he let himself down as a man or looked weak?

"Do you want me to make some appointments for you?" she asked. "I have a list of practitioners I trust."

"Are they in Denver?" he asked.

"Yes, but we can get them out here," she said with a determined nod. "Evan was clear that nothing should be seen as an obstacle to you receiving the best care possible. I can bump you up on their schedules."

He hadn't expected anything less from his friend. Or from Helga, for that matter. "How do you feel about feng shui?" If he was going to go down this road, he might as well go big.

"The studies are less clear, but personally I can tell when a room or a home is conducive to healing."

"How are we doing here?" he asked, cocking a brow.

"Not great," she said. "It's homey, but this isn't *your* home, so it doesn't have a feeling of comfort or familiarity. You also don't have any photos of you as a healthy person. Don't laugh, but sometimes that's a huge motivator. I've had a few Stage-Four cancer patients tape photos of themselves on the walls of their hospital rooms and focus on the bodies they used to have. Of course they continued with the treatments too. But they went into remission. I like to call that a full-court press."

"Under the nothing-to-lose category," he said. "But I draw the line at a cat."

They'd had barn cats on the ranch, but that was a lifetime ago, and there'd been enough reminders of the past.

"How about I bring one of mine with me?" she suggested. "It can hang around while I'm here. Wouldn't hurt anything, would it?"

He thought about it. There would be no caretaking or feeding. "I can't see a negative."

"Good," she said, giving him a broad smile. "Let's review the plan then. I'm going to set up appointments with an acupuncturist, energy healer, and feng shui expert. Anything else?"

"Is there anything I can do by myself? I can't believe I'm going to say this, but how about yoga?"

She laughed. "I don't see you and yoga working well right now. Have you heard of Qigong? It's an ancient set of Chinese movements designed to heal the body that you can do yourself. I know someone."

"You're a walking fount of knowledge," he said, sitting back in his scooter. "How do you know so much about this?"

"I explored every possible healing modality or technique when my son was diagnosed with ALS."

"I'm so sorry." Her son had Lou Gehrig's disease? "Who stays with him while you're here?"

The smile faded slowly, and that's when he knew. "He died eight years ago. But he lived longer than most people with his disease and had a higher standard of living than most. I've become a better nurse because of it."

"Was Andy his doctor?" he asked, his gut making the

linkages now.

"Yes," she said, straightening her sweater wrap. "Not all doctors are open to other healing modalities. Andy is. He's one of the finest doctors and men out there."

"Then I guess I'm lucky he's my doctor," he said.

"You owe Moira that one," she said, chuckling suddenly. "From what Andy told me, she refused to let the emergency room team work on you. She marched up and pulled him off rounds, insisting that he take care of you personally. Caused quite a scene in the hospital. She sure is a firecracker."

That she was. His chest tightened in an odd way, hearing the lengths Moira had gone to for him. She'd skied down an unskiable hill just so he wouldn't be alone, then she'd done everything possible to ensure her brother was the one who took care of him.

The doubts he'd felt earlier sloughed away. He was going to do everything to pleasure the hell out of her while he was here. She deserved everything he could give her, little though he had to offer.

"Call everyone you know," he said. "I'm ready to heal big *and* go home."

Her eye roll made him smile. "Don't quit your day job, Chase."

"I don't plan to."

When Andy arrived an hour later, Helga ran him through her assessment of his current condition while he sat in his scooter. It was hard not to interrupt, but he respected her and appreciated that she hadn't insisted on talking to his doctor without him. It was his body, after all.

"Chase has also agreed to explore many different options on the alternate healing side," she told Andy, who cocked a brow in his direction.

"I'm as surprised as you are," Chase replied. "But I'm determined to heal as fast as possible so I can get back to work."

"Run me through the plan, Helga," Andy said, listening intently.

Helga outlined everything succinctly while Andy periodically took notes on his chart. When she mentioned bringing her cat, Chase nearly groaned.

Andy looked over at him. "I won't write that in my notes. Don't worry."

"Thank you," he said dryly. "I'm afraid of what Evan might do with that information."

The man's shoulders shook, but he said no more on the subject. Then they got down to the examination, and Chase tried to remain impassive as Andy took his vitals and examined his injuries.

"The swelling around the outer edges of the casts is better," he said. "Acupuncture will help it even more. Helga, if Sarah suggest Resinol-K topically for the swelling, I'm good with it. Just don't get it on the plaster."

"I'll be careful," she said, standing at the end of the couch where Andy was doing the examination.

"I know you will," Andy said. "No one has a better touch than you, Bon—"

"Helga," the woman quickly said.

Chase was on to them. "Why did he almost call you something else?"

They exchanged conspiratorial glances.

"Evan thought it would make a bigger impression on you if we pretended my name was Helga," the woman said. "He didn't think you'd be intimidated by a Bonnie."

Was he hearing her correctly? "So he arbitrarily made you call yourself by an alias?"

"He left it up to my judgment when I met you." She gestured at him. "I agreed with his assessment. If I could have gotten away with working in a Viking outfit, I might have. You were one of the toughest, surliest patients I've ever had."

"Thank you," he said in a dry tone.

He wanted to curse. Was he really that bad? Then he remembered what Evan and Moira had said about his attitude, what a hard time he'd given Helga-Bonnie those first few days. "Fine."

"Ready for the fun stuff?" Andy asked, capturing his attention.

"Fun?" he asked.

"This is where you decide to tell me the full truth about your head." Andy gave him a pointed look. "I've dealt with people like you before. You might lie or stretch the truth to get bounced. Let me steer you away from that. You'll only end up back in the hospital with more pain in your head. The brain won't let you get away with it."

"Believe the professional here," Bonnie said.

"You think I'd lie?" he asked.

"Absolutely," they both said at the same time.

Okay, he'd thought about stretching the truth—but only a little. "Ask away. I'll answer truthfully. I'm confident the woo-woo plan is going to speed things up tremendously."

"The woo-woo plan," Andy said, pocketing his stethoscope. "I like that."

His nonchalant doctor ran him through the same set of questions they'd discussed in the hospital. They talked about the pain in his head, his moodiness, and his memory.

"I still think you need a couple more weeks to rest your brain," Andy said. "The pain is rough, sure, but the nausea is concerning. We could do another scan, but I know what it's going to show. There's still some swelling. Your call, though, if you want to go the extra step."

He shook his head slowly. "If you're sure, I don't need

anything extra. Let's focus on these other modalities and see what happens."

"I agree," Andy said, standing up. "We can do a follow-up next week. I'll call *Helga* and set something up."

He could hear the repressed laughter in the man's voice. Evan was going to hear about this when he saw his friend later. But he had to admit that this friend had been inspired in his deviousness. Clearly, he knew Chase well.

"Andy," he said. "I need to talk to you about something else."

Andy and Bonnie shared a look.

"I'll give you two a minute," she said, leaving the room.

When she was gone, he looked at the doctor. "I need another assessment. I don't think it's anything, but I want to make sure."

Andy sank back to his haunches in front of his scooter. "Shoot."

The words seemed caught in his throat, but he knew it was a bad—no, terrible—idea to keep this to himself. "There have been a few times around this injury where I've experienced sharp pain in my chest and left arm."

The man's eyes narrowed immediately.

"Chest pain? Why didn't you say anything earlier? Did you have this pain before you fell down the hill?"

He remembered how the smoke from Roger and Cora's home had made him think about the fire that had stolen his own home. "Things happened so fast. I think so, but I can't say for sure."

Andy stood up. "All right. Let's focus on the now. You said you've felt the pain after your injury too?"

"A couple of times," he said, thinking about seeing Alfie lying in that hospital bed, an oxygen mask covering his adorable little face. "I get an annual physical. My

EKG is always good. There is no history of heart disease in my family. I know I work a lot. I pay attention."

"I agree your blood pressure is pretty impressive for someone with your workload," the man said. "It's even better today, FYI, but given what you've said, I want to do a full examination, including an EKG."

He pulled out his stethoscope and put it to Chase's heart. This time he took longer to listen. When he put it back in his pocket, he lifted a shoulder. "I don't hear anything, but that doesn't always mean anything."

"I want to make sure nothing is going on," Chase said, choosing his words carefully. "But I also want to be assured that this stays between us as doctor and patient."

Andy glowered at him. "Meaning you don't want Evan to know. Shit, Chase. Do you really thinking you're just going to waltz back to work with a heart issue, should you have one? I thought you were smarter than that."

"I am smart," he insisted. "I'm having it looked at."

"You're putting me in a hell of a position," Andy said, glowering. "Not just with Evan, but with my sister. They both care about you, and since you've been a difficult patient, they're relying on me to prescribe the best course of recovery for you so you can get back to work. This could tie my hands."

"I'll abide by whatever recommendations you make if you find something wrong with my heart," Chase said. "I don't plan on risking my health. I just don't want to cause unnecessary alarm."

Andy studied him for a long moment. "I'm going to choose to believe you. I'll bring what I need to do the examination here. And I'll keep this between us. Who you choose to tell about your health is your business, but I retain the right to suggest another doctor if I feel there's a conflict of interest. Trust me when I say that keeping things from my sister *is* a conflict."

Chase respected him for that. He nodded and said,

"Let's wait until you've examined me."

Andy pulled out his phone. "I want to get this looked at as soon as possible."

They agreed on a day and time. "I'll be here. Obviously."

"You can trust Bonnie, Chase," Andy told him. "If there's an issue, we'll want to add this to the areas of treatment for the woo-woo plan, as you call it."

"All right," he said. "I'm glad to hear it. I wanted to be sure. About Bonnie. Evan is paying her, after all." It was still weird thinking of her with a new name.

"She has more integrity than that," Andy said, his mouth tight. "So do I. Just don't abuse it. Neither of us will play that game."

"I won't."

"Good, then we understand each other."

Their gazes met and held, and what Chase saw in Andy's eyes told him that Moira's straightforward attitude was hereditary.

Chapter 15

OIRA COULDN'T BELIEVE WHAT SHE WAS HEARING from her sister.

"He just walked into the gallery and asked you to come to Rome?" Moira asked into the phone after listening to Caroline's rendition of her meeting with J.T. Merriam. "I still can't believe it."

"Me either," she said. "I felt like I needed to down a scotch or something after his visit. He's like a tornado. Well, not a tornado exactly. Something powerful, but not destructive. You know?"

Didn't she? It was the perfect description of Chase. "You're going to Rome, right? Because if you chicken out, I'm going to smack you. This is the chance of a lifetime."

Moira eyed Gary, who was hovering in the doorway of her office. He gave her an awkward smile, something he excelled at.

Usually she didn't take personal calls at work, but what was a girl to do when her sister texted her with an ASAP call request? She signaled for Gary to give her a little more time. He nodded enthusiastically, but rather than return to his desk, he began pacing.

"I know it is," Caroline said, the words punched with enthusiasm. "My only concern is my schedule. Leggett needs—"

"Your time," Moira said. "It's a great gallery, Caroline, but perhaps it's time to broaden your reach. Heck, you studied abroad in Rome for a summer. It's your favorite city in the world."

"True," she said. "I'm simply...in shock."

"Well, douse yourself with cold water and call the man back."

"I'm afraid if I do it now, I'll look too eager." Her sigh was audible. "Besides, he might ask me to go to Rome today. After he finishes meeting with Evan. Did you know about that? I didn't think you did, or you would have mentioned it."

"I didn't," she said honestly. "Evan comes and goes as he pleases. Some days he doesn't come to the office because he's working on his inventions or Quid-Atch. I didn't even know he was going to Denver today. I wonder—"

"What he and J.T. are meeting about," Caroline finished for her. "If Uncle Arthur set that up—"

"Who knows with that old man?" Moira said, tapping her feet in response to Gary's caged pacing in front of her door. "Look, I have to get back to work. Bask in this, Caroline, but call that man now. Sounds like he appreciates eagerness. Love you."

"Love you back," she said and hung up.

"Gary!" Moira called. "What can I do for you?"

The young man started, as if he hadn't just spent several minutes trying to attract her attention, and then broke out into a huge smile. "Hey! Sorry if I was loitering. I just couldn't sit still."

That was Gary for you. Truthfully, it was part of his charm.

"What do you need?" she asked again.

He barreled into her office and plopped down in the red leather chair in front of her desk. "Evan wanted me to help you send out the invitations for the fundraiser."

Yeah, she'd received his email this morning. He'd included K-Barker and Quid-Atch's other competitors. Chase wasn't going to like it one bit when he heard.

"That's great," she responded. "Happy for the help. I finally stopped tinkering with the invitations. They're ready to be printed."

"I'm only doing the mailing labels really. They're not actually labels, you see, because I found a program where I can take a sample of Evan's handwriting and make it look like he handwrote the addresses on the envelopes. It's so cool. Wanna see?"

Evan and Gary were constantly using technology in ways Moira would never have thought possible. "That sounds a lot better than my idea. I didn't like the idea of printing stock labels, so I was going to ask you to handwrite the invites."

"Gah!" His face was so full of horror, she had to bite her lip to suppress her laughter. "That's so old school. It's like Evan and I told you. If you have an idea about something, we can find a technological solution that will make it easier."

Easier was a matter of perspective. She didn't like researching different applications like some tech junkie. "I'm so glad you guys know how to do this stuff. It would take me way more time."

"That's only because you have a technology block," Gary said, completely serious. "It's like you had a bad date or something and haven't gotten over it."

She started laughing. "A bad date? That's the metaphor you went for?"

"I sucked at English lit and all that grammar shit," he said with a shrug, "but I think it works."

Part of Gary's charm was that he swore about the most offhand things. "I sucked at English lit and all that grammar shit too."

"Must be why we get along so well," Gary said. "I mean, when I first met you I thought you were a little scary. But now that I've seen your chill side, we're good."

Scary, huh? "Here's the final guest list. How long do you think it'll take you to print out the invitations and envelopes?"

"No time at all. Once I input the data, all I have to do is hit the button and poof, invitations. Evan had me buy a seriously high-tech, fast printer. You have the paper, right? He said you picked out some of the fancy stuff."

She'd thought her boss would want to send out the invitations to be printed, but no, he'd told her to pick out a rich cream paper with matching envelopes. "It's in the supply closet, above the computer paper. You can't miss it."

"I bet I could," he said. "I'm like a genius when it comes to my IQ rating, but a total moron about finding things like a can of soup or my shoes in a closet."

"Maybe you need an app," she suggested, biting her lip to keep from laughing.

"That's what Evan said," Gary replied. "In the new house Evan's planning with Margie, he's got a coding system for all his clothing. You scan in the receipt from the store, and it creates an entry of the item, everything from the day you bought it to where. The app finds a picture of the item online for you to select and—"

"I get the picture," she said quickly to head off the lengthy explanation. "Why don't you try and find the paper? If you have trouble, give me a holler."

"When I have time, I'm going to use his app for our office supplies," Gary said, jumping to his feet. "Hey, Moira, have I told you recently how excited I am to be working here with you and Evan? It's like the best. The only thing that would be better—"

"Would be getting invited into the Inventor program," she said since he told her how grateful he was pretty darn often, so often it was cute.

"Yeah," Gary said with a wistful look on his face. "Or working for a company like Evan's. I can't wait to work in the defense industry."

"You're doing a great job," she told him. "Now be brave and go find that paper."

He saluted her, something he was prone to do, likely a habit he'd picked up from his father, who was an engineer on a submarine in the Pacific.

"Yes, ma'am."

He sprinted out the door before she could tell him not to call her that.

Her phone buzzed, signaling a text. She turned it over and felt a shiver shoot down her spine. Chase!

No pressure, but wanted to see if you've decided to come over here tonight. Didn't want to be underprepared in the food department. I thought I'd smoke a beef tenderloin. Helga will help me get things ready if you can bring sides again.

Her heart turned gooey at the sight of his text, but then she frowned. He wasn't supposed to be texting unless he needed something for his recovery. Who cared? He was thinking about her. It was mutual. She hadn't been able to stop thinking about him.

Was she *really* going? She'd been ninety percent sure when she'd woken up this morning, but that little human resources voice inside her head had been broadcasting messages of wreck and ruin.

Then she remembered how she'd urged Caroline to go to Rome.

She had to go. She wanted to go. Not only did she want to see him, but she wanted to kiss him again too.

She texted him back.

Yes, I'll be over tonight. Seven? You don't have to cook. I'll pick something up from Brasserie Dare on my way over. And we'll have to talk about your texting.

Not that it isn't sweet, but you're only supposed to text about your recovery.

Her body felt like it was floating when her phone buzzed with his response.

I'm within the texting rules. I'm still recovering... from that kiss last night. And I'm smoking the beef anyway. See you tonight.

The day couldn't go fast enough after that. Gary did indeed find the special paper for the invitations and then had them printed in no time. The program he'd used really did make them look like Evan had addressed them personally. The things she was learning. She would have to remember this whenever she ended up getting engaged. How much easier would it make addressing invitations?

Not that she was thinking about getting engaged.

She had a new job and a career she loved. There was no rush. Sure, her last few relationships had led nowhere, and Chase had already made it clear that there was a time limit on whatever *this* was, but it would still be a fun respite.

When she left the office around five thirty after calling in a takeout order with a six forty-five pickup time, she headed home to get ready for her date. While she didn't want to wear anything too fancy, she *did* want to feel sexy. For herself. If it worked for Chase, well, that would be the cherry on top. That meant taking a shower, splashing on a subtle perfume in a few unexpected places, creating fun, understated makeup, and dressing in comfortable clothes that flattered her.

When she entered Brasserie Dare, Brian brought out her takeout order himself. "Hey, Moira! Are you sure you don't need an entrée to go with these sides?"

She kissed him on the cheek. "This is all I need."

"Who you hanging with tonight?" he asked.

"Chase," she said, trying to keep her cool. "I thought

I'd keep him company. He's smoking a tenderloin."

"Lucky you," he said. "He must be bored out of his mind."

"He is," she responded. "I'm saving him, really."

He rolled his eyes. "I'll bet. Wait, I forgot to add your halo to the bag."

"Yeah, yeah, yeah," she said, laughing as she left.

On the way to Chase's place, she took a moment to think through her approach. Was she going to play it cool this evening? Or was she going to risk diving all in? All in, she decided. She wanted to enjoy every moment.

When she knocked on his front door, he called out, "Enter." The low command sent a pulse of heat through her.

There was already a fire going in the massive hearth. He was sitting on the couch, looking over his shoulder at her. His gray eyes were intense, as if all polite trivialities between them were gone.

She walked toward him, their gazes glued to each other. When she stood in front of him, she noted he had managed to tug on a bulky cream knit shirt, ripped at the shoulder to allow for his casted arm. It looked good on him. He had on loose brown cargo pants, one pant leg sliced in half to accommodate his cast.

Clearly he'd gone to extra effort. The beard he'd been sporting had disappeared, and his clean-shaven jaw told her he'd been thinking about another kiss as much as she had.

Why wait? she decided.

She set the takeout bag on the coffee table, which was already set for dinner, and sat down next to him. He'd positioned himself on the couch intentionally, she imagined, since his good arm was free.

"Hi," she said simply, giving him a smile.

"Hi," he said back.

Then she leaned in slowly, keeping her gaze on him.

His mouth curved, and he extended his head in her direction. Their lips met. Some part of her gave a shiver of delight in response to the teasing passes he made with his mouth. There was a nip here and a tug there, to which she responded with a playful jab of her tongue.

His good arm came around her, and she scooted closer until she was pressed to his side. He was warm, and he smelled delicious—like musk and smoke—and if he kept on kissing her like she was his version of a banana split, she was going to belt out a heartfelt moan in a moment.

Instead, she leaned back and fought the urge to lick her lips.

"I like a greeting like that," he said in a deep, husky voice, one that raised the hairs on her arms. "You look beautiful, by the way."

She glanced down at herself. Her fitted navy tunic and black leggings were sexy but comfortable. It was the knee-high black boots that knocked the outfit out of the park. "Thank you. I was thinking you looked pretty good too when I walked in."

"It's not what I would normally wear for a first date," he said with a wry glance, "but perhaps the sizeable slit up my pant leg turns you on."

Taking her time to study his leg, she said, "The plaster ruins the line for me."

He chuckled. "I decided to try and look as presentable as possible, so the scooter was out. However, that means you'll have to pour your wine and serve the food. The tenderloin should be ready. Hope you don't mind bringing it in. It needs to rest in foil for about fifteen minutes."

Since he sounded a little vulnerable asking that of her, she leaned in and gave him another slow kiss. He was smiling easier when she pulled back.

"You do look sexy, and I'm happy to arrange

everything."

"While I'm confessing, I might as well mention I have this terrible urge to ask you for the receipt from Brasserie Dare so I can reimburse you. I would never have a woman pay on a date. It...galls the crap out of me."

Oh, he was so sweet. "I can see your dilemma, but while I appreciate the offer, how about we just pretend the first date fairies paid for things and let it go? It's only a few sides."

"First date fairies," he said, stroking her jaw. "I didn't know you believed in fairies. I wouldn't have guessed that about you."

Clearly, he was too serious for flirting about fairies. "You believed in the tooth fairy, right?" she asked, liking the way he pushed her hair behind her ear.

"Until I found out who was really behind the scenes," he said, shaking his head. "It ruined all fairy talk for me."

Her lips twitched. "I'll keep that in mind."

While she didn't want to pull away from him, she forced herself to stand. "I'll grab the meat."

Her first sight—and smell—of the smoked tenderloin made her mouth water. Coming inside with it, she stopped to look at Chase. "This smells incredible. You outdid yourself."

"It felt good to be productive. How was your day?"

"Pretty good," she said, heading into the kitchen. "Let me wrap this up to rest."

While she was in there, she grabbed some serving dishes and utensils from the cabinets. Then she headed back into the main living area and unloaded the sides.

"Gary and Evan continue to blow my mind with everything they can do with technology, although I don't need to know all the details." She didn't think it would overtax Chase's brain to tell him about printing the invitations, but since it was a sore spot between them, she kept her mouth shut.

"That sounds familiar," Chase said, laughing. "One time Evan had me fly to Paris to see the newest installment of something he was inventing. After this hour-long recitation—half of which I didn't understand—he blew up all his test tubes in the demonstration, triggering the sprinkler system in the lab."

Hopefully Evan and Gary would keep any flammable experiments away from her.

"It soaked my five-thousand-dollar Italian suit and shoes. Evan didn't even notice he was soaking wet. He started cussing at what I'll call his 'inventing fairies,' to use your earlier train of thought. I had to drag him out of the lab when the Paris Fire Brigade showed up."

"Gary wouldn't cuss so much as he'd say, 'Dude, did you see that blow up?' or 'I'm on fire. How cool is that?'"

Chase had a good laugh at that. "I was a little skeptical when Evan told me he wanted to hire Gary at Artemis," he said, "but it sounds like they're two peas in a pod."

"I was as well, but he's terrific. Truly. And Evan assured me it won't impact the selection panel's decision to accept him if he chooses to apply." She still didn't like how it looked to the outside world, but it was Evan's call.

"It won't influence it," Chase said in his executive voice. "That's why Evan's not the only one who'll be deciding who's accepted. But trust me when I tell you that Evan's hardly a pushover when it comes to hiring. The head of Quid-Atch's R&D department went through eight rounds of interviews with him."

"Rajan sounds like a great guy. But that's a crazy amount of interviews."

"Of course, when I pointed this out to Evan, he said they were just chatting." Chase laughed. "I told him he'd better close the deal or Rajan would go elsewhere."

Moira finished arranging the sides on the serving

plates. "I'm going to carve the tenderloin and bring it out."

"Great," he said. "I hope you like it. I coated it with honey, black pepper, and ground lavender—Helga's idea—and smoked it with mesquite."

"That sounds...ridiculous and delicious. So you figured out a way to use the lavender, after all."

"Helga is a great cook. Turns out she's a nice woman...and that her name's not Helga." He gave her an arch look. "Something you'd know since she took care of Andy's first wife."

Oh shit, was that out of the bag? "It was Evan's idea," she said, feeling like a tattle-tale kid even as she said it.

"So I was told," he said. "I'd appreciate not being treated like an imbecile or an ogre. I told Evan the same when he called me earlier on his way home from Denver."

"Did you know he was meeting with J.T. Merriam today?" she said in a not-so-subtle attempt to change the subject. "I only know because J.T. popped in to see my sister, Caroline. Uncle Arthur put them in touch."

"Evan is hoping to buy some Merriam land here in Dare Valley for him and Margie."

"Do you know J.T.? I mean...I don't know him as an adult. He and his family stopped coming to Dare Valley when he was pretty young."

"J.T. is a savvy businessman with the heart of a lion," Chase mused. "He believes in his people, and from what I can tell, they believe in him. Of course, it's not easy working in Africa and the Middle East, but he's respected for his vision and leadership."

Moira was oddly relieved to hear his take on the man. If Caroline was interested in J.T., she wanted current references. "Do you like him?"

"Yes," Chase replied. "I don't know him well, but we've run across each other at political fundraisers and other corporate events."

"I appreciate your insights," she said, turning to finish arranging the sides on his plate and her own. "We should eat. We don't want to have to nuke your tenderloin."

"That would be a travesty."

She headed back into the kitchen and poured them drinks—a glass of wine for her and water for him—and delivered them before returning to carve the meat.

"Didn't you have a medical eval today?" she asked when she came back to the coffee table with the platter of tenderloin.

"I wasn't looking forward to talking about my injuries on our first date." His jaw locked. "But since you asked... Your brother is still concerned about the concussion. He thinks I need two more weeks to rest my brain. It was deeply disappointing."

Pausing in the act of transferring slices of tenderloin to their plates, she set the utensils aside and turned to face him, putting her hand on his chest. "I'm sorry."

"Me too."

She brought her plate onto her lap and settled back against the couch. Chase shifted forward until he was on the edge of the cushion, extending his casted leg out sideways to avoid the coffee table. He picked up his fork and started awkwardly cutting his meat one-handed. Biting her lip, she tried to decide if she should offer to help. That would gall him, she knew, so she decided to chill. While it was a slow process, he managed to get the job done. She was relieved—for both of them.

"This is really good," Chase said after taking a bite. "The combination actually works. The black pepper rounds out the honey and lavender."

"What you said." Moira plopped another piece of meat in her mouth. "Delicious."

"I'm glad you didn't bring over a soufflé," Chase

said. "Evan served it once as an entrée, thinking it was a pretty good joke because he'd promised me steak. He has a weird sense of humor."

"You don't strike me as a soufflé kind of guy," she said, spearing a thin green haricot vert dotted with slivered almonds and crème fraiche.

"I like dessert soufflés like anyone," Chase said, picking up a forkful of gratin covered in roasted cheese and cream. "But not when I was hoping for steak."

She laughed. "You and Evan seem to joke with each other a lot."

"Evan does it more with me than I do with him," he said, taking a bite and chewing thoughtfully. "He thinks it makes me less uptight."

Was he usually uptight? Yes, he was passionate about his work, pretty much exclusively so, but he was also darn good at it.

"Tell me about your family," he said, reaching for a napkin and wiping his mouth. "I haven't met everyone, obviously, but your brother is growing on me."

Andy had a funny way of winning people over—even frustrated patients. "We're pretty wacky. Well, not all the time, I guess. We're all serious about our professions, but we like to tease each other too. Matt and Natalie have this ongoing bumper sticker war, for example. Natalie won the latest round. She found one with the cutest little yellow fuzzy goslings that says 'I Heart Baby Goslings.' Matt is convinced she wants to take his Man Card away. I can't wait to see how he retaliates."

"Baby goslings, huh? I can see his concern."

"What about you?" she asked, finally picking up her wine. "Do you have siblings?"

"Only one," he said. "A younger brother named Boone. We're not close."

There was a whole heap of warnings in that recitation. She could all but feel him shore up his walls. *Interesting.*

"And your parents?"

"My dad died when I was twelve," he said, looking off into the fire. "My mom lives in Cheyenne now."

Again, his words were buttressed by a million warnings. She'd wait to ask more—if they got to that point. Right now they needed a complete change of subject. "If we were in D.C. having a first date, what would we be doing?"

His head turned, and their eyes met. Even in the firelight, she could see the frown on his face. Whatever the story was with his family, it wasn't a happy one.

"I'd take you out to a place downtown, maybe Capitol Grille. If it was a nice night, we could take a walk. I might even show you my favorite monument."

She was relieved to see his tormented look slip away. Yes, this was a safe topic. "What's your favorite monument?"

"Guess," he said, spearing a green bean and popping it in his mouth.

"That's not a fair question," she said dryly. "I've only been to D.C. once, as one of the dreaded family trips my dad used to insist on to further our education of America. I was eight, I think. All I remember is walking around until my legs ached and feeling like the heat was pressing down on me. Oh, and the ice cream cone I had in front of the Washington Monument."

"You know the monuments," he said, nudging her with his good arm. "Give it a try."

What was this? A quiz? Well, it beat the family tree talk. "The Washington Monument."

"Nope."

She thought back to all the movies she'd seen that were set in D.C. Where did people go? "The Lincoln Memorial. That's pretty impressive, right?"

"It's my second favorite," he said, reaching for his water glass. "Try again."

Were they going to sit here all night while she guessed? "The Jefferson Memorial."

He shook his head again, slowly. "While the cherry blossoms are quite lovely, it's too predictable."

Too predictable, huh? "You're not going to tell me it's the Vietnam Memorial, are you?" She remembered crying softly after their tour guide told them all the names etched on the wall were people who had died in the war. At that time, the list had seemed endless.

"Impressive and intense, but not my favorite."

She gave him a look. "Wanna put a girl out of her misery on a first date?"

He must have heard the rancor in her voice because he set his plate aside. "I'm not being very romantic, am I? Well...would you mind doing me a favor? Could you fetch me the box on the bed in the first bedroom on the right?"

A box? Chase was pinging all over the place tonight. Maybe it was due to his concussion. "Sure."

She headed over to the bedroom, and sure enough, a long white box wrapped with a red ribbon sat on the quilted bed. Curiouser and curiouser. When she returned to the den, she handed it to him.

He gestured to the box with his good hand. "It's for you."

Her heart kicked up at the thought of him getting her a present. How had he done *that*? She untied the ribbon and opened it. A bed of orange and purple-colored orchid flowers captured her attention. "You bought me flowers?"

"I'm sorry I didn't give them to you earlier." He gave a tight smile. "I forgot about them, actually. Seeing you walk in here...and then having you kiss me..."

She could have melted to the floor. "These are beautiful." She traced the orchid petals. "And rare. Where did you get them?"

"I had Bonnie call The Grand Mountain Hotel and ask if they had some orchids they could spare to brighten this place up. Quid-Atch has a business account with them, and they know about my accident, obviously, since it happened on their grounds. They were happy to send some over."

Of course, they would be, she thought. Chase was a good client.

"Thank you," she said, giving him a smile. "These are...quite a surprise." Most of the guys she'd gone out with in the past hadn't bothered with flowers.

"I'm glad you like them," he said. "Bonnie thinks I should get some flowers for this place to boost the feng shui. She might actually arrange for an expert to come by to consult me on the layout."

"You're kidding!"

"I'm serious," he said, crossing a finger over his heart. "Bonnie thinks acupuncture and a whole bunch of other healing modalities might help me get better faster. Your brother agrees. There's certainly a growing body of scientific evidence to suggest there's merit to it."

"That's a good idea. Acupuncture and energy healing helped my sister-in-law when she had cancer," she said, feeling a swell of hurt in her heart over losing Kim. "I hope they'll help you too."

"Bonnie mentioned taking care of Kim," Chase said softly. "It must have been hard on Andy and the rest of you, losing her so young."

His voice was warm and soft and threaded with emotion. When she met his eyes, she realized what it was: compassion. "Yes, it was terrible. For Andy and his young son most of all. We're so happy he's found love again, but it doesn't take away the hurt we feel when we think about Kim. Natalie was her best friend. That's how Kim met Andy."

"I'm sorry," he said, taking her hand and bringing it

to his mouth for a kiss. "Losing someone you care about is never easy."

"You said your dad died when you were twelve," she said, deciding to put it out there. "That must have been horrible for you, especially at that age."

His chest rose as he dragged in a deep breath. "It was," he said, looking away. "Did you bring any dessert by chance?"

She respected that he wasn't ready to pour his heart out. If she were in his position, she'd feel the same way. Placing the orchids on the coffee table, she tucked her knees under her and turned to face him. "Actually, I thought we could make dessert together."

His brow rose. "What did you have in mind?"

Leaning in, she kissed him on the mouth and then moved to the corners of his lips. "Something like this." Slanting her mouth over his again, she pressed her full advantage. The kiss was hot and carnal, and by the end, both of them were breathing hard.

"I like this idea of us collaborating on dessert," he said, running his good hand down her back. "You're certainly sweet enough."

"I thought you might," she said, kissing his jaw. "You shaved for me. Is it hard shaving one-handed?"

"It's hard doing just about everything one-handed," he told her, fingering the edge of her tunic.

She could tell he wanted to lift it and find bare skin. While she wasn't ready to sleep with him quite yet, she didn't see any reason not to take things a little further. "How about you show me what that one hand can do in the way of, say...touching my bare back?"

Oh, the fire that lit in those gray eyes of his. She shivered in response.

"Your bare back is a great place to start," he mused, leaning in and sucking on her bottom lip. "I was also thinking we might take a tour to another area of confectionary delight."

"For a corporate executive, you sure know your dessert terms. What kind of confectionary delight did you have in mind?" Oh, this was getting good.

"Your breasts are spectacular," he said in all seriousness. "I'll admit that I noticed them before we agreed to...ah...explore this attraction between us."

"Does it make you feel any better knowing I checked out your ass more than a few times and thought it was pretty great?"

"Too bad all I do is sit on it now." He gave a brief laugh. "I'm beginning to fear it won't be as 'great' as you claim once I get my casts off."

It touched her to think a man like him would be worried about his physique. "Oh, a few weeks can't affect a masterpiece like yours," she said with a grin. "Maybe six months."

His mouth found hers and gave her a kiss that made the room start to spin.

"You never did tell me what your favorite monument was," she said, pulling back.

She felt his hand edge up her tunic, and then a single finger traced her spine. She arched in surprise at the heat that shot through her, from her tail bone to her nape.

"It's the FDR Memorial," he commented, kissing her neck as best as he could from his seated position.

Leaning into him to give him better access, she cried out when he shifted her onto his lap. "Are you sure you're okay with me..." *Splayed out all over you?*

"I might be laid up, but I'm still strong enough to handle you and your body," he said, curving his arm around her back. He'd hiked up the sleeve and his skin was bare against hers.

Yes, she had no doubt that he *could* handle her. She watched his face for pain and didn't see any trace of it. "Why is that your favorite memorial? I don't know much about it."

He settled her more firmly against his chest. Pausing to kiss her between words, he said, "It tells the story of one man's determination to inspire a country facing the worst days of the Depression and World War II. The whole monument is like a mini-play, so to speak, with different sculptures and quotes to represent each act of his presidency. FDR was a man who fought through incredible pain and disability to lead. I admire the heck out of someone who decides not to take what life gave them and lay down in defeat."

When he talked like this, he was more than Chase Parker, corporate executive. His passion compelled others to share it. "You should give the half-time speech to one of the football teams playing in the Super Bowl."

He rolled his eyes. "I'm only stating the facts."

No, he was telling her something important, something that helped her see down to the heart of him. "He was in a wheelchair, right?"

"Yes," he said, tracing her back, suddenly lost in thought. "While more modern scholars dispute the original diagnosis, he was told he had polio at thirty-nine. One moment everything was fine, and the next he was paralyzed from the waist down. Instead of giving in, he kept going. He worked tirelessly to improve his condition. He continued to work. Can you imagine what this country would have looked like if he hadn't run for president?"

History wasn't her strongest subject, so she couldn't say much. All she remembered was that he'd been president a really long time until he'd died at the end of the war.

"That man is a goddamn hero in every sense of the word," Chase said, his voice impassioned, so much so she felt the need to reach out and touch his face.

His gaze came back to hers, and in his eyes, she could

see a bleakness she hadn't expected.

"So a guy like you can handle a concussion and two casts, right?" she asked softly.

He seemed puzzled for a moment, and then his mouth lifted at the corners into an easy smile. "I guess you could say that. When it comes down to it, I have nothing to complain about, do I?"

She could tell him it was okay to be upset he'd been hurt and limited, but this wasn't the time. "From where I'm sitting, you're pretty lucky. In a few weeks, you're going to be back on your feet with your brain intact. Right this moment though, you have a pretty incredible woman lying in your lap, offering you dessert."

The kiss he gave her was long and sweet. She felt the warmth of it spread all the way to her heart.

"You are pretty special, aren't you?" he asked. "I suspected as much, but my imagination didn't do you justice. Must be the concussion."

"Must be," she said, bringing both her arms around his neck.

"Thank you, Moira," he said as he pulled her against his chest.

She rested her head against the hard muscles there, feeling the emotion he was struggling to contain. "For what?"

"For reminding me of who I want to be," he said. "For helping me get my head out of my ass."

Now they were talking. And if discussing past presidents was all it had taken, well, she would count herself fortunate. "It's one of my finest qualities. You can ask anyone in my family."

"I'd prefer to experience it all myself," he said, cradling her suddenly in a way that was both tender and sweet.

"And so you shall."

"Our next date is going to be even better," he told

her.

"Are you already thinking ahead?" she asked.

"You bet I am. I'm a good planner," he said. "I'm going to romance the hell out of you tomorrow night. All day I was sulking a little over not being able to take you out like I normally would. Dress in a three-piece suit. Open the car door for you. You know, normal stuff."

"And talking about FDR becoming president despite his illness helped you get your A-Game on?" Goodness, he certainly wasn't a normal guy, was he? But maybe important people like Chase needed inspiration from other important people like FDR.

"Yeah. I can excel at dating you, even in my current condition. I've set my mind to it."

She shivered all over. "I'll bet when you set your mind to something, you're fierce."

"Fierce is a tame word," he mused. "Intense won't work either. How would I describe FDR? Maybe—"

She interrupted him by kissing him. And kissing him. By the time, she drew back, his whole body was tense under her. "Chase, stop with all the FDR stuff, okay?"

His smile was downright wicked. "Your wish is my command."

Then he tugged her close and took them both under in a way that made her certain *she* was the only thing he was thinking about.

CHAPTER 16

IF CHASE COULD HAVE WALKED, HE'D HAVE HAD A SPRING in his step the next morning. He and Moira had enjoyed a wonderful evening together, and damn if he wasn't feeling enthused.

Spending time with a smart, funny, beautiful woman was something to be grateful for. And he didn't see his current state as a dreaded predicament anymore. No, siree. After remembering all FDR had gone through, Chase had finally pulled himself up by his bootstraps. Since the accident, he'd been acting like a crybaby, really, and it wasn't who he was or wanted to be.

So he was laid up. He'd deal with it. Bonnie was right. Fighting his own recovery would only extend it.

When Bonnie arrived at his house the next morning, she closed the door and leaned against it. In her gloved hand was a small marmalade tabby kitten. "Chase, this is Barney. Why don't you make friends before your healing entourage arrives?"

"They're coming today?" he asked.

"An onslaught of them, yes," she said. "Both Evan's money and my connections helped. Prepare to be healed." Of course, she laughed, a light and airy sound he hadn't heard from her before.

"The tenderloin was incredible," he told her. "There's some left over for you to sample. Thank you again for the help."

She set the kitten down, and it made a beeline for him. He had to admit the little fur ball was cute. His green eyes stood out in stark contrast to his fuzzy orange and white. The kitten meowed and rubbed himself against the scooter, and Chase decided it wouldn't hurt to hold him. With his good hand, he scooped the kitten up into his lap. Pure delight streaked through him when the little thing snuggled against his belly and started to purr. He hadn't thought about it in years—no, decades— but he used to stuff barn cats in the opening of his coat during winter to keep them warm. It had always been a pleasure to run around the stalls with the cats purring against his chest.

"You're a natural," Bonnie said. "You've had a cat before?"

"We had them around when I was a kid," he said carefully, not sure how much he wanted to say. "I grew up in the country."

"Mousers," she said with a nod. "They're great at that. How was your date last night?"

He veiled his eyes. "I told you the flowers were for a friend."

"I know all the proper reasons for one person to give flowers to another. Exotic orchids are date flowers for a unique woman. Plus, you wouldn't let me put them in a vase."

Keeping his face impassive, he rubbed the cat's underbelly and felt him stretch in response. "What happens here, stays here. I don't need any commentary on things unrelated to my recovery."

Her eyes grew wide in response. "That sounded terrifying. Do you always put people in their place like that? Don't worry, Chase. You're right. What happens here stays here. I realized you didn't know that when you signaled for me to leave the room so you could talk to Andy. Just because Evan pays my salary doesn't mean I'd tell him anything you don't want me to."

Here he was holding her kitten, a sign of how much she trusted him, and he'd treated her poorly. "I'm sorry. You're right. I should have trusted you more."

"You have trust issues. Shocker. But we'll work through them. How do you like Barney? Isn't he the sweetest?"

He'd rather admit to watching a chick flick solo than acknowledge Barney's adorability. "I hope you brought food and cat litter."

"Of course," she said, chuckling. "I'm good with details. So let me run you through your schedule today. Between three practitioners, you're going to be tired."

"Go big or go home," he joked.

After she briefed him, Bonnie brought in a portable massage table and set it up in the den with a sheet.

He excused himself to text Moira. He'd gone to sleep wishing things had gone further than kissing and light touching, but he knew she wasn't the type to jump into bed with anyone. They were still getting to know each other, and right now, he was content with that. In fact, he was looking forward to learning more about her and what made her tick.

The only problem he foresaw was her wanting to know more about his background and his family. Those kinds of things were important to her. He wasn't sure what to do about that yet.

I'm texting for purely healing reasons, he began.

I'll bet, she immediately responded.

He found himself smiling. He hadn't been sure she'd answer right away—one, because she might be busy, but two, because there were plenty of people who played games when they were dating someone, and one of the most common was to delay answering calls or texts after a first date. He had never understood that. Why waste time by playing coy?

He thought for a moment, then typed, *Thinking about your snarky comments and beautiful smile boosts my immune system.* There, he liked the sound of that.

Prepare for another boost tonight, she replied.

Oh, the images that promise conjured up in his mind. *I'm counting the hours.*

Any dinner preferences? I can pick up some steaks to throw on the grill. You like roasted potatoes and spinach?

Not mixed together, he replied. *I like my meat, potatoes, and vegetable separate—like a good Western boy.*

While he wasn't used to discussing his eating preferences with the women he dated, he found it oddly intimate. Usually, he'd take whomever he was seeing to a restaurant where they could both have whatever they wanted—no discussion required. Even during his marriage with Trisha, they'd rarely eaten at home. She'd always hated cooking and cleanup.

A good Western boy? Maybe I'll need to start calling you Sam.

He stared at her text for a good minute, trying to decipher her reference. *You got me. Sam?*

Her response was immediate. *Sam Elliot, you idiot. One of the hottest Western men out there.*

Bonnie started humming, which made Barney crawl to the edge of his lap to investigate the sound. "Get back to your original position, Barney, or get down."

The tabby turned and gave him that haughty look cats were so famous for. Then he jumped down and pranced over to join Bonnie.

"He doesn't like being ignored," the woman commented, picking him up.

"I'm texting. About my recovery."

"I'll bet," she said dryly and resumed her humming.

He turned his scooter around for some privacy. *So you like old men? That's weird. And by old, I mean ancient. Sam Elliot?*

You're an old man, and I like you.

She was younger than he was. By eight years, if he recalled correctly.

Does that mean you'll watch Lonesome Dove *with me? It has two old Western men in it.* He didn't watch TV given how much he worked, but that mini-series was a classic he liked to break out when traveling long distances on the private jet.

That baby is one of my favorites. I adore Tommy Lee Jones too, but I don't think he's hot like Sam Elliot. Now Robert Duvall...

He started texting before she could finish.

I'm getting you an honorary membership to AARP when I get my online privileges back from my dad.

Okay, he was getting the hang of this texting flirting thing. It wasn't his normal. Usually he was too busy to send anything but perfunctory messages—the time he'd pick up a date or a thank you after they shared a meal or more. This felt...nice.

LOL. I still have to give Evan points for calling Bonnie Helga. Brilliant.

He had to agree. *He's a moron, but well intentioned.*

Look, I have to go. Gary wants to show me this new catering app he discussed with Natalie. He wants to use it to share information for the party. Sometimes I miss the simplicity of spreadsheets. See you later. Oh, and happy healing sessions.

There was an odd feeling in his chest, and it took him a moment to figure out what it was. He *missed* her. He... oh shit...they'd seen each other last night, but he already missed her. He felt his heart rate increase slightly.

Was he panicking?

No, he decided, it was this unusual sense of connection and longing. He didn't recall feeling this way with anyone before. Best proceed with caution.

Later then. Pick me a big steak.

But of course. Bye.

Bye.

He looked at those three letters. B-y-e. Apart they weren't anything significant, but together they meant something, like he was longing for her arrival. Yeah, he was in trouble.

"Chase," Bonnie called out. "If you're done texting, Dr. Sarah has arrived."

Right, the acupuncturist. "I'm ready."

The acupuncturist wasn't what he might have imagined. She was five ten with a runner's lean frame. Nothing woo-woo about her at all. In fact, she seemed pretty nice.

Until she had him lay out on Bonnie's portable massage table and started sticking him with needles.

"Why in the hell do you need to stick a needle there?" he finally asked, wincing from the one she'd stuck ruthlessly to the left of his right big toenail. "Isn't the cast enough torture?"

"Spleen line," she said. "You don't nurture yourself much, do you?"

Bonnie bit her lip to keep from laughing. He'd insisted she stick to his side like glue during his meetings with her so-called healing friends. "I'm a guy."

"Being a guy isn't an excuse. To some men, golfing is nurturing. What do you do that's like golf to you?"

She was like Bonnie's twin when it came to the tough-love bedside manner. "I work. That's my golf."

"Work isn't nurturing," Dr. Sarah said. "In balance, it can be, but I can tell by your liver pulse you don't have much balance in your life."

He gazed up at her quizzically from his position on the massage table. She had taken his pulse, but it had been different than a normal doctor. Instead of holding one place on his wrist firmly, she'd palpated her fingers around the area, keeping them about a quarter-inch apart. "My liver? How in the hell do you know that from my liver?"

"The liver is the general," she said. "Your general is overtaxed with too many battle plans and strategies. Don't worry. I have just the point."

She stuck another needle in him, this time in his baby toe.

"Ouch!"

"Take a deep breath," she said in a softer voice, a decided change. "You're resisting. That's why it hurts more when I put the needles in."

"Seriously? You're sticking needles in my body. Isn't it *supposed* to hurt?"

She shook her head and took another needle out of its sanitized plastic wrap. "Actually, most of my repeat clients don't feel anything unless I hit a particularly sensitive spot."

He wanted to call bullshit, but the woman had needles.

Dr. Sarah started walking around his head next, eyeing his neck in a way that made him nervous. "I thought you were just going to put needles on the areas where I have a cast."

"You hurt your head, right?" she asked, although it was rhetorical.

"Great. So you're going to stick needles in my head."

She smiled. "Yep. A lot of them. This will help the headaches, the nausea. After a few more visits—unless you keep resisting—you won't have any issues. That I can promise. Now close your eyes and try to relax."

Her demeanor was softening, and since Bonnie

trusted the woman, and he had come to trust Bonnie, he closed his eyes. From then on, the doctor worked in silence. Her fingers would gently touch the area she was planning to needle, which he realized was his cue to prepare himself.

After a while, he was surprised to feel a swirling of... what had she called it? Energy? Chi? The dull ache at the back of his head moved to the right side and then disappeared. He was amazed that such a profound change could be due to a handful—okay, more than a handful—of carefully placed needles.

She periodically reached for his good hand again and checked his pulses. He thought about making another joke about the little general she believed lived in his liver, but his body was feeling heavier. Relaxation, he realized. A deep, yawn-inducing relaxation.

"You're going to sleep well tonight," she told him. "I'm going to leave you alone for a while. Just keep your eyes closed. Take a cat nap if you'd like."

He opened his eyes to make sure Bonnie was still with him. She was standing at the foot of the table, holding Barney. When she gave him a wink, he slammed his lids closed again, not wanting her to realize how much he wanted her to stick around. Barney meowed and then he was out.

"Chase," Dr. Sarah called quietly by his ear. "Time to wake up."

He opened his eyes slowly. "I fell asleep."

Her smile was warm and sunny, he thought. Maybe it was her blond hair. She looked peaceful. Everything looked peaceful.

"We're all finished. You did great. I told Bonnie I want to see you two more times this week to build some momentum. I know you have appointments with her other faves. You're going to be back on your feet in no time."

He raised his head. Sure enough, there wasn't a needle stuck anywhere in his body. "I'm glad you take them with you. The needles."

"Of course," she said, helping him sit up on the table. "Take it easy and drink lots of water."

"Got it," he said, shifting until he was on the edge.

Bonnie was right there to make sure he didn't put any weight on his casted leg. Together they got him into the scooter.

"I'll see you soon, Chase. Bonnie, always a pleasure."

"Bye, Sarah," she said as the woman left. "Why don't you rest a little? I'll grab you some water while we wait for the Qigong master."

"Sure thing," he said, testing the rotation of his head. "Hey, I can move my head without it hurting."

"It's a miracle," Bonnie said dryly. "I told you this would work."

"All right, I like proof." He had to smile when he thought about Moira asking him for proof that their attraction was worth pursuing. It was rather nice to know it was something they both valued.

More proof came in the form of the Qigong master. Chase had kind of expected the man to be Asian. Instead, he was a short, squat, middle-aged man named Carl, originally from Minnesota. But Chase could actually feel the punch of energy when the man moved his hands.

Carl walked him through some movements designed to increase the healing in his body. They were all exercises Chase could do while sitting down.

"I won't tell you the Chinese names," Carl said. "They aren't important. Qigong is like making your own home remedy for a cold. You get to heal yourself. Nothing is needed other than the recipe."

Chase liked the independence of the practice. The movements made him feel like he was also getting a little exercise beyond the short physical therapy sessions

Bonnie ran him through every morning. And they didn't seem to require the same effort.

"I wrote out the ones for you to try on your own. To start, I'd recommend doing the movements at least twice a day. Let your body tell you if you can do more. There is no limit to healing. We only need to honor the body's progression."

"I'm all about no limits," Chase responded. "Let's go through the movements one more time. I think I have them down." In fact, his mental concentration and retention felt normal for the first time since the accident. God bless those needles and Dr. Sarah.

"You're a fast learner with a willing heart," Carl said. "You strike me as a man who likes to cut to the chase. Haha. Get it?"

"I get it, Carl," he said dryly.

"I don't like to mess around either. The more I practice Qigong, the more simple everything has become. Do you want one more key to unlocking your full healing?"

That sounded like a trick question. He found his former skepticism returning.

"I don't think he's ready for that yet, Carl," Bonnie said, and they shared a look.

Okay, he didn't like that. Not at all. "I want to know."

This time Bonnie stepped forward and studied him. She held the tabby against her belly and was stroking him behind the ears. "Are you sure?"

He found his chest growing super tight at Bonnie's seriousness. Why was she acting like this? "Yes."

She took another minute to study him. Then she turned to Carl.

"Tell him."

"It's love, Chase," Carl said in all seriousness. "You have to be willing to receive love. From yourself and others. It's that simple."

Bullshit, he thought. *Love? Really? Were Bonnie and this Qigong guy really going all cliché on him?* "Thank you for sharing that," he said instead.

"It's taken me decades to realize," Carl said. "Maybe it won't take you as long."

"I didn't think you'd believe us, Chase," Bonnie said, her gaze steady on him. "Go ahead and finish up the sequence, Carl. Ally will be here in fifteen."

The man's mouth twitched, but Chase didn't ask him why. They did the movements in tandem, and he felt his body grow warm—a warmth that almost went down to his *bones*. While it didn't hurt, it definitely felt weird.

When Carl finished, Chase shook his hand. "Thank you."

"You're most welcome, Chase," he said. "Good luck with everything."

After he left, Chase turned to Bonnie. "Why do I have the idea he won't be coming back?"

She set the kitten in his lap. "He's taught you everything he can."

Somehow Chase got the impression Carl was holding out on him. "Because of this love thing? Come on, Bonnie. We both know that's taking things a little too far."

"So you say," she responded. "How about another glass of water? Ally should be here any minute."

He decided to allow the change in subject. What grown man wanted to talk about love, anyway? Even happily married men didn't gush out loud about it. Certainly not about self-love. Hell, there was nothing wrong with him because he didn't want to be all lovey dovey.

Barney distracted him by rubbing his small, pointy head against Chase's belly. Animals knew about love, he supposed. They were naturally affectionate unless they'd experienced abuse. He'd always been able to count on the cats or dogs on the ranch.

And the horses...he couldn't forget them. His horse, Kerrick, had been a Tennessee Walker crossed with a Mustang. His gait had been unusual, but he'd had so much speed and power Chase had been able to win a few country races. His father had taken a photo of him crossing the finish line at the Jarvis ranch. Of course, that picture had perished in the fire along with every other happy memory he'd had of his childhood.

Love wasn't dependable. He'd decided that a long time ago. Respect was more important, and Chase had plenty of that.

A discreet knock sounded on the door, and Bonnie walked over to open it. The short, white-haired woman behind the door looked more like Mrs. Claus than some Merlinistic healer from Avalon. Shoot him, he'd liked fantasy novels when he was a kid.

Bonnie had embraced both Dr. Sarah and Carl in greeting, but this embrace went on for minutes. In fact, Chase found himself averting his eyes from the oddly intimate moment. They were holding other like only lifelong friends would, and it made him a little uncomfortable.

"So you're Chase," Ally said, her smile soft yet bright. "Bonnie has told me a lot about you. She said this is your first experience with a healer."

"Only if you don't count the woman who gave me that hot-rock massage in Tokyo," he joked half-heartedly. "She had magic hands."

Ally held hers out. "No magic here. And I won't even touch you with them. Does that make you uncomfortable?"

Bonnie hadn't told him about this in her briefing. Heck, now that he thought about it, she hadn't said much beyond her assertion that Ally was the real deal. Chase hadn't asked any questions. "Don't most healers...

ah...lay their hands on people?" God, he sounded like an idiot.

"Many do. Neither way is better. We all have our preferences." Her light blue eyes continued to gaze at him. "Would you prefer to stay where you are or lie down somewhere? I see Bonnie brought a table."

She could do her thing with him in the scooter? "Ah...whatever you think is best."

"How about we go over to the couch? You stay in that incredible machine you have, and I'll sit down."

A healer who sat down? Clearly he had no idea what in the hell was supposed to happen.

"Relax, Chase," she said. "I know all of this is new, but I can promise you there's nothing to fear. We're going to boost your body's ability to heal. Okay? I'll be talking to you throughout, so you'll know what's happening."

He glanced at Bonnie. "You'd better take Barney."

"No need," Ally said. "Cats are very sensitive to energy. He'll probably fall asleep in your lap."

Maybe Chase would too, like he had with Dr. Sarah.

"I'm going to leave you both alone," Bonnie said, surprising him.

"I want you here," he told her.

"You might want to speak with Ally alone," she told him. "Like you did with Andy."

He couldn't imagine why. "Stay." He didn't want to be alone with this stranger. Suddenly this whole thing felt too weird for words.

"Go ahead and stay, Bonnie," Ally said. "We want Chase to feel comfortable."

The healer walked over to the couch and sat down. Not on the edge of the seat, but reclined against the back cushions. He wheeled his scooter around until it was facing her.

"Good," she said. "I can already feel some of the areas in your body we want to work on, but I'm going to tune in to your energy field a little more. You work with a scientist from what I understand, so you know everyone has an energy field around their bodies. It's pretty amazing, actually."

He was aware of what quantum physicists called an energy field, but he couldn't pretend to know more than that. "Evan—my scientist friend—is likely better informed."

She nodded. "Sometimes I close my eyes to listen and feel what's going on with you. Don't worry. I'm not falling asleep on the job."

He had to give her points for humor, something he hadn't expected from a healer. "Take your time."

She closed her eyes. "Take a couple deep breaths, Chase. It will help you relax."

Why was everyone so focused on him relaxing today?

"You deserve some relaxation after all the hard work you've put in," she said. "Your body was trying to slow you down."

That comment pissed him off. He'd gotten distracted and careened down a hill. His body had suffered from his stupidity. End of story.

But then he felt something...something like deep relaxation settling over his body, accompanied by a soft buzzing in his ears. It wasn't unpleasant, but it was unusual.

"The bones are healing nicely," she said in an encouraging tone. "I can see the fractures reknitting. The one in the tibia is going to need a little longer, I think, than the humerus, likely because it's farther from your heart. It's not just the circulation of the blood that heals, but the energy of the heart."

Here we go again, he thought. Was she going to talk about love too?

"Your head still seems a little hot to me," she said. "That's the swelling in the brain. But it's getting better.

Sarah cleaned a lot out earlier. I can feel it."

How did she know that? His day had gotten progressively more woo-woo with each session. Maybe this was too much.

"Take a couple more deep breaths," she said. "I'm going to start with your physical issues and then get to the source of them."

The source? What could she mean by that? The source had been the tumble he'd taken down the side of a mountain.

The soft buzzing continued, but it faded to nothing but background noise as deep relaxation spread throughout his body. Soon he couldn't keep his eyes open.

"That's right," she said softly. "Just relax. There's nothing you need to do right now."

There was a feeling of tightness at the base of his skull, and then it was like someone had opened a door holding a vacuum and sucked everything out. His breath shuddered as the tightness evaporated.

"Good," she said in that same even-tempered, soothing voice. "Your head is feeling so much better. So many thoughts. So many responsibilities."

"Dr. Sarah talked about a general in my liver," he said, his tongue feeling heavy in his mouth.

"You're a master general," Ally said. "It's not just your liver. It's who you think you are. You have the gift of leadership, but you carry everyone on your back. There is an easier way for you if you want it."

He heard what she was saying, but his brain wouldn't form a reply. It was weird. He had no thoughts. Everything inside him was calm. He'd never felt this way before.

"You've done a lot of good in the world," she said. "And you've traveled. My goodness, you've seen some incredible things, haven't you? I see London, Berlin,

Paris, and another city with a red tower that looks like the Eiffel Tower."

"Tokyo," he mumbled. "Red Tower. Business."

"You're tired of doing it all," she said. "Making it all work right and successfully. Every day. There never seems to be a break. There's always a new battle to fight. Another city to travel to. Another government official to manage. Another meeting. Goodness, your whole life is a series of meetings, isn't it?"

His body slumped in the scooter as it all washed over him. He was tired, more tired than he'd ever felt. It was like he'd been walking in the desert for a hundred days. "There's never enough time," he heard himself say.

"I know," she said. "Let's lift all that responsibility off you. No more burdens. No more hard work. You don't have to carry it all anymore. It's time to let go."

Evan came to mind, not the Evan of now, but the nerdy, overgrown kid he'd been. The one who'd wanted to change the world with his inventions.

"You love the man you work with like a brother," she said. "The scientist? But you don't want to let him down. You feel your destiny is entwined with his, but you don't have to entangle yourselves. You can both do what you want to do from a place of pure freedom."

Another image surfaced in his head. Evan giving his speech about Artemis at the podium at Emmits Merriam.

"It's time to let him go, Chase," Ally said. "He doesn't have to be your responsibility. You don't have to take care of him anymore." Then she stopped herself. "Oh, I see. He's your family. You don't want to lose him."

A pain shot through his chest, and he gasped in response.

"Oh, honey," she said in a gentle tone. "I'm so sorry for everything you lost. Your beautiful home. Goodness, it looks so much like this one, doesn't it? I can't imagine how hard that must have been for the boy you were."

How did she know he'd lost his home? How did she know any of this? Bonnie hadn't said she was psychic too. The first tingling of fear raced down his spine, and the relaxation started to dissipate like smoke.

"Don't be afraid, Chase," Ally said softly. "It's okay to remember."

He saw their ranch burning in the black night. His mother's arms were around his younger brother, and she was screaming at Chase to stop throwing buckets of water too close to the fire. He could *feel* the muscles in his maturing arms trembling with exertion as he beat the front porch with a horse blanket. There was no water left, and the fire was engulfing everything in sight. Windows were cracking. The blanket he was holding caught fire, and his dad yanked him back, dragging him forcefully enough that his bare feet left lines in the dirt.

"Stop," he said, struggling against the heaviness in his body. "I don't want...to remember."

"Your father didn't leave you, Chase," she said. "He just couldn't handle his own loss. He's so sorry you felt so alone when he shot himself."

Another bolt of pain flashed across his chest. He opened his eyes and shook his head.

"That's enough." Barney jumped off his lap and scurried across the floor.

She met his gaze when he looked at her. "It's okay, Chase."

"No, it's not." He was totally at sea here. How had she known those things about him? About his dad?

"You have so much unprocessed hurt inside you, Chase," she said softly. "It's ready to heal. Your body is trying to help you."

He shook his head again. "Bonnie, I want this to stop. I want this to stop right now."

Bonnie came over to him and sank down in front of him. "It's okay, Chase. We've all had our hurts. There's no shame in letting it come out. You can't heal if you keep it inside."

When Bonnie touched his good arm, he realized he was trembling. *Trembling.*

"We're done here." His lungs didn't seem to be working properly. It took two deep breaths to release the crushing tension in his chest. "Ally, I appreciate your help, but this just isn't for me."

She gave him a soft smile. "That's for you to decide, of course, and I honor that. Bonnie, I'll just grab my purse and head out. Thank you for sharing your journey with me, Chase."

She was thanking him? He could tell she wasn't upset. Her demeanor was just as calm as it had been when she'd first sat down. Bonnie, who'd taken a seat at the other end of the couch, stood up and walked over to Ally. Again they shared a long hug.

The kitten pawed at Chase's leg, and Chase scooped him up into his lap. It was a little weird how intently Barney's green eyes were staring at him. Some of the animals on the ranch used to look at him like this, like they knew he'd had a bad day.

When Ally opened the door, he had to bite his tongue not to call her back inside. She'd said his dad was sorry for killing himself. If she knew about the fire and the suicide, could she be tuned into something greater? Like his dad's spirit? Some healers were reputed to have that gift. Channeling, he thought it was called, although he was no expert.

He discarded the notion.

Nothing his dad's spirit said would change the past anyway.

CHAPTER 17

WHEN CHASE TEXTED MOIRA TO SAY HE'D GOTTEN tired from all the appointments and wanted to take a rain check, she wanted to believe him.

But something in her gut told her that he was shoring up his walls some more. His earlier texts had been sweet and flirtatious. Even funny.

This Chase was all business.

I got worn out from all the woo-woo. Can I have a rain check?

That was all he'd written. She knew he wasn't blowing her off, but after seeing what Kim had gone through emotionally from her work with alternative medicine, she knew it could stir the pot of deep hurts. For a tough guy like him, that could be catastrophic.

Instead of responding directly to his request, she texted: *Get some rest.*

Then she went to the grocery store and bought their steaks, a bunch of asparagus to steam, and potatoes to roast, and headed to his house. This evening was no date, she told herself. This visit was about showing him that he wasn't alone. That she wasn't going to let him wallow.

She knocked on his door out of respect, but since she

didn't expect him to be wheeling around in his scooter naked, she let herself in.

He was sitting on the couch in front of a waning fire. His head immediately swiveled. "Hey! What are you doing here? I thought we'd called tonight off."

"You tried to," she said, crossing to the dining room table and putting her grocery bag on it. "I decided you still needed to eat, and since I'm your friend, I'm going to feed you. Then you can tell me what happened today that changed the charming, fun man I was texting with earlier to a bronze statue."

She heard a meow and looked down to see a tabby kitty racing across the hardwood floors toward her.

"Moira, I just want to be alone. You're better off going home. Trust me."

She crouched down, barely listening to his predictable reply. "Where did this kitten come from?"

"I'm surrounded by interfering women," he growled. "*Bonnie* 'forgot' to bring Barney home."

While Moira wasn't a cat person per se, the tabby kitten was adorable. "Hey, there. You don't look like a Barney to me." The kitten purred and head-butted her palm.

"Cats have healing power, according to Bonnie," he said dryly. "The vibrations of their purring have therapeutic effects. I didn't believe her at first, but there's scientific evidence that it helps healing bones. Who the hell knew, right?"

Moira had noticed there were plenty of therapy animals around when she'd gone to hospice to visit Kim. When it came to people suffering, she figured, why not try everything that might help alleviate it? "Bonnie is a wise woman. She brought one of her cats to Kim when she wasn't doing very well. It seemed to calm her."

He turned his head to stare back at the fire. She gave the kitten another scratch behind the ears and decided to approach the beast. Scooping up Barney, she set the little kitten down in Chase's lap and leaned down until she was inches away from his face.

"I missed you today," she said in a quiet voice, feeling the urge to shiver at her own vulnerability. "Mind if I kiss you? Or are you going to bark at me?"

His gray eyes flew to her own. "Moira. I'm really not good company."

Stubborn man, she decided, but she'd grown up around plenty of them. She pressed her mouth to his. He groaned immediately, his good arm coming around her and bringing her closer. She was afraid of leaning on his cast and the kitten, so she angled her body sideways. His mouth opened, and she responded. They dueled, their breathing changing rapidly.

She could feel the turbulent emotions bouncing around in him—anger, desperation, and urgent longing. Tracing his jaw, she slowed him down. His emotions rolled over her, and she fought to take a breath, staying with him.

Then he pressed his forehead to hers, breaking the kiss. In that one gesture, she felt all of his hurt. "Oh, Moira."

Wrapping her arms around him, she slid sideways into his lap, causing Barney to meow. Bringing the kitten onto her own lap, she rested her head against Chase's chest.

"You should walk out of here right now," he said. "I feel like I'm coming apart, and I don't want you to see it."

Her throat clogged, and she felt tears spurt into her eyes. "I'm not leaving. I had a sister who closed me out of her pain. I won't let you do that to me too."

"I should ask who that is, but I can't think of anything right now," he said, curling his good hand around her waist.

"What happened today, Chase?" she asked.

He sucked in a breath. "Bonnie's healer somehow knew about the fire. And my dad. She wasn't just a healer, that's for damn sure."

The crisp, biting tone of his voice told her this story was ripe with hurt. She thought back to the burning house they'd seen on the bench the day of his accident. Something clicked. "What fire, Chase?"

He was shaking his head against her. "I don't want to think about it, but ever since Ally left, my mind has been popping out all these memories—ones I haven't thought of in decades. I feel like my brain is my enemy."

Oh, the poor man. She tightened her hold. "Tell me. It will be easier once you let it out. Trust me on this."

"I don't want you to think less of me," he whispered hoarsely. "I don't understand why this is happening now. I will not be defeated by the past. I've never let it beat me before."

She could hear the resolve in his voice, but it was trembling in a way that indicated those walls he'd built up all around him were buckling. "It hasn't beaten you. Look at all you've done! It's just a part of you that needs to get out."

"My family lost our ranch in a fire," he said, his voice breaking. "In a matter of hours, everything we'd built was ash. Every toy I'd played with. Every family photo. Every keepsake. Even some of the animals. My horse..."

Her arms squeezed around him as she registered the agony in his voice. "Oh, Chase." She couldn't imagine losing her home, everything she'd held dear.

"Six months later the insurance company paid us a pittance. Oh, shit. I hate this part most of all."

She tightened her grip on him.

"My dad fucking shot himself by the fences we used to ride everyday when we checked on our cattle. Just shot himself. No note. Nothing."

Tears filled her eyes. His dad had killed himself? She remembered him saying his dad had died when he was twelve. What grade was that? Seventh? When she was twelve, her biggest worries were acne and whether Chris Evans would check the box that he liked her on the note her best friend passed to him in class.

"I'm so sorry," she whispered, pressing her face into his hot neck. Suddenly he was burning up. "How horrible for you."

"I've been sitting here since Bonnie left—since I all but threw her out—and all I can think about is how much I hate him. He was a gutless coward, leaving us like that."

Even though she wanted to be strong for him, she felt the first tear fall down her cheek. Now she had a deeper understanding of why he admired FDR so much. He was someone who hadn't buckled under adversity.

"It's crazy," he continued. "This happened twenty-four years ago, and all I want to do is...I don't know... beat the shit out of him for it. But that's nuts because he's dead. And get this. Ally said he was sorry. I practically threw her out too. I...I didn't believe it. But how could she know any of this shit? I've never talked about it publicly."

Moira got a chill from his words. She knew *of* Ally, and Andy had told her enough about the healer for her to believe in her gifts. Chase was right. She wasn't just a healer in a conventional sense.

"I don't know how she knows things," she told Chase. "But she did this kind of thing with Kim too. Andy says she's the full package. It's weird, but...undeniable. Maybe...I don't know...maybe this needed to come up. You were upset about the house being on fire the day we went skiing. I could tell."

"Are you saying seeing that fire caused my accident?" he asked, lifting her chin to look at her.

Suddenly she was afraid, like the answer would determine whether he would push her away or continue to let her see into this vulnerable part of himself. She didn't want that. "What do you think?"

He chuckled bitterly. "It's crossed my mind. Shit, I was hoping helping that family—"

"What family?" she asked.

His sigh sounded tortured. "I don't want you getting all...I don't know...mushy about it, but I helped the family whose house burned down. I swore them to secrecy. Their little boy was in the hospital."

And he'd reached out to help? Her throat seemed to close. Yeah, she felt mushy all right. "That was a beautiful thing you did, Chase."

"Moira, everything I've done in my life since my dad checked out has been about choosing the right road. Evan knows he can depend on me. So does everyone else I work with. I'm not like my father."

That was the rub, wasn't it? Her brothers had always worried they'd become like their dad. Dr. Hale had the tendency to get so wrapped up in work he'd forget about his family. "No, you aren't your father. You would never make the choice he made."

His expression shifted, like pain was physically washing over his flesh. "I think that too, but when it comes down to it, I never in a million years would have thought my dad would take the cheap way out. He was so strong."

She bit her lip to keep more tears from falling.

"Moira, he was my hero."

Then he pressed his face against her neck, his good hand digging into her waist.

The only thing she knew to do was hold him. There was nothing to say, she knew that. How could his dad not be his hero? Her brothers had idolized their father too. That's why they'd been so disappointed and hurt when Dr. Hale had let their beautiful and funny mom walk away from him without a fight. She was still mad at him for that. She couldn't imagine how angry she'd be if she was in Chase's shoes.

The kitten turned over in a half roll, like it was feeling neglected, so she rubbed its belly. Bonnie had been so smart to leave it with Chase. From the way he'd kept it on his lap, she knew he liked the fuzzy tabby.

They stayed that way, holding each other as the fire died out. Barney fell asleep on her lap, nestled between her body and Chase's.

"*Moira*," Chase finally said after eons of silence and comfort.

She kissed his cheek in response.

"Thank you."

She remembered what she'd said to him after skiing down a death-defying path to get to him, one most wouldn't have traveled. It was still true. Even more so now.

"I told you I wouldn't leave you alone."

CHAPTER 18

CHASE WASN'T SURE HOW HE'D GOTTEN LUCKY ENOUGH to wake up with Moira lying on his chest, the kitten tucked between them. He certainly wasn't going to look a gift horse in the mouth.

Last night, he'd been raw. More raw than he'd been in years. He blamed it on Dr. Sarah and Ally—maybe Carl had been part of the conspiracy too. Regardless, he'd felt more emotional than he had in decades.

Moira hadn't seemed to mind. Not even Bonnie's Helga persona was as tough as the Viking woman Moira had inside her. But she was tender too. She hadn't chided him for his weakness. Nor had she tried to placate him with Pollyannaisms. She'd just held him. Showed him that he wasn't alone. And the storm of emotions plaguing him had subsided while she was curled around him. He'd fallen asleep.

Clearly she'd meant it when she'd said she wasn't going to leave him.

It was weird how much that phrase had affected him. No one had ever said it to him but Moira. Certainly not his mom, who'd withdrawn into herself after his dad's suicide. Not even Evan.

He savored Moira's warmth. Sure, his leg was

throbbing with swelling after not being elevated overnight, but he could take it. He could handle anything if it meant he got to keep Moira in his arms.

Barney was purring against his chest, nestled between him and Moira.

Dammit if Bonnie hadn't been right. The cat was a comfort. Purr vibrations and healing frequencies not withstanding.

Moira's brown hair had a slight frizz to it in the morning light. If you asked him, it was adorable. Like the rest of her. She was the most incredible woman he'd ever met, hands down, and he'd met some of the most lauded bachelorettes in the U.S. and Europe.

Chase decided to savor the feeling of holding her. He had no idea what time it was and realized he didn't care—a certifiable thought for a man who usually lived according to his calendar.

He was hungry, sure, and in physical pain, but he also felt a deep, abiding sense of peace. They hadn't ended up eating any of the meal she'd brought. The grocery bags were still on the table where she'd left them last night.

Barney stirred suddenly and stood up on Moira's tummy, looking directly at him. Chase met those oddly intent green eyes until the kitten jumped off the couch, likely heading to the kitty litter station Bonnie had set up in the kitchen yesterday.

Moira made a noise and rubbed her face into his chest, creating a stirring of desire in him. She was curling around him like a cat in her own way, and he loved it.

"*Ummm,*" she drawled out, turning in his arms.

He winced as she jostled his casted arm, squashing the desire. Pain did that, he'd discovered. But then she started, like she'd come completely awake. Her head popped up, and she met his eyes.

"Morning," he said in a deep voice.

"Oh, good Lord," she said in a raspy voice. "Did I fall

asleep?"

"We both did," he answered, using his good hand to smooth back the fuzzy hair from her forehead. "You're adorable in the morning."

She leveled him a look that could have been used as a new defensive weapon in the war on terrorism. "Words to make a woman feel just super."

Easing off his chest, she looked down as if to ensure she hadn't squashed Barney.

"He's off doing his morning beauty routine," he told her.

She slid carefully off his lap, and he rolled his neck to the right to stretch the tense muscles there. Lifting his right leg carefully, he rested his cast on the coffee table.

"Oh God," she said. "You stayed like that all night? How do you feel?"

Telling her he felt like shit physically wouldn't be kind. "I feel much calmer," he said instead.

"Good," she said, hopping off the couch.

She wove in place a little, and he lurched forward to steady her.

"I'm so not a morning person."

He smiled. "Lucky for you I am."

Her hair was standing up in fuzzy tufts. There were dark circles under her green eyes. And she had cat hair across her middle.

She'd never looked more beautiful to him.

"Let's elevate your leg," she said, grabbing a pillow and helping him rest his cast on top of it. "What about your arm?"

He didn't feel it anymore. "It's numb."

"That doesn't sound good. Let's get you comfortable and hope it subsides."

She eased a pillow under his arm cast, being gentle. He shifted to make himself more comfortable. Tingling sensations started to zip across his injured arm. Shit.

He bit his lip to keep from crying out.

"I'm so sorry," Moira said, worrying her lip.

"Don't worry. It's fine."

"Bullshit," she said. "You're ready to howl."

Dammit if she wasn't right. "I am not."

"What did Andy prescribe for inflammation?" she asked. "I'm making you an egg and then giving you the pill."

Yes, she was definitely more intimidating than his nurse. "I don't need an egg." The pain was making him nauseous, and the thought of runny eggs didn't set well.

"You're having an egg," she said, marching off to the kitchen.

He considered the definition of a lost cause as his casted arm shot painful tingles through him. Dammit, why did limbs hurt so much when they fell asleep? He breathed through it, listening with half an ear to Moira banging around in the kitchen.

When Barney ran out of the room and jumped into his lap, he curled his good hand around the kitten. "She's in a state, isn't she?"

The kitten answered by settling against his belly and purring like a champion.

Minutes later, Moira brought out a wooden tray he hadn't seen filled with an egg, orange juice, and a white pill. "This had better be gone by the time I come back."

After she slipped back into the kitchen, he gazed at Barney, who had raised his head. "How can one woman be both scary and nice?"

The kitten's response was to hide its head with its paws.

The commotion continued from the kitchen as he choked down the egg. Then he popped the pill in his mouth and washed it down with the last of his juice.

Moira strode out, her hair swirling around her head like Medusa's snakes. "Good, you ate everything. I have to go home and clean up before going to work. Do you want to stay on the couch or go to bed? I can help you into the scooter if you want to head to your bedroom."

Her laser-like focus was captivating. It was one of the first things he'd noticed about her after interviewing her for the Artemis job. "I'm good here." He'd be way too tempted to grab her and pull her into that king bed with him otherwise. "Head on home."

She marched over to him and studied him. "You look like shit. Get some rest and text me later. I...take care of yourself." Leaning down, she gave him a swift kiss on the mouth.

He could feel her discomfort now. "You too."

Looking over her shoulder, she said, "We forgot the food last night."

"Don't worry about it," he said, stroking Barney's soft fur. "What happened in lieu of dinner was a hell of a lot more important."

A pink blush appeared on her cheeks. Was she embarrassed at how much closer they'd gotten? Last night, he'd fought it. This morning, it seemed like *she* was feeling uncomfortable.

"Make up with Bonnie," she told him. "No one has a bigger heart."

Indeed. She'd marooned her kitten over here just to make him feel better. "Will do. Are you coming tonight?"

"Do you want me to?" she asked simply.

He felt a slow smile spread across his mouth. "There's nothing I want more, Moira."

After last night, he was as sure of her as he'd been of Evan's first invention. There was no going back for him, he realized, even if he didn't know what that meant.

"I'll be here," she said. "Anything strike your fancy for dinner?"

Other than you? "You tell me, and I'll smoke it."

"You choose. I'm not picky." She looked at her watch.

"I need to go."

She seemed antsy, ready to jump out of her own skin. But he couldn't let her leave without showing her how much last night had meant to him.

"Give me a kiss before you take off."

Her face blanched with shock. "Oh, of course."

She crossed warily to him and leaned over. He yanked her to him, causing Barney to meow at the intrusion. Her mouth was warm and soft, and he showed her how much he was already missing her. When he was finished, she stood, panting.

"Well," she rasped out. "Have a good day."

"You too," he said. Suddenly, inexplicably, he had the desire to find an endearment for her. That was totally weird.

What was happening to him?

"Chase," she said, turning at the door.

"Moira, get your coat on," he told her.

She looked down. "Right. I forgot."

After tugging on her winter gear, she faced him again. "Okay, I'm out of here. Text if you need anything."

Everything he was and knew had been in turmoil after his session with Ally yesterday, but something was different this morning. He realized with a jolt that this was happiness.

"I will," he said, wishing he could march over to her and kiss her senseless. "Have a great day, beautiful." There, he'd found one.

A quick smile flashed on her face, tugging at his heart, and then she was gone.

This time he didn't feel so alone.

Chapter 19

MOIRA WAS FEELING MORE THAN A LITTLE WONKY BY the time she arrived home to change. She hadn't expected Chase to open his heart to her. When a strong man like him shared his hurts, it was a big deal. Colossal, really.

Her hands were shaking in the shower, and her body was cold despite the warm water. She cranked the temp up and cradled her head against the white tiles.

She'd fallen for him. In the scope of one night, he'd managed to find his way into her heart. Something no other man had truly accomplished. What was she supposed to do about that? He would be leaving soon once his body mended. He'd always been very clear about that.

Maybe they should stop things before she fell any harder, before she said something stupid like *I'm falling in love with you.* Better yet, before they made love, because she knew it would only deepen her feelings for him. How could it not?

By the time she arrived in the office, she was in control.

Or so she thought until she spilled her extra-large coffee mug all over her desk when Gary poked his head in her open door and said, "Hey, Moira."

"Shit," she uttered, watching the brown liquid soak the papers on her desk. Grabbing the box of tissues she always kept for human resources emergencies, she started wiping up the mess.

Gary had disappeared. Terrific.

"I've got paper towels," he cried, running back into her office moments later.

She jumped. Okay, she'd underestimated him. He lacked social skills, sure, but he had plenty of heart.

"You all right?" he asked. "Looks like you got up on the wrong side of the bed."

Most people knew not to say things like that, but she'd give Gary a pass. "I'm fine."

"Doesn't look like it from here," he said, eyeing her upper body. "You have your shirt on backwards."

She looked down in disbelief. "Shit. Oh, sorry."

"I'll just take these wet towels out of here for you," he said, picking them up efficiently. "You can...readjust. I'll get you more coffee. You'll be back to your old self in no time."

By ten o'clock, she'd broken a nail and knocked her shinbone on the edge of her desk. When she almost started to cry in response, she came to the conclusion that she was a wreck.

She needed to take a break. Treat herself to a really good coffee. That meant taking a quick drive to The Grand Mountain Hotel and asking Chef T to make her a cappuccino. Maybe Natalie would be free, and she could get a hug from her sis. She could use some TLC.

Gary was hovering outside her office. It wouldn't have surprised her if he'd stashed the office first-aid kit nearby in case she cut herself and started bleeding.

"I'm going out for a serious coffee," she told him. "Text me if you need anything. Can I pick you up something? A sandwich?"

He lifted his shoulder. "I'm on a budget, but thanks for asking."

"Oh, for heavens sake, Gary," she said. "It's my treat."

"I couldn't..."

"How about it's Artemis' treat then? You can walk me through the new catering app you set up for the party."

His eyes lit up. "Really? A sandwich would be great. I mean, if it's a business expense and all."

"You have the sandwich menu at The Grand, right? Text me your order. I'll bring it back." She could probably use some food too, she realized. Breakfast hadn't been on her radar this morning. Her focus had been on getting Chase fed fast so he could take his pill to stop the pain.

"That's great! Thanks, Moira. If it weren't weird, I would hug you."

She studied his eager expression. "Yeah, that would be a little weird."

"It's not that you're not pretty and all," he rushed to say. "But you're my boss and like my older sister."

It was all she could do not to laugh. "You're right. It isn't professional to hug, and for future reference, it's not professional to call your boss 'pretty.' Despite how nicely you meant it."

"Oh, shit, I—"

"I know," she said, holding up her hand. "I was only telling you since you'll be getting a job in the professional world soon."

"Right! Evan said most inventors suck at people-to-people interactions. Good thing we have you around to call us on our shit." He made a sign over his heart. "I promise to never call you pretty again."

She fought the urge to smile. "I'm glad we're clear."

"Thanks for not holding it against me, Moira," he said, punching her in the shoulder. "You're a pal."

Oh, good Lord. "Let's add friendly punches and calling your boss 'pal' to the no-go list. Just say, 'thank you.'"

He pressed his hands to his chest and said, "Thank you. With you around, I know I'm going to either get into Artemis or find a kick-ass job."

Gary still wasn't certain which path he would choose if he was accepted. He had school loans, he said, so the prospect of finding an immediate position in his field was attractive. "You know I'll help in any way I'm able."

"Awesome! Thanks. You go get your special coffee and my lunch."

That kinda came out wrong, but with Gary, things often did. "Will do. Hold the fort down."

He saluted her again, and she shook her head as she walked out. He still had a long way to go before he'd be ready for the professional world. But they'd get him there, one way or another. He really was a good kid.

When she arrived at the hotel and walked into High Stakes, Chef T's restaurant, she nodded to the hostess. "Is Chef T in the back?"

"Yes, prepping for the lunch crowd," she said. "You know the way."

She made her way to the revolving door to the kitchen and sucked in a deep breath of the savory air as she walked into the magic and madness. Two sous chefs were arguing about using shrimp heads for a stock while another chef was prepping a long black silky strip that looked like eel. Yuck. She trusted Chef T, but there was no way she was choking down eel.

"Moira!" Chef T called out. "You here for Chase's meat? I thought we were delivering it."

Chase's meat? Her brain shot to dirty places. *Down, girl.* "No, I'm here for one of your cappuccinos. I need a serious hit. I'm also going to order a couple sandwiches for me and Gary."

He kissed her cheek. "You got it. What do you want in the sandwich depot?"

She checked her phone. "Gary wants your Full Italian with provolone. I want balsamic chicken with spinach."

"You got it," he said, his eyes scanning the kitchen. "Is the cappuccino for here or to go?"

"Is Natalie free? I might pop up and say hi."

His eyes narrowed. "What's wrong?"

"Nothing."

"Don't kid a kidder. You come here during the work day for a cappuccino, and now you're asking about your sister. I know what that means."

"I had a night." *And a morning.*

"Do I need to beat someone up?" He flexed his impressive biceps, and his griffin tattoos looked ready to take flight.

"No, I'm good."

"Go see Natalie. I'll send up your cappuccino."

She kissed his cheek again, grateful for his kindness… and his offer to punch someone for her. "Thanks, Chef T."

"I've got your back," he said.

Her heart felt easier as she walked out of the kitchen. She was okay. She wasn't a wreck. People fell in love all the time—why should she treat it like it was the end of the world?

Mac Maven, the owner of The Grand Mountain, was leaving his office as she passed it on the way to Natalie's.

"Moira," he said, kissing her cheek. "What a pleasant surprise. Do you have a meeting with Natalie about Chase's needs?"

Her mind went to the gutter again. What was it about the service industry and their euphemisms? "No, just picking up some food. How's hotel management these days?"

"Pretty spectacular, especially since your boss is bringing in some A-listers for the Artemis fundraiser. We're excited."

"We're happy there's a hotel like yours to

accommodate the guests," she said. "And the fundraiser."
The decision had been an obvious one. They were asking
attendees to pay a lot of money to come to the dinner—
the food and the venue needed to live up.

"I have a meeting I need to get to," he said, checking
his watch. "See you later."

Moments later, she knocked on Natalie's door. "Hey!
You available?"

Her sister looked disoriented when she raised her
head. "Hey! I'm in spreadsheet hell. What are you doing
here?"

The best course seemed to be to shut the door behind
her. "I needed a hug."

Natalie jumped out of her chair, frowning, and came
toward her. "What happened?"

Moira put her arms around her. "I...oh shit...I don't
know where to start. I'm...falling for Chase."

Her sister's head jerked back. "Chase Parker?"

"Yes," she said, irritated by how pathetic she
sounded. "Oh, I shouldn't have come."

When she took a step toward the door, her sister
immediately stepped in front of her. "Don't act like that.
I was momentarily shocked. Come sit down."

She let her sister drag her over to her meeting table
by the window showcasing the mountains surrounding
Dare Valley. "I can't stay long. Plus, you're working."

Natalie pushed her into a chair. "Oh, shut up. Talk to
me. You're upset."

She landed hard on her bottom and rubbed it.
"Maybe TLC is beyond you." Maybe that was why she'd
come to Natalie. She wanted it straight.

Her sister gave her a look. "Spill."

"I...Chase and I agreed we were attracted to each
other, and we decided to spend time together while he
was here...which might have been stupid...given how I
feel now. But it's been a really nice few days. And then

yesterday, he told me things...really personal things." Could she be more vague or pathetic?

Natalie grabbed her hand and squeezed it hard. "Breathe. Then start from the beginning."

"I don't know that I should say." Chase was a private man, and she wanted to honor that.

"I swear I won't tell a soul," Natalie said. "You wouldn't be here if you didn't need to share it."

Because she trusted her sister, she told the story from start to finish. "I remembered how withdrawn you became after Kim died, so when Chase tried to cancel on me...it made me feel the same way. I wasn't going to let him shut me out."

"Good for you." Her sister's face crumbled, and she wrapped her arms around her chest. "And just so we're clear, I'm not shutting you or anyone else out ever again."

Moira gripped her sister's arms. "This is crazy. I haven't known Chase very long. I shouldn't feel like this."

"Love doesn't need time to make it right," Natalie said. "I knew how I felt about Blake the first time I met him. I put him in the friend zone at first, but it was only because I didn't trust myself or him. I wasted six months. I don't recommend it."

"But Chase is only here for a few weeks," she said. "When his injuries heal, he's going to go back to his life, his work. That's not here."

Natalie looked off, as if searching for the right words. There was a knock on the door.

"My cappuccino, I bet," Moira said.

Sure enough, one of Chef T's kitchen aides presented Natalie with a coffee tray when she opened the door. "Thank Terrance for making me a cappuccino too," her sister told the man. Shutting the door, she brought the tray over.

Taking her time, Moira stirred honey into her

beverage, added some cinnamon, and then took a long sip.

"If you're falling for Chase," Natalie said, "and I think you *have* fallen—you have to decide if you're going to step into it or step back. Given how miserable I was when I stepped back from Blake for a while, I wouldn't recommend it. By your own admission, Chase isn't a man who shares personal information like this, which means you're special to him. Why not talk about how you feel? If there's one thing Blake has taught me, it's that love is worth being vulnerable for."

"I hate being vulnerable," she said, taking another sip.

"I know. We were raised in the same family, remember? But we can choose differently. We don't have to end up like Mom and Dad. Can you imagine how different things might have been if Mom had told Dad she was unhappy years ago?"

Sure, she'd wondered, but there was no changing things now. Their mom had finally told their dad how much she hated being ignored for his work. He'd continued to ignore her. She'd left. There was no coming back from that.

"I don't know how to say it."

"No one knows the perfect formula," Natalie said. "Just say it. From your heart. He was vulnerable with you last night."

She hadn't thought of it that way. "You're right."

"I have my moments," she said with a smile. "Blake and I haven't told anyone, but I feel like this is the perfect time."

Even before her sister lowered her hand to her belly, she knew. Tears filled her eyes.

"If Blake hadn't been vulnerable with me and refused to let me push him away, we wouldn't be having a baby." Natalie brushed at her eyes. "Every morning, I wake up and the first sound I hear is him breathing next to me—okay, snoring some mornings, but don't tell him I said that. I know how blessed I am to have a second chance with him."

Gratitude washed over her as she reached down to touch her sister's tummy. She was going to have a new niece or nephew.

"Loving someone is everything," Natalie continued. "And now we're going to have a baby. Moira, I know how important work is, how important it is to be fulfilled as a person, a woman...but home and family...it's worth every moment of vulnerability."

She leaned in and hugged her sister. "I'm so happy for you guys."

"We were going to wait until I'm twelve weeks to tell everyone," Natalie told her.

"I won't say a word," she said, looking at her sister's belly in awe, imagining a little being growing in there. "Oh, this is so wonderful."

"I know," she said. "But back to Chase. What do you want? That's what it really comes down to. Do you think he could be it for you?"

She wanted to tell herself it was too soon, but the emotion she'd felt with him last night...it was unprecedented. "I'm scared, Natalie. I've never felt this way about anyone. If I'm being honest, really honest... when I woke up in his arms this morning...it felt right."

Wasn't that the truth when it came down to it? Being with him felt right.

"Then maybe you tell him that," Natalie said. "As someone who's married to a strong, private man, I know first-hand that they have the same insecurities we all do."

But Blake had gotten over that with Natalie, which was why he hadn't given up on her despite how hard she'd tried to push him away. Now they were having a baby. "You tell Blake good job, okay?"

Her sister laughed. "If I have to hear him boast one more time about 'getting it between the uprights,' I might have to kill him. But yes, I'll tell him. We're both... so happy." Tears filled her eyes then. "Mo, I almost blew it. Sometimes it still scares me how close I came to losing Blake for good out of stubbornness."

She found herself getting teary eyed, dammit. "But you didn't," she told her, hugging her tightly. "And now you're having a baby! It's crazy."

"You're having a baby!" a familiar voice shouted. "I knew it was coming. Oh yeah, a baby! My twins are going to have another cousin."

She and Natalie lurched apart. Jill Hale, who had the biggest mouth of anyone in the Hale clan, was standing just inside the now-open door, rotating her arms in the same direction as her hips. Moira thanked the dance gods that churning the butter had never caught on as a dance move. It was totally dorky, but so Jill.

"Shit," Natalie whispered. "You weren't supposed to hear that."

Moira's protective instincts kicked in. "Jill! Why didn't you knock?"

Jill's red hair bobbed as she continued dancing. "Mac told me you were in Natalie's office. If Blake had been visiting, I would have knocked."

"Oh, for God's sake, Jill," Natalie cried out, lowering her head to the table.

Their cousin stopped her geek-out. "What's wrong? This is great news."

"It's not common knowledge yet." Walking over to the door, Moira shut it and turned to Jill. "You listen to me. I love you, but you can't keep a secret worth shit. Natalie and Blake plan on telling everyone in their own time. Until then, you aren't going to say a word. Capisce?"

"Me? I'd never say a word."

She looked so sincere, and yet... "If you say anything, Jill, I swear on every Hale past, present, and future that you will answer to me. I will steal your private chocolate stash in your office. I will tell Brian you've developed a gluten intolerance to baguettes and croissants. And if I have to, I'll tell Uncle Arthur your dentist banned you from sweets, which means no more red hots for you."

Jill sucked in her breath. "That's so mean!"

"I'll be your worse nightmare."

Her green eyes—the Hale eyes Moira shared—narrowed. "I've had secret baby news myself. I know how precious it is. You didn't have to threaten my personal food pyramid."

Leave it to Jill to call chocolate, bread, and red hots a food pyramid. "So we're clear?"

"Crystal," Jill said. "Can I hug my cousin and express my happiness over the new baby?"

Moira rolled her eyes. "I suppose."

Like the eager puppy she was, Jill pranced over to Natalie, pulled her out of her chair, and hugged her. Then it turned into a crazy salsa dance step, which finally teased a laugh out of Natalie.

"Big congrats, cuz," Jill said. "I can't wait to meet your little one. Do you want a girl or a boy?"

"I just want the baby to be healthy," Natalie said with a smile. "And happy."

Happy, Moira thought.

She knew what would make her happy. How could she not fight for that?

CHAPTER 20

WHEN BONNIE APPEARED THAT MORNING, CHASE FELT better equipped to handle her. "You left your cat. I called to tell you, but you didn't pick up."

She bent over and picked Barney up when the kitten ran over to her. "Good morning to you too. I thought you could use a friend."

He shifted on the couch to look at her. Hadn't he expected that answer? "Well, he's your pet. I didn't like you leaving him here." Okay, it hadn't been a bad experience. The silly tabby had rolled over and over again on the rug after Moira had left, making him smile. Barney acted like he didn't have a care in the world.

Chase didn't want to get attached to him.

"Oh, that's too bad," Bonnie said, scratching him behind the ears. "It won't happen again. Are you feeling better this morning?"

Her tone was light. "I want to apologize. I acted badly. That...appointment caught me off guard."

There was extra warmth in her smile. "Don't worry, Chase. Energy healing isn't for everyone. I'm sorry if it distressed you."

It wasn't what Ally had done so much as what she'd said. After Moira had left this morning, he'd started thinking about their session again. He didn't want to believe Ally could talk to his dad, but he couldn't discount what had happened.

"Having a perfect stranger know things I don't tell anyone is distressing," Chase said, trying to figure out his next step. "You didn't tell me she's more than a healer."

"Know many healers, do you?" She had the audacity to laugh. "It's such a limited word, in my experience. I've met healers who run the gamut, but you're right, I suppose. If you want to be technical, she's a healer, psychic, medium, and empath."

"You should have mentioned this," Chase said, feeling the need to glower to make his point. "I didn't want the other stuff." Even though he couldn't stop thinking about it.

"Ally was only doing what she was called to do to help you heal completely," Bonnie said, setting Barney down. "The fact that it didn't work for you is okay. Are you ready for the feng shui expert today?"

The thought of another person coming in here and throwing woo-woo all over him made him want to grind his teeth. But if there was a chance it would help his recovery, he had to keep an open mind. "I'm clapping my hands in excitement on the inside."

"I'll bet," Bonnie said dryly.

Two hours later, Chase was using every diplomatic bone in his body not to toss Jarvis, the feng shui expert, out of his ear. The stylish black man was knowledgeable about all things feng shui, but he was also a touch dramatic.

"I don't know what these people were thinking, decorating this place. A cactus in your wisdom and self-cultivation bagua? Bonnie, it's appalling."

From the look of it, the Christmas cactus had been left in the hopes of brightening up the place with minimal watering. "It seems like a practical decision to me," Chase said. "It doesn't require much maintenance to keep it alive."

"It's *barely* alive! Wisdom and self-cultivation are the prize jewels of our experience on planet earth. A cactus says you're prickly about self-cultivation and don't plan to feed your inner self." He paused and took a good look at Chase. "Don't take this the wrong way, darling, but looking at you in your adorable little scooter...this poor cactus could give you a run for the money in the health department."

It was like the man knew him. "First, let's get something straight," Chase said. "Don't call me darling. Second, move the damned cactus then. We don't need to analyze *me* in the evaluation. This isn't my house."

Jarvis put his hand on his hip. "It's your house for the time being. I won't call you darling, but it's important to bring the right energy to each bagua, Chase."

"Look," Chase said, "I'm only going to be here for a few more weeks, God willing. Make this place healing and calm and whatever else it needs. Bonnie said it might help me recover, and as you've pointed out, I could use all the help I can get."

The man's face softened. "You do need help. You have hunting and death in your relationship bagua," he said, gesturing to the painting on the wall.

Chase glanced at it. A well-dressed man was shooting ducks. "Is that bad?"

Jarvis laughed out loud. "Bad? Not if you want to pursue women, shoot them, and then eat them."

"I'm kinder than that," Chase deadpanned, deciding he might have fun with this guy after all.

"I'll bet you are," Jarvis said, "but not by much. Let me put it this way. Do you ever want to get laid?"

"Who doesn't?" he responded. Of course, the only woman he wanted to be with was Moira. He'd known before it would be hot between them, but after last night, he expected it was going to be a lot more personal. More so than it had been with anyone, perhaps.

Earlier, after she left, he'd had a moment of wondering if he'd shared too much. But he wasn't a man for regrets or second-guessing. Telling her about the fire and his dad's suicide had felt right. She'd more than proven his trust. And from the tender way she'd held him last night, she'd more than proven her heart.

"We move the painting," Jarvis said. "Maybe to your wealth corner. You're a corporate executive type, correct?"

He looked over to Bonnie for confirmation, which Chase somehow found amusing. What had Bonnie told the man?

"He is," Bonnie said, jumping in to answer when Chase didn't.

"The hunting aspect of the painting is good then," Jarvis said, walking over to the painting. "I just don't like the death."

And so it went. Jarvis went from room to room, calling out everything from paintings to colors to the way his bed was positioned against the interior wall.

"You'll sleep better with your feet facing the outside wall," the man said with a wink. "Trust me."

Chase let him do what he wanted until he emerged from the walk-in closet with the Home Sweet Love pillow. A spike of pain shot through Chase's chest again, and he took a slow, controlled breath to control it. Good thing Andy was coming by later to check out his heart.

"This pillow! Why is something filled with such a beautiful intention languishing in your closet?" Jarvis traced the needlepoint with his finger. "This is excellent work. I would say it's an antique. We need to put this in your relationship bagua."

Chase could feel himself breaking out into a cold sweat. "No. I don't want it out."

"Why ever not, darl—oops, Chase? It's beautiful!"

"I said I don't want it displayed," he told the man.

"I know it's a little cutesy for a guy like you, but we don't have much to work with in this rental. I really think—"

"It's non-negotiable," Chase said flatly. "Put it back in the closet."

Jarvis gave him a scorching look. Good, one of Bonnie's healing minions was finally giving him something he could work with. Anger, he understood. Ego, he understood. Chase might be helpless in the face of all the love and compassion talk, but in this realm, he was king.

"I value your expertise, Jarvis," Chase said like he was handling an angry engineer, "but I can assure you that having this object in my relationship bagua will not produce any healing effects in me."

"As you wish," Jarvis said, walking back into the closet. "All done."

"If you need to bring in some additional items or colors to create better baguas, you're welcome to do so. Money is no object. I'll have Evan send you photos of my current residence so you have a sense of colors and objects more suited to my palate."

He had the man's full attention now.

"No pink," Chase said. "And nothing...what did you call it? Cutesy? Are we clear?"

Jarvis shook his head. "Perfectly. I'll make some notes and finish up. When can I expect the photos of your current residence?"

Was he really going to bother decorating this place for the remaining few weeks of his residence? Looked like. "I'll text him now and make sure they're in your hands by the end of the day."

"Brilliant," Jarvis said. "I was told to make you my priority."

Chase could see Evan saying something like that. "Then we understand each other."

Jarvis lifted a brow. "The cat is a great addition to the energy in the house."

"He's not mine," Chase said, looking over at Barney playing with his tail in the corner of the room.

"I see," Jarvis said. "I'll sit in the kitchen out of your way while I finish up my plan."

"Great," Chase said, watching the man walk out.

He felt a smile cross his lips. Man, it had felt good to tell someone how things were going to be. It made him feel like he was in charge of his own destiny again. Lately, he'd felt like everyone was telling him what he could and couldn't do.

"You were hard on him," Bonnie said, picking Barney up. "But it worked out. Jarvis is great at what he does, but he can be a bit intense. Do you want to tell me about the pillow?"

He shook his head, happy to realize it didn't hurt like it had before Dr. Sarah had made him a human pincushion. "Nothing to tell."

She made a disbelieving sound. "Your jaw locked and you started to sweat. I know you don't want to hear this, but you can't heal from pain you won't acknowledge."

"Bonnie, I know you mean well, but I'm fine."

Barney meowed.

"You're turning forty and having your ticker checked out today," she said, giving him an arch look. "Again, it's your health, but I care about my charges. I feel I would be remiss in not pointing out the incongruities between your pain and your words."

"My pain and words?" he asked.

"A pillow shouldn't make you feel pain, Chase," she said simply. "I'll go find Jarvis and make sure he hasn't added any pink cashmere throws to his list just to piss you off."

At another time it would have made him smile, but he was too worked up. Bonnie set Barney down in his lap on her way out. He wanted to hunch his shoulders. Why was everyone pushing him so hard?

Was he happy that a damn pillow made his chest hurt? No. He moved his scooter to the closet door and opened it. Jarvis had laid the pillow on top of the shelves. Chase studied it. He wished he could throw it away. God knows, he'd tried.

His mother had sent it to him as a Christmas present his freshman year of college in Boston, and he'd fought tears as he pressed it to his chest in his dorm room. There was no home sweet love in their family anymore.

Barney meowed and nudged him in the stomach. Chase shut the door on the pillow and the memories.

When Andy arrived for his checkup, Chase was in a foul mood. Feng shui hadn't had the most positive effect on him.

"Wow," Andy said, turning in a half circle. "Jarvis really did a number on this place."

The feng shui expert had moved all of the furniture around with Bonnie's help after finalizing his plan and making his shopping list. Chase had hated watching from his scooter. Then Jarvis had swapped out the paintings and various knickknacks. At the door, he'd winked and said, "I'll be back," in a terrible Arnold Schwarzenegger voice. Bonnie had laughed. Chase had thought about firing him on the spot.

As if comfort could come from a place. From the way a house was arranged.

"Do you feel more healing energy in this place?" Chase asked dryly.

Andy bit his lip. "Do you?"

"I'm all soft and squishy inside," he said, petting Barney. "Shall we get started?"

"I need to get some equipment from the car," Andy

said. "Why don't you go into your bedroom and take off your shirt? We can do the exam in there. Bonnie, you mind helping me?"

Chase knew that request was code for "fill me in on the moody patient." He propelled his scooter off to his temporary bedroom and fought another growl. Jarvis had not only changed the position of his bed—he had to admit it now had a nice view of the lake and mountains—he'd also laid a homey yellow afghan from the linen closet on the edge of the bed. Chase yanked it off violently, causing Barney to meow and jump off his lap.

"You got something against afghans?" Andy asked from the doorway.

Chase moved his scooter toward the dresser. "I don't like the color." After stuffing the blanket inside one of the drawers, he turned to face Andy.

"How did your healing sessions go?" Andy asked.

"The acupuncture and Qigong wasn't bad," Chase said, realizing it was probably time to set up another appointment with Dr. Sarah. He also needed to start incorporating his Qigong exercises into his day.

"And the energy healing with Ally?" Andy helped Chase remove his shirt and then got out his stethoscope.

"It's not for everyone," Chase said. "The whole thing was...weird. She knew things she couldn't have known."

Andy listened thoughtfully to his heart and then said, "She often does. Part of her gift. You strike me as a private man. Did the experience upset you?"

"I wish it hadn't." Few things got under his skin, but there was no denying the effect she'd had on him.

Andy took his blood pressure—a little higher than the last time, but still normal—and then gave him a full checkup. The mobile EKG was pretty cool. Evan would have geeked out.

"Your EKG is normal," Andy said. "Have you had

any other pain since we last spoke about it?"

Chase thought about the damn pillow incident with Jarvis. "A little bit this morning. When Jarvis pissed me off."

"What was he doing?" Andy asked.

There was a small smile on the doctor's face, but his eyes were intent. Shit, Chase knew he was going to sound like a moron. But Andy was here to look at his heart. He needed to be as forthright with him as possible. "We were arguing about his desire to include a stupid pillow in my relationship bagua."

"I can see how that might piss you off," Andy said. "What was wrong with the pillow?"

He felt everything inside of him tighten. "It was too homey. I mean, do I look like a homey kind of guy to you?"

"Where's the pillow now?" Andy asked. "Maybe I can take it off your hands. If it's pissing you off this much, it probably shouldn't be around the house."

Sweat broke out across his skin. "Don't worry about it. I hid it."

"Really, Chase, I should take it with me. Where is it? If it's that awful, I'll put it in the trash with my exam gloves."

He couldn't let that happen. "I told you not to worry about it."

Andy put his hands on his hips. "You're getting pretty upset here. I feel like I'm missing out if I don't see this pillow. Is it ugly? Or just offensive?"

The very sight of it offended Chase, but it wasn't ugly. His mom had *made* that pillow. "It's just me. I don't like it."

"Seriously, can't I take a peek? I need a good story for my nurses, and it sounds like this pillow might be just the thing."

"Really, it's no big deal," Chase said. His voice

had risen to an uncomfortable level, and he mentally chastened himself. He needed to keep a lid on his temper. Andy didn't deserve this attitude from him, plus the guy was Moira's brother. Given how much she was coming to mean to Chase, he needed to be on his best behavior.

"Man, this is really pissing you off, isn't it? And all over a pillow. I've really gotta see this, Chase."

"I said no," Chase said in a hard tone.

A jolt of pain shot through his chest, and he bit his lip to keep from crying out. Andy was on his knees in front of him in a second.

"Are you having chest pain?" he asked.

"It's like the other times," Chase barked out. "Like a bolt of pain shot through my ribs and then disappeared."

Andy took his pulse. "Maybe we should go to the hospital. You can't manage a stress test right now given your injuries, but we could do a CT test. It's possible you could have plaque in the blood vessels of your heart."

"My cholesterol is normal," Chase said, shaking his head.

"So we discovered when you came to the ER," Andy said, rubbing his chin. "Chase, I hate to press you on this, but I'm going to seriously recommend you let me see this pillow. It's elevated your heart rate, caused you to sweat and be flushed, and given you chest pain."

He looked away. "It's embarrassing."

"Never be embarrassed when it comes to your health," Andy said. "No judgments here. Where is it?"

Hanging his head, he said, "In the closet."

Andy opened the door, disappeared for a moment, and then returned with the pillow. "This wasn't what I expected, I have to admit. What about this pillow upsets you this much?"

Shit. He felt the rawness of his emotions tumble forward. "Evan brought it from a closet in my house in Virginia. My mother made it."

Andy's mouth opened for a moment before he finally spoke. "Okay," he said, "I'm going to sit down on your bed, if that's okay, while you tell me about this. One thing I've learned about the body is that when it's hurt or upset, there's often a charge somewhere causing all of it. More doctors are coming to believe in the mind/body connection, and I happen to be one of them. It's important for us to talk about this."

Chase took a deep breath. "Ally stumbled on some stuff that made me upset too, but dammit, I've put all of this behind me."

"Have you?" Andy asked. "Don't take this the wrong way, but this is a really nice pillow your mom made you."

Chase was embarrassed to feel his throat thicken. "It was the one item my mom managed to save from the ranch. I hate that she sent it to me after I left Wyoming for college. I don't know what the hell she was trying to do."

Andy held the pillow to his chest, the words facing outward. "What happened to your ranch, Chase?"

He could smell the smoke suddenly, cloying and choking. All these years later, it tickled his throat and made him cough. "It burned down."

"I'm sorry," Andy said. "How old were you?"

"Twelve." After that night, he'd never felt like a kid again. He'd stepped up, taking extra jobs so he could his mom pay for their small apartment in Cheyenne. Every spare minute had been spent studying—even then he'd known it was his ticket out.

"I can't imagine," Andy said. "Must have been hard on your family."

"It didn't get any easier when the insurance company cut us a miserable check for the loss, one that wouldn't allow us to rebuild." Chase looked longingly at the door, wishing Barney were in his lap. And that was just stupid. He was a grown man. He didn't need comfort from a cat.

But Barney was here, so why not?

He wheeled to the bedroom door and opened it a crack, hoping the kitten would get the message. Reaching for his shirt, he awkwardly tugged it on. Andy stood to help him.

"What did your family do after that?" he asked.

Chase looked up at him and made himself say it. "My dad shot himself on our land."

Shock washed over Andy's face. "God. I... I'm no stranger to loss. You know about my first wife, Kim, I expect. Sorry is such a shitty thing to say—trust me, I know—but I am. Were you the oldest?"

He nodded. "My younger brother was seven. He... took it hard. I tried to motivate him to do well in school so he could go to college. Boone got into trouble. He was thirteen when I went to Harvard. He got into a rough crowd. Started drinking and doing drugs young. He's an addict living in a trailer park outside Carson City. We don't speak. I tried a few times, but he...only wants money for drugs."

But Chase had his security consultant check in on his brother from time to time. The sad truth was, he was pretty sure it was the only way he or his mother would know if his brother ODed and died.

"And your mother?" Andy asked.

"I bought her a house, and we talk at Christmas and on our birthdays," he said, feeling his chest tighten at the reminder of how remote their relationship had become. "She has a sister she's not terribly close to, but it's somewhere to go on the holidays."

"What do you do around that time of year?"

"I work," Chase said. "But I don't totally deprive myself. Usually I'll fly to one of Europe's finest capital cities and take a walk after having a nice meal somewhere. When Evan was in Paris, I'd meet him there for a holiday brunch. Suffer through his wacky white elephant gifts."

Sometimes, though, Evan would buy him a serious gift, something he knew Chase would like. A twenty-three-year-old bottle of Pappy Van Winkle or an engraved Montblanc pen he could use to sign the multi-million-dollar contracts he won for Quid-Atch with their team.

"Evan sounds like he's become your family in a way," Andy said. "I know he's joked about you being the older brother he never had."

Chase flashed back to what Ally had said about Evan. Somehow in the turmoil, he'd forgotten. "He's finally found his feet. He doesn't need to look up to me anymore, and I don't need to take care of him."

Andy's mouth lifted in a half-smile. "Sometimes it's okay to have family take care of us a little. Chase, when Moira first found me after your accident, she said you'd gotten distracted by the house that had caught fire on the bench. I remember you saying that's when you first noticed the chest pain. You'd never experienced it before that day?"

He shook his head. "I take good care of myself despite my work schedule."

Andy set the pillow aside. "I can bring you in for more tests, but I honestly think your chest pain is related to unprocessed emotions about the loss of your family. What did Ally say?"

"It's like you're twins," he said dryly, feeling his chest tighten. "I can't...I don't want this to come up. It's done. I've put it in the past where it belongs."

"Trauma doesn't work that way," Andy said. "I know from personal experience. I don't usually talk about losing my wife, but I feel like it might help you some. You're a tough guy, and I respect that. I'd like to think I am too, but losing Kim shattered me. She was the love of my life, and we'd just created the most beautiful son together. I finally had my family. And then my partner in all of that was gone."

Chase's throat thickened. "I'm sorry for your loss."

"Thanks," he said, shaking his head. "I'm good, really good. And the reason I am is because I let myself grieve. For a while there, I bawled my eyes out every night after I put my kid to bed. I kept doing it until it slowed down and then finally stopped. My son, Danny, deserved to have a dad who had an open heart, and I couldn't do that if I bottled all my emotions up."

Chase's father had chosen a different route, and look how that had worked out for him and his brother. "Your son is a lucky kid."

"We're both lucky," Andy said. "Now I'm engaged to another wonderful woman. I guess what I'm saying is that you shouldn't give up on home and family."

"I don't want a home and a family," Chase said. "There's nothing wrong with it, but it's not for me. Work is my life."

Andy smiled. "Your anger at the pillow your mother saved from the fire suggests otherwise. The question for you is: do you want to stop being pissed off by this pillow?"

When he put it that way, Chase felt stupid. "I guess. Because I can't throw it away, and I can't stand the sight of it."

"You're going to hate what I'm about to prescribe, but here goes." He held up his hands, smirking a little. "Don't hurt me."

Something about the glib way he said it reminded Chase of Moira. He felt a tug of longing. Suddenly Barney slipped through the open door and leaped onto his lap. "I was waiting for you," he told him, scratching the kitten behind the ears. Barney's purr rumbled against his chest.

"That kitty is cute," Andy said. "Bonnie has the best cats, I swear. Now, here's what I suggest. Work with

Ally. You can talk to a psychiatrist too, but I'd start with her. She can help people release emotional blocks in... unique ways."

Yeah, she was unique all right. "Ally knows things."

"Exactly," Andy said, brightening up. "You can't hide from her. It's alarming at first, but once you trust her, she can take you where you need to go."

"Where is that?" Chase asked, cupping the kitten's head in his hands.

"To a place of peace about the past. I have a feeling your chest pain will go away too. But we can do more tests if you'd like."

"Did you go to Ally after Kim died?" he asked.

"No," he said. "I handled mine the old-fashioned way. Like I said, I cried a lot. When I got pissed I'd shred paper or go for a run. I was pretty angry with her for leaving me, even though I knew she didn't want to go. I imagine you were pretty angry with your dad."

"He took the coward's way out," Chase said.

"Ally can help you," Andy said. "I wouldn't suggest as much if I didn't believe it."

Chase nodded. "She said..." God, was he really going to say this out loud? "She said my dad was sorry. Does she really...hear things from people who've passed?"

"Some of my patients have told me she's been able to give them messages from loved ones," Andy said, nodding. "If she says she's heard something, I'd believe her. She's one of the kindest, most ethical people I know. Ally wouldn't have let you think her name was Helga, for example."

Chase's mouth twitched. "This wasn't the medical examination I expected today."

"Me either," Andy said, reaching down and petting Barney. "But that's what I love about life. You never know what the next curveball is going to be."

That was one way to look at it. "Thanks for coming

all the way out here, Andy. I know you're busy at the hospital."

"I had to," Andy said. "Moira is my family, and she's asked me to take good care of you. When she or anyone else I care about asks for something, they get it. Holler if you need something. Otherwise, I'll check in on you next week, and we'll reassess your work schedule. You'll probably be able to start up again slowly. Work a quarter time, maybe half—if you let Jarvis feng shui the rest of the house." He gave an exaggerated wink.

"Funny," Chase said.

"I like to leave my patients smiling," Andy said as he left the room.

Barney jumped off his lap and then leaped onto his bed. "Hey! Get off there. I sleep there."

The kitten nudged the Home Sweet Love pillow, which Andy had left on the bed, and snuggled against it, purring softly.

Chase left the pillow where it was and sat quietly watching the scene.

CHAPTER 21

WHILE CAROLINE WORKED WITH ARTISTIC TYPES, SHE did not have the cliché temperament. There wasn't a spontaneous bone in her body. Ask any of her siblings.

She'd been stewing about her schedule. How in the world was she supposed to give over three hundred paintings her complete attention in one long weekend? J.T. was insane.

Staring at the legal pad she'd used to create a mini-list of important considerations, she traced the line about her vacation hours. Thirty-three and a half hours, meaning not quite eight days. She usually took a week off in the spring to go somewhere fun, even if it meant doing something simple like heading south to a house in Taos or Santa Fe. Such great art there, and the food...

Could she take three days off and head to Rome? It simply wouldn't be enough time to review the collection, and she couldn't possibly stay with J.T. She barely knew the man.

But she wanted to get to know him better, and not in a completely professional way. That was the rub. If she was going to look over his art and listen to his ideas for this museum he was planning, she needed to get a grip on herself. Needed to control her reaction to him.

But he was so hot. There was no denying that.

She picked up her cell phone and called Uncle Arthur. He knew how to cut to the chase.

"Arthur Hale," he answered in his normal gravely voice.

"Hi, it's Caroline," she said.

"Caroline who? Give me your last name, girl. What am I, a rolodex?"

He sounded so put out, she smiled. "It's your niece."

"I know who it is," he said, laughing. "I was yanking your chain. J.T. tells me you haven't accepted his offer to go to Rome yet."

He was speaking with J.T. about her again? She wasn't sure she liked that. "Hence my call to you. Do you really think I can give this collection in Rome a professional look in a long weekend?"

"I think you can do whatever the hell you want to," Uncle Arthur said. "Why are you dithering? You young people make everything harder than it needs to be. I don't know what you'll do when I'm not around to kick you in the pants."

"Don't talk like that." The thought of not having her crotchety old uncle around to give her a hard time—to inspire and push her—made her sad.

"It's life, child," he said. "We all die. You want my opinion? Call J.T. back. Go to Rome. See the art collection Emmits began before I was born. And have a good time. J.T. is a nice boy. You might hit it off."

She frowned. "Are you matchmaking, Uncle Arthur?"

"Never," he spat out as if the very thought was repulsive. "Have I ever tried to set any of my kin up? No. Do you know why? Because your heart knows its mate. Maybe not at first. But it knows. Never doubt that. But you know art, and so does J.T. This art museum is important, Caroline, and it will bring even more attention on Dare Valley. I have faith the attention will be favorable."

She looked down at the pad in front of her. "I'm not sure about my vacation time—"

"Great balls of fire, Caroline, what is there to consider? You take your vacation and ride first class to Rome. So, you'll be tired when you get back. Who cares? You're not even thirty yet. What the hell are you worried about? Losing beauty sleep?"

"I'm turning thirty this year," she said, and to her, it was a big event.

"Well, take it from an old man with less time left than you, live! Not just a little. But a whole heck of a lot. Soak the world in. Time goes by so fast, Caroline. You blink, and you're my age, picking out cemetery plots."

Her face creased into a frown. How morbid he'd been lately. "Are you sure you're okay, Uncle Arthur?"

"I'm fine, but I'm hanging up. This call is wasting precious seconds of the time I have left. You decide what you want to do and do it."

Sure enough, he clicked off. "Live a little" was a phrase she was good with. But "a lot" seemed scarier.

She looked at the thirty-one paintings they had in the gallery. They had a reasonable collection, but it wasn't even close to the size of J.T.'s. What would it be like to see a collection of that size and scope? To help guide him in such a colossal undertaking?

Okay, she was going to see them. She would keep it professional. No drooling over his Italian sense of fashion or the charming dimple in his cheek. Correction. She'd never even noticed his dimple. Caroline Hale, the art expert, didn't notice things like dimples on business associates.

And that's what J.T. Merriam was.

She took his card out of the top drawer in her desk. The international number looked complicated, which almost made her chicken out. But she looked up how to call someone in Rome. She dialed in the 011+39+06 and the rest of his number, and it rang. Whew!

Tapping her foot, she listened to the unusual ring tone.

"Hi Caroline!" he said after she identified herself. He sounded pleased to hear from her. "I've been waiting patiently for you to call. My brother, Trev, says hi, by the way. He tried to wrestle the phone away from me. I think he wanted to apologize for the childhood mud incident too."

Did he have to be so charming and personable? "Tell him a bottle of wine is an acceptable way of apologizing for getting a girl covered in mud."

"I wasn't the one—"

"Shut it, Trev," J.T. said. "Sorry, he was trying to listen. We were watching a soccer game on the couch. I'm heading out onto the balcony to get away from him."

The sound of honking cars and people cheering carried over the line. "What's going on?"

"Roma just won," he said, giving a few whoops himself. "In a tie breaker."

"Soccer," she said, picking up her pen and fiddling with the end. "So I—"

"Decided to come, right? If not, I'm going to have to fly back over there right now so I can make another effort to convince you in person."

"That sounds a little extreme," she said. Her heart was racing in her chest, but she wasn't sure if it was because of his offer, which did make her nervous, or *him*. "But it makes me wonder, why me? I mean, you could hire anyone to look over the collection. I'm small potatoes when it comes to the international art scene."

He laughed. "Well, let me tell you. I have had the big potatoes look at the art. Shut up, Trev, I swear to God, she came up with the potato metaphor. Go back inside.

Sorry. My brother lives to torture me. Back to your question. I know on good authority that our collection is excellent. What I want is to make it special to Dare Valley."

His impassioned tone told her he meant every word.

"My great-great grandfather loved that town. And so did the rest of the family. I did too, until we stopped going there. When I talked to Uncle Arthur again, the... shit...how should I say this? The nostalgia of the place came flooding back to me. The Merriams and the Hales put Dare Valley on the map. I thought...working with you might bring that full circle."

Every art lover was a romantic in some essential way, and she understood what he meant. "It's why I love art really," she told him. "It makes me nostalgic for other times. Whenever I look at a portrait, I wish I could meet the subject. It's like artists capture a moment so other people can long for it for eternity."

"Exactly! That's how I feel."

She could feel the chill bumps rising up on her skin. "I need to speak with my boss about time off, but you can count me in."

"Good," he said. "I'm glad. I was afraid I was going to have to unleash Trevor on you."

Huh? "I don't know what that means."

"People who know us both say that he's the more suave and dynamic one," J.T. said. "They're mostly correct. Look, I have to go. Said charming twin is opening my Armand de Brignac Brut Rose Champagne. Trev, that's a ten thousand-dollar bottle of champagne! I know Roma won, but seriously... Sorry, he's a nutcase. Wants to take a bottle out into the streets with the other crazies tonight and burn cars and shit. Save me."

She couldn't help but laugh. "A ten thousand-dollar bottle, huh? I can't imagine."

"I'll make sure we have one when you come," J.T.

said. "Talk to your boss and let me know what makes the most sense for your schedule."

"Don't you need to check your schedule?" she asked.

"No, I resigned from my position a couple of days ago," he said. "It was time for a new adventure. I'm focusing all my energy on this museum."

Well...that certainly meant he was serious. "Oh...should I say congratulations?"

"Sure. That's how I'm looking at it. Otherwise, I'll stay depressed."

She couldn't imagine him depressed. "Have fun with your brother. I'll call you when I know more."

"Great," he said. "Good night, Caroline."

Something in the way he said that made her wish she could go into the streets with him and his brother and drink champagne to celebrate something as silly to her as a soccer game.

CHAPTER 22

THE MINUTE MOIRA WALKED OUT OF THE OFFICE, A little later than usual given her jaunt to see Natalie, she called Caroline from her car.

"Hey! I got your text about having news. Speak."

Her sister laughed. "I told J.T. I'm coming to Rome to see his collection. I'm stroked."

"And you're clearly celebrating," Moira said, heading to her house. "I think you mean 'stoked.' What are you drinking?"

"Second glass of champagne. I bought a bottle. How often does a girl agree to up and go to Rome to see over three hundred paintings with a gorgeous, charming man?"

Gorgeous, huh? J.T. was hot, undeniably, but her sister sounded *interested* in his hotness. Usually Caroline went for soulful, artistic types. Maybe J.T. had that going for him too. Moira didn't know much about him after all these years. "When do you leave?"

"I need to talk to Kendra tomorrow. Of course, I can't tell her what I'm up to. She'll want a piece of the action. You know how she is."

Kendra Wolst had three ex-husbands—all famous artists. All divorces had purportedly happened for the same reason. She'd been more interested in their art than in their persons. "Smart."

"J.T. is going to send a private plane for me," Caroline said, giggling. "It's like a dream."

"Hold tight, Cinderella," Moira said. "Your coach turns back into a pumpkin at—"

"Oh, don't be a party pooper," she said. "*Party pooper, party pooper—*"

"I am so not listening to you sing that song. I gotta run. Talk to you later. Love you."

"Love you. Wish you were still in Denver. I...kinda miss having you here."

She gripped the steering wheel as her sister's loneliness crept over her, filling her with longing. How many times had they met up during the week when they'd both lived in Denver?

"I miss you too, but I'll see you soon. We'll celebrate then." Likely with Natalie and Blake's news about the baby. She couldn't wait until everyone else knew.

"All right. You headed to see Chase?"

"Yes." She wanted to change first. Pick up one of Brian's roasted chicken meals to go.

"Have fun. Love you."

"Ditto."

She hung up, wishing she were closer to her sister so they could grab a quick drink, but a small voice in the back of her head told her she still would have gone to Chase. Now that Natalie had helped her set aside all of the details and focus on what she wanted, she felt drawn to him.

She wanted Chase. It was time to tell him as much.

When Moira arrived at Chase's place after stopping off to pick up their takeout, she was a stewpot of nerves. She'd changed her shirt three times before finally settling on a red cable-knit sweater and jeans.

It was a frigid night, and she only knocked once

before entering the house. Barney greeted her.

"Hi," she said, reaching down to pick up the kitten after closing the door. "You're still here."

"The experts agree he's good for me, so I let him stay," Chase said from his usual position on the couch in front of a blazing fire. "Who am I to disagree?"

She walked over to him after depositing the takeout bag on the dining room table. He didn't look like he was freaking out over last night's revelations, but he looked downright somber in a loose navy T-shirt and tan cargo pants. Still, he was so heartbreakingly handsome... He made an effort at a smile.

"I can't tell if your agreement about Barney staying comes from defeat or acceptance," she said. "What happened? Because it's hard to ignore that someone moved some furniture around in here. I doubt it was Barney." The kitten meowed and rubbed his head in her palm.

"I was feng shui-ed today," he replied with a roll of his eyes. "Your brother also joined the rest of my so-called healing professionals in urging me to deal with the fire and my dad's suicide."

God, that had to have been tough. Sitting on the couch next to him, she put her hand on his good knee. "You've had a day then. Maybe we can make it a little brighter now that I'm here."

"You brighten up everywhere you go," he said, taking her hand. "I noticed it before we...agreed to be together."

How lovely. Leaning in to kiss him, she kept her eyes on his. He shifted until their mouths met. The kiss was slow and gentle, yet super hot. Moira found herself getting sweaty under her winter coat. She'd been too eager to get to him to pause and take it off.

When they ended the kiss, she smiled at him. "I'm going to hang my coat up. Do you need anything?"

His mouth turned up in a half smile. "Besides more

kissing?"

That comment punched her in the gut. "Happy to address that in a sec, but yes, anything else? I picked up a roasted chicken dinner at Brasserie Dare. We should eat tonight for a change."

"Sounds good," he said, taking Barney from her and scratching the kitten behind the ears. "I don't need anything else at the moment."

After stashing her coat, she poured a glass of wine for herself and cuddled against his good side in front of the fire. Moment of truth time. "Chase?" she said softly, her heart beating out of her chest.

He shifted to put his arm around her and then kissed the top of her head. "What?"

The gesture gave her more courage to speak her mind. "I wanted you to know how much it meant to me that you shared your story last night. I...it was brave and...it really touched me that you trust me like that. I... want you to trust me."

Shifting so he could see her face, he gazed at her with those gray eyes of his. "I do trust you. More than I understand sometimes."

She traced his jaw. "I've fallen for you...more than I can understand. I want...to be with you."

"I thought we'd already covered this," he said, smiling.

He'd given her an opportunity to chicken out, to pretend she hadn't meant it that way. But she could hear Natalie's voice urging her, *Tell him.* "It's stronger now. Last night changed things for me. For us, I think. Is that weird?"

"Weird?" he asked, kissing her lightly on the lips. "No. Everything seems so different. I'm not in my normal life or normal place—hell, even my clothes are weird—and yet, I have you here...and this damn kitten. Let's not talk about the healing contingent right now.

I'm uncomfortable much of the day, but never with you. Even though I have moments where I'm..."

She waited for him to finish his thought.

"I'm not used to any of this, Moira," he finally said. "The last woman I trusted was my mother, and she let me down. I've...put a hell of a lot of faith in you."

"I'm not going to mess that up," she said, feeling a tug in her heart. "But there's something I want to tell you."

He tilted his head to the side. "I'm listening."

Heat suffused her cheeks. "Okay, here goes. I like you. A lot."

His brow lifted.

She took a deep breath. "More than I've liked anyone so far. I...don't want to put a time limit on us. This. I... know you're going to leave soon. Once you get well." Oh, she sounded so awkward. "I don't want that to stop us from pursuing this—if we still want to. Does that make sense? I...oh shit. I might be falling in love with you. Is that weird enough for you?"

He seemed to take an equally deep breath. "I... that's...unexpected."

She started shaking her head immediately. "Okay, I know it's a lot to take in. We've only been 'together' for a few days, but I couldn't concentrate at work this morning after leaving you. I spilled coffee all over my desk. Heck, I ended up visiting my sister for some advice. I never do that."

"Moira—"

"No, hear me out." She had to be truthful. Not just for him, but for herself. "My sister, Natalie, had a horrible time when we lost Kim. She didn't want to deal with her grief. She shut everyone out, including her husband. But she's dealt with it, and they're back together. They're happier than ever. I...God, what am I trying to say here? What I feel for you is scary, but it's also really wonderful."

He touched her cheek, and her eyes flickered back to his. He was watching her closely. "I couldn't agree more."

"It's just...I want to be with you. I thought that...well, since you told me something you've never shared with another woman...you might not want to put a timeframe on us either."

"I honestly don't know how we'll make things work long distance," Chase said. "It's not like Dare Valley is a quick flight to D.C.—even with my private plane. And then there's my travel schedule. But I don't want to put a time limit on us, Moira. I...I'd like to have these damn casts off so I can take you out for dinner at some point."

His good hand curled around hers, and she took it. It felt like a handshake of some kind, sealing his intentions.

"I wish I could show you how much I want you," Chase said, "but you deserve a lover with all his abilities."

Heat stole through her. "I've told you I'm all for being creative."

"That you have," Chase said, kissing her lightly on the lips. "But I want better for you. For us. Setting aside the timeframe helps with that."

It did indeed. "I want—"

A knock sounded on the door. She jerked her head toward it as it swung open. Evan had a shopping bag in his hand.

"Hey! You two having dinner? Cool!"

Moira tried to jerk her hand back from Chase's, but he wouldn't release it. She looked at him and then back at Evan.

"Yes," she said, her throat suddenly dry. "Would you care to join us?"

"I think Evan can head on home to Margie," Chase said. "Once he drops off whatever he brought."

Evan's brow rose. "Margie is totally on board with me hanging out with you tonight. I feel bad I haven't been around as much the last couple of days. Quid-Atch is more than a full-time job. I don't know how you do it, Chase."

He took a couple of steps closer to the couch where Moira was pressed intimately to Chase. She tried to scoot away, but Chase wouldn't release her.

"Moira and I are having dinner," Chase told Evan. "Maybe you can swing by for lunch tomorrow?"

She wanted to die on the spot. "No, I can go. You two have dinner, and I'll—"

"You're staying," Chase said, squeezing her hand. "Evan can take a hint."

His shoulders started to shake with laughter. "I can, yes. I think this is really great. Moira is—"

"Leaving," she said, standing up.

Except Chase had a firm grip on her hand. Damn him. "*Chase.*"

"No, you're staying. And since you're so uncomfortable, let me lay it all out. Evan is an adult. He knows you don't technically work for me or for Quid-Atch, so there's no problem. He also understands we're both too professional to let this affect our work."

Yet, here she was blushing to her roots in front of her boss. "Maybe I should let you two discuss this."

Evan waved his hand. "No, Chase is right. There are no two people I trust more to have good sense in a situation like this. Just...don't tell Gary. Since he thinks of you like an older sister, he might be a little weirded out by this, Moira."

Oh, good Lord. "You got me, Evan. I was planning on telling Gary about me and Chase first thing tomorrow morning."

Evan barked out a laugh. "All right, you two wild and crazy kids. I'll leave you alone and head back to the wife. Have a good time."

Wild and crazy kids? She'd smack him if he didn't

sign her paychecks. Instead she gave a weak smile and watched him leave.

Chase laughed. "Good thing I have one good hand. You're not easy to keep a handle on."

"Let that be a lesson to you," she told him. And, after checking that the coast was clear, she proceeded to kiss him senseless.

CHAPTER 23

WAS THERE ANY CITY MORE MAGICAL THAN ROME? Caroline could scarcely sit still as the plane descended, lowering through magical clouds until blue sky surrounded her on all sides. The sun beamed bright orange rays of sunset. The flight had been close to ten hours, and she wondered how J.T. had simply hopped on a plane to Denver last minute given the extensive travel time.

She'd left Friday night and done her best to sleep in the bed in the master suite on the plane. What a luxury that had been. According to her time zone calculations—Rome being eight hours ahead of Denver—they were arriving on time, shortly after five o'clock. The landing was flawless, like everything had been so far, from the driver who'd picked her up to take her to the airport to the plane's crew.

Her personal flight attendant helped her deplane. As she walked down the stairs, she caught sight of J.T. jogging toward her in what looked like olive corduroys and a brown cashmere sweater.

"Hey!" he called out, arms wide open. "You're here."

He met her at the bottom of the stairs. That dimple she'd decided not to notice winked at her, as big as his smile.

"Hi," she said, feeling a little awkward in the face of his super-charged personality.

"I'm so happy to see you, I could kiss you." He gave a cheeky grin. "Italian style, of course."

She turned her cheek to him, feeling warmth spread across her face, as he did just that. "I'm happy to be here. Your plane is incredible."

"Glad you like her," J.T. said. "I'm partial. We've been together a long time. Come. Giacomo is getting your bags."

She'd only be staying for three days, so she'd brought a single suitcase. "You didn't have to pick me up. I could have taken a cab."

"Nonsense! What kind of host would that make me? Plus, I plan to spend all the time I can with you."

From the way he was looking at her, so openly excited, she knew he meant it. "Are we heading to the paintings straight away?"

He waved his hand. "I'm no slave driver. I expect the crew fed you, but how about a glass or two of wine somewhere before I show you the collection? There's this trattoria I adore with the best view of Rome. Unless you're tired and want to nap?"

She made a raspberry sound. "Nap? I'm in Rome for three days! I don't plan on sleeping."

He waggled his brows. "Good answer. You can sleep on the way back." Extending his arm to her like an old-world gentleman, he said, "Come on, Caroline. Let's go have some fun."

It didn't take long for Caroline to decide she rather liked his idea of fun. They sat at a corner window table in a quaint trattoria as the sun went down, and the wine was as bold and engaging as Caroline's companion. They were through a whole bottle before she knew it, and she had a pleasant buzz going. When he moved to order another, she shook her head.

"I'd better not," she said. "I'm a lightweight in the liquor department."

"Wine isn't liquor," he said, shaking his head in disagreement. "It's like Galileo said. 'Wine is sunlight, held together by water.'"

"You sound like my sister-in-law, Jane," she said, watching as their swarthy waiter appeared with another bottle. *My God, are all the men in Rome gorgeous?* "Hi," she said to the server.

She could tell J.T. was laughing silently from the way his shoulders were shaking. "You are a lightweight, but that's okay. I'm a pro. We'll make a killer combination. You were telling me about Jane."

"She can pick the maker and year of just about any French wine blindfolded. Or was it blind tested? I can't remember."

"Good thing she's married then," J.T. joked. "Sounds like my kind of woman. Catch me up on your family. It's been a long time since those magical summers my family spent in Dare Valley."

And so she caught him up. He seemed to eat up all the news about the expanding Hale family and the additions to the booming town.

"I've been hearing from Uncle Arthur for a few years now about all the new businesses. It sounds like it's becoming a small town with cosmopolitan flavor."

She took a moment to consider that. "That's a good description."

"Tell me more about the businesses," he said.

Their conversation about Dare Valley took them into a late dinner at a cozy restaurant solely lit by candles. She was floating by now and had laughed so hard at J.T.'s quirky comments and jokes her stomach hurt. But she made a decent dent in her meal of shaved scallops with black truffle—to die for—a mushroom risotto that redefined mushrooms, sea bass with braised endive, and salt-crusted pigeon, something J.T. insisted was the best meat entrée on the menu. He wasn't wrong.

By the time dessert rolled around, a scrumptious ricotta cake topped with brandied plums, she'd told him everything about her family. She'd even told one of her favorite childhood stories about Matt and Andy jumping into a pit of mud after torrential rains, pretending they were having a mud bath.

"Since you like mud and all," she told him, finishing the last bite of her cake.

"I even like desserts that look like mud," he said, holding up his spoon, covered in chocolate hazelnut pudding. "You're not safe around me."

She gestured to the casual navy dress she'd worn with gray leggings and tan suede boots, an outfit she was happy to have worn on the plane since there hadn't been a break to change for dinner. "You'll get thrown out of this place if you so much as put a dollop on me."

A mischievous glint flashed in his piercing green eyes. "Don't think you're safe. I know the owner."

"Oh, I'm so scared," she said, waving her hands dramatically.

"Up for a cheese plate?" he asked.

"No freaking way," she said, patting her belly. "I'm set to explode as it is."

"I'd appreciate a warning so I can duck out. I hate watching people explode."

She laughed and sat back in her chair, looking at him. "You're fun."

His wink was downright illegal. "I like you too. Let's get the check. I'll bet you're jet lagged."

"I've lost all sense of time and space," she said, giggling. "I'm a little tipsy."

He leaned in and whispered, "I noticed, but don't worry, you're safe with me."

After paying the bill, they made their way to his private car. In the back seat, he turned to her. "Sure you don't want to stay at my house? I have a room all ready for you, and I make a fabulous truffle omelet."

She was tempted. Too tempted. "Let's stick with the plan," she said, and then looked out the window to give herself time to breathe.

At the hotel, he insisted on walking her in. "Wait! I forgot my bag."

She made a move to turn back to the car, but he stopped her. "Giacomo has everything," he said. "Don't worry. And I already had him check you in while we were at dinner."

"What if I'd decided to stay with you?" she asked, only to immediately regret it.

His dimple winked at her, and he shrugged. "No biggie. I'm all about rearranging things last minute."

She wondered how many times he did just that. Probably a lot, given how handsome and charming he was. She wasn't immune to those qualities in a man, but it was something else about J.T. that really pushed her over the edge. He was funny. And he listened.

Give her a lace fan to cool herself down.

They grew silent as they went up the elevator to her room. She realized it was the penthouse when the light on the switchboard illuminated P. "You're kidding."

"You deserve the best," he said, leading the way down the marble hallway dotted with giant gold-bordered mirrors.

"This is really lovely, but..."

She broke off as he opened the door. All of Rome seemed to be lit before her. She was conscious of her gasp. "It's beautiful. The windows..."

The penthouse seemed to be made of glass. A fire was lit in the green marble fireplace, and discreet lighting gave it a warm glow.

"I may never leave." She wandered, as if in a trance, to the wall of windows.

"She's beautiful, isn't she?" he said, coming up to stand beside her. "Every time I come back from a trip, it's like her arms are always open to welcome me."

She noted Rome's famous sites, at once lit and in shadow. "I don't know how you could ever leave. It was hard for me when I studied here for that one summer in college."

He made a humming noise. "For a long time, I didn't think I *could* leave, but things change. I've been feeling I need to find a new home if I'm going to find what I'm looking for in life."

Turning to him, she regarded him in the half-light. "What's that?"

His mouth curved up, and he tapped her on the nose. "That's a conversation for another time. I'll..." His eyes dipped to her mouth, but instead of spanning the distance between them, he took a step back. "I'll see you in the morning, Caroline. Just call me when you're up and about. Tomorrow, we start on the paintings."

She realized her chest was tight. There was no trace of humor on his face now. Instead he was radiating a magnetic intensity.

He wanted her, she realized.

A quiver started at her feet and surged upward.

She wanted him too.

"You can feel it too, can't you?" he asked, stepping close again. "I wondered. I've been trying to keep things on a platonic level, but I've wanted you from the moment I walked into the gallery and saw you looking at that painting. Before I even saw your face. The way your brown hair trailed down your back. It was like an oil painter had used a harder brush stroke to capture your curls. Then there was your waist, the way it dipped into your hips. I was...caught."

She bit her lip, completely entranced.

"You aren't the girl I remember throwing mud at."

"You aren't the boy I remember either."

He tucked his hands into his pants pockets and rocked on his heels. "Maybe for the moment we should keep our focus on the art until...you've seen all the paintings."

It wasn't difficult to know what he meant. But God, seeing him standing there like he was, his body a testimony to strength and beauty, smelling like citrus and musk, she wanted to throw all caution to the wind and enjoy him. Every last inch of him.

"This museum in Dare Valley is...the most important thing I'm doing right now," he continued. "I've made some big changes recently to make it so."

She thought he was referring to something more than resigning from his job, but didn't feel she had the right to ask.

"Plus, I don't want to make you uncomfortable." His green eyes locked on her. "I asked you to come here in good faith. Your good opinion means a lot to me."

His good opinion was equally important to her, she realized. She remembered what he'd said about people in art circles. The last thing she wanted was to devolve into a cliché. Maybe...once they'd looked at the paintings, they could have another conversation. She broke out into a sweat imagining it.

"I believe that's wise," she said, fisting her hands by her sides. "The art should be our focus. Especially as important it is to you, your family, and Dare Valley." She felt a surge of pride and loyalty when she said the name of her hometown. This museum *was* important. And Uncle Arthur had brought her in to help. She wasn't going to spoil that.

J.T. kicked at the marble floor as if testing its polish. "I'm glad you agree. Good night then, Caroline."

A quick smile flashed across his mouth, and then he walked out before she could wish him the same.

Pressing her hand to her wildly beating heart, she realized this trip had already changed her.

And she hadn't even seen the paintings yet.

CHAPTER 24

EVAN ARRIVED AT THE CABIN EARLY ON THE FROSTY
Friday morning after he walked in on Chase's date with Moira. Not that Chase was surprised.

"Good morning," Evan said cheerfully, picking up Barney, who'd run over to greet him, with his free hand. "I brought you some of Margie's cinnamon rolls. How are you feeling this morning?"

"Great," he said. "I'm planning on smoking some elk today. Chef T sent some over this morning."

Clearly everyone had gotten up early. Including Moira, who'd texted him for twenty minutes before she'd headed into work. Before his injury, Chase had rarely texted. Now he was starting to see what people liked so much about it. There was an art to choosing one's words when flirting with a woman in a string of messages.

Moira was good at it. Chase had more than caught on.

After some playful kissing and creative touching last night, he was a little hot and bothered. But he still thought she deserved a man who wasn't encumbered by plaster. Now that the time limit was off, there was no reason they couldn't wait a little longer to make love. As a goal, there was nothing better. He planned to use it as a motivating factor to get through more rounds of needle therapy. He was still trying to decide what to do about Ally. Bonnie and Andy clearly thought she could help him, but she'd made him feel so raw. He wasn't sure he could go through that again.

"Where's Bonnie?" Evan asked, looking around and whistling.

"She's calling a few of my healing practitioners to set up more appointments," he told Evan, who clearly had something on his mind. "In the kitchen."

"That's great," Evan said. "I've been reading up on a few other things you might try. There's a chance I can modify a Tens device."

"What's that?" he asked.

"Transcutaneous electrical nerve stimulation," Evan explained. "It's a type of therapy that uses low-voltage electrical currents. It helps with firing up muscles that have atrophied. But it also works with the brain—"

"You want to rig me up to some device that shocks me?" he asked. "No way. The needles sound safer. Let's appreciate that a moment. When did my life become so messed up that needles became my best option?"

"It's not—"

"No, Evan," he said, wheeling forward in his scooter. "Now, why are you here?"

His friend lowered the kitten to the ground, and Barney raced across the floor and bounded into Chase's lap.

"You're dating Moira," Evan said, shoving his hands in his pants pockets. "I know it's none of my business, but you helped with Margie."

"Under duress," he reminded his friend. "She called me and pretty much begged me to get in touch with you."

"I was a heel," Evan said, wincing. "But everything worked out, partly because of your help. Like I tried to say the other night when she was here, I'm totally cool with you and Moira being together. Not that I need to be. But she's great, right? I mean, I'm not into her, but I can see why you would be. She's super smart, a fabulous businesswoman, and she's pretty. Do you need me to buy you condoms or anything?"

Chase wasn't often shocked, but that segue took him aback and then some. "What?"

Evan hunched his shoulders in the perfect imitation of a cringe. "It's not like I wanted to ask, but here you are, house-bound. It's not like you can go out and buy them yourself. I didn't know if you kept any in your wallet, but you can't store too many there—"

"Evan please stop speaking," Chase said.

"I'm only trying to help, although I'd give you points for having sex in your current condition. Did you ask Andy if you were healthy enough for sexual activity?"

Evan sounded like one of those ED ads. Chase was going to kill him. "He's her brother," he snarled, "and no, I didn't. I know my body. And that's the last I'm going to say on this topic."

"Whew!" Evan wiped his forehead. "Good, because I had trouble falling asleep thinking about this talk. But I had to be a friend. I needed you to know you could count on me like that."

"And I never want to," Chase said. "Ever again."

Evan started to laugh. "I mean you know I love you... That's a lot of love."

Chase couldn't help himself. He started to laugh too. "More than I can handle."

"Moira probably has all the love you can handle and more."

That comment received his best glower.

"What I mean is," Evan said, holding up his hand like a peace offering, "should you and Moira fall in love and such, maybe you'll finally consider what I've been wanting all along."

Chase didn't like the way Evan was staring at him. He had on his puppy expression.

"What is that?"

"Don't get mad, but I've been hoping you might move here for real." Evan ducked his head. "Permanently. I mean…now that I know what family means because of Margie, I want you to be here. Shit, you know you're my family, right?"

Chase felt his throat close.

Evan came closer to his scooter. "Now that you're finally more open to talking about what happened when you were a kid, I…I want you to have a sense of home again. This is a great town with some great people, Chase. Everyone has opened their arms to me. I know they'd open their arms to you. Even without Moira."

Good God. Had Evan really convinced himself it was a possibility?

"I mean, how could they not include you?" Evan asked, smiling crookedly. "You're the best man I know."

"I told you that you needed to stop putting me on a pedestal, Evan," he said with a sigh. "I'm just a man. Who runs your company *in Virginia.*"

"You could run it from anywhere," Evan said. "Think about it. Now, I'll stop pressing you for the moment because judging by the way your jaw is clamped, you might bite your tongue."

Chase had to consciously relax the tension in his jaw. Truth be told, it made his neck hurt. "Don't hold out hope on this one, Evan. You know you're like a brother to me, but I still run your company."

Evan pulled out a chair from the dining room table and brought it over. "I've been thinking about that," he said, sitting down next to him.

Dread pooled in his belly. His friend wasn't planning on taking that away from him, was he? "I'll be back to work as soon as I can."

"I know that," Evan said. "You look green. Did you think I was going to fire you? Chase, I can be something of a mad inventor, sure, but I'm not certifiable. I've been thinking we should call ourselves a family business. You and me. Like brothers. Equals."

Chase felt his body grow heavy at the thought. "We're not related, Evan."

"Why is blood the only indication of family? When people marry, they make a family. Why can't two men who feel like brothers call themselves a family?"

Chase could think of all sorts of reasons. "Evan, people already know we're friends. This would confuse our shareholders and our clients."

"I don't think so," Evan said, putting his hands on his knees. "It's not like I want to put out a press release. I just...want you and everyone else to know how I feel. Chase, I want you and I to create a legacy. I look at everything Arthur Hale and Emmits Merriam have done here in Dare Valley, and I want the two of us to create a legacy like that. Something that's going to keep helping the world long after we're gone."

Chase never thought about things like that. He'd seen early on how someone's life's work could disappear in an instant. "We don't have to be family to create something sustainable. By the way, how did your meeting with J.T. Merriam go?"

His friend shook his head. "He politely turned down my offer. Seems he has his own plans for the Merriam land they still own in the valley. Margie was crushed, but I told her we'd find something else."

Chase wondered how much, if anything, Evan knew about J.T.'s meeting with Caroline and decided to ask outright. "What do you know about his plans?"

Evan was silent for a moment. "This is all confidential, but I don't think he'd mind me telling you. He's working with the university's administration to finalize the details of a new art museum that will house the Merriam art collection. I guess he and I both kinda love the idea of bringing more science and art to Dare Valley. There's a poetic justice there."

Poetic, huh? Evan always had been a romantic. "It will certainly bring in a lot more tourists to Dare Valley. I wonder how the long-time residents will feel."

"From what J.T. said of his discussions with Arthur Hale, there will be some resistance. It helps that the university is so well respected."

"And that J.T. is like the prodigal Merriam son returning to Dare Valley," Chase said.

"He announced a couple of days ago that he was stepping down from Merriam Oil," Evan told him. "Didn't say why."

"Africa and the Middle East aren't an easy beat," Chase said, stroking Barney. "Maybe he was burned out."

"Maybe."

Chase could appreciate the problem. He'd been feeling a little burned out these last couple of years.

"I also need to share some news you aren't going to like," Evan said, resting his elbows on his knees. "I didn't think you'd want me to wait on this one. Promise me your head won't explode. It's about the bid."

Chase's eyes narrowed immediately. "Spill it."

Evan started tapping his feet. "Gopal Urwod backed out on us."

Gopal was the project candidate they'd chosen for the giant government contract they were bidding on, a man Chase had spent a lot of time with recruiting. "What? He fucking signed a letter of commitment. I negotiated his salary, his benefits package. How could this happen?"

"I don't know!" Evan said, standing up and pacing. "Rajan said the guy called him up and started listing concerns."

"What concerns?" Chase asked, but he already suspected.

"Don't explode. He said he was concerned about your accident and ongoing health," Evan said. "I tried calling him personally, but he wouldn't listen to me."

"Give me your phone," Chase said, holding out his good hand.

Barney leaped off his lap and ran into the kitchen.

"I don't want this hurting your brain," Evan said.

"Evan, if you don't give me your phone now, I will run you down with this scooter. We can't lose Gopal. I know who's behind this crap about my health. Maurie Wallins of K-Barker."

"Rajan thinks so too," Evan said. "And so do I. Gopal wants this position, and everyone in the industry knows Quid-Atch and K-Barker are the firms to beat."

"It's going to be won by Quid-Atch," Chase corrected him. "Your phone, Evan."

Evan nodded. "But just this once. You're not ready to get back to work yet." He handed his phone over.

Chase didn't bother to respond. He called Rajan for a debriefing. Before their call was over, Chase's gut was writhing with anxiety. It sounded like Gopal had made his decision.

Only Chase wasn't going to let him off that easy.

He called the man and went through the expected pleasantries before addressing the topic at hand. His head was splitting by the time he hung up the phone.

Evan was resting his head in his hands. "I hate shit like this."

Chase didn't want to rub the back of his neck in front of Evan. No need to tip him off to the pain he was experiencing. "You know how competitive government contracting is, and when we compete against K-Barker, it tends to get dirty. Maurie likes it dirty."

"From the gist of your conversation, do I understand

Gopal is back with us?" Evan asked.

"You heard what I told him," Chase said. "We have a signed letter of commitment from him, pre-dating anything he might have signed with another company—although he wouldn't say so outright. I also have emails with a negotiated salary and benefits package. If he doesn't go with us, I'm putting his name in anyway and letting the selection committee draw its own conclusions about what happened. It's a risk, but if we let K-Barker bid with him, they'll be hard to beat. Gopal needs to understand that this sort of behavior will ruin his reputation with our colleagues in the Defense Department."

"But how can we have him run the project after this should we win?" Evan asked. "It's clear we can't trust him."

Chase sadly agreed. "Normally I wouldn't do it this way, but we have no choice if we're going to win. We bid with him. Once we win, we replace him after six months. Our Defense Department colleagues won't be happy, but I can handle the fall-out. In the meantime, have Rajan and his team start looking for another candidate."

"Will do," Evan said with a sigh. "Sometimes I wish we were in a different business. All I ever wanted to do was have enough money to create my inventions and share them with the world. I hate government contracting."

Chase laughed. "So do I, but it puts bread on our proverbial table, so to speak. Evan, it's the way governments—not just the U.S.—do business. Otherwise, people like Maurie would be bribing officials with planes, trains, and automobiles in exchange for contracts. This is a fairer system."

"The system still sucks," Evan said darkly. "How's your head?"

"Great," he lied. "Feel like I could handle three more

calls like that."

"I've known you long enough to know when you're lying," Evan said. "My phone."

Chase handed it over.

"Please don't say this wouldn't have happened if you'd gotten injured," Evan told him. "I don't want you blaming yourself."

"I blame Maurie," Chase said. "This is how he plays the game. Are you ready to cancel his invitation to the fundraiser?"

Evan looked down. "Chase, the invitations already went out."

"Call and say this one was made in error," Chase suggested. "Maurie will know why. Gopal is going to have called him after our chat, remember?"

He secretly reveled in imagining how the call would go down. Maurie deserved that and worse for being so unethical.

"We can't rescind an invitation," Evan said. "That would be playing his game."

"Give me your phone again," Chase said, not believing what he was hearing. "I will happily rescind it."

"We're better than that, Chase. Don't you want to smile in his face at the fundraiser, knowing we got Gopal back?"

That would put Maurie's over-priced knickers in a wad. "I still don't want him showing up at the fundraiser, especially after this."

"Let's stay the course," Evan said with a sigh. "He can't do anything to us at the fundraiser. He wouldn't dare."

Chase wasn't so sure.

CHAPTER 25

ON SATURDAY MORNING, MOIRA CAME OVER TO CHASE'S cabin after his acupuncture appointment with Dr. Sarah. She'd offered him a drink, and he'd joked that he was afraid the liquid would escape from the puncture marks.

The silly side of him only warmed her heart more. Then there was the way he was with Barney. Despite his grumbling, it was obvious he was happy about Bonnie's decision to delegate the kitten to him for the duration of his stay in Dare Valley. From the constant purring the kitten emitted from Chase's lap, she could tell the feeling was mutual.

"How is Caroline's trip going in Rome?" he asked.

"Ridiculous," she told him. "The pictures she's texted me all look amazing. And the food!" Her sister hadn't said anything about the art, except that it would take decades to properly appreciate the paintings. Regarding her companion, J.T., she was oddly cool. Moira knew what that meant. Something was up between them, but Caroline was striving for professionalism.

Moira understood. But she was so grateful she'd decided to take a chance with Chase.

"Barney seems to like you," Chase commented, using

his good hand to tickle her under the ribs.

She jerked, making the kitten, who'd been on her lap, stand on all fours and arch his back. "He won't if you keep that up."

"Since we're waiting to have sex until I'm free of all this plaster, I have to find innocuous ways of touching you."

He did? For a smart man, he was so simple sometimes. She disengaged from him, causing Barney to jump down. Turning to face Chase, she tugged off her aubergine-colored sweater. Today, she'd made sure to wear a fabulous apricot-colored padded bra since she was a little sensitive about her flat-as-Kansas chest. The push-up style gave her a little cleavage and the color worked well with her skin tone.

"How's this for innocuous?" she asked, reaching for his hand and bringing it to her right breast.

"I believe the creator of that word had a different definition in mind," he said in a deep voice, one she'd learned to recognize as cautious.

Deciding it was time to encourage him to see past his injuries, she stood and shimmied out of her fleece tights. They were sitting close enough to the fire that she wouldn't turn into a ball of goosebumps.

"Your lingerie matches, I see," he said, taking his sweet time looking her up and down. "My God, you have gorgeous legs. How have I never noticed that?"

"Because I'm five-two," she said. "No one notices my legs first. I'm also not exactly endowed in the boob department, despite your comment about my breasts being fabulous. Thank you for that, by the way."

He ran his finger up her thigh, making her body turn to liquid. "How is it you're selling yourself short? That's not the Moira I know."

"Because I'm a girl, you idiot, and most of us have some insecurities about our bodies." Then a light bulb went on. "Like you do right now with yours. You *think* that I'll find you less manly with two casts on, but you're wrong. While it's not ideal, it doesn't make me want you any less."

"I'm happy to know that," he said dryly.

Sitting next to him cross-legged, she faced him. He was watching her with those intense gray eyes while she was turning into a puddle on the inside. Deciding he wasn't going to initiate anything, she tugged on his plaid shirt. "Let's get this off you."

"Moira, we've talked about this," he said, stopping her hands. "I don't want to make love to you until I can do it properly."

"And I appreciate that," she said, leaning in to kiss him on the mouth, "but you're forgetting that I have the power to make love to *you* properly. I think you just need to lie back and let me."

He grumbled while she took his clothes off. Goodness, he had a marvelous chest. She gave him a gentle push, urging him to lay supine on the couch. After arranging one of the pillows under his arm cast, she looked down at him.

"Comfortable?" she asked.

"You think I'm making love to you for the first time on a couch?" he asked, glaring at her. "Give me a little credit."

"Oh, don't sound so put out," she said, pursing her lip for effect. "This isn't a bad gig."

His good arm gripped her waist, sending bursts of fire up her torso. "Whoa."

"No it's not."

"What was I saying?" she asked, feeling hot all of the sudden.

His fingers stroked her skin. "You were taking charge."

"I was, wasn't I?" And he seemed to be letting her.

That made her smile. "How am I doing so far?"

"Really good," Chase said, sliding his arm around to trace her spine. "This is hard for me."

She raised herself up until she was straddling him. "I can tell," she said, rocking a little against his impressive hardness. She'd forgotten how good foreplay could feel.

He groaned and caressed her back. "I wasn't talking about that. Being hard around you is a given."

"How nice." She wanted to shimmy in celebration.

"I meant letting you take charge like this when I don't feel like I'm pulling my weight. But we need to talk about something first. Birth control."

She was glad he'd broached that conversation. "Right! I'm not on the Pill right now, so I brought condoms. Are you good with that? I was waiting to see how long-term this was going to be before I went to the doctor."

"I'm good with condoms for now," he said carefully. "And I had a clean bill of health in the hospital—like always."

"I haven't been with anyone in three years, and I'm good too."

He traced a line across her stomach, making her shiver. "Why so long? You're beautiful."

"I don't let just anyone touch this body," she told him. "I hope you realize how special this is."

His eyes darkened. "I do. I hope you know how special you are to me too. Moira, I..."

She froze at the hoarseness in his voice.

"You're starting to mean the world to me." He reached for her hand and placed it over his heart. "I wouldn't let just anyone see me this way. Or take charge like this."

For Chase, it was akin to the most romantic declaration he could make. She found she was ready to make her own.

"I love you, Chase."

His face closed for a moment, like a curtain had been drawn over his emotions. Then he gave her a slow smile. "I don't know if I can say that. I haven't told a woman that. Ever."

How was that possible? "Not even your ex-wife?"

"I told you we had a different relationship."

She couldn't imagine living like that. "You take your time. I have it on good authority you excel at everything you set your mind to."

He regarded her very seriously. "You're right, and I keep letting the past run this reel of my life, don't I? You deserve better than that. Moira, you deserve everything. I want to give that to you."

She leaned forward over his chest until she could caress his jaw. God, she was getting misty-eyed. "That's really wonderful of you to say."

His chest rose under her, and he let out a long breath. "I love you too, Moira. Whew! I said it. Man, that was... intense. I'll do better with practice."

Oh, she was so going to cry. She curled around him, and they held each other. "I didn't expect you would say it," she whispered into his ear.

He gave a hoarse laugh. "My whole life seems totally upended right now, but one thing I know for sure is that I like being with you. Moira, you've helped me...feel happy again. I like how you're not intimidated by me, how you don't want anything from me. That's been my interaction with women for a long time."

Given all of his power and money, she wasn't surprised. "Well, aren't you lucky your whole life got upended? You deserve to be happy, Chase. Remember how you said you cared about my happiness?" Maybe that early comment of his had foreshadowed all the possibilities between them.

"Moira, I don't know where this is going, but I want to explore it." He cupped her bottom with his good hand, squeezing it while rolling his hips under her. "And God, do I want to make love to you. But please. Not on the couch."

She was a frisson of nerves after that maneuver of his. "All right. I'll get the condoms while you make your way to the bedroom. We'll figure it out, Chase."

"Damn right, we will."

And they did.

He couldn't use both hands to caress her, but he used words to arouse her to a fever pitch, describing what he loved about her body and all the things he wanted to do to her. The man was downright inventive.

When she finally took him inside her, she arched her back and gave a low cry at the fit. They were perfect together.

"Oh, God," he moaned, straining to sink higher inside her. "I need more of you."

She had been careful, balancing so she wouldn't accidentally knock one of his casts. Shifting a fraction, she lowered until he reached the hilt. This time it was she who said, "Oh, God."

Then she started to move, slowly at first, but when his hand gripped her waist urgently, she gave in to a faster pace. She could feel him straining under her, doing his best to lift when she fell, but it couldn't be easy for him with his injuries.

"Are you okay?" she asked, panting.

His eyes locked on her face. "No. God. I need you to come for me."

Okay, that was hot. "Trust me, it's going to happen."

"Lean back," he growled, and suddenly his good hand was caressing where they were joined. She arched again as a surge of energy rocketed up from her toes. Crying out, she came. Hard.

She was aware of his hand shifting, and then he was changing the angle of her body over him. He cried out, coming under her in deep pulses. She folded over him.

"Oh, my God," she said, everything tingling beautifully. "Oh, my God."

"Yeah," he said, caressing her spine. "Oh, Moira."

He was breathing as hard as she was by the time she rolled off him. "If this is how you do things when you're injured, I can't wait to see what you'll think of when you're free of these casts."

Turning his head on the pillow to look at her, he smiled. "I'm going to blow your mind."

Oh, she liked a man who excelled. "I can't wait. You... this...it's like the best gift ever."

"I love you, Moira," he said, reaching for her hand.

She took it and pressed it to her heart—where it belonged. "I love you too."

CHAPTER 26

CHASE WAS JARRED FROM SLEEP BY A SOUND. IT TOOK him a moment to register that someone was knocking on the front door. He groaned as he turned over. His bad side screamed. Shit, that hurt.

"Who is that?" he heard a sweet voice ask.

"If we ignore them, they'll go away." Opening his eyes, he couldn't help but smile at her. "You're adorable with your hair sticking out." Normally he didn't notice such things, but with Moira, he noticed everything.

"That's not the most complimentary thing to say to me after last night," she said, raising a brow at him.

"You're beautiful and fierce and completely sexy," he said, frowning as the knocking on the door ramped up again.

"Do you want me to get dressed and get that?" she asked. "Or would it be weird if I answered the door?"

"After last night, it wouldn't be weird at all." He loved her, and part of him wanted to shout it from the rooftop. He still couldn't take it all in.

She slid out of bed and looked around. "Ah...this is awkward. My jeans and shirt are in the den, and the front door—"

"Has window panes on either side," he said, seeing

her dilemma. "Grab one of my robes. In the closet. It will take me twenty minutes to get dressed, and I'm not starting the process without knowing if it's just a determined UPS man needing a signature or something."

Laughing, she dashed into his closet and came out wearing his navy floor-length robe. "It's like I have a train behind me. Okay, I'm going out."

Chase wondered at the time. He heard voices, and then heavy footsteps heading his way. Evan appeared sheepishly in his bedroom doorway, holding up a bakery bag.

"Fresh croissants?" he asked. "I'm sorry to intrude. Really, I am."

"Evan, what in God's name are you doing here?" Chase asked, pulling himself up against the headboard and tucking the sheet around his waist.

"I thought it would be safe to swing by. It's noon. Are you okay?"

Chase scowled at him. "Let me repeat. Why are you here? Not that I don't like seeing you, but this is my first morning with Moira."

"I'm sorry for interrupting," Evan said. "And even sorrier for bringing you another work problem. Something happened with Gopal."

Chase's gut tightened. "Tell me."

"It seems Maurie told him that K-Barker is going to submit him on their bid as well since they also had his letter of commitment and a salary package negotiated. Gopal believes him."

Maurie was pulling out all the stops. "Shit."

"Exactly. Gopal knows it will hurt his reputation with our defense colleagues if he's put forward on two bids. He's withdrawn from both of us."

"But we had him first! Our letter of commitment says so. Let me call him."

Evan shook his head. "I talked to him for over an

hour after Rajan did. He won't change his mind."

"So we're out the best candidate for the bid," Chase said in a tight voice.

"Maurie is as well," Evan said, rubbing his forehead. "That's got to be a small comfort."

"It's not," Chase said. "This is a victory for Maurie and K-Barker, and he knows it. Gopal had better not go with anyone else."

"He won't," Evan said, shaking his head. "I want to hire him direct to Quid-Atch before Maurie does. He's vulnerable right now, knowing his ethics are in the toilet. I think we can bring him on and bid him out on another high-profile bid in the future. We'll just have to watch him like a hawk to make sure he can be rehabilitated. Rajan agrees that it's a good plan."

Chase looked at his friend in shock. "I like the way you're thinking, Evan. Especially the hawk part. Work with Rajan on what to offer him salary-wise. I don't want him making bank because of this error in judgment. He doesn't deserve to be rewarded."

"Gopal doesn't think you'll forgive him," Evan said, coming further into the room. "You might need to make the offer personally."

"I can do that," Chase said. "I'm fairly certain Andy is going to green-light me to return to at least quarter-time work this week. God, I can't wait to dive back in." But there was another part of him that felt tired just thinking about it.

"Me either," Evan said with a gusty sigh. "Running Quid-Atch is harder than I imagined. Forget what I said about you moving here."

Chase felt a ripple of surprise go through him at Evan's about-face.

"Just kidding," his friend joked, his shoulders shaking. "I'm more hopeful than ever after seeing Moira here this morning. I'm going to leave you these croissants and slink out the front door. Moira and I were a little embarrassed to see each other."

Chase could imagine. "Don't you dare discuss our personal relationship with her. I mean it, Evan. I don't need your help on the logistics issue in our relationship."

Except that wasn't quite true. He needed help from someone. Something. After she'd gone to sleep last night, he'd stayed awake. How were they going to continue seeing each other? Even if he didn't live so far away, he worked long hours and traveled internationally. Something was going to have to give. He didn't know what it was.

"You know my vote," Evan said. "You move here. Rajan is open to the idea, by the way."

The look Chase gave him made him shift his weight. "Don't you dare start talking to our personnel about moving operations out here without my agreement. You'll cause a panic, Evan. People have established lives in the D.C. Metro area. Kids in school. And we have partners who are used to seeing us show our faces frequently."

"We don't have to move everyone," Evan told him. "I think we can create a way to make this work."

Chase's head was starting to hurt. "I don't want to talk about this right now, Evan. We keep things as they are for the moment. When I feel differently—"

"Chase, I want R&D out here with me," Evan said. "Maybe not everybody, but the lion's share. I've given it a lot of thought, and I don't want to keep traveling back and forth like I have in the past, staying in D.C. for weeks at a time for testing and the like. This is my home now. I want to invent here and have the rest of my team here to support my efforts."

So he'd been thinking about moving Quid-Atch for personal reasons, ones separate from his desire to bring Chase into the Dare Valley fold.

"Can we discuss this when I don't have a concussion? Or my..." He was too old to call Moira his girlfriend. "Moira is here."

"Of course," Evan said, waving his hand. "I'm sorry for springing it on you like this. I was a little off balance about Gopal. We can discuss it when you're back to full speed."

Judging from the way everything was starting to unfurl, from the problems with the bid to his friend's wild idea about moving R&D, Chase had better get back in the saddle soon. "We'll figure things out."

He only hoped Evan would be able to put Quid-Atch's best interests at the forefront instead of his own. That was leadership.

"Okay," Evan said, placing the bakery bag on the edge of the bed. "I'll be going now. Have a great day. Are you sure you don't need me to buy you—"

"No!" Good God, would his friend give the condom thing a rest? "We're fine. I'll see you later, Evan."

His boss and friend looked down in the mouth as he walked to the doorway. "I'll let you know if there are any new developments on the bid."

That statement brought him back. "Can you bring me Rajan's top three candidates for Gopal's old position? I want to see what we have to work with."

Evan looked down. "You've seen all the best candidates. We haven't found anyone new to consider that matches all the personnel qualifications."

Chase stroked his jaw. They'd been recruiting on this bid for over six months. Gopal had been far and away the best candidate. "If that's the case, we might have to bid Rajan."

"No way!" Evan said immediately. "He's the head of R&D. Irreplaceable. Especially with MAL-77 being finalized."

Evan wasn't telling him what he didn't know. "We

may not have a choice. Evan, we need to win this bid. It's not just the money. If we win this contract with the Defense Department, it'll put us at the forefront of the government's new military initiatives. We'll be positioned for every upcoming bid for the next five years, maybe ten if...*when* we perform like rock stars and win the extension."

"Chase, you and I have agreed to keep Rajan exclusive to Quid-Atch operations. He can bill time on this project, but not run it full-time."

"Gopal might have changed that," Chase said.

"I can't get on board with this one," Evan said, shaking his head. "We need to find another solution."

Chase wanted to throw something, but the only thing within reach was the croissant bag. There would be something unsatisfying about throwing that. "That's hard to do with me laid up. You're asking the impossible here. We haven't found a better candidate than Gopal. The person doesn't exist."

Evan's eyes turned frosty. "Then I'm prepared to lose the bid. Rajan is vital to our efforts at innovation and invention. If we bid him on this project for the full five years, it'll hurt Quid-Atch's efforts for the next twenty. And I'll be really unhappy. You know I don't invent when I'm unhappy."

That was true, but he didn't like Evan manipulating him that way. "Let's table this for the moment. Rajan can keep looking for another candidate, but I need to speak with him ASAP. Losing Gopal has a huge impact on our technical approach."

Evan sighed and crossed the room to hand Chase a phone. "You can call him from this phone. Only him."

The urge to growl was tough to suppress. "Only him? You expect me to be Quid-Atch's savior, but you're treating me like I'm twelve years old."

"I'm sorry," Evan said, his scowl pronounced. "You

aren't the only one who wishes it were different. We're all making compromises, Chase."

He walked out. Chase wanted to call him back, but he was tired of reassuring Evan. No one ever reassured Chase. He was the one who did that for everyone. And he was tired of it. Right now, part of him wished he could simply disappear and let someone else handle things.

Instead he called Rajan. Their head of R&D was as upset as he was. Chase didn't have to put the option on the table. Rajan himself said he would be willing to be bid in Gopal's place if it would help them win.

"Evan doesn't want that," Chase told him. "But we're both realists. I don't see us finding a better candidate, especially with the clock ticking."

They both knew how important this position was to their technical approach for the bid. Time couldn't be wasted recruiting for a Hail Mary.

"What about Evan's idea to move R&D out to Dare Valley?" Chase asked. His gut told him Evan had probably broached the subject already. If he was wrong, at least he could get his two cents in first to try and stave off disaster. "Who else knows?"

"You're putting me in a tight spot," Rajan said. "I told Evan he needed to speak with you about it first. I work well with both of you."

"I know," Chase said, "and I'm sorry for this, but I need to know, Rajan. A move like this is big."

"Yeah," Rajan said. "I don't think he's said anything to anyone but me. But since Evan moved to Dare Valley and...well..."

"Spit it out."

"He's been more hands-on," Rajan said. "Everyone has been wondering what it would mean long-term."

How could they not wonder? Evan could change their whole world, moving parts of Quid-Atch out west. "I'll need to handle that kind of rumor in person—the minute I get back to HQ." Of course, he and Evan would have to come to some kind of understanding first. God, he hated thinking about it. The rare times he was at odds with Evan were always awful.

"That would be best," Rajan said.

"In the meantime, I should be able to dig into other priority items this week after the doctor clears me to start working some. I need you to outline the three areas that need my immediate attention."

"Besides your health?" Rajan joked. "You'll have my report tomorrow."

Even though it was Sunday, Chase thought. He hadn't expected anything less. "Rajan, when do you see your wife and kids?"

The man laughed. "I can hear them in the other part of the house, Chase. My wife and kids know how important my job is. I see them when I see them."

Where was this concern over Rajan's work-life balance coming from? "I need to go, Rajan. It was good talking to you. I appreciate you keeping things rolling while I've been out."

"Chase, no one can keep things going but you. This unexpected leave of absence proved that. Gopal isn't the only one who's been worried. I think Maurie has been filling some of our clients' ears with concerns. I had a defense official ask a few too many questions about your time off."

It felt like a rubber band had been snapped into his brain. "That bastard."

"It's a smart move on Maurie's part," Rajan said. "He likes to go in for the kill."

"Yes, he does," Chase said. "Keep your ear to the ground for me. Nip anything that comes up until I'm back."

"I will," Rajan said. "I'm going to write up your report now. Get better. Evan says you're doing acupuncture.

It's an age-old tradition. I do it myself when my ulcers act up. Hate medicine personally."

"And I love needles," he joked. "We're a pair."

He hadn't known Rajan suffered from ulcers. He wondered what other work-induced symptoms of stress the rest of their employees were experiencing. Something to handle when he returned.

"Expect the report, Chase."

"Thanks, Rajan. Talk soon."

After hanging up, he could feel his energy flag. There was no easy solution to any of the problems facing him. Usually he had a laser focus and cut through obstacles. All he wanted to do now was run off to some island with Moira and never come back. He laughed at himself. Yeah, that would last for a day.

"Are you okay?" Moira asked from the doorway, holding two cups of coffee. "You don't look any happier than Evan did when he left. Want to talk about it?"

He rubbed the tension encircling his neck. "Unfortunately I can't. It's Quid-Atch business and falls under—"

"Your top-secret clearance," she said, coming into the room and handing him his coffee.

He hated saying it after the closeness they'd reached last night. "I would tell you if I could, but there's no reason for us both to be depressed." Then he had a thought. "Has Evan talked about moving parts of Quid-Atch out here with Artemis?"

Her green eyes widened. "No. Is he?"

Chase instantly felt better. If Evan had only talked to Rajan, the problem wasn't as great as he'd feared. "I shouldn't have said that. Sorry. I'm..."

"Tense?" she asked, setting her coffee on the bedside stand. "Worried? You look like you did the first time I met you—minus the naked part."

Leave it to Moira to make him smile at a time like

this. "Did I look tense and worried then?"

"No," she said, worrying her lip. "You looked like you spent every second of the day taking names and kicking ass. But now that I know you better, I think that's how you react when you're tense and worried."

He hung his head, not bothering to tell her she'd gotten the phrase mixed up. Was that how he wanted to continue to live his life? At this particular moment, he wasn't so sure. "Sometimes I don't know what we're working for. Like today's current problem. Someone decided to be unethical and undercut us, ruining all our hard work."

"That must be exhausting," she said, rubbing his good shoulder. "Is there anything you can do to change it?"

"Doesn't look like it. Not right now, anyway." Maurie had tied him up quite nicely this time. What he wouldn't give to drag that man behind a horse for a few miles.

"Then can you come back here and be with me?" She sat beside him on the bed. "I'd like to have a good day, just the two of us. Having you all to myself is a luxury. You mentioned smoking the bacon that finished curing. I'm even bowing out of a Hale family dinner."

He thought of Rajan writing a report for him on a Sunday as his family enjoyed the weekend in other parts of the house. He'd never interacted much with Trisha in their home. Would the same thing happen to him and Moira if they ended up staying together? Different lives under the same roof?

"I want to spend time with you too," he said. Especially since it would be a lot harder as soon as he got Andy's clearance to work. "But if you want to see your family today, you should. You can meet me here afterward. It's not like I'm going anywhere."

She undid the robe she was still wearing and slid it off, rising over him. Situated as he was against the headboard, their eyes were level. "I want to be here."

He leaned in to kiss her. "Me too."

"But I need your phone first," she said, making an attempt to smile. "Boss' orders."

Taking her mouth in a drugging kiss, he showed her how little he cared about handing over the phone and how much he wanted her.

But part of him feared things would change after he returned to his normal life. Whether he liked it or not.

CHAPTER 27

MOIRA WAITED UNTIL TUESDAY MORNING TO CALL Caroline. Her sister had texted about her trip, sure, but she wanted first-hand material. She was on her way home from Chase's to get ready for work, and she figured Caroline would be getting ready too.

"Okay, spill it," she immediately said when her sister picked up the phone.

"What can I say?" Caroline responded. "It was a whirlwind. Incredible. Life changing. The paintings were...*are*...some of the most beautiful ones I've ever seen, and the way J.T. wants to group them is pure brilliance. He's got such vision. Dare Valley is so lucky to have this museum coming. I can't wait to visit it myself. Oh, Moira, it's going to be like nothing you've ever seen. J.T. is going to tell stories with the paintings and use famous quotes and historical facts on the walls alongside them to do it. The whole concept is so artistic."

Caroline sounded like she was walking on Monet-inspired clouds. "I'm glad you're so happy. Working with J.T. agrees with you." Hoping her sister would continue without prodding, she paused. She darn well knew there was something going on with Caroline and J.T., and she intended to hear about it.

"He's amazing, Moira," Caroline said, a sigh wrapped around her voice. "Like no one I've ever met. I'm... sometimes at a loss for how much I like him."

"Like him, like him, or *like him, like him*?" she asked, turning onto the main highway to drive into town.

"You sound like Natalie," Caroline said, a frown in her voice. "She prodded me about J.T. too. Yes, I *like him, like him* and he feels the same way, it seems. But we're going to focus on the paintings, which is practical. He lives in Rome, and I live here. It's not like we're thinking about getting together or anything..."

Moira could hear the *but* coming from a mile away. "And yet it's all you can think about."

"I'm trying not to, but it's hard," Caroline said. "It's like I got hit by a runaway train and was swept along on a magical ride."

"If a train hit you, you'd be splatted all over the place," Moira said, chuckling. "No magic in that. But I see what you mean. When are you going to see the next stash of paintings? The one in California?"

Her sister's sigh was audible. "I don't know right now. Soon, I expect. Of course, Kendra is going to suspect something if I ask for another long weekend off too soon."

"Who cares? It's your vacation time." Sometimes the work ethic their parents had raised them with sucked. "It's not like you're lollygagging around."

"You sound like Uncle Arthur," she said, laughing. "Who says 'lollygagging' anymore?"

"I do, apparently," Moira said, joining in her sister's laughter. "It's a great word. More people should use it."

"How are you and Chase?" Caroline asked.

She'd been ready for this question. "We're in love, actually. I'm still a little in shock. We spent the whole weekend together—"

"I *heard* you missed dinner at Matt's," Caroline said,

and she could hear the smile in her sister's voice.

"I did," Moira said, smiling herself as she drove down Main Street. The sidewalks were still sparse except for the early morning traffic at Don't Soy With Me. People were grabbing coffees to start the day. She'd get one at the office.

"And..." her sister drawled.

"I had the best time possible." Spending the whole day in bed with Chase had been a hell of a lot of fun. "It's a little scary how easy things are between us."

"Easy is scary?" Caroline asked. "But I know what you mean. I felt that way with J.T. It's like I've known him forever. I want to listen to every one of his stories, see every masterpiece he loves."

"You want to share yourselves," Moira finished, understanding perfectly. She and Chase seemed to be breaking open all sorts of barriers between them, emotionally and physically, and it was the most transformative experience of her life.

"Yes," Caroline said. "Moira..."

"What?" she answered, hearing the vulnerability in her sister's voice.

"I wanted to make love with him so much," she confessed. "I've never felt that way about anyone. Or so fast. He...the first night after I flew in...he called it out there and said he felt it too, but the project is really important to him and... Oh, heck, he didn't want to lose sight of that or change gears on me when he'd asked me to come to Rome for professional reasons."

"So you need to make the move," Moira said, nodding to herself. "What do you want to do?"

"Go out with him," Caroline said. "Slather him in pesto sauce and eat him up."

"Dude," Moira said as she turned onto her street, "did you have to bring in a visual?"

"Yes! When I tell you I wanted to be with J.T., I'm

serious. You and I aren't the type to jump right in and do the horizontal mambo, as Jill would say, but Moira..."

Their cousin certainly had a way of talking about sex. Always had. "I know. As someone who's dancing a lot of mambo right now, I can testify that it's pretty spectacular with a man you feel that way about."

"Oh...I wondered. Good for you! When do I finally get to meet him?"

She'd been thinking about that after this weekend. Her family was important to her, and Chase was important to her. "I don't know exactly. He's got a lot of pride about being laid up and getting around in a scooter."

"And yet, it seems like you don't think it detracts from his appeal whatsoever," Caroline said.

She pulled into her driveway and opened the garage. "Hang on. I need to take you off hands-free. I just got home."

"I wondered at the echo," she said.

Moira grabbed her bag from the passenger seat. "It doesn't matter to me, but then again, I can't smell him without wanting to rip his clothes off. The casts aren't ideal, but they haven't stopped us."

"Plus, you have a doctor brother you can call if you're too rough with him." Caroline started laughing.

"Funny. Like I'd call Andy if *that* happened."

"Mo, I need to get going," Caroline said. "I want to hit an early morning butt blaster class after all the food I devoured this weekend."

"You're not going to get rid of me so easily. We didn't talk about the food. Was it good?"

"Does God exist?" her sister quipped. "I already made Natalie salivate."

"When did you talk to her? I waited until this morning to call you out of respect."

"Ha! Natalie has always been more tenacious. She

called last night. I was super jet lagged, but she wouldn't take no for an answer."

"It's the Hale way. How did you leave things with J.T.?" Moira asked, heading into her bedroom. She needed a shower before work.

"I'm supposed to give him a date for our trip to his parents' place in Napa Valley."

Moira started stripping off her clothes in her bathroom. "Sounds like that'll be an interesting trip. Book it fast. Tell Kendra you have a man in your life. It's kinda true."

"You know Kendra," Caroline answered as Moira turned the shower on. "She thinks the sky is going to fall if I'm not around."

"That's only because she doesn't like to work," Moira said.

"Which is why she's the gallery owner. I really need to run, or I'm not going to make my class."

"I'm naked outside my shower stall," Moira said with a laugh. "Run."

"Glad we didn't Facetime," her sister said. "Love you."

"Love you too."

Moira set the phone aside after they hung up and then looked in the mirror. She was sexy, dammit. Sure, she'd joked about her flat-as-flapjacks chest and how short she was, but right now, all she could see was her own beauty. Her skin was dewy, likely from all the orgasms she'd been having. Her curls seemed more perfect somehow, and her eyes... The green was rich and deep and clear.

It was because she was happy, she decided. She had a fabulous job, doing something she believed in, and they were about to launch their first event. Then there was this other part of her life, still so new—she had a wonderful man to spend time with. He liked to snuggle, she'd discovered. When she'd teased him about it, he'd confessed it was a first for him. They were experiencing so many firsts together.

She never wanted it to end.

CHAPTER 28

CHASE WAS GETTING USED TO HIS NEW SURROUNDINGS and new routine. Jarvis had feng shuied the hell out of the house, and even Chase had to agree it was more appealing, from the soft colors in the new window draperies to the even softer textures of the cashmere throws on the couch and in his bedroom.

Even more encouraging, Andy had approved him to work a quarter time. Of course, to the doctor, that meant ten hours a week. Chase explained his normal work week consisted of one hundred and twenty hours, on average, so they needed a different number. Andy hadn't bought that. He'd held the line at ten.

Rajan's report had been extremely helpful in determining where Chase should spend the precious time he'd been given. They were still looking for the right person to bid in Gopal's place, but Chase still suspected it would come down to Rajan. Of course, he hadn't told Evan that.

His boss and friend had restored his cell phone to him, but he'd found a way to limit it to only ten hours of calling time. Evan had been pretty proud of his continued ability to alter technology to out-fox Chase, as he liked to say. Chase had been less pleased.

With the work, Chase's headaches returned, which made him more than impatient. Acupuncture took away the pain, but it was a Band-Aid. Cooking also seemed to help, which he found interesting, and so did being with Moira. It wasn't only the sex—although it was the best sex of his life—it was the contentment he felt when they were together. He was happy when he was with her or thinking about her.

But one glance at the Home Sweet Love pillow Jarvis had set in his relationship bagua, and his head started hurting and his chest grew tight.

He knew what he needed to do.

So he told Bonnie to call Ally and make another energy healing appointment for him.

By the time the older woman arrived on Friday morning, he was sweating from nerves. It felt like an elephant was taking teatime from atop his chest.

"It's good to see you again, Chase," Ally said softly as she approached him on the couch. "Looks like you and Barney have become fast friends."

The tabby kitten nudged his hand to remind him to continue scratching behind its ears. "Yes. I want to apologize again for the other time."

Today, she was wearing a simple navy sweater and jeans. Funny, how it seemed so...normal. Then he almost laughed. What was he expecting, a turban and a crystal ball?

She waved her hand in the air and smiled at him. "There's nothing to apologize for, Chase. Letting go of the past is hard for many of us."

"I thought I already had let go of it," he said cautiously.

"Forcing your memories into a box and sealing them off is different than letting them go," she said. "You feel better than you did last time. There's a nice pink light around you. You've found a woman to love. I'm happy for you."

A pink glow? Good God, he might as well sign up for an ashram in India. He glanced over at Bonnie, whose lips were twitching. "Did you tell her that?"

"No," Bonnie said, picking up her coffee cup from the dining room table. "Why would I? You haven't told me anything."

That much was true. Bonnie continued to help him prepare and smoke the meat he cooked for his meals with Moira—something he loved doing—but beyond that he'd said nothing about her. What was he supposed to say? *Hi Bonnie, Moira, the love of my life, just left the house after another night of mind-blowing sex? How was your night?*

Please.

"I'm going to drink my coffee in the kitchen," Bonnie said, casting him another smile.

"You do that," he said, tucking Barney more securely in his lap. While he was still nervous, he felt more comfortable with the idea of being alone with Ally than he had last time. "Can we sit on the couch?"

"Whatever is most comfortable for you," she said, joining him.

He shifted his body onto the cushions, hoping physical comfort would ease the tension in his chest.

"You're anxious," she said, gazing at him. "We'll address that first. Take a few deep breaths."

The pleasant buzzing sound settled over him, and he felt calm spread through his body. He had to take some extra deep breaths to release what felt like trapped balls of air inside him, but soon he was sinking back into the couch, his muscles completely unwound.

"Your bones are healing nicely still," she said. "Not as hot as last time, which is good. Less swelling, right?"

He nodded. "But there's still itching." It drove him nuts sometimes unless he focused his mind elsewhere.

"That's only natural. I'll show you something you can do to help that when we're finished. Now, close your eyes."

They'd been flickering open and shut as the calm rolled through him. "Are you...are you going to talk to my dad?" He had to ask her. He'd been unable to think about anything else in anticipation of this appointment.

"We'll see if he comes again," Ally said, giving him a soft smile. "I'm going to be silent for a while. You just lie there and keep breathing."

He was aware of the soft buzzing for a while, and then he felt like he was floating outside his body. Was this supposed to happen?

"Relax, Chase," she said, as if reading his mind. "There's nothing for you to do right now but be here."

There was pressure at the base of his skull, like a rubber ball pressing there, and then it faded to nothing. He wondered if she was working on his headaches. But before he could give it any thought, a flash of pain seared through his head. An image of their house burning to the ground, smoke trailing out of his room, flashed into his mind. God, he'd loved his room, from all his books like *Robinson Crusoe* to the prized BB gun he'd named Wild Bill.

Sorrow swallowed him whole. "I don't want to remember this."

Ally's hand touched his good arm. "Your mind wants to let it go, Chase. Are you ready?"

In that moment, he wasn't sure. Suddenly he was standing in front of their house, watching the flames envelop everything in sight. His mother stood between him and his little brother, holding both of their hands. Chase's dad was on his other side, squeezing his free hand. It was the last time his father had touched him. He'd stopped hugging or kissing any of them after that night.

But it wasn't the only "last" for them, Chase realized. It was also the last night they were a family.

By the time the last flames had turned their home to ash, the family he'd known, the family he'd loved, had disappeared forever.

"I wish it had never happened," he whispered, shocked to feel tears begin to roll down his cheeks. "Oh, shit." The hurt was so huge, pressing upward, seeking release.

"I know you do," Ally said softly. "Take my hand. We'll let it go together."

Somehow the hand that curled around his didn't *feel* like her hand. It felt like his dad's, the tough and callused one he remembered.

Another memory flashed through him. He was holding his mother and brother's hands as they watched his father's coffin being lowered into the ground. He could feel his brother squeezing his hand, gripping it to the point of pain, while his mother's grasp was limp, as if their dad had taken all the life from her by killing himself.

"I want my dad back," he said aloud, but it wasn't his voice. It was the voice of that twelve-year-old boy he'd been. "He shouldn't have left us. How could he have done that to us?" Searing anger shot through his gut. "He was a coward."

A hand gripped his, hard enough to wrest his attention from the memories. Again, he felt those calluses.

"Your dad is here, Chase, and he wants you to know how sorry he is for what he did. He wasn't doing it to hurt you. He simply couldn't keep going. When he lost your home, he thought he'd lost everything. Now he knows you and your mom and brother were the most important things, not all the work he'd put into the ranch. He wants you to forgive him. It's up to you if you're ready to do that right now."

In his mind, he could see his dad standing before him. Like Chase, he was tall and broad in the shoulders. He wore that constant five o'clock shadow he'd always had in life.

"I'm sorry, son," Chase heard the man say.

A chill washed over his skin.

"Please forgive me." His dad approached him, shadows under his dark eyes. "I've been waiting for you to realize how sorry I am. I...couldn't cross over until I made amends with you and your mama and brother. I've still got a ways to go with them."

Chase felt like his brain was split in two. He wanted to believe his dad was talking to him. Another part thought he was making it all up.

"I'm real, son," his dad said with a crooked smile. "There's a lot you can't see from your side of life. It took me some time to realize what had happened, but now I know why I couldn't go into all that light. I was too ashamed about what I'd done. I can't go until I make things right."

The words were shocking and mysterious, and Chase wanted to inch back from them.

Then his dad extended his hand to him. "I'm so proud of you, son. You've become an incredible man."

Chase's heart started pumping so loudly he could hear it in his ears. "You still shouldn't have left us," he said, realizing he'd whispered it.

"I know," his dad said, re-extending his hand. "Will you forgive me, son? You can think on it if you need to."

Then Chase's mind filled with images of how his dad had been after the fire. They'd lived with his dad's cousin for a few weeks, and his dad had tried to find work. One day, he'd overheard a heated argument between his parents. His dad had told his mother that all he wanted to do was ranch his own land. He needed his own cattle, his own spread. He didn't want to work at the feed store in town for the rest of his life. They would rebuild once the insurance money arrived. After Chase's mother stormed off, his father had put his face in his hands and cried.

Chase had never seen him cry until that moment, and he'd been too scared to go to him.

He felt more tears spill down his face. Felt that callused hand grip his again. His heart was pumping so hard and so fast he was panting.

Pain squeezed his heart, and awareness flooded into him as the memory of the last time he saw his dad surfaced. His dad had just opened the check from the insurance company. His mom had started crying. But his dad had simply stared at the check with something akin to horror in his eyes. Then he'd set it aside and walked off like a robot. Chase had called his name and run after him, but he hadn't heard him.

His dad had driven off in their pick-up truck moments later and never returned.

"Oh, Jesus," he cried, feeling the hurt crash through him.

His dad had been hurting so badly he hadn't seen another way out. The loss of their home and their life had broken him completely.

"I'm sorry," he heard his dad say again.

Chase was floating then, and everything seemed to grow still around him. He felt warmth surround him. Love, he realized somewhere in his consciousness. It was how he felt when he was with Moira, that giant feeling of contentment and happiness rolled into something powerful and mysterious.

That was when he knew he could do it.

"I forgive you, Dad," he whispered.

His dad stepped forward and touched his face. There were tears in his eyes. "I love you, son," he said.

Then he disappeared.

There was a whoosh, like a gust of wind blowing open a door, followed by the most powerful stillness he had ever experienced.

There was no sound. No movement.

But he was enfolded somehow. The peace was endless and all encompassing.

He stayed like that for what seemed like eons. There was no time. No past. No future. Only him.

And all was well.

Like a balloon falling slowly back to earth, he felt himself start to come gently back to himself. He became aware of his body. Every nerve was tingling pleasantly. His chest felt more open than ever, and he felt himself smile.

Everything was okay.

Barney nudged him in the belly, and when he went to remove his hand from Ally's, he realized he wasn't holding it anymore.

Then he wondered if he ever had been.

The kitten was purring against him, and damn it all if he didn't realize how much he loved that little guy too.

When he finally opened his eyes, Ally was watching him. Her eyes were like two shining stars. "Welcome back, Chase. How do you feel?"

"Good," he answered, sitting up a little straighter. "Calm."

The soft buzzing was abating, he realized, and again, his rational mind wondered what in the world this was all about. He supposed it didn't matter. He felt better. He couldn't logically explain what had happened to him, but something had, something powerful and profound. He wasn't going to pick it apart.

"That's wonderful," Ally said, patting his good hand. "Let me show you what you can do when your skin starts to itch under the cast."

She demonstrated how he should brush his fingers

up and down the area in question, not touching, explaining it would move the energy in the same way as scratching would. He was more open to believing her after their session.

When she rose to leave, he reached for her hand. "Thank you, Ally."

That mysterious smile flashed on her face, and he wondered again at the mysteries this woman, this healer, connected to on a daily basis. "You're most welcome, Chase."

Bonnie left him alone for a while after that, and Chase sat in front of the dying fire with Barney in his lap. He felt like he'd been given a part of his life back.

He couldn't wait to tell Moira.

CHAPTER 29

MOIRA CHECKED HER COUNTDOWN METER. THE fundraiser was in three days, and they were in the final preparations.

Chase was getting his casts off today, and they were being swapped for a sling and walking boot. It wasn't ideal, but he'd be more mobile this way. Of course, for Chase, this meant he'd look more presentable in the Italian suit his tailor in D.C. was specially making for him. She was happy he was happy.

He'd been different after that incredible session with Ally. Forgiving his father had changed him. Hearing the details of what he'd experienced had given her chill bumps, but when it came down to it, all that mattered was that it had helped him.

He hadn't had any headaches or chest pains since that session—even though he'd had a follow-up appointments with Ally and Dr. Sarah to, in his words, keep everything on track. He considered it the reason Andy had increased his work week to twenty hours, still not enough if you asked Chase.

"Yo," Gary called in her doorway. "You cool? How was your meeting with your sister and Chef T?"

As far as she was concerned, Natalie and Chef T

were catering rock stars. They were preparing a beef tenderloin with wild mushrooms and sea bass with hazelnuts and white wine as entrée choices, paired with crispy polenta cakes and asparagus bundles wrapped in prosciutto with thyme sprigs.

"Observe my cucumber-like demeanor. Everything is good to go for the fundraiser. I even squeezed in a walk-through of the space with Jill and Abbie. The flowers arrive day of, but they're starting to set them up today."

"Awesome," Gary said. "Hate to break your bubble though. Our musicians backed out last minute."

She shot out of her chair. *"They what?"*

"Just kidding!" he said, laughing. "You should see your face."

Coming around her desk, she drilled him in the chest. "Don't you ever do that again."

"Ouch," he gasped, dancing away from her. "Fine. I won't. Man, you're vicious."

"When you pull that kind of joke, I'm more than vicious." She made her face go deadpan. "I'm your worst nightmare."

"I swear I will never josh with you again," he said in all seriousness.

Gary either forgot that promise or had never meant to honor it in the first place. For the next two days, he played one practical joke after another on her. There was the fake spider hanging above the toilet in the women's bathroom. She'd tried to leap away from it and had promptly tripped on the pants around her ankles. He'd smeared mashed bananas on her office phone—something she'd discovered only *after* pressing it to her face to call Evan with a briefing report. Then there was the exploding can of worms he'd stuck into her tin of green tea in the break room. He said it was to help her chill, but only Gary would think jump scares were relaxing. Still, the pranks were kind of funny, and they were a welcome distraction.

Of course, she'd tried plotting her revenge, only to discover she sucked at practical jokes. Luckily, she had two siblings who excelled at them. Matt and Natalie had both been liberal with their advice. So when she handed Gary the sandwich she'd brought him from Brasserie Dare, she waited just inside her doorway as he opened the package at his desk.

The girly scream he emitted made her clutch her belly with laughter.

"You stuck plastic flies in my sandwich?" he cried out, dashing out of his office and appearing in her doorway, holding out the items in question.

"You know what the song says, 'I don't know why he swallowed the fly...' Oh, wait, I do. Because he played practical jokes on his boss."

"You are so dead," he said, getting in her face. Then he grimaced. "I didn't mean it like that."

She couldn't stop laughing. "I know you didn't."

"But I would highly recommend you refrain from saying that to anyone you work with," she heard a familiar voice say.

Chase appeared behind Gary, who lurched around.

"Oh my God, you're like the big boss, like—"

"Chase Parker," he said, holding out his good hand to shake.

She thought about warning Chase. Gary shook hands hard enough to make a zombie's wrist snap off.

"Mr. Parker! It's an honor." He tucked the offending sandwich under his arm to take Chase's hand after shoving the fake bugs into his pants pocket.

Moira's shoulders started to shake.

"Evan says you're even a greater man than he is, and Evan is like the shit." Gary grimaced. "I mean Evan is a visionary, a genius—"

"I know what you mean," Chase said, stopping the

over-exuberant handshake. "You can let go of my hand now, Gary."

He released it immediately. "I'm sorry. I get a little excited. Working here is like the best time of my life, and Moira is—"

"The shit," Chase said, his lips twitching. "I'm well aware of that. Why don't you call out for a sandwich free of bugs—on Artemis, of course—while I speak with this genius right here?"

"You bet!" Gary saluted him.

Moira bit her lip to keep from losing it.

"Can I get you anything, Mr. Parker? I heard abut your accident. Ice? A pillow? You're looking great actually." A plastic bug fell to the floor—one Gary must have missed. "I'll just...clean this up."

Chase stepped over the bug and shut Moira's office door behind him. "You have a peculiar way of inspiring morale." Then he started to laugh. "Remind me to never engage in practical jokes with you. I knew you'd think of something."

She found herself grinning. All she wanted to do was kiss him and wrap her arms around him. Should she? "Natalie and Matt gave me ideas. They're scary really. You need to meet them. How about tonight? You're back on your feet and looking very good, I might say."

He looked over at her, and she paused, feeling anxious around him suddenly.

"Ah...this is weird. I'm second-guessing things right now. I want to kiss you and hug you and...tell you how much I love you, but I'm at work. Is *that* okay?"

"I don't pay rent for this facility," he said, shifting his weight. "So long as we don't throw everything off your desk and have wild sex, I think we're good."

Heat tore through her. "That was low. You know I would have serious ethical qualms about that."

"So do I," he said, "but it doesn't stop me from

thinking about it. God, it feels good to be out of the house and free of all that plaster."

"How did you get here?" she asked.

"Bonnie is outside in the car," he said. "I asked her to make a stop here after we left the hospital. I wanted you to see my new getup."

He proudly extended his black walking boot. Then he gestured to his brace, rapping on it with his good hand. "The marvels of plastic."

"You had her stop here on the way back from the hospital so you could model for me?" God, she loved him.

He turned around slowly in a circle. "I wanted to stand on my own two feet before you and tell you how much I love you. I couldn't have gotten through this ordeal so easily without you."

"I was just thinking about how much I love you," she said, putting her hand on his chest. "And...I'm glad it was easier for you."

"Know what else?" he asked her, smoothing back the hair behind her ear.

"What?" she answered.

"I've been cleared to work forty hours a week, adding ten extra hours each week moving forward." Then he frowned. "Of course, it's still not enough time to get everything done. It's going to take me weeks to dig out."

Her heart squeezed. That meant he'd be leaving, right? She'd known it was coming, and she was happy he'd be able to reclaim his life. She just didn't know what that meant for them yet. "That's wonderful. I know how much you've been looking forward to that."

"Yeah," he said, but his tone lacked its usual certainty.

"It'll be fine," she said. It was a reassurance they both needed.

"Of course it will." He pulled her against his chest. "I'm not letting you go, Moira, even if I am going back to work."

"Of course, you aren't," she said, injecting some humor into her voice. "Especially now that you know I'll put plastic bugs in your sandwich if you mess with me."

Kissing her on the top of the head, he tightened his hold on her. "All I could think of when I got this great news was how I couldn't wait to share it with you."

It was the same way for her. She called or texted him every time Gary pulled a particularly Machiavellian joke, and after the outrageously delicious lunch she and Evan had enjoyed yesterday at Brasserie Dare, the first thing she'd done was call Chase.

"Does that mean you'd be open to meeting my family tonight? They can bring pizza and beer over to your house if that's more convenient. Caroline is coming in tonight for the weekend."

"If you don't mind, I'm tired of being cooped up." He traced her face. "How about we do it at your house? I've never been there. I'd...like to make love to you in your bed."

Everything tightened up down south. "That sounds like a plan. I'll be your chauffeur. Oh shit. My place is a wreck since I've been staying with you. And Caroline will have to stay with Mom. Okay, you need to go. I have a lot to do. In addition to making sure this fundraiser rocks."

He kissed her nose. "It will. Don't worry about me getting to your house. I'll find my way there."

"You sure?" she asked.

Gesturing to himself, he said, "I'm an independent man again."

After he left, she sat down in her chair, unable to dispel a slight sense of unease.

Would an independent Chase love her and want her as much as the old one had?

CHAPTER 30

No two ways about it—when the Hales got together, it was a party, and a rowdy one at that. Somehow word had gotten out about Chase meeting Moira's family—everyone blamed Jill—and the whole *extended* family had been invited as well. That meant there was a passel of children in addition to all of the adults. Jill and Brian's twin girls were chasing after Danny and Keith, their older cousins, who were trying to teach the little girls how to play a game of tag. So far, it had been hit or miss. The girls were only interested in chasing the young boys, not being chased, and they emitted high-pitched squeals guaranteed to puncture an ear drum when the boys wouldn't run away.

Sure, there were a lot of people, but he'd heard about most of them from either Evan or Moira, so he was well prepared. The open affection in the family was palpable—just like Evan had told him. He felt both immediately welcomed and like an animal on display in the zoo for the first time. He'd been to hundreds, no, thousands, of parties. He'd even mingled with heads of state, but this was a little disarming.

What would it be like to have a family this large?

Moira's immediate family was especially kind to him.

Her mom, April, kissed him on the cheek and said she'd been praying for his recovery. Her brother, Matt, shook his hand and offered to share embarrassing childhood stories about Moira, which had earned him a punch in the gut from his sister.

And then there were the sisters. Natalie promised to keep everyone in line at the fundraiser if Moira fell down on the job, but it was obvious she was joking from the way she slung her arm around her sister as she said it. It was easy for him to connect with Caroline, who enjoyed the wonders of Rome as much as he did. He met all of the in-laws as well, speaking about wine with Jane, world events with Lucy, and professional athletics with Blake.

But his sense of ease faded a little when Natalie and Blake announced they were expecting a baby. He didn't feel he deserved to be privy to such a celebration. After that, he tried to stay out of the way.

"Sometimes it gets so crazy at one of these shindigs," Peggy McBride said, sidling up to him. "I'm afraid I'm going to have to arrest people for disturbing the peace."

Dare Valley's sheriff was a no-nonsense police officer to the core, which Chase quite appreciated. She was married to Mac Maven, owner of The Grand Mountain Hotel. "I don't think you have enough handcuffs," he said.

"Don't be so sure," she told him.

"I actually believe you," he replied, smiling as he caught Moira wink at him from across the room. She was shoving beer bottles into a large red tin filled with ice. He'd offered to help her before, but she'd told him to mingle.

"You're wise to believe her," Mac Maven said, putting his hand on his wife's shoulder. "Whenever Keith or I step out of line, we watch to make sure she's not pulling out the handcuffs."

She gave him a look. "You're so full of it, Mr. Poker."

"She likes to sweet talk me," Mac said, laughing.

Peggy caught his lapel and kissed him hard on the mouth. "How's that for sweet talking?"

"Are you two *kissing* in front of Chase?" Moira asked, racing over. "Please! It's his first party with us. Out of everyone, I thought you two would behave."

"Me too," Jill Hale said, bouncing over with a bottle in her hand. "Get a room, guys. Chase needs a drink. I asked Andy if a beer was okay. He agreed that it was, so here's one of my favorite micro-brews."

"Thank you," he said to Jill, taking the beer from her. He fought a wince when he read the label. Pumpkin ale? God help him.

Evan looked over and pointed furiously in the redhead's direction.

"What's he doing?" Jill asked, tilting her head to the side.

"I'm not sure, honestly," Chase said.

Moira leaned close to his ear. "He's warning you to beware of Jill. As if you don't already know. I still can't believe she invited everyone without asking me."

"I'm sure she meant well." Other than her abominable taste in beer, she did seem to have a warm heart if you could put up with her enthusiasm. Plus, he could handle himself. His biggest problem at the moment was his right leg. He shifted on his feet. He loved standing up again, but his ankle was swelling badly, and there was a line of pain throbbing up to his hip.

"You might want to sit down," Andy said from behind him. Could he read minds like Ally? "You can't go from zero to ninety in one day. Remember that for work too."

Chase wasn't so sure having his doctor present at his first party was a good thing. "Thanks for the advice."

"That means, FU, Andy," Jill said laughing.

Moira punched her brother in the arm. "Nice one, bro. Chase, come over and sit by Uncle Arthur."

He'd been introduced to the man earlier in the evening. All of the Hales and honorary Hales had lined up in a crazy receiving line so Moira could make the intros. It had been a little weird. She'd never referred to him as her boyfriend or alluded to their relationship, but people knew why he was here.

As he approached the couch, he had to brace himself. Everywhere he looked, there were babies. Okay, only two, but it was a lot for a man who couldn't remember the last time he'd been around one. Arthur was holding a baby dressed in green, and the woman Chase recognized as Rhett Butler Blaylock's wife, Abbie, was holding the other, a girl dressed in a pink and white polka-dot onesie.

Arthur nodded to the vacant space beside him. "Join us, Chase. This is Jared Arthur McBride, my great-great grandson. My granddaughter, Meredith, and her husband wisely named him after me."

Chase fought a sigh as he sat down and stretched his boot out. The baby looked slightly older than Abbie's daughter from the way he was babbling, and his four front teeth were visible when he smiled at Chase.

"Your leg hurts like a bitch, doesn't it?" Arthur asked.

"Arthur!" Abbie said. "Little ears."

"Oh, bah! Their ears are too little to decipher words yet. Watch this, Chase. Jared, you're a sweet little one. Did you know that there is horrible poverty in this world?"

The baby continued to smile at the man who was speaking to him in a sing-song voice.

"See, Abbie," Arthur declared. "So long as you say things in a nice voice, babies still smile."

Chase wanted to laugh, but Abbie seemed so put out, and he didn't want to offend the new mother. "You have a beautiful baby," he said instead, gesturing to the infant on her lap.

"Thank you," she said, tucking the baby higher up on

her shoulder. "This is Clara. She's our delight."

"Sure is, sugar," Rhett Butler Blaylock said, appearing behind the sofa. The world-famous poker player was the kind of man who commanded attention. Topping out at six foot six, he had a lusty laugh and a Southern drawl that carried across the room. He and his elegant wife seemed like a textbook case of opposites attract.

"For years I thought poker was my life," Rhett said, "and then these two angels appeared. Lady Luck seems a mite small in comparison now."

Chase had heard the same from most of the other people he'd spoken with tonight—some of whom he'd already met. Every one of them—men and women alike— had been focused on their careers until they'd met their spouses. Moira's brother-in-law, Blake Cunningham, had even retired from the NFL to give his full attention to his marriage before finding a new, more balanced career. It made Chase consider something he'd never imagined. Was it possible for him to find some kind of healthy balance between a career and a home life?

During his last energy healing session with Ally, she'd told him that he was at a crossroads in his life. Part of him didn't want to keep working at such a punishing pace, but he didn't know how to change. How to find a way to be fulfilled both personally and professionally. Right now, he had trouble envisioning what shape his relationship with Moira would take once he left Dare Valley, and he hated thinking that.

"If you're going to hang around this motley crew, you need to be able to hold a baby," Arthur said, transferring Jared onto Chase's lap.

Alarmed, he immediately gripped the baby. "I only have one good arm," he said, wishing the older man would take the infant back. "Maybe I shouldn't—"

"Jared likes to cuddle," Arthur told him. "Tuck him close to your body, and he'll do the rest."

Chase hadn't held a child since his brother was little, but sure enough, the baby curled into his chest. Much like Barney did, he realized. Then the little boy turned his head and looked up at him. He grinned, his teeth showing, and grabbed Chase's shirt.

"He likes you, and he's as good a judge of character as his great-great grandfather," Arthur said. "You ever think of having one?"

Shock rippled through him. "No. Never."

But there wasn't as much conviction behind that word as there would have been if someone had asked him the same question before the accident.

"It's because of your work, right?" Arthur asked.

"Yes."

"I managed to have an amazing career with a wife and a family," Arthur told him, playing with his great grandson's hand. "I tell these young people all the time that they overcomplicate life. Want to hear my secret?"

Chase leaned in closer. "Please."

Arthur harrumphed. "You make time for what's important. You decide you *can* have it all, and so you do."

Chase wasn't convinced.

"Bring in people you trust to work with you," Arthur continued. "Then delegate what you can to give yourself more time for the personal stuff."

Chase was *already* delegating. His time off had only shown him how many of Quid-Atch's critical functions required his personal attention.

Arthur was looking at him over his rimless glasses. "If you have a great partner in life, you'll have balance on the home front too. In my generation, I saw women burn out all the time from trying to be a full-time parent, homemaker, and career woman. Their husbands didn't help at home, which is hogwash if you ask me. What man can't handle a load of laundry and bathing his own kids?"

"You're very forward thinking," Chase told him.

"I've got sense," Arthur said with another harrumph. "A true partner helps you have the time you need to do what makes you happy. And you do it right back for them. Hell, that's what love is, son. Makes everything easier."

There was that word again. *Love.* Chase fitted the baby closer when he lurched up on his lap. He glanced up to see the twin girls running toward them. Jared gurgled and clapped his hands.

"Mia. Violet. You slow down."

The sternness in Arthur's voice had them doing just that. "Okay," they both said with toothy grins.

"Just like their mother, Jill," Arthur said. "She was a handful, but some of the most fun you'll ever have with a person. With this generation, we got two duplicates of her. And I love them like crazy. Come here to Great-Grandpa, girls. Have you met Chase?"

"Hi," the twin on the right in purple said.

The one on the left in pink said, "Chase," and waved at him with her little hand. "You hurt. Need Band-Aid. Mama has it."

She looked so concerned, he said, "This boot is my Band-Aid."

The little girl bent closer to look at his walking boot before clambering up onto Arthur's lap and patting Jared, who giggled.

"This is pretty far away from the boardroom," Chase said, wincing as a string of drool from Jared's mouth soaked his pants.

"And yet it's not a bad gig," the older man said, scooting over to let the other twin sit between them. "I like knowing there will be Hales in the world after I go. I have high hopes that one of these little girls will have black ink in her veins."

Chase smiled, loving the newspaper allusion. "You like the idea of your family continuing to run your newspaper." He thought back to what Evan had said about wanting them to be a family business. To create a legacy.

"It would be nice, but it isn't necessary," he said, squeezing one of the girls in a hug. "I want them to be happy. I got lucky enough to have a few family members who love the newspaper business as much as I do. Who am I to ask for more? My legacy is set. It gives a man of my age peace."

Chase thought of his own father. He'd talked about Chase and Boone ranching the same land his father and his father before him had ranched when they'd come West to stake their claim. "You seem to have gotten everything you've wanted."

"There were bumps, but you get your shovel and fill them in. I expect this accident has been difficult for you. Not easy for a man to be limited. I have a damn cane to contend with and achy joints. But I don't let them stop me."

"No, I'm not the kind to accept limitations either," Chase said, watching as the twin in purple touched the little boy's face, making them both grin. "They really are cute."

He felt weird saying it, but it was true.

"At this age, they're even cute when they spit up," Arthur said. "Doesn't last long in a human lifespan. Moira has her eye on you, I see. She's a doll. Can be sweet or tough as nails if the situation calls for it. Like all the Hale women, I'm proud to say."

Chase looked over, and sure enough, Moira was watching him with a soft smile on her face. She was talking to her sisters and her mom, who were also surreptitiously watching him. The expression on her face was filled with an emotion at once soft, warm, and fierce: love.

It was still hard to accept. He'd been without it for so long, and he didn't completely trust he wasn't going to lose it again. He made the effort to give her an answering smile.

"You're holding a *baby*?" he heard a familiar male voice ask.

He looked to the right and saw Evan and Margie. "Arthur forced him on me."

"Bullshit," the older man said. "You could have forced him right back."

"Arthur!" Abbie cried out suddenly, breaking off her conversation with her husband, who laughed when the older man winked at her.

"That would have seemed rude," Chase said, trying not to laugh himself. "But he's easy. Rather like Barney actually."

"You would liken a baby to a kitten," Evan said, shaking his head. "Arthur, we need to talk Chase into staying in Dare Valley with us."

Chase felt everything within him grow still. Evan hadn't brought up his plans to move Quid-Atch's R&D to Dare Valley again, but here was the proof that he was still thinking about it.

Chase glanced at Arthur, whose brow was cocked. "Evan's got an active imagination. He's spinning this tale about how we can remain prosperous if we move our successful defense contractor company outside D.C. to a small town in the West."

His friend's face fell. "I don't think it's a tale."

"If you're good enough at something, people don't care where you work from," Arthur said. "Everyone back East told me I couldn't create a successful national newspaper out here."

Evan started to smile.

"But no one was used to you being out East," Chase

argued. "And you don't have clients or government counterparts like Quid-Atch does."

"That's true," Arthur said, helping one of the twins off his lap when she started to climb down. "It sounds like you two have a lot to work out."

Evan wasn't smiling anymore. In fact, he looked downright grim.

"We always work things out," Chase told Evan. "Right?"

He nodded, but the gesture lacked conviction. Evan looked worried, and suddenly Chase felt the same way. Their visions of running Quid-Atch had never been this different.

Looking around the room, Chase tried to remember that all of these people had careers, ones they cared about. But they didn't run a global billion-dollar enterprise like he did. They didn't have the weight of thousands of jobs and lives and careers on their shoulders. In that moment, icy dread filled his belly.

He didn't believe another way was possible.

And then he caught Moira's gaze on him, and the ice slowly began to dissolve.

She made everything *feel* possible.

The big question seemed to be: could he turn it into reality?

CHAPTER 31

MOIRA SNUGGLED UNDER THE COVERS WHEN HER alarm went off. "Not yet," she cried out. But her day-of checklist for the fundraiser was already rolling through her mind.

A warm hand touched her side, one she had come to know by heart, stopping the details.

"Good morning," Chase said in a deep voice.

She opened her eyes, eager to get her first look at him. Like always. Waking up with Chase had become one of her favorite things. So had making love. Last night, she'd discovered a couple of new ones. She'd loved seeing him mingle with the other people she held dear, and while she didn't know what to make of it, she'd loved watching him hold baby Jared. Darn it if she wasn't glad Jill had invited everyone, after all. She planned to tell her cousin as much after the fundraiser was over.

"How long have you been awake?" He looked a heck of a lot more alert than she felt.

"A while," he said, smiling when she rolled over to face him. "You know I only sleep four or five hours."

And yet he'd been sleeping seven or eight hours since she'd started sleeping with him.

"I've been looking around your bedroom," he said.

"I didn't notice it last night with the party and our after-party..."

She shivered as memories washed over her. He'd been more mobile with his new sling and boot. That, coupled with his typical creativity and determination, had quickly reduced her to a puddle.

"You like homey," he said, pointing across the room. "I like the sayings you have sprinkled around your place. They suit you. Funny and sweet and a little...crazy. Especially the one over there that says, 'I Kick Ass, And Then I Kiss It.' I might have experienced that first-hand last night."

She laughed. "Matt got that placard for me after I gave him the what-for for talking about joining a law firm he hated because it was 'distinguished.' I told him to choose a firm that made him happy. I'm happy to say he followed my advice."

"I like your brother," Chase said. "I expect he makes a good mayor. Easygoing on the surface, but highly watchful. He doesn't miss much, does he?"

Chase had summed him up neatly. "That's why we call him Matty Ice. I'm glad you..." Oh crap, she was getting a little emotional.

He rolled carefully onto his good side. "What?"

She found it difficult to meet his eyes. "It was nice to have you meet everyone."

"I can see why Evan is so big on your family," Chase said. "It's a wonderful group of people. You're lucky, Moira. Thank you for including me last night."

She wanted to keep on including him, but she reminded herself to take things slow. Seeing him hold her cousin's baby had given her a few flashes of a possible future down the road, one where he'd been holding *their* baby at a family party. That vision had shaken her to the core, even though it only confirmed what she already knew.

She loved him and wanted to be with him forever, if he'd have her. She just didn't see how that was going to work with his career in D.C. and hers in Dare Valley. She wasn't going to quit a job she loved and follow him there. He wouldn't want that either. And her family was here.

What the hell were they going to do?

"It's a busy day for me," she told him, refusing to get riled up by the future. "You going to be all right on your own?"

"I promise not to get arrested," he joked. "Tonight is going to be perfect. I can't wait to see you there after my meetings wrap up."

"I am going to do great," she affirmed. "After all, I kick ass, and then I kiss it."

"Maybe you have a little time to demonstrate that for me again before you have to leave," he said, his gray eyes staring directly into hers.

Desire filled her belly. She leaned in to kiss him. Their tongues danced, and she found herself growing urgent. Really urgent.

"I want you," she told him, gently pushing him to his back. "Right now."

He caressed the bare leg she threw over him. "Do your best."

He'd said that before, and she liked that he'd made the saying positive instead of the negative, "Do your worst."

She slid a condom over his hardness and then eased him inside her and arched her back. "God. It always feels so good."

Rolling his hips under her, he groaned. "Yes. Move, Moira."

She took them on a wild ride. By the time they were finished, panting and grinning at each other, she gave in to the sudden urge to tickle his belly.

He jerked at her touch. "Stop that!"

"Do you know how much I love you?" she asked, feeling joy explode through her. "So much I want to tickle you and hug you until we're both laughing like crazy people."

Taking hold on the hand on his stomach, he eyed her suspiciously. "Who's feeling playful this morning?"

"I am," she said, realizing how precious the feeling was. "And on what I thought was going to be one of the most stressful days ever."

He tugged on her hand to settle her onto his chest. "Do you have any idea how beautiful you are? How special? Moira..."

This time she felt *his* vulnerability. "What?"

"You've been the best thing to happen to me in a long time. I'll always be grateful for that."

He'd started out great, but she wasn't sure how to read the rest of his comment. It was like he was already leaving her. A sharp stab of fear drove her to her feet.

"I need to shower and dress. I can drop you off before heading in. Lots to finalize."

"Get going," he said, pulling her down for one final kiss. "I don't want to be the one to blame if the details don't come together brilliantly."

"That's my responsibility," she said, heading to the bathroom to get ready.

Throughout the day, she continued to supervise the last-minute preparations for the fundraiser. Gary was a huge help, doing everything from moving tables that needed to be adjusted a few feet to the right of the stage to tracking down a 9V battery for one of the musician's electric violins.

Abbie had done a bang-up job with the flowers. The wine-colored tables were topped with towers of white orchids in three-foot-high glass vases lined with sea shells. Natalie was running a tight ship with the catering staff, and she and Moira exchanged a high-five every time they crossed paths. Even Mac came in to check on the progress.

"I know you could have used the university's ballroom since Artemis is going to share its campus," he said, "but we're happy you chose The Grand."

"I knew our elite guests would enjoy the ambience of your beautiful hotel," she told him. "Besides, most of them are staying here, so it's easier for them. Plus, your food is better than the university's."

He laughed. "I would hope so. Between Chef T and your sister, I know you're in good hands. Have a wonderful fundraiser, Moira."

"Thank you, Mac," she said.

As promised, Evan arrived at around three o'clock, four hours before the official start time, to check things out. He'd been in meetings all day.

"Hey! This looks like one hell of a party." He unbuttoned his suit jacket. "Do you think I could snag a late invite, or would I need to crash it?"

She laughed, watching as Gary ran over to his hero's side. He'd been working hard with her all day, as eager to make this fundraiser a success as she was.

"We've hired Peggy to bust any crashers," she said, biting her lip to keep a straight face.

"We did?" Gary asked. "I didn't know that. Man, that's super cool!"

Evan slapped him on the back. "She's joking." Then his whole face turned tense. "Of course, if Chase had his way, we would have hired her."

"Holy shit," she heard Gary say.

"Maurie!" Evan quickly called out. "The party hasn't started yet."

Moira bristled at the sound of the man's name. Turning to look over her shoulder, she watched as a distinguished silver-haired man in a perfectly cut suit strolled toward them. Of course, she'd looked up pictures of him online, wanting to be alert to his presence because of how much he upset Chase. He was nearing fifty, she'd read, and recently freed of his third marriage to a woman half his age. Strikingly handsome, his teeth flashed white as he smiled at their small group.

"I thought I'd swing by and say hello before things got too busy," Maurie said. "Evan, it's good to see you. I was so sorry to hear about Chase's accident. Is he able to make it tonight?"

It sounded like he meant every word.

"Of course, he's coming," Evan said. "You know Chase. Nothing is going to stop him."

"Of course not," Maurie said, shaking his hand. "One of the strongest, most determined men I know. I admire the hell out of him. And you too. Evan, Artemis is going do a lot of wonderful work in the world. Before you tell me more about how it came to you, please introduce me to your friends."

Maurie turned to look at Moira, and that was when she felt the hairs rise on the back of her neck. This man looked at a person, and he oozed charisma. She'd realized he would have to have "something" to be as successful as he was. But this? She hadn't expected it.

"Maurie Wallins of K-Barker. Please meet Moira Hale, the amazing and talented director of Artemis," Evan said. "We're lucky to have her."

"Not a relation of the famed Arthur Hale?" Maurie asked. "But you must be. The coincidence would be too great in such a small town."

"He's my great-uncle," she said.

He extended his hand to hers. When she met it, he held it. "Arthur has interviewed me a few times in my career. He's one of the canniest journalists I've ever met. I read his Op-Ed every Sunday. Great stuff. Evan was smart to bring you in. I'll bet you're as marvelous as your great-uncle."

Moira didn't know all the details of Chase's dislike for the man. Granted, they were competitors, but this man didn't seem like the devil incarnate or even a slick used car salesman.

"Thank you," she said, disengaging from the handshake. "He's a great role model. Maurie, this is Gary Frehlich. He's one of the brightest engineering students here at Emmits Merriam. We're also lucky to have him working with us part-time at Artemis while he's finishing his doctorate."

Gary thrust out his hand. "Mr. Wallins! It's an honor to meet you, sir. Wow. I'm in the same room as Evan Michaels and Maurie Wallins. If I died right now—"

"Please don't, Gary," she told him, putting her hand on his arm to calm him a touch. "We need your help."

Maurie shook Gary's hand and pumped. "I like your enthusiasm, young man. Are you going to be one of the inventors at Artemis?"

"Maybe, sir," Gary said. "I'm graduating in the spring and still trying to decide whether I want to apply for Artemis or jump right into the workforce. I'd love to work for R&D at a company like Evan's. Or yours, of course. Quid-Atch and K-Barker have been my dream companies since I was a sophomore."

"You should give me your resume before I leave," Maurie said. "Oops. Sorry, Evan. Was that out of line? I must have been swept away by this young man's enthusiasm. Of course, you'd love to have him work with you."

"I only want Gary to be happy," Evan said with a brief gesture of his hand. "If that's with Quid-Atch, Artemis, or even K-Barker, that's up to him. I'm happy he's decided to be with us for now."

Moira took note of Evan's response. Again, she remembered Chase and Evan's disagreement about inviting Quid-Atch's competitors. Evan seemed to view them as less of a threat than Chase did.

Maurie clapped Evan on the back. "That relieves my mind. Gary, you decide what will make you happy like Evan says. If you want to give me your resume tonight, please feel free. And Moira, it was a pleasure to meet you. I hope we can speak more tonight at the party. Is your great-uncle joining us, by chance? I'd love to catch up with him."

She smiled, remembering her uncle's complaints about having to iron a suit for tonight's shindig. "Yes, he is. Big news for the paper."

"Indeed," Maurie said. "I'll let you all get back. So happy I ran into you early."

As he strode off, Gary did a dance in a circle. "Holy shit. Holy shit. That was Maurie Wallins. I mean like, wowza." He put a hand over his heart and swayed in place. "You guys are the biggest shit in the whole fucking world."

"Gary," Moira said, biting her lip to keep from laughing. "Let's try to leave out those words tonight around our guests."

"You mean I can come to the party?" he asked.

She hadn't really thought about it, so she glanced at Evan for approval. He was still looking at the ballroom doors Maurie had passed through, lost in thought.

"Evan?"

"Sure," he said, rebuttoning his jacket. "I need to get going. It looks like the preparations are coming along. Moira, do you need anything?"

"No," she said, "I'm good. Last rounds are at five thirty, and then I'm off to get dressed."

"I'm going to get Chase," Evan told her. "We have some meetings with a few people before the party starts. Text me if something comes up."

Like she would interrupt their meetings for anything less than a disaster.

"See you later," Moira said. "Seven o'clock sharp, remember?"

"Would I be late for my own party?" he asked. "It's Margie I feel bad for. This sucker is going to stretch way past her normal bedtime."

"I doubt Margie's worried about that," she said.

Evan clapped his hand on Gary's shoulder. "I meant what I said. I can't promise you anything, but you know how much I value you. You know you can use me as a reference for a job. And Moira here too. Except for the invention program at Artemis, of course."

"Moira explained conflicts of interest to me," Gary said. "Thanks, Evan. I feel like I'm Dorothy in *The Wizard of Oz*, walking on the Yellow Brick Road."

"Don't wear the ruby slippers," Evan told him. "See you both later."

After Evan left, Gary grabbed Moira by both shoulders. "Do you think I have time to run back to my dorm and print off my resume for Mr. Wallins? Shit, I need to change too. Oh my God, is my one suit going to be okay? I wore it for my grandpa's funeral. It's—"

"Gary, it will be fine," she said, checking her watch. "Everything looks like it's on track."

"It's pretty great of Evan to be so cool about me giving Mr. Wallins my resume, don't you think? He was my hero before, but now... He's like Jesus or something."

"I doubt he'd enjoy being likened to the son of God, but I get your point. Go on, Gary. And make sure you print that resume on high-quality resume paper. Not the regular kind you turn in to professors."

"Resume paper?" he asked. "What the hell is that? Oh my God, I'm going to screw this up, aren't I?"

Because she loved Gary, she put her hand on his back to calm him. "I have some resume paper at my house from when I was applying for jobs. Let's wrap things up here, and then we'll get it."

"Moira, you're the best!" He kissed her quickly on the cheek. "You're my new hero. I mean...my future has never looked so awesome."

Hearing that made her all the more convinced she was exactly where she was meant to be, working in Dare Valley as Artemis' director, helping young people like Gary. Some aspects of the future might still be a question mark, but at least she knew that.

CHAPTER 32

CHASE WAS SEEING RED. IF HE'D BEEN A BULL, HE WOULD have stomped the ground underneath him and charged straight toward his mortal enemy, Maurie Wallins. As if the mess with Gopal hadn't been bad enough, the man was now trying to steal one of their most critical teaming partners on the bid.

"Let me remind you, Douglas," he told the president of their largest subcontractor, "that you committed to Quid-Atch's bid over a year ago. We outlined a scope of work and a range of the possible level of effort—something you know I don't usually do—in the teaming agreement." Douglas Gadwershay, president of GreenSolutions, always drove a hard bargain, but he was pushing the limit this time.

"This isn't personal, Chase," Douglas said, tapping the massive table in the conference room they sometimes rented for business meetings like this at The Grand. "You know we work with both you and K-Barker depending on who we think is best positioned to win. We're not dropping out of the bid to join Maurie's team, but we have serious concerns about how things have been handled with Gopal. You know he worked for us in Brussels. He's really upset about being caught in the middle between Quid-Atch and K-Barker."

Chase wasn't alone for this shit show—Evan, Rajan, and Darren, Quid-Atch's VP of Operations, were also at the table—but he was running it. He let silence hang over the table for a moment while Darren reached for his water glass. Evan wasn't normally present for this kind of meeting, but Chase had thought it best to bring the full complement of Quid-Atch's executive team to show Douglas they meant business. Losing Gopal for this bid had been a blow. If GreenSolutions backed out, they'd lose the contract, no question.

"Gopal put himself in the middle when he signed a letter of commitment with K-Barker after committing to us beforehand," he said. "Douglas, it's not public yet, but as a gesture of good faith, we've offered Gopal a long-term contract with Quid-Atch, and he's accepted. Evan felt he would be a good asset to us despite this incident."

Douglas glanced at Evan. "I'm happy to hear that."

Evan nodded in response.

"But let's stick with the matter at hand," Chase continued. "You're asking for a greater share of this bid than we both agreed to months ago, and we just don't have it to give. We have other subcontractors."

"They aren't as key as we are, Chase," Douglas said, and he wasn't wrong. "This is a competitive bid. I want our level of effort to reflect that."

"Thirty percent more than reflects that, Douglas," Chase said. "And you damn well know it."

Douglas stared him down. "Maurie Wallins offered us forty percent recently, as I told you. Given your sudden leave of absence and Gopal's departure from your bid, we're not sure you have the edge to win."

Because Maurie was playing dirty and going after the arrangements Chase and his team had worked so hard to put in place. "You're trying to hold me hostage here, Douglas, and I don't like it."

But Chase couldn't walk out. Douglas ran a highly respected company of technical consultants that excelled in areas in which Quid-Atch was weaker.

"We're not saying we're going to jump ship like Gopal did, Chase," Douglas said through his perfect white teeth. "We only want to discuss amping up our role as a way of bolstering our collective chances to win this bid. Maurie is being more than aggressive this time. You need to have an answer for him. We think we're that answer."

Rajan released his breath slowly, audible enough for Chase to hear. Usually Rajan was the epitome of calm. He was the only person Chase knew who closed his office door and meditated for fifteen minutes during the work day.

"You shouldn't be discussing this bid with our rival, Douglas," Chase said, "and you damn well know it."

"We were talking about another project we have together with NATO," Douglas said, lying to his face. "You know Maurie. It simply came up."

Calling bullshit wouldn't get them anywhere. They needed to come to an agreement that would work for both of them. Damn it all to hell. Douglas had them by the balls, and he knew it.

"You've had your say," Chase said, "now I get to. Douglas, we do value what you and GreenSolutions bring to this bid and the rest of the projects we work on. None of us wants to damage our overall long-term working relationship, do we?"

Douglas shook his head. "Of course not, Chase. We never meant for you to think that."

"Good," he said, putting his hands on his knees to ground his anger. "I will promise to do my best to increase your level of effort. I can't give you a figure right now. You know how much things change as we work the budget. But you have my word. Are we good now?

Because I don't want to be looking over my shoulder tonight, wondering what you and Maurie are cooking up in the corner at the fundraiser."

Douglas smiled at him, the kind that said he appreciated holding Chase's balls and wouldn't squeeze any more tonight. "You have nothing to worry about, Chase. When Maurie and I meet at the party, the only talk we'll have is about our mutual enjoyment in golf."

Chase ground his teeth and smiled. "Wonderful. Then let's call this meeting to a close for now. Evan and I have some other business to see to before the fundraiser."

"Of course," Douglas said, rising. "See you there."

As soon as the door was closed, Rajan shot out of his chair. "Dammit! I want to strangle Douglas. He's always trying to re-negotiate and cut new deals."

Chase rubbed his forehead, finally showing his tension. His head was pounding. "I hate it too, but you know they're the best at what they do. That's why we have to put up with them. Not all our partners are our bosom buddies. That's government contracting for you."

"I think I'm still in shock," Evan said, standing up and putting his hands on his hips. "Is this how most of our partners are?"

"Not all of them, but yes, quite a few," Chase said, rubbing the back of his neck. "You don't usually see this side because you're inventing. We work with partners who want and need to make money. It's not a party all the time, but it's the way the system works."

"The system sucks," Evan said, frowning. "Why are we doing this? I mean, maybe we shouldn't go after government contracts anymore."

Rajan turned his head sharply to look at Evan. "What?"

Darren set his water glass aside with a loud clack.

Chase leaned back, striving for calm. "Evan, that's

high-minded, but not practical. You create inventions with military and defense applications. You can only legally sell products like that through government contracting."

"Right now, I'm questioning everything," Evan said. "Hell, I didn't want to tell you this because I knew it would raise your blood pressure, Chase, but Maurie waltzed into the ballroom earlier during setup and met Moira and Gary. He sweet-talked her and waxed poetic about being a fan of Arthur Hale's work. Then he turned to Gary and all but offered him a job on the spot, making sure it was okay with me first, of course. What the hell else could I say but yes?"

So Maurie had already made an early move, and on Moira too. Gary was small potatoes as far as Chase was concerned, but it was still an affront, although nothing like what Maurie had pulled recently with Gopal and Douglas.

"Is steam coming out my ears?" Chase asked, changing tacks.

Rajan nodded. "Yes. Mine?"

"Yep. We won't even ask Darren how he's feeling since we know."

"I'm thinking of bringing back tarring and feathering," Darren said, rubbing his forehead. "Especially if we have to bid Rajan in Gopal's place."

"I won't have it!" Evan barked out. "Not after seeing the kind of filth he'd have to work with. He's a genius, and they don't deserve him."

Rajan's face rippled with shock. "Thank you for that, Evan, but I've told you both I am happy to serve the greater good of Quid-Atch."

"GreenSolutions and this bid are not the greater good of Quid-Atch," Evan said, raising his voice with each word. "I did not create this company to work like this. Jesus, no wonder your head exploded, Chase."

"That was my concussion, Evan, but let's not quibble. It's always been like this. We have some great partners, ones who do a good job for us and honor our agreements, but issues like Douglas or Gopal are a dime a dozen." He wasn't going to mention any of the assholes they worked with *after* they won the government contracts. Evan was acting volatile enough.

"But people like Maurie and Douglas threaten our competitive edge, and they suck up the wellness and happiness of the people I care about. That's you, Chase, and Rajan and Darren."

"We know what we're dealing with," Chase said. It sickened him to think about it, but he'd been dealing with situations like this one for nearly a decade. It was the part that made everything seem worthless. "This will pass. We'll put forward the best bid possible and keep doing what we do."

"No, we don't," Evan said, his voice more emphatic than usual. "We won't have to go through this if we offer something no one else can sell."

Jesus, Boy Wonder was spinning tales all over. "One invention won't keep the company afloat, Evan," Chase told him. "We sell technical expertise and services to our country and our allies around the world. You don't get revolutionary ideas fast enough to bring in the capital we need to remain solvent."

"I've gone through our past financials," Evan said, shocking him. "When I do invent something new, the invention raises our corporate finances by thirty percent."

"In the past, yes," Chase said cautiously. "But we've expanded. We might reach a net gain of twenty-five percent with MAL-77, but I'm not betting the farm on it."

"What if we start working in a field that few companies are working in. One that's vital to the world's market?"

"What field?"

The smile Evan gave made him sit up a little straighter in his chair.

"Alternate energy."

Rajan's eyes turned feverish, and Darren leaned forward in his seat.

"All right," Chase said. "You have our attention. Do you want to walk us through what you're thinking?"

Evan glanced at his watch. "I'd love to. Let me grab my co-presenter."

That had Chase standing up. He had more than an idea? "Evan—"

"Trust me, Chase," Evan told him. "And you can trust our mystery guest too."

He opened the door, and in walked J.T. Merriam. Chase sat back down, partly out of shock, as the two men shook hands. Evan introduced Rajan and Darren to him and then J.T. walked over and gave Chase a firm handshake, looking him square in the eye.

"It's good to see you again," J.T. said.

"I can't say it's not a surprise to see you," Chase said, cocking a brow at Evan. "I thought you two met in Denver about some property."

"We did," Evan said, "but J.T. had this other idea he'd been tugging on and thought it might interest me."

Chase didn't appreciate hearing Evan had been making plans behind his back for the better part of a month with a man he barely knew. "I heard you resigned from your position at Merriam Oil & Gas and were planning on building an art museum in your spare time."

J.T. flashed him a genuine smile. "You're well informed."

"It seems a little odd to me that you might be an advocate of alternate energy, being a Merriam and all." Chase crossed his arms. "Your family swims in oil and gas."

J.T. nodded. "True, but it's a dwindling pool. It's not a renewable energy source, and the cost keeps rising. It's time to look for new energy solutions, ones more efficient, cleaner, and less political than the current ones. Evan thinks he can help with that."

Time to get down to brass tacks, Chase thought. "And what are you planning on offering to this effort, J.T.?"

The man held out his arms. "What I have in abundance. Money. Loads of it."

"J.T. wants to invest five hundred million dollars into this new venture, Chase." Evan put his hand on J.T.'s shoulder. "I would run the R&D. Rajan would be my right arm. There would be no government contracting. We would be like Apple. We would sell our products on the open market."

Holy shit, he was talking about closing down Quid-Atch, the company Chase had spent every waking moment striving to grow for the past ten years. "And what products would that be?" he asked cautiously, glancing at Darren, whose eyes had narrowed considerably.

"How about renewable batteries for homes as well as energy solutions for cities around the world? Smaller, more practical and affordable solutions using solar and wind power?"

Chase fought Evan's excitement. This vision would be a huge sea change. It was just like Evan to forget he already helmed another fully operational company with layer upon layer of responsibility. One that couldn't just be left by the wayside or transformed into whatever vision he'd formed overnight.

Evan unbuttoned his jacket. "All we need is a man with an incredible reputation, experience with making start-ups successful, and tested sales ability. This is going to happen in Dare Valley, by the way. J.T. thinks his great-great grandfather, Emmits Merriam, would want to have the company here, where he began to share his larger vision of the world through the university. That works for me since I've also made my home here."

Chase found he was holding his breath. Was Evan talking about creating a brand new company or altering Quid-Atch's corporate mission? "And do you have someone in mind for this position?"

Evan put his arm around J.T. and gave Chase a conspiratorial grin.

"You."

CHAPTER 33

WHEN CAROLINE RECEIVED MOIRA'S TEXTED REQUEST to help her deal with her makeup, she turned to give Andy and Danny the news.

"Moira needs help painting her face," she said as the young boy zoomed around the room making airplane sounds. "I'll be back in a while. Can you wait a little longer on the pizza?"

"Sure," Andy said, picking up a few of Danny's toys scattered in the corner. "Lucy might appreciate a little more time to touch up her photos. She's been working nonstop to meet her deadline. I was surprised she wanted to leave her cave to meet Chase last night."

"I know Moira was grateful," Caroline said.

Everyone had been on pins and needles about Lucy taking off to Lebanon for a week to take photos for a calendar about Syrian refugees. The trip had been heartbreaking, according to Lucy, but well worth it.

"Maybe you want family time, given how much Lucy has been working," Caroline said.

Danny let his toy fall to his side and gave her a puzzled look. "You're our family, Aunt Caroline."

Andy kissed her on the cheek. "Yes, she is. She's slow sometimes. Go help Moira. I'll feed the munchkin a snack if I need to."

"Great! See you later."

She dashed to her car and drove to Moira's house. There was a red Ferrari FF parked out front. Must be Evan. Only he would drive a car like that around Dare Valley.

Knocking on the door, she waited for her sister to answer.

"Hi," Moira said, opening it and welcoming her with a hug.

"You're all dressed and made up," Caroline said in a dry tone. "You look beautiful, in fact. I'm glad you took my advice on the navy dress, but am I missing something here? This hardly seems like a fashion SOS."

Moira put her hands on her shoulders and led her into the house. "Yes. Don't be mad. He's very persuasive, and I like him. Okay, I've gotta run. Have fun."

"What?" Caroline asked as she watched her sister grab her clutch and run out of the room. "Moira!"

"Hey, beautiful," she heard a familiar voice say.

She spun around to see J.T. standing in the doorway to the den. She felt a little light-headed suddenly, not only from the shock of seeing him, but also because he was wearing an Armani tuxedo. *Glory, that man was gorgeous.* "Oh my God! You're here! Why are you here?"

His smile was so wide that a dimple appeared in his right cheek. "I was in Dare Valley last minute and couldn't pass up the chance to see you. Thought it might be fun to surprise you. Moira thankfully agreed to help. How are you?"

"Ah...good. Fine. What..." She was babbling.

"I really need to greet you the Italian way," he said, taking one step toward her. Two.

Her heart crested to aerobic levels, and when she caught a whiff of his musky cologne, she had to firm up the weakness in her knees.

The smile faded from his face. He put his hands on her shoulders and simply looked down at her. "I missed you." Then he slowly kissed first her right cheek and then her left.

He surprised her by pulling her to him instead of stepping away. When he wrapped his arms around her, she found herself clutching him back. "I missed you too."

He traced her spine with a finger, sending a frisson of desire racing through her. "I'm glad. I wondered if this was a dumb idea—showing up last minute for the fundraiser so I could see you."

Leaning back to see his face, she was captivated by the intensity she saw there. "You used the fundraiser as an excuse to see me? I'm..." What the hell was she? "Flattered."

"You should be," he said grinning. "Even Trev assured me this move couldn't be construed wrong."

The full weight of his words settled over her, but instead of inflaming her fast-beating heart, it calmed it. "You couldn't wait until after I saw the other paintings?"

He shook his head. "No. I realized something a few months ago—the knowledge came at a price, but it's changed my life. You don't wait on joy. And Caroline, for me, you are pure joy."

Warmth exploded in her chest. "That's...I'm..."

"If you say you're flattered one more time..." He cupped her face. "Caroline."

"What?" she asked, settling closer to his body.

"Nothing. Just Caroline. I'm going to kiss you. Last chance to divert me."

She couldn't help it. She laughed. "Divert you? I can't imagine anyone doing that."

His face grew serious. "You could. I mean it. Once I kiss you, I'm going to want to be with you. Today I set even more plans into motion to bring me stateside again. Which I will tell you about later, if that's okay.

I still want your help on the art front and with a whole bunch of other things, but mostly, I just want *you*."

Her throat thickened, and she touched his face. They had details to work out, certainly, but although she was a detail-oriented person, she was content, for once, to let the details wait.

"Caroline Hale, where have you been all my life?"

He kissed her slowly at first, gently. Pressing his hand against the small of her back, he made her aware of how much he wanted her. Heat fanned out from the place he touched until she felt engulfed in a blissful fire. His tongue traced the seam of her lips, and she opened her mouth to heaven.

When he finally leaned back, he was smiling. "Well... that was better than even my over-active imagination could conjure up."

He'd been thinking about kissing her too? "I couldn't agree more."

Wrapping both arms around her, he rocked them in place. "Interested in being my date tonight?"

She linked her arms around his neck. "I'd love to, but your spontaneity has its limits. I don't have a suitable dress."

He made a raspberry sound with his mouth. "Is that your only concern? Give me some credit. My spontaneity has no limits. Come with me."

Her heart pounded in her chest as he drew her into Moira's dining room. She stopped short at the sight of a large golden dress box wrapped up with a giant red bow. "You didn't. You couldn't."

"I did," he said, picking up the box and holding it out to her. "Let's consider this repayment for the dress I threw mud on."

"How long have you really been planning on this?" She raised the top of the box and set it aside. "Are you sure you know my size?"

"I've been thinking about this for a few weeks—since Rome. I called your sister earlier to ask her where you were before I left Denver. And *please* give me some fashion credit. I told you Rome has given me a taste for fashion. I know something about sizes."

She parted the white tissue paper and gasped. The white strapless dress was dotted with gold crystals, and the fashion designer label boggled her mind. "Oh, my God! It's beautiful! J.T., I'm..."

"Flattered?"

"Speechless," she said, carefully drawing the dress out of the box and holding against her body. Sure enough, it looked like a perfect fit. "You're..."

"Crazy?" he asked, grinning.

"Wonderful," she said with a sigh. "But yes, this is a little crazy."

He kissed her lightly on the mouth. "I told you before. Welcome to my world."

Right now she couldn't imagine anywhere else she'd rather be.

CHAPTER 34

EVERYONE SEEMED TO BE ENJOYING THE FUNDRAISER SO far. Evan was holding court in one corner with a group of people she recognized as a combination of corporate executives and what Gary had called "mad inventor types." One of the guests had won the Fields Medal, another the Nobel Prize in Physics.

She felt totally intimidated—not her normal.

Perhaps it was because her mind was elsewhere. Chase seemed to have fallen off the face of the earth. He hadn't responded to any of her texts. Granted, she'd known he was in meetings with Evan and a few other people, but she'd thought she'd hear something. And Evan was here, wasn't he?

Looking around, Moira spotted Caroline walking into the ballroom with J.T. Holy crap, she looked gorgeous. Almost regal. And her dress... J.T. had been so endearing, enlisting her help in surprising Caroline. Her intuition had told her that her sister would be overjoyed, so she'd gone along with the ruse. J.T.'s arm was around her sister's waist, and there was no mistaking the attraction between them. Then he made her laugh, and happiness radiated from both of them.

"Is that our sister?"

She turned to see Natalie carrying a tray of champagne. "What are you doing out here, serving?"

"Chef T said he saw Caroline walk in with some good-looking guy when he was coming back through the lobby from checking a shipment. I had to see for myself. Take a glass of champagne. You look stiff."

A glass of bubbly sounded divine about now. "Nat, that's J.T. Merriam."

"Shut up. That's the mud slinger? Seriously, some people have all the luck in the genetic lottery."

She started laughing. "Reformed mud slinger."

They both watched them for a moment, then Nat whistled and said, "She's in deep with him. And he, her. Rome really must have been a weekend."

"I'm happy she's happy," Moira said.

"Why didn't I know she was his date tonight? I thought she was supposed to be having pizza with Andy and company."

"She thought so too," Moira said with a grin. "J.T. wanted to surprise her. He came in last minute."

"Where did she get the dress?" Natalie asked.

Moira spotted Chase coming into the ballroom with a man she didn't recognize. She took a step toward him before registering what she was doing. "I can't talk about this right now."

"And people are starting to wonder why I'm not serving," Natalie said, transferring her tray to her other hand. "We'll pick this up later."

"Sounds good," she said, already walking away

As Moira drew closer to Chase, anxiety rippled through her. There were hard grooves around his face indicating tension. She was so used to seeing him smiling, she realized. He caught sight of her approaching.

"You look beautiful," he said, leaning in and kissing her cheek.

She placed her hand on his good arm and met his

eyes. "You okay?"

He glanced at his companion. "Today hasn't gone like I expected. Have you met Rajan Singh, Vice President of Research and Development at Quid-Atch? Rajan, this is Moira Hale, Director of Artemis, and the orchestrator of tonight's amazing fundraiser."

Gosh, he was smooth. She'd rarely seen this side of him. Even though his sling was slightly visible under his tuxedo jacket, he radiated power. Chase Parker, global entrepreneur, was in the house. And he'd never seemed more distant from her.

Turning to Rajan, she extended her hand. "It's a pleasure to meet you. You work with Evan a great deal, from what I understand."

He nodded. "And Chase. The fundraiser seems to be going great. Congratulations."

"So far. Evan told me to keep an eye on a few people known to consume a little too much bubbly," she joked.

"Is my name on the list?" Rajan asked with a charming smile.

Chase chuckled. "You wish, Rajan. But tonight I might need to add my own name to that list. God, I need a drink."

The defeat in his voice pulled at her heart. What had happened? "Why don't you come with me, Chase? I'll find you a special bourbon."

He touched her arm, but then his gaze shifted to a point over her shoulder and he instantly tensed. She turned to see why.

"Chase!" Maurie called.

She felt him remove his hand from her immediately. While she understood he was trying to look powerful in front of the man he considered a competitor, it was hard not to feel slighted.

"Maurie," he said, stuffing his good hand into his pocket.

Moira wondered if he'd done it to avoid shaking hands with Maurie.

"You know Rajan, of course," Chase said.

"Of course, one of the most brilliant minds at Quid-Atch."

Maurie shook Rajan's hand, smiling the whole time.

"You don't need to introduce me to Moira," he told Chase, reaching for her hand and holding it. "I met Artemis' charming director earlier. Is your uncle, Arthur, here yet? I've been keeping an eye out and haven't seen him yet."

She actually hadn't either, but she'd been preoccupied. "I'm sure he's around somewhere."

"Likely talking to all of the incredible people you've invited to this event," Maurie said, smiling grandly at her. "I'm honored to be among them."

She could feel Chase simmering beside her, so she tugged her hand away from Maurie.

"If you'll excuse us, Maurie," Chase said, taking a slow step backwards. "Moira was just taking me to see something."

"So soon? Chase, I wanted to see how you were feeling. Your arm and leg look to be healing nicely. How is your head, though? Concussions are such a nasty business."

A razor-edged smile flashed across Chase's face. "So are some of the games you've been playing recently, Maurie. You'd be wise to remember what happens when my ire is invoked."

Moira stiffened at his tone while Rajan stepped closer to Chase as if ready to stand beside him in battle.

"I have no idea what you're referring to." Maurie flashed another smile, but this one didn't reach his eyes. "You'd be wise to remember those kinds of comments are defamatory. No one at K-Barker deserves to have such accusations leveled at them."

"You keep saying that, Maurie," Chase said, shaking his head, "but this isn't our first rodeo. Need I remind you?"

Moira wondered again what had happened between them.

"The roots of that business came from within your own home," Maurie said. "But let's set all that aside tonight. We're at a party, and we don't want to ruin Moira's big event talking about the past. My dear, thank you again for the invitation. I wish you a wonderful evening. Rajan, always a pleasure. Chase."

With a half-bow, Maurie turned and walked off.

Rajan shook his head. "Incredible."

"That's one word for it," Chase said tightly. "Since I can't stalk off to the bar for a drink after that confrontation, let's mingle a little until people stop watching us."

Were they watching? She casually scanned the crowd. Sure enough, there were a few pointed glances in their direction. Evan was still speaking with a few VIPs, but he kept darting glances in their direction.

"Have you met Senator Jawakski?" Chase asked her. "He's on the Appropriations Committee. I won't say he's a good friend, but he's respectable. Can't say that about all politicians."

No, they certainly couldn't. For the next thirty minutes, Chase introduced her to politicians, scientists, and even the defense ministers of France and Germany. Of course, she'd put together the guest list, but meeting so many august people in person was a totally different ball of wax. She felt like a fish out of water.

Caroline seemed to be having a fabulous time, and every time Moira darted a look at her, J.T.'s hand was on the small of her back. Of course, Caroline dealt with famous artists and art collectors all the time. Moira tried not to feel down on herself. She would get used to these kinds of people, these kinds of events.

This was her new world as the director of Artemis. And it was also Chase's world.

"I think we can safely find me a drink," he told her as they left the last group of people. "Rajan, why don't you make sure Evan isn't talking about anything other than Artemis tonight in his speech? I should have looked it over."

"It will be fine, Chase," Rajan said, his mouth tight.

"I wonder," Chase replied. "Let's go, Moira."

"Do you want to tell me what's going on?" she asked as she led him through the ballroom to the server entrance. Natalie would be able to find Chase a good bourbon.

"Not here," he said. "Later, you can tell me about your first encounter with Maurie. I'm glad he found you so charming."

His comment was laced with menace, and she didn't like that one bit. "He was the one who appeared out of nowhere earlier. I know you have some kind of feud going on with him, but don't drag me into it. He was pleasant to me."

"Of course he was," Chase said. "You work for Evan and me."

In all their time together, Chase had never referred to their business relationship that way. It didn't feel good. "I know you've had a tough day, so I'll make allowances, but you need to know I don't appreciate the way you're speaking to me right now. I haven't done anything to you."

Silence hung between them as they stepped into the kitchen, where Moira's sister was checking the line of salads waiting to be served for the first course. It was a visual warning that dinner was close to being served.

"Natalie! Chase needs your best reserve small-batch bourbon. Neat. Can you get him one?"

Natalie gave her a thumbs up and crooked her finger at one of the servers dressed in black.

Turning to face Chase, Moira said, "I need to get Evan to encourage people to find their seats. Are you okay to wait here?"

"Of course." Chase stopped her on her way to the door. "I'm sorry. There are things you don't know. Just... don't talk to Maurie. Okay?"

Angry heat made her skin prickle. "What am I supposed to do if I run into him? Give him the cut direct? Come on, Chase. I'm a professional. I thought you knew that."

His hand wrapped around her arm. "I know you are, but Maurie isn't. Moira, I'm not asking you. I'm telling you. Maurie is off limits."

She tugged her arm away. "What's wrong with you tonight? You're acting like a jerk."

He rubbed the back of his neck. "I don't mean to be. I'm feeling a little besieged. Go do your thing. Maybe a drink will calm me down."

Walking away from him, she took deep breaths to center herself. Evan was in the middle of a power crowd that included Maurie, a sight that made her want to snarl. Sure, Chase could order her not to speak to Maurie, but did the same rules apply to Evan? No, siree.

"Excuse me, Evan," she said, sidling close. "It's time."

He nodded. "Folks, if you could find your seats... I need to make an announcement."

Taking Moira's elbow, he led her up the steps to the raised podium. "Ready?"

"Yes," she answered, smoothing her hands down her sides.

"Good evening, ladies and gentlemen," Evan began. "I'm delighted everyone could join us for The Artemis Center's inaugural fundraiser."

There was a spattering of applause as conversations

stopped around the ballroom.

"As you know, I created this center to be on the forefront of invention and innovation, supporting the world's brightest young minds as they tackle the world's biggest problems. I'm honored to be joined in my vision by Moira Hale, Artemis' director."

He stepped back and gestured to her, and she smiled as more people applauded. Moira caught Caroline lifting a glass of champagne to her, and the sight of her sister eased some of the tumult in her belly.

"We're also delighted to announce dinner is ready to be served, so if everyone would find their seats, we'd be most grateful. I'll be speaking more about Artemis after you've had a chance to enjoy The Grand Mountain Hotel's fabulous cuisine. Thank you."

For the rest of the night, Moira refused to allow anything to distract her from doing her job. She sat next to Evan at the head table, and when Chase chose a seat that was as far away from her as possible—or so it seemed—she merely nodded at him. He was between Rajan and another man Evan had identified as Quid-Atch's vice president of marketing and sales, and whatever they were discussing only deepened Chase's glower. She caught Evan watching the scene as well, but he kept up a steady conversation with the chancellor of Emmits Merriam University.

Evan's speech was particularly inspiring, and it helped reaffirm her happiness in being on board.

When the official evening had concluded, a line of people appeared to meet her. She mostly listened as the people spoke—some scientists, some corporate executives, some politicians. There were a lot of nuances beneath the small talk, she soon realized. People knew she had Evan's ear, so many of them were telling her information they hoped she would convey to him.

Her head was hurting by the time J.T. finally barreled

in on a conversation.

"Mind if I steal her away, Senator Pollard?" he asked. "I haven't had a chance to speak to her all night, and I need to head out shortly."

As J.T. drew her away, she asked, "You're really leaving? For Rome?"

"Good God, no," he said. "Your sister told me to rescue you. She said you were reaching your limit on the mingling meter."

That was one way to put it, she thought. "It wasn't all that bad."

"Moira!"

Suddenly Maurie was intercepting them.

"I wanted to thank you for hosting such an incredible evening," he said, reaching for her hand. "You're going to do incredible things here at Artemis. I can't wait to see."

She found herself fearing Chase would see her with him, but then she shook it off. He had no right to give her orders like that. There was nothing underhanded about this.

"Thank you for coming, Maurie. I hope you have a safe trip back to Washington."

"I wish I could take tomorrow off and ski," he said, giving her a wink. "The slopes look amazing here."

"They are," she replied. J.T. urged her with his elbow to move on, but before she could say her goodbyes, Maurie took a good look at her companion and said, "Aren't you J.T. Merriam?"

He nodded. "I am. I don't believe I've had the pleasure."

"Maurie Wallins of K-Barker," he said, shaking the man's hand. "You just resigned your position with Merriam Oil & Gas, didn't you? How are you hooked up with Ms. Hale and Artemis?"

"I've known the Hale family since I was a kid, and

Moira was kind enough to invite me since my great-great grandfather created the university Artemis is attached to. Thought it would be nice." He leaned closer to Maurie. "Plus, her sister is my date. Childhood sweetheart. You know how it is."

Color her surprised. He was laying it on thick.

Maurie chuckled. "Indeed. Good for you. I didn't know the Merriams still had connections in Dare Valley."

"Are you kidding?" J.T. said. "My family has been part of Dare Valley for decades. It'll always be like a second home. Maurie, I hate to cut this short, but I kept my date waiting, and she's probably wondering what's keeping us."

Moira decided to help him out. "You don't want to get on my sister's bad side."

"Of course," Maurie said, slapping him on the back.

Once they were far enough away, she said quietly, "You lied six ways to Sunday back there. Why?"

"I don't want him to start wondering why I'm here," he said. "Not a big deal, but it would be better if he doesn't think too hard about it."

Why wasn't anyone making sense tonight? First Chase had gone off the rails, and now J.T. "I don't understand."

He gave her a wink. "I know. But you will. Don't worry. I'm just being paranoid."

Was she really supposed to settle for that explanation? "Because of Maurie?"

"No, I'd have said that to anyone." He kissed her on the cheek. "Okay, you're free. Do you need any help wrapping things up? I can take Caroline home and then come back for you."

Her brow rose at this. "And just where is Caroline's home tonight?"

He chuckled. "Your place, she said. Ah...she thought you'd be staying at Chase's, and she worried we'd keep your mom awake talking into the night."

Was that all they were planning to do? *Hmmm...*

"I'll be fine," she said, though part of her wondered if she *would* be staying with Chase. He was in such a rotten mood, and she didn't like the way he'd talked to her earlier, especially since he'd spent the rest of the night ignoring her. "If I end up staying at my house, is that going to be a problem?"

His mouth twitched. "No. We'll whisper like church mice...or drive back to Denver. I couldn't get a room at The Grand last minute. The only flaw in my spontaneous plan."

"You seem pretty quick on your feet," she said, gesturing to his fancy Italian shoes.

"When you're a reputed mud slinger, you have to be," he said. "Thanks again for your help earlier."

"You're welcome. Like I told Natalie, you're a reformed mud slinger."

Laughing, he headed out of the ballroom. She looked around to see if Uncle Arthur was still present. She hadn't said more than two words to him before dashing off to talk to the various guests. She turned and nearly ran into Gary.

"Moira! I was waiting for you to finish up. I'm sorry, but I need your help."

"What's the matter?" she asked.

He held up the burgundy resume folder she'd given him along with the resume paper. "I didn't give Mr. Wallins my resume."

"Oh."

"He was always talking to someone, and I didn't want to barge in on one of his conversations... You know?" He bounced on his heels. "I really wanted to give this to him."

"Why don't you leave it at the front desk for him?" she suggested.

"Will you go with me? I thought of that, but I wasn't sure they'd take it from me. I mean, he's a famous guy, and I'm a nobody."

Moira put a hand on Gary's arm. "You aren't a nobody. You're a PhD student with a bright future ahead, and one of the best office assistants I've ever had."

"Really?" he asked, his necktie a little crooked after the evening.

"Really," she said. "Come on. We'll get this resume delivered."

Chase's warning about Maurie came to mind, but he was being ridiculous, wasn't he? Besides, Evan had approved this.

As they passed the bar in the lobby, Gary grabbed her hand, his grip so tight she almost squealed.

"He's in the bar!" Gary exclaimed. "Oh, my God. I'm going to hyperventilate. Oh, my God."

"Calm down, Gary," she told him.

He thrust out the folder. "You give it to him. I can't do it."

Maurie was having drinks with someone. "We'll do it together."

"I've sweated through my shirt," he said, opening his suit jacket. "I'm a mess. I sweat when I get nervous." His stomach gurgled. "Uh-oh. I...need to find a bathroom. I also get tummy problems when I'm nervous."

This was a new side of Gary, one they'd have to work on before he started his way up the corporate ladder.

"Okay, I'll give it to him." He went to hug her, and she stopped him with a hand. "Let's keep it cool."

"Right! Thank you, Moira. You're the best!"

She shook her head as he darted off toward the restrooms. Heading into the bar, she made her way to Maurie. *Keep it quick. Just give him the folder.*

"Excuse me, Maurie," she said quietly from behind him.

He turned on his bar stool and broke out into a smile. "Moira! How wonderful to see you. Have you come to have a drink with me?" He gestured to the man beside him. "This is Albert Mann, the director of the National Academy of Science."

She nodded to the older man. "I'm afraid I'm still closing things down for the event, but I dashed out to find you. Do you remember the young PhD student you met earlier with Evan and me? You asked him for his resume, and he wanted to make sure you didn't leave without it."

"Of course, Gary, right? A bright kid. Is he here? I'd love to buy him a drink."

She wasn't sure Gary would impress a future employer in his current state, but that wasn't her decision. "If I see him, I'll be sure to pass on the invitation."

Moira extended the resume to Maurie. "I'll let you two get back to your drinks."

Someone snatched the folder from her hand before Maurie could take it. Her head swiveled automatically, and her heart stopped when she saw that it was Chase.

"I thought I'd made myself clear earlier," he said, staring Maurie down. "Stop messing with my people."

Maurie stood up. "You're making a fool of yourself, Chase. Must be the concussion. There's so much concerning scientific evidence on the negative impacts of a concussion on a person's behavior."

Moira appreciated Maurie trying to help Chase save face. Right now, it was more generous than he deserved.

"Chase—"

"Stay out of this, Moira," he said in a tight voice. "You and I will talk later."

She felt like he'd slapped a dunce cap on her head and put her in the corner for bad behavior. How dare he!

"Maurie, I'm talking to our legal department first thing tomorrow," Chase ground out. "You've crossed the last line."

Maurie shook his head. "Moira, you should find Evan and ask him to help you take Chase home. I'd offer, but my presence here seems to be agitating him. Albert, let's find another place to continue our talk. Good luck, my dear."

Chase got in Maurie's face as he tried to step aside. "You don't wish her luck. You don't speak to her."

Moira grabbed his arm. "Stop this! Stop this right now!"

Maurie took full advantage of the distraction, putting his arm around Albert and leading him away. As soon as they were gone, Chase slapped the folder on the bar.

"I told you not to speak to him," Chase whispered under his breath. "But this? I didn't see it coming."

She looked around the bar. Given the late hour, there was only a cluster of people present. "Not here." She couldn't rip into him in public.

"I don't want to talk about this," he said. "Ever."

"Too bad. I'll meet you at your house once I'm finished here. After you open that folder you're so upset about."

His gray eyes smoldered.

"Open it," she ordered.

He flipped the burgundy folder open. The way his eyes widened in shock should have made her feel better. It didn't, though.

Maybe nothing would.

CHAPTER 35

CHASE ARRIVED HOME TO FIND BARNEY AS OUT OF SORTS as he was. The poor kitten was curled up in the center of Chase's old scooter, and he gave him a mournful look when he burst in through the front door.

"I'm sorry," he found himself saying as he picked up the kitten. "I know you were alone a lot after Bonnie left today, but I had a miserable day too." On the way home in one of The Grand's private cars, Chase had concluded today ranked in his top five worst days of all time.

Evan was talking about concluding their work in government contracting, and he and J.T. Merriam had planned what sounded like a new company—or a revised Quid-Atch, dammit!—behind Chase's back. If he hadn't been so out of the loop lately or tied up with Moira, this might never have happened.

Right now, he didn't know which way was up, and to make matters worse, he'd learned over dinner that Maurie was causing trouble with their government contacts in Berlin and London by suggesting Chase's leave of absence might be a sign of some bigger issues at Quid-Atch. After hearing Evan's crazy, obscure plans, he had to conclude Maurie was on to something.

It didn't help one bit that Maurie was doing *everything*

he could to undermine Quid-Atch's competitiveness and rattle him—something he'd obviously succeeded in doing. When he thought of their altercation at the bar over what had turned out to be Gary Frehlich's resume, he was ashamed of himself. It hadn't been one of his finer moments, but the sight of Moira handing that son of a bitch a business folder had been enough to break him. His mind had flashed to Trisha in that instant, and he hadn't been able to stop himself from going nuclear.

And Moira...she was rightly pissed at him, but part of him thought it was her own fault. If she'd stayed away from Maurie like he'd asked, this never would have happened. Sure, she didn't know any details, but she should have listened.

His phone rang, so he set Barney down and pulled it from his pocket. It was Evan. Not being one to put off a call, he picked it up.

"You rang?" he said. Though he could hear the sarcasm in his own voice, he didn't feel the urge to dial it back.

"I heard about your fight with Maurie in the bar," Evan said. "Are you okay? I won't ask what happened. I've heard from both Moira and Maurie. Your enemy expressed his deep concern for you given your behavior tonight. I know you were upset, but what in the hell were you thinking?"

"You don't want to call me on the carpet right now, Evan," he said. "I acted poorly, and I know that, but we're facing bigger issues right now. Maurie is doing a great job of undermining Quid-Atch beyond just the bid. I spoke with a few of our international partners at the fundraiser, and I need to fly to Europe to handle some problems he's created."

Everything seemed to be falling apart around him, and he was having trouble mustering the energy to roll up his sleeves and wade in again.

"You're not cleared for international travel yet," Evan said quickly. "Let me go—"

"No," Chase shot back. "You're talking about changing everything that's made Quid-Atch successful. You're the last person I'd send. And don't talk about all your new ideas to our board of directors, Evan, because they aren't going to like it. I sure as hell don't."

Silence permeated the line for what seemed an eternity. "You think I'm trying to undermine you? I was trying to come up with a better business strategy that wouldn't see you hitting a wall, competing against assholes like Maurie. One that wouldn't keep the people I care about from spending their whole lives away from their families."

"Are you talking about getting rid of Quid-Atch or completely changing our mission? I'm confused, Evan, and really pissed off."

There was an even longer silence on the line. "Honestly, I don't know. All I know is that I don't like the way things are and think we need to do something different."

Chase couldn't believe what he was hearing. "Until recently, you never cared what it took to make Quid-Atch successful. This is how it is, Evan. You can't just change your mind. We have legally binding contracts and thousands of employees! Also, it's totally unprofessional to discuss these *new ideas* with an outsider and not me."

"Dammit, I thought we were better friends than this," Evan said. "Chase, J.T. brought these ideas to *me* when we had lunch in Denver. He's going through a major philosophical overhaul about doing business too. I agree with him across the board about the politics and greed. I think his ideas are damn good, and I also believe they're financially viable. Can we sit down and talk about them? Today was just a primer. You're the one who always creates the plan."

He walked over to the window to open it, needing fresh air to cool him down. "I don't have time. I'm leaving for D.C. in the morning with Darren and Rajan. Once I assure everyone at HQ that the sky isn't falling, I'm going to fly to Europe and start knocking on doors. We're in trouble, Evan." He still wasn't sure what to do about Maurie's sabotage plans, but he'd think of something when he talked to legal in the morning.

"Andy hasn't cleared you for full-time work yet or travel," Evan said. "I want—"

"You don't want to get in my way, Evan," Chase said. "I'm going to hang up before I say something I might regret, but you might reflect on how you want to work with me moving forward. You can't keep things like this from me. And come morning, my phone and email had better be *fully* operational."

Pocketing his phone, he felt Barney paw at his leg. When he picked him up, the kitten crawled into his tuxedo jacket. "You cold? I'm blazing hot." He wished he could go for a run. Usually it helped him burn off his anger. And he was mad as hell at Evan for pulling this shit on him.

Headlights appeared in the driveway, and he laid his forehead against the cold window pane. What was he supposed to say to Moira? Right now, his whole life seemed to have fallen apart.

She didn't knock. No, she barged in with a gust of cold air. Her face was flushed, and he knew she was pissed. Barney, who'd popped his head out, ducked back under the jacket after taking one look at her.

Moira slammed the door and then stalked to the dining room table and set down her clutch. No, threw it.

"How dare you!" she began. "I've been trying to see your side of things since I left the hotel, but I can't get past how much you just insulted me. Someone you said you respected professionally. Worse, someone you profess to love. Did you really believe I would hand something confidential to Maurie Wallins or anyone else? Especially after sharing your bed?"

The force of her anger washed over him, and he felt the pain in his head crescendo to epic proportions. Screw legal, he decided. If he didn't tell her, she'd never understand. "My ex-wife shared my bed, and she still gave Maurie confidential information. Of course, she also slept with him."

Shock rippled across her face, and she wrapped her arms around herself. Score one for him.

"I didn't know," she said in a strained voice.

"No, you didn't. I'm legally not supposed to talk about it to anyone. I didn't act well earlier. I know that, and I'm sorry. Maurie is already doing his damnedest to make the most of my loss of judgment."

Her hands fell to her sides, and he could tell her anger was waning. His was changing too, and the hurt he felt had teeth.

"Why wouldn't you listen to me when I told you not to talk to him?" he asked. "Why couldn't you trust I had a *really* good reason?"

She looked down and took her time before answering. "Because Evan said it was okay. I was only giving him a resume after Gary turned into a total mess about it. *A resume.*"

He shook his head. "It's never just a resume with Maurie. You and Evan got played today, and I stepped right in to execute my part as well. That stops now. Maurie is orchestrating an insidious plot to undermine me—and Quid-Atch—at every turn."

He couldn't mention the fact that Evan seemed to be as well.

"Well, you certainly helped him tonight, didn't you?" She glared at him. "You hurt me, dammit."

He felt his throat thicken and fitted Barney closer

to him. "You hurt me too, Moira. And you weren't the only one today." He took a deep breath, thinking about Evan. "I'm leaving tomorrow morning. After hearing all the shit that's going down with Quid-Atch, I have a lot of holes to plug if we're going to continue to be successful."

She clenched her hands into fists by her side. "I see. What about us?"

Pain radiated through his chest, but after all the work he'd done with Ally, he knew it wasn't physical. He would find a way to deal with it somehow. "I love you, and I'll always be grateful for our time together, but this has been an interlude out of time. There's no way we can be together in reality, not with the way my life is—or yours. I have responsibilities I've neglected, and Quid-Atch is suffering from it. A lot of people depend on me. I can't let them down."

He watched as she closed her eyes and bit her lip. Everything in him wanted to cross the room to her, comfort her, tell her there was a way for them to both have what they wanted. But that would be a lie.

Isn't that would he'd realized today? He *couldn't* have everything he wanted. It didn't matter how much he wanted it.

"I see you've made up your mind then," she said, finally opening her eyes. "Good luck getting everything squared away at Quid-Atch."

She crossed over to the table and picked up her clutch. He fitted Barney even closer to him as he watched her walk to the door.

"Goodbye, Moira," he said softly.

Her hand closed around the doorknob. She took a deep breath before looking up and gazing at him one last time. "Goodbye, Chase."

He moved to the window to watch her pull away and stood there until the pain in his body grew too great to bear.

CHAPTER 36

MOIRA DROVE HOME ON AUTOMATIC PILOT. PART OF her couldn't believe Chase was ending things between them after everything they'd experienced together. It was exactly what she'd feared, but she'd thought their love was stronger than that. She'd thought he was committed to finding a way for them to be together without compromising their careers.

After hearing how horribly his ex-wife had betrayed him, she was afraid he'd never truly be able to trust her. Hadn't he proven that at the bar when he'd grabbed the folder from her hand? He had deep issues influencing his life, but it wasn't her responsibility to fix them.

She wasn't even sure she could.

When she pulled into her garage, she stayed in her car. God, Caroline was inside there with J.T. She thought about going to Natalie's house, but this was her house, dammit. All she wanted to do was curl up in her bed.

The door to the garage opened, and she saw Caroline and J.T. in the doorway. Fully clothed, thank God. Her sister jogged forward and opened her car door.

"Moira, are you all right?"

She shook her head. "It's over. He's leaving. He..." Oh, God, the pain was rising over her, as unstoppable as a tide.

"Oh, honey," Caroline said, leaning down to her level. "Come on. We'll get you into a hot shower, and then you can tell me all about it."

She wasn't sure she wanted to talk about it at all. Right now she was desperate to forget the way Chase had clutched Barney to his chest while telling her they were through. How could that stupid man love a cat and not her?

"He's a fucker," she told Caroline, letting her sister help her out of the car.

"Of course he is," Caroline said, putting her arm around her and leading her inside. "How could he possibly leave you if he wasn't?"

"Tell me who he is," J.T. said, "and I'll beat the crap out of him."

"Chase Parker, CFO extraordinaire, hothead, and stupidest man on the planet," she told him.

"Consider it done," J.T. said. "But I feel like I might have added to his bad day."

Right now she didn't care. "Doesn't excuse him."

But her rage sloughed off inside the shower, replaced by a deep sadness that sent tears cascading down her cheeks. Caroline finally pulled her from the shower and dried her off as she cried. Then she wrapped her in a fuzzy pink robe, laid her on her bed, and put her arms around her.

"He's so stupid," Moira repeated over and over again. "I can't believe I fell in love with him."

She fell asleep with everything hurting, and when she woke up in the morning, she was sure lead had filled her veins. Caroline was gone, and she felt tears pool in her eyes when she remembered her sister's kindness the night before.

She needed coffee and another hot shower. Today, she'd take it easy and wash Chase out of her hair, so to speak. Tomorrow she'd start anew at Artemis and focus on all of the good stuff in her life.

Leaving her bedroom, she heard whispering coming from the kitchen. When she entered, J.T. and Caroline looked up. Both were still wearing their clothes from the night before. An empty bottle of wine and two glasses sat between them.

"Have you two been up all night?" she asked.

Caroline rose from her chair and hugged her, not saying anything. When Moira shifted her gaze to J.T., she caught him frowning. He'd said something last night about adding to Chase's bad day. She wondered...no, Chase was no longer her concern.

"I'm making coffee," she said after releasing Caroline. "Want some?"

J.T. nodded and rose. "I'm going to take a shower and change, if that's okay. I need to leave soon as well, but I'll take that coffee to go."

She looked at the two of them. "You're just going to leave too?" What was wrong with some men? Suddenly she wasn't so sure about J.T.

"I'm going to give Chase a ride to D.C.," J.T. told her somberly. "Evan and I have a plan. I can't promise I'll be able to change his mind on the personal front, but I'll do my best. I can be pretty persuasive when I put my mind to it."

Shocked, she watched him wink at her and then leave the kitchen.

"What in the hell?" she asked.

Caroline wrapped her arm around her waist and said, "Isn't he wonderful?"

Moira planned to reserve judgment after her own experience with Chase.

CHAPTER 37

CHASE WAS COMPLETELY PACKED BY THE TIME BONNIE arrived. He could have had her stop coming after his casts were taken off, but since neither she nor Andy had raised the issue, he'd let it ride. He'd come to enjoy her company.

Today it ended.

And so did his time with Barney.

Cupping the tabby kitten in his lap, he closed his eyes and savored the soothing purr. He couldn't believe he'd gotten so attached to this little fur ball, or that he felt emotional about leaving him behind. But he did. He was feeling emotional about everything, it seemed.

Especially Moira.

All night he'd lain in bed, his head pounding, his chest tight, wishing he'd handled things differently. Been calmer. More apologetic. Kissed her one last time.

Bonnie arrived on time, and Chase stood to greet her with Barney cradled in his arms. She looked at the suitcases by the door.

"You're leaving," she said simply. "I wondered if you'd jump the gun. You're still not completely healed, but I imagine you know that."

"The bones will heal the rest of the way, and so will my

head at some point," he said, although after yesterday, he feared the headaches were going to be stronger than ever. He'd been so hopeful the acupuncture and healing sessions would permanently banish them, but now he knew they were triggered by work.

"You heart may not heal if you leave now," Bonnie said. "From the greenish cast of your face, I'd say things are finished with Moira?"

Bonnie had never minced words, but this time she'd managed to pull his chain. "That's not your concern."

She shook her head. "Despite how hardheaded you can be, I've come to like you, Chase Parker, so I'm going to tell you what I see. You have two roads ahead of you, the one you had and a new one of your own making. Do you really want to go back to your old life? How was it working for you? Were you happy? Because you were a bump on a log when I first set eyes on you, and in the past weeks, you've changed into a much happier, more enjoyable man."

Something inside him was moved by the rightness of her words, but he couldn't let it affect his decision. Quid-Atch's interests were in trouble, and it was largely his fault. Maurie had made sure of that.

"This is vacation. It was a sojourn from reality," he said, mimicking what he'd said to Moira.

"Reality is what you make it," she said in a strong voice. "I had high hopes you had the courage to make yours into something new."

For a time, he'd thought so too, but that was over now. "I have people who depend on me. Leaders don't always have the freedom to do what they want. That's something Evan doesn't understand." His boss and friend had the luxury of spending years, if needed, to turn a wild thought into reality. Not everyone could live that way. Nothing would get done.

"I think Evan has the right idea about life from what

I can see," she said, "and he certainly cares about you. Maybe he has more of the right answers than you think."

For himself perhaps, but not for Chase and certainly not for Quid-Atch. Chase felt Barney paw at his stomach. "I've appreciated you letting me spend time with your cat." He made himself walk over to her with Barney.

Her round face turned stern. "Barney isn't my cat, Chase. Evan said you used to like them when you were a kid, so he asked me to find one for you. He even named it after a barn. Get it? Barn cat?"

"But how did he know?" Chase asked, shifting his weight. "I—"

"You might ask him," she said, shaking her head.

Suddenly a light bulb went on. Chase suspected Evan had arranged for him to have a rental that looked like his old house. Thinking about his friend's kindness, of the efforts Evan had gone to for him, made Chase wish they weren't at odds at the moment.

Bonnie came over and patted him on the shoulder before turning away again. "I'm not one for goodbyes, so I'll head out since you're leaving too. I wish you all the love and happiness in the world, Chase. I'm just not sure you'll accept it."

"Wait!" he said as she walked to the door and opened it. "I can't take Barney with me. I travel. I work—"

"Not my problem," Bonnie said. "But if you give that cat away, you'll discover I can live up to the fearsome name of Helga."

He followed her onto the porch, but she wasn't stopping. "This is ridiculous!"

"I couldn't agree more," she called out as she got into her car.

Looking down at Barney, he shook his head. "Evan got you for me? What in the hell was he thinking?"

He knew what his friend was thinking. This was another of the Pollyanna inventor's crazy schemes.

Checking his watch, he noted he had ten minutes to get ready before Rajan and Darren picked him up. Time to check his phone. Sure enough, it was fully operational.

Chase made his way through the house one last time, checking to make sure he had everything. He felt a tug of longing when he looked at the smoker on the back patio. It had been fun, exploring that hobby again. Maybe he could buy one for his house in Virginia.

Except he was never home.

He hated that house.

The last item he needed to make peace with was the Home Sweet Love pillow. He'd wanted to give it to Bonnie, but the damn woman had shocked him by leaving without taking Barney with her. He'd forgotten all about it. While he didn't want to leave it, he couldn't bear to take it either.

He'd give it to Moira. That was it. She liked homey things with sayings on them. Her whole house was full of them. He'd never given her anything, he realized. Well, maybe she could remember him fondly someday. And if he couldn't give her his heart...

He wrote a quick note to her before he changed his mind.

Dear Moira,

You know the history of this pillow my mom made and everything it survived. I want you to have it. I hope one day the words will become your reality.

Chase

He looked at the letter. Reality? Isn't that what Bonnie had just said? He picked it up to ball up the paper and start over, but couldn't. He really did wish her Home Sweet Love.

It just couldn't be with him.

He heard the crunch of tires on the snow and left the note next to the pillow. He'd text Evan about it getting it to her.

Looking around the house one last time, he had a moment of deja-vu. In one frame, he saw the home he'd grown up in, the one that had been taken away by fire. In another frame, he saw the home he'd enjoyed these past weeks, cozied up in front of the fireplace with Moira, Barney curled up on his lap.

Chase wasn't meant for home and hearth, but this time he wasn't being forced out by an act of nature. He was leaving it of his own accord.

A knock sounded on the door, and he crossed the living area to open it.

J.T. Merriam filled the doorway. "Hi! There's been a change of plans. Rajan and Darren had to leave earlier. I have my plane in Denver, and I'm going to give you a ride to D.C."

Chase wanted to punch him in the mouth for his interference—at Evan's request, he expected. "You're just going to give me a ride? I can wait for my own plane."

"Look, I know you're probably more than a little pissed at me, and Evan too. In your shoes, I might feel the same way. Hey, is that your cat? What a sweetheart. Is he coming with us?"

Barney took the opportunity to jump into the man's open arms. Chase wanted to growl. "I need to focus on Quid-Atch business right now."

J.T. scratched the kitten behind the ears, obviously a total pro. "I'd like you to hear me out. Plus, you need the ride. Why wait a few more hours when I'm offering my plane?"

"You aren't going to change my mind about anything," Chase said, giving him a pointed look. "Not that I completely understand what the hell Evan is thinking right now."

A dimple appeared in J.T.'s cheek. "You might be surprised. We have a lot more in common than you realize. A few months ago I had a major gut check—like your accident seems to have been for you. It's made me look at everything differently. Let me put your bags in the car. I'll tell you everything on the way to Denver. If I haven't convinced you to listen to more, you can take my plane without me. All I ask is that you send it back for me so I won't be stranded here. Agreed?"

The man knew how to drive a hard bargain. "Agreed. And yes, we're taking the cat."

"Great! I love them. Been trying to decide if I want to get a dog or a cat. I might just get both because why the heck not?"

No wonder J.T. and Evan were chatting about working together—they were both off their rocker. He let the man grab his bags and turned to take one final look at the house.

As he closed the door, he felt like he was closing the door on two chapters, the past he'd loved and the future he'd dreamed about for only a moment.

CHAPTER 38

OR THE LAST TWO WEEKS, MOIRA HAD DONE NOTHING but run her brains out in her spare time. Saturdays had turned into extra-long burn fests. At exactly eight o'clock in the morning—weather permitting—she met her brother-in-law, Blake, and Andy and Matt for a ten-mile run.

Until Chase had broken her heart, leaving her with nothing but his Home Sweet Love pillow, she'd never been serious about workouts. In running, she'd found a new calling. It never failed her. Despite how busy her mind was or how hurt her heart felt, everything inside her calmed by mile two. She felt lighter, more focused. Less emotional.

She ran during the week by herself or with one of her running partners—depending on who had time—and being around a bunch of guys was refreshing. No one asked her to talk about her feelings. Well, except for Andy, but he didn't press her about it. She'd told him she needed time to sort through things on her own, and he'd accepted that.

The rest of her family had been supportive, of course, with surprise visits punctuated with bread, chocolate, or wine—the three most important breakup foods on the planet, if you asked Jill.

Evan didn't press her either. He'd taken Chase's pillow back when she'd refused to accept it and hadn't said another word about it. They saw each other at family events and when he came to Artemis, of course. But he'd relieved her mind by telling her she was solely reporting to him—not Chase.

Apparently Chase had nothing to do with Artemis anymore.

She wanted to know why, of course, but she managed not to ask.

As for what Chase was up to, she had no idea. Quid-Atch business, she expected. It didn't matter. It was none of her concern now, and whenever she found herself missing him, she'd take a moment and breathe through it. Or eat a piece of chocolate and remind herself she was better off without some stupid man.

Gary was also a sweetheart, telling her he planned to do everything he could for the rest of his life to thank her for *trying* to give Maurie Wallins his resume when he'd turned into a sweaty, gurgly mess. Fortunately, Evan had shared his concerns about Maurie's ethics with Gary, prompting the young man to exclaim, "Man, I really dodged a bullet there." Perhaps sensing her occasional somber mood, Gary kept up the practical jokes, and she retaliated in kind. He'd never know how grateful she was for his easy, fun presence at the office.

Every day, she continued to implement the initial phases to make Artemis the most impressive center for invention and innovation on the planet. And she felt proud of that.

This Saturday morning, they were running in twenty-degree weather laced with a cold north wind. She made sure to watch for ice on the path that fanned out from The Park of Sunset Dreams, the park Matt had personally named after becoming the town's mayor. He and his wife, Jane, had met here with their dogs and fallen in love.

"You're on fire today," Blake said, keeping to her pace, something he often did.

"I love running," she told him. "Can't believe it took me this long to discover it."

She and Blake settled into a silent rhythm. He was always by her side, a comforting presence, which she knew was intentional. Matt and Andy were shooting the shit in the rear like usual.

It was another great day to be in the Hale family, she decided.

By the time she waved goodbye to her men—as she liked to think of them—she was feeling lighter. Not happy. She hadn't felt that since she and Chase had quit each other. But it was a start.

There was a familiar red Ferrari FF in front of her house, and she had to smile. Caroline never knew when J.T. was going to pop up, and that mostly delighted her. He had revealed himself to be a real gentleman. He'd told Caroline, who'd in turn told Moira, that he didn't want to move things forward until he could ensure there were no secrets between him and Caroline. Which meant he'd put the brakes on their physical relationship until he could reveal the full extent of his super-secret plans.

When Moira walked into the kitchen, she shook her head. "Please make yourself at home, J.T."

He turned from his place at her stove and grinned. "I think your apron looks pretty good on me."

Caroline gazed at him adoringly. "When you make me pancakes, you can wear anything you want."

"I have bacon too," he said to Moira with a wink. "Oh, and I brought you a treasure trove of goodies from Rome. Don't tell Natalie. I'm afraid she might kill me for not sharing."

He'd become reacquainted with everyone in the

Hale family in the past two weeks, and there had been a lot of talk about the old times when the Merriams had been a force to be reckoned with in Dare Valley, working with the Hales. In fact, J.T. became downright nostalgic whenever the topic came up. He and Uncle Arthur were tight these days.

"I'm going to take a shower," she told them. "Make sure there's coffee for me when I return."

J.T. winked. "Already planned."

Moira gave in to the luxury of stretching her muscles in the steamy shower. By the time she finished dressing, her stomach was growling. She decided to forgo makeup for the moment but eyed her wet hair. Well, it wasn't like she cared what J.T. thought.

Walking out of her bedroom, she headed into the kitchen. "My coffee had better be ready," she called out, knowing to announce her presence to the lovebirds.

When she walked in, she stopped short. Chase sat at her kitchen table, Barney on his lap. J.T. and Caroline were nowhere in sight.

"What are—"

"Hello, Moira." He set the kitten down and stood up, looking completely healed from his accident.

His gray eyes met hers, and she could feel every grain of hurt fill her, like sand filling an hourglass. There were deep grooves around his mouth, which seemed to be struggling to form a smile. He couldn't quite pull it off. Had he decided to stop in and see her while in town to meet with Evan?

Barney jumped at her leg, and it jarred her out of her reverie. She bent down and picked the kitten up. "What are you doing here, Chase?"

He reached behind him and turned around with the Home Sweet Love pillow in his hands. "You wouldn't accept it, Evan said."

The sense of calm she'd felt after her run faded as

hurt bubbled up inside her. "It was wrong of you to give me something so personal. Usually people ask for things back from each other when they stop seeing each other."

He raised his brows in the equivalent of a shrug. "I don't seem to do what normal people might do in similar situations."

Well, wasn't that a wordy entreaty? Suddenly, she felt deeply exhausted. "I don't have much stomach for bullshit right now. If you're here to ask me to accept your mom's pillow because you can't live with it yourself, don't. The problems you have with that pillow and your past aren't my concern anymore, Chase. I can't imagine why you'd come here at all. Personally, I'm exhausted."

"I am too," he said, sitting back down in his chair. "I've been working like a maniac—against your brother's orders, mind you—to try and get everything done so I could come and talk to you. Moira, there's so much I want to tell you."

The hopeful note in his voice put her back up. "I no longer want to listen. Look, I'm not your friend anymore." It broke her heart to say it. "I don't mean to be unkind, but I can't be. I wish you well, Chase. Just... Please don't come over here the next time you come to see Evan."

"I didn't come to see Evan," he said, setting the pillow aside and reaching for a piece of paper. "I came to see you. To show you something."

He held it out to her, and she eyed it suspiciously. She could see the Quid-Atch letterhead from where she was standing.

"Please, Moira," he said. "I know you're still hurting, and you have every right to be angry with me after what I did to you—to us—but this is my way of showing you... Well, read it, dammit. Sorry. Please, read it."

Barney ran over to him, and Chase scooped him up onto his lap. She remembered how he'd sought comfort from the kitten before. Taking the paper from him, she started to read.

FOR IMMEDIATE RELEASE

Quid-Atch Enterprises is proud to share the following announcement. Long-time chief financial officer, Chase Parker, is stepping down in his current capacity to work with Evan Michaels, Quid-Atch's founder and president, on an exciting new venture in collaboration with reputed entrepreneur and visionary, J.T. Merriam. Parker will be taking the reins as president of a new company called Infinity Energy dedicated to creating renewable energy solutions. The company will be located in Dare Valley, Colorado.

She had to stop reading. Her hands were shaking so hard she couldn't make out the rest of the press release. Chase was standing up, and he took the paper from her hands.

"You're—"

"Starting a new job, here in Dare Valley," he said, trying to smile. "You don't have to forgive me now—or ever—but I hope you will."

He took a step closer, and she watched his Adam's apple bob as he swallowed.

"I've bought the house I stayed in while I was injured," he said, his voice hoarse. "I've spent the last two weeks ironing out a plan with Evan and J.T. and the rest of the executive team at Quid-Atch to make things right. I didn't want to come to you until I had something solid to present to you, to offer you. Moira, the day I left you... It was the worst day of my life."

She felt stupid tears fill her eyes and looked down at the floor. Barney was staring up at her, almost like he was entreating her to forgive his friend.

"I thought I had to save Quid-Atch, take care of everything and everybody, give the company my whole life. Again. Then J.T. showed up to fly me back to D.C., and he talked to me." Chase ran a hand through his hair. "He understood what I was going through. He'd just gone through it himself."

She shook her head. "What? I'm confused."

He put his hands on her shoulders. "I wanted more, and I couldn't see a way to have it. J.T. had found a way—for himself—and because of Evan's...I'm calling it friendly support and not annoying interference...there was a way for me too. Moira, I'm sorry. For spouting off like an asshole about Maurie. For walking away from what we had. For everything."

The heat of his hands was as scorching as the pleading look in his gray eyes.

"Can you forgive me? Will you be with me again? Will you...make a home with me? I'm still a little scared to reach for it ..."

His hands caressed her skin then, and her heart settled. There was no other way to describe it.

"But I want to make a home with you more than I want anything, and I won't let my fears stop me."

He looked her straight in the eye and she felt the punch of his emotion all the way down to her toes.

"I love you, Moira, and I don't want to ever be without you again. Will you please—"

"Oh, shut up," she said, hurling herself into his arms. "Shut up, shut up, shut up." Cupping his face, she looked right back at him. "I'll forgive you if you swear to me that you'll never leave me again."

His mouth turned up at the corners. "Moira, I plan on being buried here. Is that enough assurance for you?"

She kissed him hard on the lips. "We really need to find you a positive pill, don't we? Oh, Chase, you're leaving Quid-Atch. Are you sure? It's such a big move."

He smoothed his hands down her back, pulling her against him. "When I left you, I wasn't sure Evan intended for there to still *be* a Quid-Atch, but we worked it out. Quid-Atch will remain, but we're rethinking many of the ways we've been doing business. As chairman of the board, I'm still going to be involved in those decisions, but not the day-to-day running of the company. And yes, I'm sure. One hundred percent, headache-free sure."

It was then that he smiled, and she knew. He was happy.

"I loved what I did for Quid-Atch," he continued, "but I didn't want to keep working like that for the rest of my life. J.T. pointed out that plenty of other executives do."

She was going to kiss J.T. Merriam the minute she saw him. "He has a way about him, doesn't he?"

Chase nodded. "But Moira, you were the first one who helped me believe I could have more. Want more. And I want you."

She let out a slow breath. "I still don't want to be the sole reason you gave it up."

"Barney will remind you that you aren't."

She couldn't help but laugh through her tears.

Leaning down, he kissed her softly on the lips. "I made peace with not ranching like my father and his father did. I love the country. Always have. But I never completely let go of wanting a home, the kind that comes with a woman I adore and the children we make together."

Her watery eyes tracked to the pillow on the table. "Home Sweet Love, huh?"

He nodded. "I finally asked my mom a few weeks ago why she'd sent it. She..."

His emotion was palpable, and her heart clutched, thinking about what a big step it had been for him to ask her about that traumatic time.

"She said...ah...she sent it to me, hoping I would remember what she and my dad had once, what we can all have when we find the person we're meant to be with."

She felt the first tears roll down her face. It was all too wonderful to believe. She wanted to spin around in a circle, but mostly she wanted to lay her head against his chest and listen to his heartbeat for the rest of her life.

"That's how I feel about you too," she said, her voice breaking. "But if you ever change your mind—"

"I won't." He traced her cheek. "What Evan, J.T., and I have cooked up with Infinity Energy has given me a new spark. It's a totally new business model, and one much more suited to the kind of life I want to lead. With you."

She wrapped her arms around his waist. "I just realized J.T. set me up."

Chase smiled at her. "You mad?"

Her answering smile couldn't be contained. "Livid. Who's replacing you?"

"Before your human resources brain starts to worry, you should know, we're initiating a quiet—but thorough—recruitment process on Monday. You might have gotten an early look at the press release we plan to send out."

"Seems like things have moved a little fast," she commented, happy to be in his arms again.

"Not fast enough to suit me," he told her. "Every day away from you was hell. I don't ever want to go through it again."

"Me either," she said with a noticeable sniff.

"Since I'm moving to town, I was hoping you might go out on a date with me."

She linked his arms around his neck. "In public? What a novel idea."

He kissed her on the mouth again. "I have a few others. One involves finally making love to you without any casts or slings. Would that appeal to you, Ms. Hale?"

Her whole body seemed to have become an overflowing champagne fountain. "That works for me."

"And would you consider spending the rest of your life with me? Make your home with me?"

She had to take a moment to answer through her clogged throat. "I'd love that most of all."

As they kissed slowly, thoroughly, she fell into the moment with him, letting go of the last of her hurts, letting him all the way back into her heart.

"And when the time is right," he said between kisses, "will you help me give the pillow my mom made to our children when they're grown?"

Their whole life stretched out before her. She could see them holding hands as they walked away from one of their children's homes after Chase worked his smoker magic at another BBQ. They'd return to their own home, the one they'd built together on an intention.

Home. Sweet. Love.

"Yes, Chase."

Together, they sealed the vision with a kiss.

EPILOGUE

J.T. LOCKED UP THE BUILDING THAT HELD THE ART collection currently housed at his parents' Napa estate. Everything had been arranged to fit his new vision for the museum in Dare Valley. He was ready to show Caroline the rest of the paintings when she arrived tomorrow.

But there was one he couldn't bear to put in the museum. No, he'd asked for it to grace the new home he had in mind, the one he hoped Caroline Hale would share with him one day.

He walked through the south vineyards back to his parents' home. After letting himself into his father's study, he came to a stop in front of his most favorite painting of all.

Since childhood, he'd been captivated by the portrait Emmits Merriam had commissioned of himself. It depicted him after he'd first struck oil. His great-great grandfather had wanted his descendants to know where they were from, what he'd built for them, what he'd entrusted to them.

In the portrait, Grandpa, as everyone had called Emmits, was dressed in dark jeans and a rumpled white work shirt. His cowboy boots were covered with oil from the well he'd been working. On Grandpa's face was a smile of pure joy as he raised his oil-covered hands to the blue sky and brilliant sun. The Oklahoma prairie stretched behind him.

J.T. had always thought Grandpa was raising his hands in praise, but his brother Trev thought he was giving thanks for the offering the earth had bestowed upon him. They still argued about that point, but honestly, it was all in good fun.

"I'm headed back to Dare Valley, Grandpa," he told the man he'd always wished to know. "The Merriams belong back in Dare Valley."

The light changed in the room, the sun emerging from the earlier clouds to radiate light on every available space, including the dimple in his grandpa's right cheek, the one J.T. had inherited from him.

"And I'm in love with Uncle Arthur's great-niece, Caroline," he said, grinning as he thought of her. "You'd love her, Grandpa. She's everything beautiful in the world."

Approaching the painting, he carefully lifted it off the wall.

"And you're coming with me too, Grandpa."

He thought Emmits would like that.

Uncle Arthur sure as hell would.

Dear Reader,

This book is truly special to me, not only because I was able to spend time back in Dare Valley and give Chase his story after so many of you asked for it, but also because I was able to share more about the beauty of healing. As many of you have read online, I have my own healing gifts. The funny story behind this book was my editor's reaction to Ally. She couldn't believe one person could have so many gifts. We both laughed when I told her I was just like Ally, something she hadn't fully understood before. The joy of this story was showing how one person could decide to change their life and have people with gifts help him. It's always a joy to see.

If you enjoyed this story, I would love for you to post a review since it helps more readers want to pick up this story and enjoy it themselves. When you post one, kindly let me know at ava@avamiles.com so I can thank you. Thank you for spreading the word!

There are a lot of wonderful surprises coming up, including J.T. Merriam's return to Dare Valley in THE SKY OF ENDLESS BLUE. I can't wait to share it with you.

Thanks again for being part of the family.

Lots of light and joy,

Ava

ABOUT THE AUTHOR

International Bestselling Author Ava Miles joined the ranks of beloved storytellers with her powerful messages of healing, mystery, and magic. Millions of readers have discovered her fiction and nonfiction books, praised by *USA TODAY* and *Publisher's Weekly*. *Women's World Magazine* has selected a few of her novels for their book clubs while Southwest Airlines featured the #1 National Bestseller NORA ROBERTS LAND (the name used with Ms. Roberts' blessing) in its in-flight entertainment. Ava's books have been chosen as Best Books of the Year and Top Editor's Picks and are translated into multiple languages.

57198091R00215